THE MASKS AND THE DANCER

BEA PAIGE

GRITTY, ANGSTY, DANGEROUS ROMANCE

THE MASKS AND THE DANCER

TRIGGER WARNING

Dear Reader,

If you're reading this then you've already fallen into the dark and depraved world of The Masks. Book two of their duet is even more of a clusterfuck of darkness.

You've seen glimpses of The Masks past in book one of the duet, well this book will delve into the abuse they suffered in more detail and it will give you an insight into why they are the way they are, and more importantly, just how hard they have to fight against their pasts to be the men Christy deserves.

Ultimately, this is a story about redemption. It's about finding humanity when it's been stripped from you so cruelly. It's about human emotion. It's about love.

That most of all.

This won't be an easy read, book contains graphic abuse, memories of child abuse, dub and non-con, suicidal ideation, blood and knife play and other uncomfortable situations. Please read at your own discretion.

Much Love,
Bea xoxo

BOOK PLAYLIST

If you're familiar with my books you'll know that I love a book playlist. **The Masks and The Dancer** can be found on Spotify.

There are two ways of spreading the light: to be the candle or the mirror that reflects it.
   ~ ***Edith Wharton***

Leon - aged fourteen

"WHAT ARE WE DOING HERE, FATHER?" I ask as we step out of the car, the air releasing from my mouth in little white clouds. It's cold here in Devon, though not as cold as Scotland. It rarely gets warm there, or perhaps it's just Ardelby Castle that's always so bleak.

"We're here to deal with a loose end," he replies, staring at the quaint cottage we've pulled up outside of. It's situated at the end of a long, winding dirt track and is surrounded by a copse of trees that hide it from the fields beyond. Frost dusts the neatly clipped lawn, the moonlight making it sparkle like the uncut diamonds my father acquired last week.

"Loose end?"

"Yes. Open the trunk," he demands, adjusting his cufflinks and straightening the sleeves of his suit jacket before pulling on a pair of black gloves that he'd picked up from the dash of the car. You wouldn't catch my father wearing anything other than an expensive tailored suit. An expensive, tailored, *black* suit. Everyone knows black hides the blood stains better.

"Yes, Sir," I respond, nodding my head.

Despite the anxiety churning my stomach, I do as I'm told. I've learnt the hard way that disobeying a direct order from my father is a first-class ticket straight to a beating. I've suffered at the hands of his cruelty many times over the years, and taken a beating, or five, for both of my brothers, so I know how much it hurts.

I'd do it again. Better it's me than Jakub or Konrad.

Swallowing down the bile burning my throat, I open up the trunk. There's nothing but two gas cans filled with petrol and a pile of rags. I peer around the trunk, "Father?" I question, confused.

"Bring what's in the trunk, *here*," he barks, his focus on the cottage.

There are no lights on, no sounds coming from the building and no vehicles parked in the small drive just off the dirt track. I'm assuming that whoever lives here isn't home, or at least that's what I'm telling myself. Ever since he ordered me to accompany him on this *business* trip to Cornwall, I've been on edge. I may still be a child, but I'm not an idiot, I know that phrase is used as a euphemism for something violent. He rarely deals with business, and has a raft of men who clear up *loose ends*, and do so on a regular basis in his name. Whatever this is, it's personal to my father.

Malik Brov, The Collector.

A man who takes what he wants regardless of the consequences. It doesn't matter what it is, if he wants it he'll take it. Property, jewellery... *people*.

Especially people.

The Collector deals in diamonds and gold, bricks and mortar, flesh and blood.

"Leon!" he snaps.

Spurred into action, I tuck the rags under my arm and carry the gas cans over to my father, placing them on the ground at our feet. As I rise upwards, a sudden gust of freezing air lifts up the hair at the nape of my neck, scattering shivers down my spine.

I don't like this.

Reaching back into the car, my father grabs another set of gloves, handing them to me. "Put them on, then lay out the rags, and cover them in petrol, " he instructs.

"Yes, Sir," I reply, pulling on the gloves. They're soft, supple, and made of the finest Italian leather, but I know he isn't asking me to wear them because he's concerned about my hands getting cold. We're here to do damage, and wearing gloves prevents any fingerprints being left behind.

"Douse them thoroughly, and make sure you don't splash your clothes," he warns me, before picking up one of the gas cans and pushing open the rusty iron gate. The squeak is carried off in the wind that is making the trees surrounding the cottage bend under its power.

I nod tightly, watching him as he walks up the path towards the cottage. He pauses at the front door, resting his hand against the wood briefly before opening the cap of the gas can, twisting on the nozzle attachment and pushing it through the letterbox. When he pulls it out a few seconds later, he steps back and pours petrol over the front door, making sure to cover it completely, then proceeds to splash more petrol over the window frames on either side. Looking over his shoulder at me, he jerks his chin, talking quietly.

"Bring the rags. Put a few through the letterbox, but leave

one hanging on the outside so we can light it. Then meet me around the back." He doesn't bother to wait for me to respond, intent on completing the job.

Grabbing the now fully-saturated rags, I hold my arms out to the side so none of the petrol dripping from them splashes me, and push open the gate. As instructed, I slide several wet rags through the letterbox, then follow my father around the side of the house. By the time I've caught up with him, he's standing at the back door pouring more petrol through a cat flap before discarding the empty can. It bounces a couple of times on the frosty grass, spilling the remnants of its contents before coming to a standstill. For a moment I'm struck by a large pond at the bottom of the garden, the full moon reflected in its inky darkness. What I would give right now to slide beneath its depths and never surface again.

"Put the remaining rags through the cat flap," my father says, pulling my attention back to him and the job at hand.

I do as I'm told, relieving myself of the rags and grateful, at least, that I'm no longer holding onto them. Straightening up, I take a step back and wait for further instruction. I couldn't tell you what thoughts are running through his head, but mine? I'm hoping that there isn't a living soul in this house, least of all a cat.

"Take your gloves off unless you want to go up in flames," my father says, looking pointedly at my hands.

"Why?" I'm not asking him why I should remove my gloves, I'm asking him why we're here at the other end of the country, in the middle of the night, setting light to this cottage. More specifically, why he chose me to accompany him.

He snaps his head around, looking at me sharply. "Your gloves, Leon. Take them off and light the damn rag." His tone of voice brooks no arguments and I know better than to disobey him.

"Yes, Sir," comes my well-rehearsed reply.

Yes, Sir...

Whatever pleases you, Sir...

Beat me, Sir...

Yes, I deserve it, Sir...

I am worthless. Just like you say, Sir...

With a stuttered intake of breath, I peel off the leather gloves and chuck them on the mat by the back door, then take the lighter from my father. Our eyes meet, and his coal-black ones spark with annoyance.

Fuck.

I'm still learning to keep my emotions in check, to dampen my feelings, to turn them off, and with every beating it gets easier. But sometimes, like today, my face reveals my emotions. I have to get better at wearing a mask. When it comes to Malik Brov, there are three rules my brothers and I must *always* stick to or suffer the consequences: never show emotion, never display weakness, and always follow his commands.

"Do it!" he demands.

At least this time I don't flinch.

Flipping the lid on the zippo lighter, I press my thumb against the flint wheel and force it to turn. A flame appears, wavering in the breeze. I feel the warmth of it and wonder how something that can save lives also has the power to end them.

With one jerk of his chin, I step towards the sodden rag and light it, stumbling back at the ferocity of the flames that crackle and leap, instantly fuelled by the petrol. The heat is intense, the flames a wild beast coming alive right before our eyes. It's gaping maw is filled with destruction, heat, and poisonous smoke as it devours everything in its path.

Stepping back, I watch in fascination as the flames lick up the wooden frame of the door, crackling and hissing as it catches fire to the ivy climbing up the wall. The flames spread with ease, and within seconds the room beyond the back door is engulfed.

"Burn in Hell, *witch*," my father says, cocking his head as a slow smile spreads across his face.

Noticing that I'm studying him, he jerks his chin. "Go around the front, light the other rags."

Swallowing hard, I nod, backing away from him slowly as he steps towards me, that familiar look in his eye. "And make it quick!" he adds when I'm not moving fast enough.

Twisting on my feet, I run as though the very devil is at my back.

Perhaps that's because he is, a little voice inside my head taunts me.

I shut that thought down, concentrating instead on the task at hand. When I reach the front door, I can see the red and orange glow of the fire through the downstairs window. The flames haven't yet reached the front of the house, but it won't be long. I watch it spread across the floor and walls, a living breathing organism intent on destruction as it consumes and annihilates.

Stepping closer to the rag, I hold up the lighter, the sharp teeth of the flint wheel biting my skin, but something stops me from lighting it. Over the shattering of glass, and the roar of the flames, I swear I can hear a soft cry coming from inside the house.

My whole body stiffens as I listen, straining to hear over the decimation of the fire.

"What are you doing, Leon?" my father asks as he steps into my peripheral vision.

A beat later a high-pitched scream shatters the air, confirming my worst nightmare. Despite the rising heat, my blood runs cold. Ice cold.

"No!" I choke out, shock making me forget my place as my father's servant. His slave.

"Light. The. Rag," he insists.

I don't move.

The screaming gets louder.

The fire fiercer.

Black smoke works its way up into the air taking my breath along with it.

"Light the damn rag," my father orders.

But I can't seem to move. Even breathing has become difficult, and it has nothing to do with the smoke.

My father steps closer to me. A monster dressed in the finest suit money can buy. "She. Must. Die."

"I t—thought it was empty."

"You thought *I'd* come all this way to set light to an empty house?" My father barks out a laugh, shaking his head. "You know me better than that."

He's right, I do.

The screams come again. This time punctuated with calls for help. It's hard to tell, but I think I can hear two voices. Both female, one younger. A mother and a daughter, perhaps?

"Who are they?" I whisper, still stuck in the same position. Still unable to move.

"That's irrelevant."

There are more screams, more calls for help. I can barely make out the words over the roaring flames, but I know that whoever's inside, my father *fears* them. I see that written all over his face. Whoever they are, they must be powerful for a man like my father to come all this way to kill them.

"But—"

"If you don't do as I say, there will be consequences."

The screams that pierce the air are blood-curdling. Bile burns the back of my throat. I shake my head and lift my thumb off the flint wheel. "No."

"No?! You dare tell *me*, no?"

"I—I won't do it." Lifting my chin, I look into my father's eyes. "No," I repeat, firmer this time.

"I thought you might say that, *son*," he snarls, emphasising the fact that I'm not his flesh and blood, that I am disposable, unlike Jakub who he'll beat until he's on the verge of death, but will never kill. Jakub has Brov blood running in his veins. I'm just a poor farmer's son taken by The Collector as payment for a debt. I've only survived this far because, up until now, I've always done everything my *father* wanted.

Not this time.

"If you don't light the rag, Jakub's dog will die."

"There are people inside!" My stomach churns at the thought.

The screams get louder and I swear I can hear the little girl call for her mama. I start to tremble, her screams scoring my skin, tearing it apart just like the flames tear apart this cottage. I feel like I'm inside along with her, drawing in clouds of black smoke into my lungs.

I can't breathe.

"Mama, Mama, Mama!"

My father doesn't even notice her pleas, or if he does, it has no effect. He narrows his eyes at me. "Then his precious Star dies."

"So be it," I whisper, dropping the lighter to the floor. Jakub loves that dog. She's the only thing that keeps him sane, and I've just signed her death warrant. But what choice do I have?

Above us a window is shoved open and a girl, no more than eight or nine, leans out, plumes of black smoke billowing out of the window behind her. "Help me," she cries, her face and hair covered in ash and soot, her eyes and teeth bright white against her blackened skin. She looks like a demon crawling out of Hell.

Only she isn't a demon. She's a child. An innocent *child*.

"Help!" she screams, gasping for breath, her tiny frame shaking as she coughs and splutters, tears streaming down her face. "Please, help!"

She doesn't look down, oblivious to us standing below her as the smoke wraps around her in a suffocating blanket. It won't be long until the poisonous fumes kill her.

I have to do something.

I *have* to.

There's a tug in my chest, one I can't even begin to understand.

Looking from her to my father, I make a snap decision.

"She's just a kid," I say.

"There will be consequences!" he warns, his black eyes narrowing. "Leon!" His teeth grit and his nostrils flare but for some reason, right at this moment, I'm not afraid of *him*...

I'm afraid of what will happen if I don't save *her*.

"Mama!" she screams, disappearing back into the house and spurring me into action.

Looking around frantically for something to break the glass, I eventually spot an ornamental stone nestled amongst the shrubbery beneath the window. Wrapping my hands around it, I lift it against my chest then with as much strength as I can muster, throw it through the window. The shattering glass is loud, but not loud enough to drown out the girl's screams.

"I'm coming!" I shout, elbowing out the shards sticking upwards from the frame before climbing over the ledge. The newly broken window causes a vortex of smoke to billow outwards, blinding me momentarily as I lose my footing and slam into the hardwood floors, my knees cracking. A jolt of pain rushes up my spine and I curse loudly as a shard of glass embeds itself in my knee.

There are more screams, but her cries are drowned out by the sounds of the building creaking and groaning as the fire consumes it bit by bit. Crouching low to the ground, I cover my nose and mouth with my jumper and move towards the door that opens into the hallway. The heat of the fire is a vicious animal to my right as I take a step towards the stairs.

"Stay there, I'm coming!" I yell, uncertain if she can hear me, but calling out regardless.

"Wait!" a broken voice, hollowed out and hoarse, begs me.

My gaze flicks towards the sound and I stumble back in shock as a woman steps out of the flames, her body wrapped in a halo of fire, her clothes are alight, her skin blistering and bubbling. I don't even know how she's standing, let alone talking, but she is. My mouth opens in a silent scream as the heat of the flames quickly engulfs everything behind her.

"Please. Let her *live*," she manages to choke out, the words garbled, bursting like bubbles from boiling lava as she falls to her knees and raises her hands imploringly. With the next breath she's entirely consumed by the flames. Death has taken her now.

"Mama!" the girl cries as her mother's body is stripped of skin and muscle before my very eyes. The smell of burning flesh makes me gag, and I watch as her eyeballs pop from the sheer heat of the flames.

I don't think about the danger.

I don't think about the brutal consequences I will endure for disobeying my father.

I don't even think about the possibility that I might burn alive myself.

All I can think about as I run towards the little girl is why her mother begged me to let her daughter live rather than asking me to *save* her.

Years later, it all becomes clear.

CHAPTER ONE

Thirteen.

AS I ENTER THE LIBRARY, The Masks look up at me from their position by the open fire. The light from the flames casting them all in a hellish glow.

They're monsters, demons.

Brutal. Beautiful. *Broken.*

Heaven knows I've tried to help, but no potion or elixir that I've brewed has worked. Try as I might, some wounds are too deep to heal. They fester and putrefy, infecting a person's soul, stripping away humanity until all that's left is a vessel for darkness to thrive in.

I tore open their wounds thinking that would be the only way to help purge them of their pain, their sins, but my actions just allowed more darkness in.

Where's Christy? I ask, scribbling across the notepad that I carry with me everywhere.

"*Zero* is in the Room of Fantasies, with the others," Konrad replies, stressing his given name for her.

Why? She isn't part of The Menagerie, I write, ignoring the look Leon gives me.

He's close to the edge. He has been for days now, and I have to force myself to remain resolute, strong in the face of his wrath, just like Christy has done since the moment they brought her here.

Jakub places his own drink on the table, before unbuttoning the top button of his shirt and loosening his tie. "We have our reasons, Thirteen."

I shake my head, my mouth pursed, my confusion evident. *No!* I write, angrily tapping at the word with the end of my pen, then instantly regretting that I've allowed my feelings to show.

Leon bares his teeth at me for even daring to object.

"Listen—!" he begins, but Jakub rests his hand on Leon's arm, cutting him off.

"You are here as our guest, but do not, for one minute, assume you have any right to question what we do with *our property*. You understood the terms of your place here. That hasn't changed."

I huff, scrawling another quick response. *I understand that, but...* I begin, then stop myself from writing what I truly want to say, feeling wholly frustrated with myself and my inability to verbalise my thoughts. No matter how much I wish to, the sounds won't form, the words lost to a traumatised child.

"You've become too attached," Konrad states, watching me closely.

I shake my head, flicking to a clean page. *I care about all of the Numbers.*

"But this is different," he persists, cocking his head as he reads my words. "This isn't just your need to heal those who hurt, this is more. Tell me I'm wrong."

Isn't it that way for you? I deflect.

Konrad takes a sip of his brandy, opening his mouth to answer only to be cut off by Jakub, who seems intent on silencing his brothers tonight. "No," he interjects, his jaw tight, rigid with tension. "She remains *Nothing* to us."

Schooling my features, I nod. I despise the names they've given Christy, but I cannot allow them to know how I truly feel because it will only raise more questions that I'm not willing to answer. That I *can't* answer, at least not yet.

"That performance was another act of defiance, and as such, Nought needs to be taught a lesson," Leon adds. "She doesn't hold the power here, we do. She doesn't rule us, *we* rule her. She is nothing but revenge. No more, no less."

So this is a lesson? I ask, hope blooming in my chest with every letter I write.

A lesson implies that she will remain alive to learn from it. However cruel The Masks' lessons might be, however twisted, however much it pains me to witness what Christy has had to endure, at least she is still alive to endure it. To fight back. Where there is fight, there is hope for all of them. She's the only one strong enough to face them, to make them see what they've become. She's already proven just how much of a force she is.

"What's it to you? In fact, don't answer that, Thirteen. We're done with your questions."

"Leon," Jakub warns, but it's lost on deaf ears as he approaches me.

Even Konrad isn't making a move to stop Leon. Not that it would matter anyway, their control over him is waning. They know it as well as I do, and we all know that when Leon loses his last shred of humanity he will become the ultimate monster his father, The Collector, had raised him to be. Once one falls, the other two will surely follow.

Shaking my head, I step back, holding my hands up in a bid to urge Leon to wait. We're not done here, there is one more thing I need to do. It's the *real* purpose for my intrusion. I came here to deliver a letter that I've been entrusted to keep safe until this very night. It remains sealed, the envelope discoloured with age, the corners bent and torn. I reach for it now, tucked safely inside the pocket of my skirt and pinch the paper between my finger and thumb.

"Out of respect for your gift," Jakub says, his voice terse, making Leon falter in his approach, "And all that you've done for the Numbers, I will forget about your desire to question our actions tonight. Go to bed, Thirteen."

Wait! I plead with my eyes.

"Leave us. Now," he bites back, striding over to us both and gripping Leon's shoulder, preventing him from getting any closer. Of the three, Jakub and I were closest as children. That lingering affection, however minuscule, saves me now.

Except I can't leave. I won't, not until I've done what I came here to do.

Shaking my head, and ignoring the darkness leaching into Leon's gaze, I pull out the letter from my skirt pocket and shove it towards him. My instructions were clear, deliver this letter to The Masks on this very night, no matter the cost.

"What's this?" Leon asks, his voice strained and his gaze sharp, deadly beneath the black mask he wears.

"Looks like a letter," Konrad remarks dryly as he joins us.

Jakub releases Leon from his grasp. "From *whom*?"

With shaking fingers I write my response, then slowly turn the pad around. *Nessa, Christy's mother.* I'm met with silence as my response sinks in, then Leon blinks a few times as though coming out of a trance.

"Nought's mother is dead!" he shouts, his reaction as explosive as expected.

I school my features, turning all the fear inward and giving off that serene, calm-like state that I've perfected so well. *Yes, she is.*

Leon snorts in derision. "Why the fuck would Nought's mother send *you* a letter from beyond the grave?"

Not beyond the grave. She sent it before she died to my grandmother, who gave it to me on her deathbed. I was instructed to give it to you today, on this very night, I explain, my fingers aching from writing so fast.

Jakub flicks his gaze at me, his shock reflecting his brothers', before returning it to the letter still gripped in Leon's hand. "What does it say?"

I shake my head, writing my answer down quickly. *I haven't read it. It wasn't meant for my eyes.*

"But it was meant for you to deliver it to us fifteen years after Nessa's death?"

It's a rhetorical question filled with sarcasm and more than a little distrust, but I answer truthfully nonetheless. *Yes.* I nod.

"You should read it, Leon," Konrad interjects, eyeing me with suspicion. "Nessa has clearly gone to great lengths to get it to us, so it must be important. Right, Thirteen?"

This time I don't dare reply, I simply wait. A shiver tracks down my spine as Konrad turns his attention back to Leon, handing him his flick knife. Leon slides the blade beneath the flap, pulls out the letter and begins to read it out loud.

To Jakub, Leon and Konrad,

You might be known as The Masks to many people, but I shall refer to you by your given names and not the name you

gave yourselves. I do this because those names belong to the boys you once were as much as they do to the men you are now, and perhaps that small reminder will be enough to persuade you to let my daughter live.

By now you will be questioning how a dead woman, long since buried beneath grass, soil and stone can possibly know your intentions. The answer is both as simple as it is complicated. Let me explain.

My name is Nessa Dálaigh. I am the second daughter of Brennan Dálaigh, aunt to Arden Dálaigh and best friend to Aoife O'Brien, Cynthia's mother, or as you now call her, Thirteen.

"Zero is a *Dálaigh?*" Konrad's nostrils flare as he swipes a hand through his hair. "That did not come up in our background check on her. Fuck!"

Jakub holds his hand up, his jaw clamped shut as he jerks his chin at Leon, urging him to continue. Leon nods tersely before reading on.

As you know, Thirteen's father, Niall O'Farrell, was a close acquaintance of your father, and like your father he was a troubled man, corrupted by power and twisted by the darkness he harboured inside.

He stole my friend, just like you stole my daughter.

Aoife fought her attraction to Niall, but over time she fell in love with him. But unlike your father, Niall still had a streak of humanity, one that her love helped to bloom. Four years after he stole her, she died in a bitter war between the two families. Thirteen witnessed her mother's death and never spoke from that moment on. She is the silent one and your only friend in this life.

I tell you all of this for one reason only: I fear if nothing changes, history will repeat itself.

Leon pauses, catching my eye. My mother wasn't the only person to die that night. Both of the warring families lost people they cared about. It was a bloodbath, one I wish to forget. I swallow hard, forcing the memories of that night back into the padlocked recesses of my mind as he continues to read.

Please understand, there are no coincidences when it comes to fate. Our families were destined to cross paths. We are tied together, your family and mine, the Dálaighs and the Brovs. Just like the O'Briens and the O'Farrells were.

Like the roots of The Weeping Tree, our fates have been intertwined for years. Hate and fear feeding violence and revenge. My brother, and Arden's father, Michael, will be another victim of this bitter war. He too will be murdered by The Collector, a year before your father burns me alive. I know that because I've seen it.

There is a blade with a handle made of his skin that you display in your home. This is proof of how far our families are willing to go for revenge. That act of violence brought to life three brothers-in-arms who are much like yourselves. Tortured souls bound together by death, violence, and hate.

You know them as the Deana-dhe.

The three men exchange looks, and for the first time since arriving here, I see a brief flickering of fear in their eyes. The Deana-dhe are men whispered about in private rooms. They're the shadows in the corner of your eye, the assassins who move like ghosts, unseen, feared, violent. They're both real and imagined. They're the gatherers of secrets and deal in lies and half-truths. They're the monsters who slay monsters. They're stuff made of legends, and unbeknownst to The Masks, are the men I've run from.

Jakub clears his throat. "Read," he demands.

It pains me to know how much blood has been spilled, how many people hurt, and how many lives snuffed out, and for what gain?

I still don't have the answer to that question.

What I do know is that Fate has played her part well, and she has plans that even I cannot see beyond.

"What does she mean, see beyond?" Konrad snaps, ripping the letter out of Leon's hold. He reads on silently, his face paling. "This can't be true..."

"What can't be?" Leon asks, taking back the letter and reading out loud once more.

I am what you call, a seer. I can look into the future, but my daughter's life is unclear beyond this night, the night you read this letter.

Unclear, but crucially, not over.

I have questioned myself many times over the years about my role in your destiny with my precious daughter. I have battled with my need to protect her. I've made mistakes, changing our names, hiding from my very own family and taking aid from Christy's father—a man who I never should've fallen in love with—in the hope that he would save us both. But I should've known that Fate always catches up with those who run from her, punishing them for it.

Do my actions make me a bad mother, knowing that I've kept so many things from Christy? That I've hidden part of her true family from her? I don't know the answer to that. What I do know is that fate is written in the very marrow of our bones, and the cells in our blood, and no matter how much we might

try to change our path, we will always end up at the same destination. Always.

Leon's head snaps back up as he glares at me. "What kind of game is this, Thirteen?"

No game, I write quickly, shaking my head. *I didn't write this letter.*

"Bullshit!" Jakub snarls. "Did the Deana-dhe put you up to this?"

No. They are enemies of my father. I have <u>nothing</u> to do with them.

"But they're not your mother's enemies!" he throws back. "The Dálaighs are close to the O'Briens."

My mother is long dead, I point out. *My father has kept me away from them all. You know that.* I swallow hard, willing him to believe me.

"And yet here you are delivering a letter from a Dálaigh," Konrad points out, prying the letter from Leon's hold and continuing to read, but not before giving me a look. A look that tells me that my position here has become tenuous.

Leon made a choice to save my daughter from the fire. Your father killed Star just like he warned Leon he would. The day he shot her dead was the day you became The Masks. You did it to protect your hearts from the true monster, your father.

Every action has a reaction. Every decision has a consequence.

Whether I like it or not, whether you accept it or not, Christy was meant to come into your lives, as you were meant to come into hers.

That cannot be unwritten, and nothing I could've done would have changed that fact.

Nothing.

Still, I write this letter in the hope that somehow the truth of your connection will ensure her future. I suppose this is my last attempt at trying to protect her.

But how do you ask three soulless men to allow your child to live?

Pleading won't help.

You are your father's sons after all.

What I do know is that there are bigger forces at work here, bigger than your father's hate for a heart filled with kindness, bigger than your need to exact revenge on a woman who had nothing to do with his death...

Understand this, there is as much truth in a legend as there is in a fairytale.

Break the cycle once and for all.

Let. Her. Live.

Nessa.

Konrad's arm drops to his side, his fingers releasing the letter. I watch as it flutters to the ground, the sound of it hitting the wooden floor loud over the deadly silence that has descended around us.

CHAPTER TWO

Jakub

RED IS a colour I've seen in varying shades over the years.

It's the bright scarlet of blood trickling from the wounds my father inflicted on my body. It's the deep hibiscus of a bruise blooming across my skin from his fists. The blush of my cheeks as he ordered me to fuck women whilst he watched. It's the cherry, rose and ruby of the cunts that I was forced to pleasure as a teenager with my mouth and tongue. It's the rust of a manacle wrapped around my ankles and wrists whilst my father flogged my back raw to teach me a lesson.

It's the port wine stain of Nothing's birthmark, blooming darker from my touch.

It's the fire that took her mother's life and scarred her back.

It's the rich merlot of Star's blood and brain matter that haunts me still.

It's the red mist that settles over me now.

With a roar, I pull back my fist and slam it into Leon's face. He stumbles backwards, shock quickly replaced with anger of his own.

"What the *fuck*, Jakub!" he shouts, pressing his fingers against his split lip, spreading the scarlet over his chin. Behind me I hear Thirteen suck in a breath as his mask slips. He adjusts it quickly.

"Get the fuck out!" I shout at her. She starts to write on her notepad, but I grasp her wrists. "No. You've done enough! Push me again and you'll see what I'm capable of doing to those who keep secrets from me."

Her face drains of colour. *No*, she silently begs, shaking her head. *Please.*

"Get the fuck out now or find yourself strapped to a fucking cross alongside Nothing!"

No. Wait! her expression implores.

"Get out of my sight!" I snap, backing her out of the room and shoving her into the hallway beyond before slamming the door in her face. The moment she leaves, the three of us rip off our masks.

"This is some bullshit," Konrad remarks. "Thirteen's fucking with us. Her and Zero are in on this together."

"Shut your fucking mouth," I snap, holding up my hand to silence him before focusing back on Leon who's staying suspiciously quiet. "Tell me *everything*. Right the fuck now."

"I told you everything that night we had dinner in the courtyard with Nought. I set the fire. Nessa died. I pulled Nought out. There's nothing left to say other than the fact I didn't know she was *that* girl. I only began to suspect the night she showed us her back."

"But you didn't tell me about Star! You *never* told me about that!"

"What difference would it have made? I can't change what happened."

"I deserved to know."

"And now you do," he replies, gritting his jaw. "There is nothing left to say."

"And yet here we are, surrounded by so many secrets that this room is thick with them," I bite back, snatching up the letter and casting my gaze over the pretty cursive. I screw it up in my hand, crumpling the paper into a tiny ball before throwing it into the open fire. It turns to ash within seconds.

"I had no idea that she was a Dálaigh, *is* a Dálaigh," Leon says, crossing his arms over his chest.

"Right now, that isn't what concerns me the most. You've kept things from me."

"Look, I'm sorry about Star. I made a choice based on a foolish boy's feelings. That boy is gone now, as is Star. It's been years, Jakub."

"I'm not talking about the dog. I'm talking about *you*."

"Why do I concern you?"

"You've hidden how you *feel*."

"What?!" he snaps.

"You *want* her."

"Of course I want her. We *all* do!" Leon retorts with a sharp laugh, glancing at Konrad who's watching us both in a state of shock. "Need I remind you, that you were the one who broke our agreement first. You feasted on her pussy then put your dick in her mouth. *You* broke our agreement. You want her just as much, more given you couldn't fucking control yourself!"

"That isn't what I meant. We all want to fuck her, but you... You've developed *feelings* for her," I accuse, getting in his face. I've been ignoring that fact for days now, but seeing his expression as he read the letter just now... that's only confirmed what I've feared all along. He feels something for her.

He *feels*.

Feelings are dangerous.

Poisonous.

Not. Fucking. Allowed.

He can fuck her, torture her, use and abuse her, but *want* her for more than that? No. No fucking way. We haven't built what we have here for it to be destroyed by a piece of ass, no matter how fucking tempting she may be. No matter how much she fulfills our fantasies. No matter what a dead woman supposedly said from beyond the grave.

No matter how much you want her as well, that treacherous voice inside my head goads.

I push it away, locking the thought up with all the other ones that have been brought to life since her arrival. They've no business being in my mind.

Leon barks out a laugh. "Says the man who ran off to the forest to beat himself black and blue just so he could be in her presence. I think you're projecting, *brother.*"

Without giving it a single thought, I pull my arm back and punch him again, relishing the feel of my knuckles splitting from the force of hitting his jaw. His head snaps to the side, the loud crack of bone meeting bone reverberating around the room.

"You fucker!" he roars, punching me in the eye and splitting my eyebrow before Konrad pulls him off me, getting an elbow to his cheek for the trouble.

I raise my fist, ready to throw another punch, but Konrad steps in between us, pushing us both back. "ENOUGH!" he shouts, forcefully shoving us apart.

The three of us stare at each other, chests heaving, fists

curled. Despite everything we've been through at the hands of our father, there hasn't been one thing that has made us fight like this. Except *her*.

Which is precisely why she must die.

"She's supposed to be Nothing..." I say eventually, scrubbing a hand over my face.

"She is. She means *nothing* to me. I know how I feel," Leon says, striding over to the antique drinks trolley and pouring himself a three-fingered shot of bourbon before knocking it back in one gulp. We all notice how his hand shakes. That never happens. *Ever.*

"Do you though?" Konrad asks, his voice strained, troubled, as he flicks his gaze to me.

"What?" Leon slams the glass back on the table, his body coiled tightly as he turns back around to face us.

"You called her by her name, brother," Konrad reminds him. "And when she reminded you of that fact you lost your mind. You..."

"I what?" he snaps.

"You *cracked.*"

"It was a slip of the tongue. A fucking *mistake*. She pissed me off."

"It was more than that," Konrad insists.

Leon shakes his head. "No—"

"Then prove it," I say, forcing the words out, even though they burn my throat. I hate that. I hate that those words hurt. I shouldn't give a shit about what I'm asking Leon to do. I shouldn't fucking care, but I do, and that's the problem.

"Prove it?"

"I need to see you prove it. End this, tonight."

"You want me to kill her... *tonight*?" Leon's face blanches.

"Wait, what about our agreement?" Konrad asks, gripping my arm, his fingers digging into my skin as he stares at me.

I look pointedly at his hand, understanding in that moment that both of my brothers are guilty of feeling more for Nothing than they should, whether they want to admit that or not. "Konrad," I warn.

"She's ours to *use*, remember?" he counters.

"It's too late for that now. She's a *Dálaigh*. She's our enemy, regardless," I point out. "Perhaps if she wasn't, I might have let her live. I would have kept her for us. We could've had our fun. But knowing this only reinforces what I already know to be true," I shake my head.

"And what's that?" Leon asks.

"That she's already got beneath our skin."

Konrad swipes his hand through his hair. "*Our* skin?"

"I drugged her and chained her to the cross for a reason. It wasn't just to teach her a lesson. I needed to be certain of how she was affecting us. Everything else that's happened since that moment she swallowed Thirteen's elixir has only compounded my feelings. In fact, it's shone a fucking light on them."

"And what do you feel?" Leon asks, his voice deathly quiet.

"Unbalanced. Unsteady. Out of control. Not myself. She's messing with my head," I say, tapping my finger against my temple roughly. "Just like she's messing with both of yours. This needs to end. *Tonight*."

"Fuck!" Konrad roars, his outburst unsurprising.

Picking up my mask, I fix it back into place. "Tell me you don't feel the same, and I will call you a liar." Konrad presses his mouth into a hard line, his silence telling me all I need to know. "I thought as much."

"And the letter? What Nessa said..." Leon asks, swallowing hard.

Turning my attention back to my Leon, I jerk my chin at his discarded mask. "It's bullshit. Put your mask back on, you have a job to do. It's time to finish what you started, Leon. *She. Must. Die.*"

Konrad picks up his own mask and slides it over his face. "And fate?"

"We live by our own rules. We are The Masks, and The Masks bow down to no one, not even fate."

"MASTER, the Baron is taking liberties with Zero," Five says as we approach the Room of Fantasies, our masks fixed back in place, our suits straightened out and, more importantly, our emotions buried fucking deep. Later I will purge those emotions, but first we must deal with this mess.

"Is he now?" Konrad replies, unnaturally calm.

His expression gives nothing away, but I know him. I see the way his jaw is clenched tight and his back is rigid. I see his fingers curling into fists. I feel the tension rolling off him. I understand what he's going through because I'm going through it, too. So is Leon, given the look in his eyes.

She. Is. Ours.

No one gets to touch her but us.

No one.

Five flicks her pretty golden eyes to my brother, her fingers sliding over the knife strapped against her thigh. "You wish me to send him a warning?"

Leon nods before I'm able to answer. "Yes!" he snaps, his teeth grinding.

"We need him alive. Be certain to miss all the vital organs," I add. The Baron doesn't deserve a swift death, Five will injure him and we will finish him off the only way we know how, violently.

"Of course," she agrees.

The sound of Twelve singing greets us as we stand outside the room. Her voice is crisp, mournful and full of heartbreak. Another man might feel guilty for causing such harm, but I'm not like other men. Guilt, remorse, empathy, they're not feelings I indulge in.

They were beaten out of me a long, long time ago.

At least I thought they had been.

Right now the thoughts that are running through my head are ones of rage and anger but also, confusingly, possessiveness, ownership and the distinct and uncomfortable sense of *guilt*.

I, Jakub Brov, feel guilty.

Not for Twelve who's heart is breaking. Not for Thirteen who I handled roughly only minutes ago. Not for the Numbers who are being fucked raw by the men and women inside this room. Not even for Leon who's lip I split.

But for the woman I call Nothing.

That realisation makes my head fucking spin and I hold out my hand, pressing it against the brick wall. It takes everything in me not to throw up the lavish dinner we just indulged in not an hour before as I steady myself and try to fight off this unfamiliar feeling. I need to get my head straight. Guilt has no place here. It's weak. I am *not* weak.

I. Am. Not. Fucking. Weak.

"Master...?" Five says, drawing my attention back to her. She's clearly just asked me a question and I've not heard a damn word of it. I look at her blankly.

"I want the room cleared. Injure the Baron and get the others out. We'll finish him off ourselves," Konrad says, because I can't seem to find my fucking voice.

He flicks his gaze to me and I give him a terse nod before confirming his order. "Do it."

"And Zero?" Five questions, looking between the three of us.

"She stays with us," Leon says more than a little possessively.

"Understood."

Pushing open the door, Five moves silently into the room on bare feet. Her ability to move about unnoticed is one we've taken advantage of over the years. Since our father brought her home, she has become our eyes and ears on evenings such as this. Her skills as a knife thrower, combined with her talent for remaining unseen has made her invaluable to us. In another life, I've no doubt she'd have made an excellent assassin. Picked up by my father in the backstreets of Calcutta, her exotic beauty had attracted him first, then once he'd witnessed her talent, he paid a handsome price for her, making her parents rich beyond their wildest dreams. That kind of money was too much of a temptation and they sold her without hesitation.

Fools.

It never ceases to amaze me how easily people will sell their own flesh and blood if the price is right. Though Five didn't seem to mind. Of all the Numbers, she was the most willing to settle into her life here. We trust her implicitly.

Konrad reaches for me, resting his hand on my arm. "Jakub?"

"Keep in the shadows for the moment," I instruct, ignoring his concern before stepping into the room. Without even meaning to, my attention goes straight to Nothing. I don't notice the fucking going on in the cages around the room or pay any mind to the rest of our clients standing naked just beyond them. Nor do I hear the sound of Twelve's haunting voice.

All I can see, hear, and smell is her.

Nothing.

The rise and fall of her chest. The pants of her breath as air is forced from her lungs through fear and, I suspect, a healthy dose of anger. Her distinct scent that's both sweet like vanilla and musky like her sex. It consumes me.

She becomes my sole focus.

"That motherfucker," Konrad grunts as he too focuses on her and the man who's abusing her.

Nothing's eyes are wide, her mouth is parted on a silent scream, her dress ripped down the middle, and crouched before her is the Baron, suckling on her tit and pulling on his limp dick as he moans and groans, imagining his own daughter no doubt. Bile burns my throat at the thought. We cater to a raft of sexual fantasies here at Ardelby Castle, the Numbers fulfilling those with ease, but I draw the line at fantasising over children. That's just another reason he'll die tonight.

"Oh yes," the Baron moans as he gropes what doesn't belong to him.

She is ours.

Right at that moment the truth of those words barrel into my fucking chest. They're no longer a flippant comment used to show ownership, but something deeper than that, something everlasting.

I feel those words like heavy boulders crushing my rib cage. They're weighted with meaning.

I can't fucking breathe.

The Baron needs to die. Nothing needs to die.

Then and only then will I be free.

We watch in sick fascination as the Baron sucks and pulls on her breasts, oblivious to the impending danger, too caught up in his own twisted fantasy to notice death has come for him.

He groans.

And the red mist descends once more.

It's all I can do not to steal the knife from Five's hand and throw it at the disgusting child abuser myself. I want to ruin him. I want to make him pay for touching her. For hurting her.

These emotions are foreign to me, alien. I don't fucking want them.

"Master?" Five whispers, she's still within the shadows too, waiting for my instruction.

"Do it!" I hiss.

Five's knife is impaled in the Baron's shoulder before I can even blink. He falls forwards into Nothing from the impact, the sound he makes as he pushes off of her is like a stuck pig, which seems fitting because it won't be long before he's squealing like one.

Five steps into the dim light cast by the thousands of candles lit around the room, her fingers feathering over another knife strapped to her chest. The fucking stops and the last lingering note from Twelve's lips hangs in the air like a portent.

Everyone in the room stills.

Every single one of them knows what's about to happen.

The Baron is about to die.

Little do we know, it won't just be him who'll be weeping blood tonight.

CHAPTER THREE

Leon

"WE CAN'T ALLOW you to live," Jakub says, his words ringing in my ears as my fingers circle Nought's throat, my thumb pressing against the unsteady thrum of her pulse, my palm squeezing over tendons and muscles.

"Time's up, Nought," I whisper against her lips.

Her eyes widen in shock. Her lips parting as she gasps for breath.

Not yet.

I loosen my hold and her breaths are frantic as she desperately tries to draw air back into her lungs. Behind me Konrad and Jakub look on, waiting for me to end this game of cat and mouse. The air is thick with the metallic scent of blood, with fear. Behind us the Baron is nothing but an empty sack, his innards spilt out over the floor. The Numbers are gone, entertaining our guests in another part of the castle.

It's just us.

The Masks and The Dancer.

"Leon," Jakub warns. I hear the impatience in his voice. His need for this to be over and done with, but there's something else too, something close to... *regret*, maybe?

I ignore him and his confusion, struck by the colour flooding back into Nought's lips. Caught by the way her birthmark lightens as she draws oxygen into her lungs. Captured by her different coloured eyes and the way they beg me to stop. She is undoubtedly beautiful regardless of her flaws, *because* of them. Truthfully, everything about her rouses something within me, and I can't help but bury my nose into her hair and breathe in deep.

Fuck, I'm drawn to her.

I'm drawn to her in a way I can't explain.

There's this pain in my chest every time I'm near her. I don't understand what it means. It fucking hurts, but it also reminds me of something else... It reminds me of what it feels to be alive. For the better part of my life, I've been dead inside. Until her, until she came back into it.

She has cut me to pieces and made me bleed.

She has held up the mirror and made me see.

She woke me up.

"I want you so bad, Nought. I want to crawl inside of you and make you mine. But I can't. I fucking can't. I have to end this now for the sake of us all. I *have* to. You don't belong here."

Pulling back, I cup her cheek with my free hand, my fingers around her throat stroking her gently, reverently. Her eyes are brimming with tears, her pupils blown so wide that there's almost no more colour left. For a moment I'm struck by them, by the dark pools, glittering under the candlelight, so like the pond that I carried her into as a child.

She's breathtaking.

She. Must. Die.

Those three words spin around and around in my head as Jakub's command merges with my father's voice travelling all the way from Hell. The Collector is always there in the back of my mind, reminding me every day of who and what I am.

A monster.

"I have to finish what I started, Nought. Don't you see? It's the only way to set us all free."

Behind me Konrad says something, and even though I hear the words I make no sense of them. Right now it's just me and her, just us. Exactly like it had been when I'd laid her down on the damp grass the night of the fire. Our story, hers and mine, has come full circle. Perhaps her mother had been right, perhaps fate has brought us together for a reason?

Break the cycle once and for all... Let. Her. Live.

Nessa's plea lingers in my mind as I hold Nought's life in my hands. Do I release her and allow her to live, or tighten my grasp and finish this once and for all? Right now there is no pressure around her throat, just indecision and the feeling of her pulse thumping beneath my fingers.

"Tell me what I should do..." I whisper.

Kill. Her. My Father's voice strikes like a bullet to my temple. I'm blinded by the pain of it. *Kill her and end this.*

My fingers flex then tighten. She chokes.

"Shut up!" I whisper through gritted teeth, my heart pounding, my head spinning, my fingers releasing.

A tear drips from her long lashes and slides down her cheek and I can't help but lean in close so I can lick it from her skin. It tastes of broken things, of shattered hearts and quiet suffering.

Something inside my chest hurts. It *hurts* so bad I want to rip open my own rib cage and pull out whatever it is... and yet, like a drug, her fear makes me shake with power. It fuels the monster. It feeds the need I have to destroy and annihilate, to crush and break, to throttle and squeeze, to *kill*. I am my father's greatest weapon, moulded into a tool used for pure evil, to harm, to destroy, just like he taught me. I've always obeyed his orders.

I've killed. I've ruined. I've crushed.

And once upon a time I *saved*.

That wasn't you. You are not that weak, good for nothing boy. You're a monster now, and monsters kill. Kill. Her.

"Shut up!" I grind out, louder now. My fingers tighten then loosen, tighten then loosen as I battle with myself, with these thoughts, with these feelings that are both abhorrent and alien.

Kill her. End this, he snarls inside my mind.

Why won't he leave me alone? Even after death my father still haunts me. Like a worm feasting on the rotten meat of my blackened heart, he lives within me. I used to be okay with that.

I used to pride myself in the fact that a piece of him was alive in me... But now? Now I'm not so certain.

This is wrong!

This is who you are. Fucking kill her!

"*I* am the master of her fate. *I* hold her life in my hands," I say out loud, not understanding why I feel the need to do that, but doing so anyway.

It isn't her mother who sent a letter from beyond the grave who has the power to persuade me to stop.

Not Jakub who stands behind me waiting for me to end this.

Not Konrad who vibrates with a need so strong he's desperate for her last breath so he can fulfill his fantasies and bring her back to life.

Not my father whose ghost haunts me daily.

I am in control.

I can *choose*.

Let her live, end her life.

Live or die.

Right and wrong.

Good and evil.

Monster and angel.

Who am I?

Nought draws in a shaky breath, still alive, still pleading with her eyes.

She can't fight back.

She can't cut me with her words.

She can't strip me bare with her courage.

She can't hurt me with her pity or her hate.

She can't hold up the damn mirror and make me see.

She can't make us want her if she's dead.

Because Jakub was right, I *do* want her. She makes me wish for things I cannot have. She makes me crave softness, kindness, warmth... *love.*

Love.

Fuck!

FUCK!

Love hurts. Love is a mother selling you to pay off her debts. Love is feeling, and feeling is pain. Love is poison. It's suffering and heartbreak.

Love is weakness.

Kill. Her. Do it! his voice shouts. My fingers tighten.

I can see the agony in her eyes. I can see the pain and the desperation. The utter terror.

I can also see the rage.

It burns brightly, fiercely.

If looks could kill, I would be dead.

She *hates* me.

And I deserve nothing less.

I'm the monster she believes me to be. I always was.

But why does that hurt so much? Why does it kill me to know that's the truth when only days ago I revelled in that fact... *Why?*

She stares at me, her eyes filled with tears that tip over her lashes and down her face in streaks dripping onto my wrists.

Drip, drip, drip.

So many tears. I remember the ones she cried years ago when I laid her down on the damp grass. When we had both been children unknowingly caught up in a war between our two families. She had looked at me like I was an angel and for a moment in time, I had allowed myself to be her hero.

Could I be that now? Could I save her?

Time ceases to exist as I contemplate that thought. There's nothing but me and her, just us. And somehow I'm back in the past again, the tip of my nose pressing gently against hers as we look into each other's eyes...

"I thought you were dead."

"I'm not?" she replies.

"No, you're not." I smile. "You're stubborn."

"Who are you?" she croaks, and I find myself grazing my fingers over her cheek. The pain is gone from her eyes, and a sweet kind of serenity replaces it instead.

"I'm nobody. I wasn't here. You won't remember me when you wake up."

"Because I'm dying?"

"Maybe." I pause, cupping her cheek, before leaning over and pressing my lips against her ear. "If you survive, don't remember me."

Sirens ring in the distance, help is coming. Maybe it's too little too late.

I hope not. I hope she lives. I doubt she will.

My heart squeezes, jackhammering in my chest.

"That's impossible," she replies, blinking up at me as I pull back. "How can I forget the boy who has eyes so green they're like the fields of Heaven themselves? You're beautiful."

Her words both sting and soothe. I've never considered myself beautiful. Worthless. Ugly. A burden. A dissapointment. But never beautiful. Never that.

"I'm not beautiful. I'm far from beautiful. Inside I'm rotten to the core."

"Are you wearing a mask then?" she blurts out.

"Perhaps I should..." I respond solemnly.

"No, you're an angel," she murmurs, her voice weaker now.

I shake my head, sadness overwhelming me as a hot tear slides down my cheek. "No, I'm not an angel."

"You're the angel—" Inside my chest, my black heart stutters to life. I release the pressure. "I won't do it," I murmur, blinking back the memory. "I won't kill her."

"STOP!" An unfamiliar, raspy voice screams, breaking me from the trance I'm under and forcing me back into the present, back into my body.

I let Nought go, my palms and fingers prickling as though burnt.

Bruises bloom like chains around Nought's throat and I'm struck dumb by the dark blue of her lips, the lifelessness of her eyes.

"No! NO!" I stumble backwards, my legs unsteady. Bile burns my throat as realisation dawns. I double over, throwing up.

"What have you done?! My God, what have you done?!"

It takes me long moments to realise that it's Thirteen who's talking. Thirteen who hasn't spoken a single word since she was a child. Thirteen, who is frantically unlocking the manacles around Nought's wrists and ankles. Five is with her, helping her to lay Nought on the floor whilst I stare at her lifeless body. I stumble towards her as feelings bombard me. Feelings that I've shoved so deep I'd forgotten how much they hurt.

Remorse, guilt, longing, regret. Fucking *despair*.

And it hurts like nothing ever has before.

I'd take a thousand lashes, a hundred cuts, dozens and dozens of cigarette burns, whippings and degradation. I'd take all the punches, kicks, and slaps my father has ever inflicted. I'd even take the handle of a knife repeatedly shoved up my arse over this kind of pain.

Nothing hurts like this. *Nothing*.

A roar rips out of my throat, it tears me open, splitting me down my middle from chin to groin. The pain of it feels like a hatchet has hacked open my chest and all my innards are pooling out of me. I feel as though I'm dying.

I *want* to die.

I killed her.

I killed Nought.

No, I killed *Christy*.

"No! No! NO!" I shout, falling to my knees as I crawl towards her. My hands move over her body frantically. Reaching for her face, I cup it gently. "Come back to me. Come back to us, Christy! Fuck! Christy, come back to me!"

"Leon!" Jakub shouts, gripping my shoulders, dragging me away from her.

He's in shock. He's confused by my reaction. I can hear it in his voice. Fuck him. FUCK HIM! I climb to my feet, rounding on him.

"Get the fuck away from me! This is you! This is *your* fault!" I roar, shoving him off me. Foolishly, he takes a step towards me. "Leon—"

"Don't fucking come near me!" I spit, grasping his shirt in my fist and lifting him up off the floor. His hands wrap around my wrists, his fingers digging into my skin. We lock eyes and for just a moment I see the same pain reflected back. We're *brothers*. But I will kill him if I have to.

Konrad is between us in seconds. He grips my throat, getting into my face. "Put. Him. Down."

I drop Jakub like he's burning coals, not because I don't want to hurt him but because I *do*. I want to fucking kill him right now.

Konrad gets into my space and presses his forehead against my own, forcing my mask to dig into my skin. "What are you doing, brother?"

"What you're both too chickenshit to do!" I retort, baring my teeth, willing to go head to head with both of my brothers in order to protect the woman who's fucked us up worse than The Collector ever managed to do. I don't understand my reaction any better than they do. All I know is that I *have* to protect her from them, just like I had to save her from the fire. "I'm protecting her!"

"Protecting her?" Konrad shakes his head, and there's pain in his voice before he quickly swallows it down. "Brother, you've *killed* her."

"Enough!" Thirteen shouts, her hoarse voice cracking.

I shove Konrad off me and watch as she lowers her ear to Christy's mouth. "Stay the fuck away from me," I hiss at him. "Thirteen?"

She holds her hand up for silence. "Let me listen!"

Jakub takes a step towards Thirteen and without hesitation I pull out the handgun that I always have holstered to my chest on nights when we have guests. "Move one more step and I'll fucking shoot."

"Leon!" Jakub growls.

"Stay fucking back!" I warn, flicking off the safety.

I'm all too aware that I've just crossed a line with my brothers, but I don't give a fuck. Right now, I can't even breathe. I don't want to breathe, not unless she's breathing too. When Thirteen draws back and presses her fingers against the pulse point in Christy's neck, I pray for a fucking miracle.

She shakes her head.

"No!" I refuse to believe it. "Bring her back."

Thirteen nods, looking up at me as she positions Christy's head. "Keep them away."

Konrad's gaze flicks to Christy. I see the longing in them and his desire to bring her back to life. His crazy God complex is a sickness. He's sick. We all are. "Don't you fucking dare!"

"It's not like that!" he protests.

"Bullshit! Move!" I order.

My brothers step back. They know me, they know I'll pull the trigger if I have to. Jakub doesn't utter a word, but I can see how disturbed he is by the turn of events. Konrad doesn't know how to act or who to back. Alongside his sick need to heal what he's broken, there is an emotion he's failing miserably to hide. *Remorse.* I can see it written all over his face. Right now he's battling his own demons as much as I am, even if he doesn't realise it yet.

I was always the biggest monster, the one with the blackest heart and the coldest soul. Nothing fazed me. You want me to chop off a man's dick and feed it to him? I'd do it. You want me to string up an enemy of my father's and peel his skin off slowly over days? I'd do that too.

Yet here I am.

Here *we* are.

I don't like what I'm doing. It's wrong to threaten my brothers, to go against every code we live by, but I can't seem to stop. The monster in me howls in pain, lashing at my insides as it tries to force me to lower my hand and stand beside the only family I've ever known.

But I can't.

If I do that we'll have no hope of bringing her back because, despite those conflicting emotions, I can't risk trusting them. Allowing her to live goes against everything we've ever been taught. She's a threat and we've always been taught to take out any threats.

Jakub knows it. Konrad knows it. As do I.

The difference is, I'm saying no more.

Me.

It has to be me. I have to be the one to protect her, just like I've always stepped in to protect my brothers. I'm the only one who can do that now.

Beside me Thirteen instructs Five. "When I tell you to, I need you to give Christy thirty compressions to her chest, just like I taught you, okay?"

"Okay," Five agrees.

Thirteen nods, tipping Christy's chin back and placing her head in the correct position before nodding at Five. "Now."

Five places one hand in the middle of Christy's chest, between her breasts, and the other directly on top of it, then laces her fingers and compresses her chest thirty times in quick succession. When she stops, Thirteen pinches Christy's nose then breathes into her mouth, twice. I see her chest rise and fall with each breath.

"Live," I grind out as Five repeats the next round of compressions and Thirteen breathes life into her lungs. "Live, goddamn it!"

"Brother, let me help—"

Konrad tries to move towards me but I shake my head. "Don't!"

They repeat the sequence twice more, then Thirteen tells Five to wait as she reaches for the pulse in Christy's neck. The room falls silent. Time stills.

"She's alive. I can feel her pulse. It's faint, but it's there," Thirteen says, her voice raspy with relief as she gently checks Christy over. I watch as she takes off her cardigan and covers Christy up with it. "There are tonics in my room that will help. I need to give her one right now before we move her. Five," Thirteen says, looking at her, "You know the one I mean. I keep it in the gold vial beside my recipe book in the left drawer of my desk."

"I'll go now." Five nods, rushing from the room.

"Fuck!" I exclaim, relief floods my veins. I drop my hands, my head hanging in shame.

My brothers are on me in an instant, and before I know what's happening, Jakub has snatched the gun from me and Konrad has his knife pressed to my throat, the blade digging into my skin. I feel the sharpness of it, the droplet of blood as it slides down my throat.

"This ends tonight," Jakub says, raising the gun and aiming it at Christy's chest.

"Jakub don't!" I shout, struggling in Konrad's hold. The sting of the knife pulling me up sharp.

"Don't make me do this, Leon," Konrad begs.

"Fuck you, *brother*," I spit. "Slit my throat. Fucking do it!"

Jakub steps towards Christy and I jerk in Konrad's hold, the knife pressing deeper. "Brother, please," Konrad begs, his lips pressing against my cheek, his arm wrapped around my chest as he pins me in place.

More blood trickles from the cut. The sharp pain forcing me to think. I can't help her if I'm dead.

My brain frantically tries to come up with a way out of this, but right now the only solution I see is killing my brothers in order to save her.

Turns out I don't have to.

"Stop. Everyone stop!" Nala shouts, holding up her hands as she runs into the room, directly towards Jakub. Her lips are trembling, her eyes brimming with tears as she looks at Christy, at Thirteen, then between the three of us. "You didn't?" she whispers, focusing on Jakub, understanding in that moment what's happened.

"What's that on your hands? Is that blood?" Jakub asks, ignoring her heartbreak and disappointment and focusing on her trembling fingers.

She nods sharply, her hands dripping with thick, viscous blood. "Yes."

"Yours?"

"No, Sir."

"Did something happen to one of the clients?"

"No," she shakes her head, her hazel eyes flashing with concern.

"The Numbers?"

"No."

"Then whose blood is it?"

She swallows hard. "It's The Weeping Tree's."

"What?!" he snaps.

"It's bleeding," she whispers.

Konrad's hand drops from my throat at the same time Jakub steps back. I see the look that passes between them. The disbelief. The horror. The fear.

"The Weeping Tree only ever cries tears of blood when a

virtuous soul, pure of heart and mind dies beneath its boughs," Thirteen reminds us gently, repeating the legend that we all know so well. She looks up at us all imploringly. "Do you get it now?"

"But that makes no sense. Nothing is here in this room with us, not in the courtyard beneath the tree—" Jakub points out, shaking his head as he takes another step backwards. Putting space between him and Christy.

"Yes, it does," I say, my gaze resting on the wooden frame she was shackled to. "Don't you remember the storm when we were kids? Lightning struck The Weeping Tree. It lost two of its largest branches..."

"Father had this frame built from the wood," Konrad adds, the knife he's holding slipping from his fingers and clattering to the stone floor as understanding dawns.

For a beat no one speaks as we all try to make sense of what's happening.

Jakub shakes his head, gritting his jaw, the gun still aimed at Christy. I can feel his turmoil, the indecision. He's not as immune to Christy as he's leading us to believe. He *feels* too.

"Jakub, just wait," I implore.

"No!" he snaps. "Why should that make any difference to what happens now? It's a *story*, make believe, and even if there was any truth in it we all know that kindness has only ever brought sorrow to this family. Nothing's changed! She has to die."

"*Everything's* changed," Thirteen insists.

"Don't kill her. Don't do it," Nala begs, tears streaming down her face. "I told Christy you weren't all bad. I told her what you did for me. I begged her to see the good in you."

"There is no good in me," he bites back, his chest heaving, his hand shaking as he keeps the gun aimed at Christy.

"But there *is*, your father knew that, too," Nala counters, her jaw chattering as she steps between Christy and Jakub, blocking his aim.

"You don't know anything. Get out of the way, Nala."

"I know you saved me. I know you took care of me."

"I'm not that person anymore," Jakub retorts sharply, shaking his head.

"I know that he was cruel to you," Nala continues. "That he *lied* to you."

"Lied?" I ask, frowning.

"Yes," she replies, flicking her gaze to me before focusing back on Jakub. "He only told you part of the legend."

"Part?" Jakub snaps, glancing at Konrad and me, searching for answers. I have none.

"Yes, your father didn't want you to know the truth."

"What truth?" Jakub asks.

"*The Weeping Tree only ever cries tears of blood when a virtuous soul, pure of heart and mind dies beneath its boughs...*" Nala reiterates, wiping at her tears. "But that isn't everything. He left out the most important part—"

"And you know this *how*?" Jakub asks, still refusing to lower the gun even though it's now pointing at Nala's chest, the girl he saved from the brink of death in the forest. The girl we all cared for and protected before our father found out about her existence.

"Grandfather. He told me..." Her voice breaks as she lets out a sob.

"Go on," Konrad insists, striding over to Jakub and placing his hand on Jakub's arm, forcing it to lower.

Nala nods, swiping at her tears. "*...And when her heart stops, theirs will beat once more, and the cycle of violence will end for good.*" Her voice trails off as she looks between us.

Thirteen draws in a breath. Shock giving way to understanding. "Oh my God, don't you see?" she exclaims. "Nessa didn't ask you not to kill her daughter, because she knew that was inevitable. She asked you to *let her live* because she wasn't certain that you would."

CHAPTER FOUR

Jakub

"MASTER, what can I do for you?" One asks me as I push open her door and step into her private quarters a few days later. She's wearing a sheer red gown, her bare pussy and breasts on full display. Behind her the sun is setting through the window, dousing her in a fiery glow. Even her obsidian hair is stained with red. She looks like the Queen of the Damned, a fucking demon.

Perhaps she is.

We lock gazes and despite my cerise mask hiding every inch of my face, she reads me expertly. "How many lashes?"

"Until I bleed."

She nods, taking the leather whip from me, her fingers brushing against mine as she does so. It's an intentional move and I shiver from her touch, not because it turns me on but because it brings back memories I'd rather forget. Our past relationship is pitted with abuse and a struggle for dominance. By the time I walked away from her, I was the victor.

Coming back, however, gives her the upper hand.

What the fuck am I doing?

It's a question I've asked myself over and over again as I've made my way towards her room, and each time I come up with the same answer. I need to take drastic measures because if I don't, I may just lose my fucking mind.

It's only been three days.

Three days since Nothing was strangled to death then brought back to life. Three days of losing my sanity over a woman who should mean... who *does* mean nothing to me. Yet here I am, seeking absolution from the one person I vowed never to go near again. A trip to the forest hasn't helped. My back is raw and covered in welts and weeping scabs from self-flagellation, but even that has done nothing to ease my torment.

Nothing has worked.

Nothing...

I grit my teeth at the very thought of her. She infiltrates my every waking moment. She even steps into my dreams, taunting me with her scars, her fight, and the emotions she conjures within the dark, festering wound that serves as my heart. I'm in agony, unable to function on any kind of level, let alone how I'm used to. I don't know who the fuck I am anymore.

The only thing I'm clinging onto is the fact that I want her gone. Right now, I'm using One to purge her from my system so that I can face Leon and remove her from our lives and this world permanently.

"Jakub?"

One reaches for me, pressing her fingers against my arm. My eyes snap to hers as I return to the room, thankful that the ability to read someone's thoughts is make-believe just as much as seeing into someone's future is. I don't believe that Nessa had such a gift anymore than I believe that I'm not a fucking monster. There's more to her letter, to this whole fucking mess than meets the eye, and I intend to find out what it is just as soon a I can get my fucking head back on straight.

"Where would you like me to do it?" One asks, her voice gentle even when her eyes are hungry, *ravenous*. We both know that she's been waiting for this moment for years and here I am giving myself up to her on a fucking platter. I would've asked Konrad to do this if he wasn't so fucking wrapped up in his own torment down in the dungeons. We're each so caught up in our own turmoil that we haven't considered how the other is fairing. I don't even want to think about Leon. My own fucking brother choosing *her* over us. If I had a functioning heart, it would surely break.

"Jakub?"

"My chest."

"Your chest?" she queries, her cheeks heating as she licks her lips.

"That's what I said!" I snap back, shucking off my suit jacket and chucking it on the chaise lounge positioned at the end of her bed before removing my shirt swiftly. I wince as some of the newly formed scabs rip off with the material.

Her eyes lock onto my pale blue shirt and the blood staining it in patches. "You've been to the forest?"

"Yes," I reply, striding over to the spot in her bedroom where two leather wrist straps are hooked onto the wall, arms length apart. I hear her suck in a breath as she views my shredded back.

"It didn't work?" she asks me as I secure my left wrist and wait for her to do the same to my right.

"I'm here, aren't I?"

"Is it because of the legend? Are you troubled by what happened with The Weeping Tree?"

My head snaps up. "That has fuck all to do with you. Know your place, One."

"I just..." She sighs, fingering the knotted leather handle of the whip as she considers what to say next. Another man might believe her act of contrition, the dip of her head, the blush to her cheeks, the sag of her shoulders, the way she makes herself smaller. I do not. One is calculated. She's seeking information that she has no business in trying to obtain. Yes, The Weeping Tree might've wept 'blood' but no one but Thirteen, Five, Nala and my brothers know what actually happened in the Room of Fantasies, and that's the way it's going to stay.

"The Weeping Tree is diseased. What you see isn't blood, it's *sap*. Nothing more. If you question me about it again, there'll be consequences."

She nods, approaching me, the leather whip grasped in her hand as she studies me in that hawk-like way of hers. It's little wonder my father chose to keep her rather than disposing of her the same way he did all the previous women he brought home before her. She's made from the same mould as him.

Her *love* for the Numbers—and I use that term loosely—is twisted in a way they refuse to acknowledge. One's a product of abuse just like many of the Numbers are, the only difference is they've all been coerced into staying here, whereas One remains of her own free will knowing what this place is all about, understanding the truth of it. She's as fucked up as my father, as *we* are. She's manipulative, dangerous and only kept in line because of the tenuous relationship we share. What I'm doing now is risky. I'm fully aware of that fact, but needs must, and I *must* rid myself of this sickness.

Right the fuck now.

I cannot afford to be weak, not if I'm to maintain what we have here.

Placing the whip at my feet, One reaches for me and raises my arm, fixing the leather strap around my right wrist. Her fingers are cool and my skin instantly pricks with goosebumps, reacting to her touch. She's like the frost that comes right before the snow falls, freezing everything in its path, sucking the life from it. Warmth isn't something I've ever experienced from another human being, or at least if I had, I don't remember it. Whilst One and I have shared many intimate moments over the years there has never been any warmth or affection. Only pain and control.

Gritting my teeth, I lean my head back against the wall, watching her under hooded eyelids. Her lip twitches with a smile that she immediately hides with a perfectly posed bite of her lip when she notices me staring at her.

"It's been a while, so forgive me if I mess this up, Master," she says, her eyes dropping to my mouth then lowering as she feigns submission. One is many things, but she is not a submissive, not by any stretch of the imagination, but I go along with it nevertheless. Her acting is distracting, if nothing else.

"I'm certain you'll pick it back up very quickly," I reply tightly as she trails her fingers along my arm, over my shoulder and down my chest, finally resting on the buckle of my belt as she squats to pick up the whip.

My cock fucking shrivels up at her nearness, and I'm pretty sure my balls rise back up into my body, too afraid that she might go against my wishes and suck them into her mouth just like she did so many times when I was a boy.

"If you'd like I could—"

"No!" I cut her off, glaring at her as she licks her lips.

"As you wish, *Master*."

There's a subtle change to her tone of voice, one that raises my hackles. Someone who doesn't know her as well as I do wouldn't even notice it. But I do. One false move and I could tip the power balance between us. I have to play this out the right way so I can get what I need and she can remain a loyal Number, happy to maintain what we've built here.

"What I wish for is for *you* to provide me with much welcome relief. The death of the Baron has caused us some issues that I hadn't foreseen," I lie, "And I need you to take my mind off them for a while. It is you I seek at this moment. No one else. Only you."

Her spine straightens with the compliment and she rises up slowly, her gaze fixed firmly on mine. "Then I am happy to serve you, Master. Your wish will forever be my command. I am *yours*," she says, knowing full well that she's never, *ever* been mine.

Unlike Nothing.

Gritting my jaw, I choose to ignore One's subtle act of defiance alongside that bastard voice in my head that is getting louder and louder with every passing day. When my father was here One wouldn't have dreamed of overstepping the mark, but these last two years since his death she's become more and more emboldened.

"Are you ready?" she asks me, her dark eyes roving over my bare skin.

I can almost hear her thoughts. She wants to inflict pain. She wants to draw out the teenage boy who used to sob when she beat him. Over the years, it was One as much as my father who taught me how to take the pain and turn it into something powerful. I was sent to One every time I'd become emotional in a way that didn't fit my father's ideals and One would beat it from me until I learnt to turn my feelings off. Every bruise, every lash, every cut, every spark of pain that caused my tears eventually evolved into something else. I'm grateful to her, to my father for doing that. It's allowed me to live a life free from the chains of human emotion. Until now.

"Do it."

"How many lashes?"

"You will whip me until I tell you to stop."

"Yes, Master."

Stepping backwards and to the side, One releases the tail end of the whip. It drops to the floor, the tip dragging over the wooden floorboards as she holds it in her hand. With one curt nod of my head, she raises her arm, pulls back then strikes me as hard as she can, her pert tits wobbling from the force. The sound of the whip cracking against my skin is what I experience first, followed shortly by the sensation that I seek. Pain registers, and with it a brief, mind-altering release.

A release that's short-lived, because despite the throb and the endorphins that follow, it's the initial sharp sting that I relish. That's where Leon and I differ. He seeks a state of nirvana that comes *after* a severe beating, where the mind detaches from the body and it feels like you're floating. I seek the intensity of the pain in the *moment* that it happens. It's fleeting, brutal, and exactly what I need to prevent myself from feeling any damn thing, to keep me in the present.

One raises the whip and strikes me ten more times in quick succession knowing that I prefer my lashings this way instead of drawing them out. When she raises her arm to strike me a twelfth time, she hesitates.

"More?"

"Am I bleeding?" I grind out between breaths, trying to focus on the pain, pissed off that she's stopped.

Her gaze locks on my chest. "A little across your right pec."

"A little is not enough. I told you. I want to *bleed*."

She nods, and this time is unable to hide the smile that spreads across her face. One loves to inflict pain as much as I love to feel it. She finds satisfaction in it, and I find relief. Or at least that's what I'm hoping for because, even now, all I think about is her.

Nothing.

And there is no relief where she's concerned, only agony.

"Then bleed you shall."

One strikes me hard, and I feel my skin tear. The pain is intense but it barely registers against thoughts of Nothing that barge their way into my consciousness.

She *died.*

And for just a moment my world had fucking ended right there with her. I would've fallen to my knees like Leon if his reaction to her death hadn't pulled me up sharp. It was like looking into a fucking mirror. He'd reminded me in that moment what it means to truly feel.

Weak.

He'd become weak, and I'd made a choice to remain fucking strong.

Being here will only help me to maintain that strength.

Bullshit, you're here because Nothing makes you want more, and no amount of lies or lashes will hide that fact, my internal voice taunts.

"No!" I bite out, pressing my eyes shut as I try to bury the thought.

"Should I stop?" One asks, misunderstanding my outburst.

"No! *Harder!*" I demand, my fingers curling around the restraints as I try to ground myself in the moment here, right now with One.

But it's no use. Nothing still invades my thoughts as I

remember how she'd judged us all that night she'd danced for us in the library.

"You're sick. How can anyone find pleasure in pain? How can you?" she'd accused.

My skin trickles with sweat, stinging the open wounds that now crisscross both my chest and back as memories of that evening come hurtling back. Nothing had been appalled by the pleasure Leon received when I'd whipped him for disobeying my orders, and had refused to give him the final lash on my command. Instead she chose to receive it, to save herself from that small act of violence. She'd pissed me off and I hadn't held back. I whipped her as hard as I whipped Leon. Only she proved how strong she truly was by not making a sound, by turning back around to look me dead in the eye and asking me if I was done.

She hadn't cried. She hadn't thrown up. She hadn't cowered. She didn't break.

Then she'd danced like a fucking angel who had endured savagery and conquered it, and in that moment I knew we were all fucked.

Just like I know I am now.

"More!" I roar, and more is what I receive.

One doesn't stop until my chest is a bloody mess and I'm barely conscious.

CHAPTER FIVE

Christy

"MAMA, IS THAT YOU?" I blink back the fog, rubbing at my eyes.

"Hello, my darling girl," she replies, holding her arms out to me.

I don't hesitate, I run into them, pulling her close and burying my face into her hair. "Oh, Mama!" I cry, a sob releasing from my throat.

"Hush, child. We have no time for tears," she says, grasping my shoulders and gently guiding me back onto a wooden bench that I hadn't noticed before now.

"No time?" I swipe at my eyes and blink away the tears, a deep sense of longing making it hard for me to breathe as she settles beside me.

"You need to listen to me," she says, clasping my hands in hers. I marvel at the warmth of them. She feels so alive.

"Where am I?" I ask, confusion settling in as I look around me. The white mist clears revealing the cottage I spent my childhood in and the garden my mother loved to tend. A warm sun heats my skin and the pond at the end of the garden sparkles under the sunlight.

This is home.

"Somewhere you don't belong," she replies, swiping a strand of hair off my face, sadness and love filling her eyes.

"I don't?" I question, blinking rapidly as her grip loosens from around my fingers. When I look down at our joined hands, mine are rapidly disappearing. "Wait! No!" My heart stutters, my chest aches. Swallowing becomes painful.

"Christy, there is no time. Listen to me now."

The urgency in her voice makes me focus, and I nod, forcing myself to ignore the pain in my heart, my chest, my throat.

"I need you to remember who you are."

"What do you mean, I know who I am—"

She shakes her head as if to say that I don't. "You must remain determined in the face of distrust, and courageous in the face of brutality," she continues urgently. "You must always show them what is right and what is wrong. You will not be a victim, never that my darling girl, but I am asking you to see that there is strength in forgiveness, bravery in compassion, and hope in redemption."

I frown, her words making me angry somehow. Then I remember why... The Masks. My hand rises to my throat as I try to understand why it hurts. All I know is that it has something to do with them. "You want me to be kind to those monsters? You want me to have compassion for the men who hurt me? You want me to be tender when all they've been is cruel?" I ask, shaking my head in disbelief.

"I want you to teach them to be the men they were always

supposed to be before the real monster stripped them of what it means to feel loved, what it means to be human. I want you to heal each other. This cycle of pain and hurt has to end. It must."

"And what if I can't do that?" I ask, knowing in my heart all I feel is anger, disappointment, rage.

"Oh, my darling, but what if you can?"

"But..."

She presses a kiss against my cheek. "It's time to go now. Stay strong..."

I AWAKE WITH A START, my lungs filling with oxygen that burns, not soothes, as I gasp for breath. Reaching for my throat, bitter tears sting my eyes at the memory of my mother's words. She wants me to heal *them*? I would scream if my throat didn't hurt so much.

Why does it hurt so much?

"Shh, it's okay. I'm here," an unfamiliar voice says, as I blink away the tears pooling in my eyes. "It was just a dream."

"Not a dream," I croak, focusing on the woman before me as gentle hands ease me back onto the mattress. She frowns at my response, cocking her head. I blink, not understanding how she is suddenly talking. "Thirteen, is that you?"

"Yes." She gives me a soft smile, concern filling her eyes. "How do you feel?"

"You're talking..." I state, surprised at hearing her voice, making me forget everything else momentarily. It's not what I expect; there's a soft lilt to it, an accent. Irish maybe?

"I am."

"How?"

She reaches for a cup on the side table, offering me a straw.

"It will hurt to swallow for a little while, but this tonic should help you to recover quicker," she says, not answering my question.

My lips part and I suck, the sudden need to slake my thirst taking over. The liquid is warm, but not hot and tastes pleasant, sweet. But she's right, it hurts to swallow. The muscles in my neck feel bruised. I reach up to touch my throat, pressing gently against the skin and wince from the pain. "What happened?"

"You don't remember?" she asks, placing the cup back on the side table.

"No. I—I don't. I just feel..."

Strange. Not really here, somehow. Like part of me is still with my mum in that vision... Was it a vision? It felt real, like I was with her, and if I was with her does that mean I was... *dead*?

I force that thought away. Refusing to acknowledge it or the sadness it makes me feel at leaving her. Instead I allow other emotions in, focusing on them instead. They're strong, powerful.

"What?" Thirteen persists, gently stroking my hand.

"I'm angry. It *hurts*," I reply, and I don't just mean physically, as I rub my palm against my chest and try to figure out if my heart aches because of the vision, or something else. I suspect it's both.

"You've every right to be. I'm so sorry. It never should've happened."

"What shouldn't have happened?"

"I didn't think..." She shakes her head. "I'd hoped that they wouldn't... I thought the letter would be enough to make them stop."

"The letter? What letter? Make who stop?"

"From your mother to The Masks."

"You had another letter from my mother, for *them*?" I whisper, drawing my hand out of her hold. My jaw begins to chatter as I try to unravel my confused thoughts. Why would my mother write a letter to The Masks?

"Six months before I came here, I was given three letters by my grandmother on her deathbed. One was addressed to me that I was instructed to open there and then. One was addressed to you that I was instructed to give to you two weeks after you arrived here, and one was addressed to The Masks that I was told to give them the night you were taken to the Room of Fantasies three nights ago."

"Three nights ago?" I repeat.

"Yes. You've been in and out of a drug-induced coma."

"A drug-induced coma? Why?"

"So you could rest, recover. Do you remember anything about that night?"

I frown, trying to focus as bits and pieces slowly come back to me. "I remember dancing in The Menagerie. I remember One playing the piano and Six and Seven singing whilst I danced... I—I don't remember much else." Memories rapidfire in my brain like parts of a movie edited to confuse and baffle the audience. I see Jakub holding a tiny bottle. I see Leon covered in blood, I see people fucking, I see Konrad with rage in his eyes. I remember feeling *numb*, but none of it makes any sense. "I'm not sure... It's confusing."

"Something happened after the show," Thirteen begins, squeezing my hand, her grey eyes round and filled with guilt.

"Tell me," I whisper, a sudden feeling of dread that's quickly accompanied by a deep well of rage spreading through my veins. It's so powerful I can almost taste it. Why am I so angry?

"Leon—" she begins, only to be cut off as the door to the room opens behind her. My focus moves from Thirteen to the door, the door of a room I don't recognise. The furniture is all dark wood, there are no pictures on the walls, none of Thirteen's equipment or drying flowers and herbs, nothing but bare stone. This isn't Thirteen's room.

Panic floods my system.

"Where am I?" I ask, focussing on Thirteen and not the monster who enters the room. *He's* the reason I hurt. I might not remember exactly why but my physical reaction to his presence is enough to tell me I'm right. I'm certain of it.

"My private quarters," Leon answers, cutting off Thirteen as he places the tray of food he's carrying on the bureau to his left. Today he's dressed in a pair of dark blue jeans, a purple shirt with the sleeves rolled up to his elbows and a purple eye mask with gold flecks scattered across the surface. To many he would be attractive, mysterious. To me, he's a monster dressed to confuse and entice. My heart hiccups inside my chest and a sudden rush of fear and hate blooms like wildfire under my skin. It's worse than before. I've feared him, hated him, but this is something more.

"No!" I shout.

"Christy, listen to me," Thirteen says, reaching for me as I push up onto my hands and shuffle backwards on the huge bed.

"Keep him away from me! KEEP HIM AWAY!" I shout, my throat raw.

Leon stiffens, scowling at me before flicking his gaze to Thirteen. "I brought you food. Nala said you were hungry, Thirteen."

"I don't care why you're here! Get out!" I scream, ignoring the pain in my throat. I know that he isn't someone I can talk to like that without consequences, but I don't care. Fear and anger make me reckless.

"Leon, she's not ready," Thirteen implores gently, twisting

her body away from me and holding her hands up to Leon like she's trying to tame a wild animal. He bares his teeth at her, rocking on his feet before glaring at me. I can see the internal struggle he's fighting. There's a dark kind of need in his eyes, but also something else, something new, something close to empathy. It's what holds him back, what stops him from doing what he truly wants. "Please, Leon. Give her time."

"It's been three days already. I *need* to talk to her," he counters, taking a step closer.

"Not now, okay? Not now," she begs, shaking her head.

"Right now," he counters.

"Get. Out!" I demand, panting now, my gaze locking with his. I reach for the glass next to the bed, pick it up and throw it at him. He ducks and it shatters against the wall. When he straightens, his eyes darken and the lines between his eyebrows deepen.

"You'll have to speak to me sooner or later. I'm the only one standing between you and them," he says before twisting on his feet and striding from the room, slamming the door behind him.

My breaths come out in short, sharp bursts as my chest heaves and tears stream down my face. I swipe at them, feeling unhinged, confused, angry, *afraid*.

"What did he mean by that?" I ask, pushing the duvet from my legs that Thirteen is trying to cover me with. I slide off the bed, banging into the side table and a leather armchair as I move. My legs feel weak. I feel weak.

"He means Konrad and Jakub. He's protecting you," Thirteen explains, rising to her feet, approaching me cautiously.

"*Leon* is protecting me from *them*?" I shake my head, still backing away. I'm so confused. My thoughts are in turmoil. Something doesn't feel right. "You're lying!" I accuse, knowing deep down that he's the one who hurt me the most. So why would he need to protect me from his brothers if hurting me is *their* sole purpose?

"No. I'm not. Leon—"

"Strangled me to death!" I shout, remembering suddenly what's been just out of reach. My hand flies to my throat, my eyes widening as Thirteen reaches for me. "No! Don't touch me!" I spin on my feet and run towards the opposite side of the room and to a door that leads to who knows where. Yanking it open, I step into a huge bathroom with a tub the size of a large jacuzzi sunk into the floor, and a vaulted ceiling made entirely of glass situated directly above it. Sunlight streams into the room and I slam the door shut, locking it.

"Christy, please don't be afraid of me. I'm your friend. I won't let him hurt you," Thirteen pleads through the door.

"You already did!" I shout back, my knees buckling beneath me as I slide to the tiled floor. "You already did." I repeat quietly, staring at my reflection in the mirror opposite as I press against the deep purple fingerprints that ring my throat. Fingerprints he made with his hands.

The hands that killed me.

CHAPTER SIX

Christy

STRIPPING OFF MY COTTON NIGHTGOWN, I lower myself into the huge bathtub, desperately needing to get clean, and grateful at least that I'm no longer wearing the chastity belt. I don't know who removed it, and I don't care. I'm just glad to be free of it. Resting my back against the porcelain, I bring my knees up against my chest and wrap my arms around them, wishing I could be enveloped in my mother's arms again.

"Mama, why couldn't I stay with you?" I whisper, tears pooling in my eyes as I rest my cheek against my knees and try to unravel my jumbled feelings of loss, anger, confusion and disappointment. I want to believe that what I saw, what I felt, was my mother reaching out to me from the afterlife, but if it was true and that was her, then why would she tell me to go back? Why would she ask *me* to heal *them?* Why would she want me to be compassionate and kind after everything they've done to me?

She wants me to fix the unfixable.

How can I? How can she ask me to do that?

They're monsters.

A sob escapes my throat, followed by a loud keening. I sound more like a tortured animal than a human. I *feel* like an animal, caged, abused, beaten down, broken.

They hurt me.

They used and abused me.

They tied me to a cross and allowed another man to touch me.

I held up the damn mirror and what did they do? They smashed it to pieces.

They. Broke. Me.

I died.

I *died*.

My whole body shakes as I sob. It won't stop. I can't stop crying. It's a purging of my soul. It all comes pouring out of me. All of the frustration, the grief, the pain, the absolute loss of seeing my mother again and losing her once more.

It's knowing that I'll never leave this place. That I'm a prisoner who'll only escape through death at their hands. It won't be swift, there'll be no mercy.

It will be painful.

"Christy, please, let me in," Thirteen says, banging her fist against the door. She's been there on the other side of the wood for as long as I've been hiding in this bathroom. It's been hours.

"Go away!" I shout between sobs.

"Christy. Open the door! Please," she begs, rattling the handle.

I don't find any comfort in her voice. I feel numb to it.

There's so much I don't understand about her role in all of this. Sinking lower in the water, I ignore Thirteen's pleas. I ignore the echoes of my mother's voice telling me to stay strong.

Instead, I search for oblivion, because there is no hope for me.

I can't run because they'll catch me.

I can't stay because Grim and Beast will die if they come here.

There's only one way out.

Making a decision, I slide beneath the surface of the water, finding peace in the muted silence as my eyes drift shut and I open up my mouth, accepting death on *my* terms.

But that escape is taken from me, too.

Firm hands grasp my upper arms and yank me upwards, pulling me above the surface of the water before thumping me on the back, forcing any water I've inhaled out of my lungs. I cough and splutter, unable to feel the pain of it. Where normally the slightest touch to my back would cause unbeliev-able pain, now there's nothing. I don't have to switch it off, it simply ceases to exist. Is it because something more traumatic has happened to me and I no longer feel the phantom pain? Perhaps.

Blinking back the sting in my eyes, my knees collapse beneath me as I wheeze and gag, whilst a firm arm wraps around my waist. With every intake of breath, I mentally shut down. I fold in on myself, like a piece of paper made into a deli-cate origami bird incapable of flying away. I'm trapped, destined to crash against the bars of this cage, crushed bit by bit.

"No more," I mumble, my throat hoarse, only vaguely aware that I'm now being held within strong arms, cradled against a firm chest that belongs to a man that has killed me once and saved me twice.

Leon.

He's as familiar to me now as my own skin. He's the boy I once thought was an angel and the man I now know to be a monster. He's still wearing the purple mask I saw him in earlier, the green of his eyes popping against the opposing colour.

"You can't leave," he says gruffly, his mouth brushing against my forehead, the water sloshing around my naked skin as he lowers us beneath the surface. My fingers press against the material of his purple shirt, it's sodden.

I stare at my hand, pressed against his chest. I should punch him, scream, pull off his mask and rip at his skin with my nails.

I should fight him off.

I do none of that.

All my fight has depleted.

Every last ounce of strength has drained away.

I'm neither tense, nor relaxed in his hold. I just am.

He senses that, his fingers gripping onto my upper arm and thigh, bruising my skin no doubt.

But I feel nothing. I feel *nothing.*

I've become everything they wanted.

"Leon, let me take her now," Thirteen says, as she kneels beside the bath and urges him to get out. I hadn't even noticed she'd entered the room.

"No. Give me a minute."

"I can't do that."

"You *will* do that. I won't hurt her," he insists.

"But I—"

"Get out. Now, Thirteen!"

She hesitates. I can hear the rise and fall of her breath as she makes a decision. I don't intervene. I don't care if she stays or goes.

I don't care.

"I'll be just in the other room, Christy. I *promise*."

I'm vaguely aware of her quiet footsteps as she leaves me with the man who took my breath and stopped my heart only a couple of days ago. That should hurt. It doesn't. My vision blurs, not with tears but with apathy. Sounds become distant as I sink into myself, my head resting against his chest as I stare off into the distance.

"Stay with me," Leon demands, the tenor of his voice exacting.

I don't answer. Not because I'm feeling stubborn or because I want to get a rise out of him, but because I have no energy left to form the words. I half expect him to react with brutality, with cold, hard hatred. To shake me into action.

He doesn't.

Instead he rests on a ledge beneath the surface of the water and balances me in his arms, grabs a cloth from the side of the bath, and begins to wash me with it.

"She brought you back, you know. Her and Five. I watched her bring you back after I took your life..." He sighs, letting out a tremulous breath as he washes my face, a frown creasing his brow as the cloth passes over the chain of bruises around my throat. Jewellery his hands decorated me with.

He's gentle as he passes the cloth over my breasts and stomach.

He's shaking when he dips it between my legs and cleans me there.

Every now and then a word or a phrase sinks into my consciousness as he repeats those steps.

Broken.

Protect you.

Monster.

Dying.

Cut me.
Fucked up.
Hurt.
Want you.
Sorry.
Angel.
Lost again.
Mirror.

When he drops the washcloth in the water, and adjusts me in his arms, gently cupping the back of my head as he helps me to float, I find myself staring up into his eyes. I don't look away. I don't do anything other than let him support my weight in the water. Above him, the last of the day's sunlight pours through the glass ceiling, the sky a deep purple edged with pinks and oranges.

"Even now I want you like this. *Broken* like this. I want to sink into you. I want to fuck you. God, I want to fuck you so bad," he mutters, a host of emotions scattering across his face like shadows through a darkened room. "I'm not a good person. I'll never be a good person, but I *will* try to be. I'll fucking try if it means I get to keep you." His gaze roves over my naked skin, from my face to my chest, to my stomach, to my pussy and back up again. Need flares in his eyes, quickly followed by shame, then anger. He's fighting his natural instinct to take, to maim, to steal, to *hurt*. He's flooded with need, with emotion, with contradiction.

Yet I'm hollow. I don't feel.

Not fear.

Not embarrassment or shame.

Not hate.

Nor anger.

I'm *empty*.

He could take advantage of me right now and I doubt I'd feel a thing.

He could take my virginity and cover his dick with my blood, and I wouldn't even notice.

He could kill me and I'd let him.

Yet, he does none of those things. Instead, he gathers me in his arms, climbs out of the bath and carries me back into the bedroom, laying me down on the bed.

"She needs to rest," Thirteen says, entering my peripheral vision. I don't need to see her expression to know that she fears for me. She doesn't trust him not to hurt me again.

"And she will," he replies. "I'll make sure she does."

"It would be better if you leave. Give her some space." Thirteen's voice is filled with trepidation, as though she's expecting him to revert back to the man we both know so well.

I don't doubt that he will, I just don't care if he does.

"No, I'm not going anywhere. I respected your wishes and gave you time to heal her. It didn't work."

"It's only been a few days. Healing takes time, Leon. The physical wounds will fade, the emotional ones, the mental scars, they take so much longer."

"She just tried to kill herself, Thirteen. I'm not leaving her in your care for a moment longer."

"And why do you think that is?" she asks. There's no anger in her voice, just a sad kind of truth.

"I know why. I want to fix it."

"I'm not sure you're the right person for the job," she replies, brutally honest. "I'm not sure any of *us* are."

Leon growls, the rumble rising up his throat threatening. "Don't start that with me again. She is not going home. She is *mine*."

"Konrad and Jakub would beg to differ."

Leon grits his teeth so hard I can hear the sound it makes, like stones being scraped against one another. "Konrad and Jakub can go fuck themselves!"

"You know this reprieve won't last. They'll come for her, Leon. Then what? Will you kill your brothers?"

"If I have to," he grinds out.

Thirteen throws her hands up in the air, shaking her head in frustration. Still I remain mute, numb. I hear what they're saying but don't react to it. "Really? When it comes down to it, you'll take your brothers' lives?" she asks him.

"I'll do what I have to do. I always have..." His voice trails off as he looks at Thirteen. "Violence is the only language I understand."

"Is it?" she asks him softly.

He shakes his head, cutting his gaze to me whilst addressing Thirteen. "You can stay, or you can go, but my mask is coming off and if you see my face, you know as well as I do that you'll *never* leave here."

"Leon, *please*," Thirteen implores.

"It's your choice. Make a decision."

"Christy, I—" she begins, her voice cracking.

The emotion in it stirs me enough to turn and look at her. She's devastated. She doesn't want to leave me alone with Leon, but equally she doesn't want her future to be confined to this castle.

I don't blame her for it. She still has a chance to be free. I can't take that away from her.

"Go," I whisper, forcing my mouth to move.

She reaches for me, grasping my hands and pressing a kiss against my cheek. "I won't do that." Pulling back she glares at Leon. "I will sleep on the chaise. I will look away from you, but if anything happens and I'm forced to look upon your face then

I will take the punishment for it. I will remain here for the rest of my days. I will never leave Ardelby Castle."

"You would do that for Christy?" Leon asks, confusion mixed with a little dash of awe.

"I would do that because it's the *right* thing to do."

With one last wavering smile at me, Thirteen turns on her heel and strides across the room settling on the sofa. Once her back is to us both, Leon removes his mask, dropping it onto the floor beside the bed then turns his attention back to me.

"You're still wet. I'll dry you," he states.

I don't protest, instead I remain still as he grabs a towel from somewhere to the left of the bed and begins to gently run it over my body. I can hear the way his breath becomes more and more laboured with every stroke. Again I expect him to take advantage.

Again, he doesn't.

And I don't react to his touch. Numbness gives me respite from everything. I'm grateful for it.

"There, you're dry," he mutters, pulling away for a moment. I can hear the sound of him removing his wet clothes and I fully expect him to be naked as I feel his weight dip the mattress as he lies down next to me.

"I won't touch you," he rumbles, leaning over me as he pulls up the throw folded over the end of the bed and lays it across my body. The material is soft and smells of lavender and berg-amot. I draw in a deep breath, allowing the scent to wash over me.

As he tucks the throw around me like a cocoon, I turn my head to face him. He's bare-chested and wearing a pair of jogging bottoms, and my eyes rove over his chest taking in the black reed tattoos, before flicking back up to meet his gaze. A flop of dark hair is falling into his eyes as he looks at me in much the same way he did right before he wrapped his hands around my throat and squeezed the breath from my lungs. I shiver involuntarily, residual fear causing a low moan to break free from my mouth.

"I won't touch you. I promise," he repeats.

If I had the energy I would laugh because who can trust a promise coming from a man who takes whatever he chooses regardless of the consequences. All I can do is continue to stare at him, my gaze roving over his face. His mask is gone but a new one sits in its place, and I don't know if this one is real or not. I can't trust myself to know the truth. Right now he's a man caught up in a tight bundle of agony. His dark brows meet in a frown, his nostrils flare under a strong nose. His plump lips part as his chest heaves with every breath. His cheeks, chin and throat are covered in a dark stubble. His neck has a cut right across it, a thin scab showing evidence of a fight I've no memory of.

"What happened?" I find myself asking.

"Konrad." He swallows hard, his Adam's apple bobbing under his skin. "He held a knife to my throat when I tried to stop Jakub from killing you again."

"I see," I mutter, uncertain how I feel about that. Mixed emotions serve up a cocktail of thoughts that I don't have the stomach for.

"I'm sorry," he whispers out, brushing the tip of his nose against mine gently. It's a moment of purity, truth, *remorse*, that should comfort me. It doesn't. For a moment he hovers above me, staring down as he waits for me to acknowledge his apology. When I don't, he gives me a sharp nod, then draws back, settling down beside me. Both of us stare up at the ceiling. After a beat he speaks. "You're right to be afraid. I've given you every reason to fear me, Christy. But know this, you're mine whether you want to be or not. You were the moment I pulled you from the fire."

"And your brothers?" I question, the words thick, heavy on my tongue.

"Are still trying to figure out whether they want to fuck you or kill you."

"So nothing's changed then," I croak.

"You're wrong. *Everything's* changed."

I heave out a sigh, the truth of his words sliding into my bloodstream and sparking something to life within me. I'm not sure what the feeling is, but it's no longer just apathy and numbness that sits heavy in my chest. It's so much more than that.

"Do you understand what I'm saying?" he asks.

"I understand," I whisper, giving Leon my back as I turn on my side and hold onto that tiny spark of life in my chest like it's a lifeline. It's only when my eyes drift shut that I truly understand the feeling for what it is...

Vengeance.

CHAPTER SEVEN

Christy

A FEW DAYS LATER, I'm tossing and turning in bed, haunted by dreams of my mother, of Grim and Beast, and of sweet baby Iris. Their faces linger in my consciousness as my eyes snap open, and I smother a sob that tries to escape my throat by stuffing my fingers into my mouth.

I miss them so much.

Blinking away the tears that have formed, I bite down on my fingers. Hard.

No more tears. No more self-pity. No fucking more.

Four days ago I tried to kill myself.

For four days I've barely eaten, hardly slept. I've gone through the motions, acting weak whilst I build up my defences slowly, minute by minute, hour by hour.

Leon has hovered around me, barely leaving my side, tracking my every move. Even Thirteen hasn't been able to persuade him to give me space. He's wound-up tight, every atom of his being on high alert as he waits for me to attempt to take my life again.

I won't.

Not today, not tomorrow, nor the day after that. I'm going to be strong. Stronger than ever before. That's the one thing I can do for my mother. The *only* thing.

Because I sure as hell can't do what she's asked of me.

I can't. I won't.

Adjusting my position, I turn onto my back. The room is pitched in darkness, a slither of moonlight cutting through the gap in the curtains allowing me to make out the outline of a man sitting beside the unlit fire, his head in his hands.

Leon.

Wrapped up in shadows, Leon grasps his hair with his fingers, and I see glimpses of the muscles in his back tensing and flexing as he rocks back and forth, back and forth. The black reed tattoos come to life across his skin as he drowns in his sorrow.

I should look away, but I can't seem to take my eyes off him.

I'm transfixed by his grief as he tips his head back and lets out a silent scream. The veins in his neck pop, and tears fall from his eyes like pieces of jewelled moonlight.

My God, he's a shattered man. Utterly devastated. Broken.

If I didn't know him, if I'd never experienced what I have with him, then I would've felt drawn to help him, to soothe the pain he feels. To comfort him. Hold him.

Yet I do know him. He *killed* me.

I can't get past that. He deserves every last ounce of sorrow.

Every. Last. Ounce.

Flicking my gaze away I look across the other side of the room at Thirteen, who's sleeping with her back to us, her thin frame covered by a dark woollen blanket. She has remained by my side since I woke up, refusing to leave me alone with Leon. I'm grateful, but there's still a large part of me that doesn't know how to feel about her. I have so many questions that I haven't been able to ask since I tried to end my life.

My stomach churns at the thought. I hate that I felt that way... so *numb*.

So lost. So completely crushed.

"I wanted you dead," Leon says quietly, drawing my attention back to him. I stiffen, half expecting him to attack me. Instead he continues to speak, staring off into the distance, his voice pitted with sorrow. "I wanted you dead because you made something live inside of me. You made my heart beat again," he continues, fisting his hand and bashing it against his chest.

"You have a heart?" I question, shaking my head at the thought. "How can you possibly have a heart? You're a monster."

He swipes at his face, pressing his fingers against his eyes before focussing back on me. "I want you to know that I hate myself for what I did to you. I will hate myself until the day I die. There are no excuses. I know what I did, what I am. I'm *sorry*."

I feel the truth of his apology despite hating him and all the ways he hurt me. "They're just words," I say.

"You won't believe me, but I did stop. I remembered what it felt like to save you when I was a kid. How you looked at me back then like I was more than nothing. You said I was an angel. I wasn't. I'm not. I never will be. But for a brief moment in time I'd been kind, and it had felt *good*." He lets out a sad laugh, shaking his head at the concept. A slight breeze blows through the window, shifting the curtains and highlighting his face in silvery moonlight, and for the briefest of moments we lock gazes. My heart lurches but my head shuts those feelings of pity down.

"I don't care. I want you to suffer like I have, like I *do*," I say, my whole body trembling as he rises to his feet. I watch him as he climbs onto the bed and lays down beside me.

He's built to kill. He's muscular, lean.

Powerful.

I'm well aware that he has the ability to overpower me and there'd be nothing I could do about it. I'm the most vulnerable, and yet he's the one crying.

Not long ago he would have attempted to kill me for seeing him like this. But he doesn't do anything other than wipe at the tears on his face, then look at his hand as though he doesn't understand how they got there.

"I don't blame you. If I were in your shoes, I'd feel the same way. I'd want to kill me, too."

"How do you know I won't still do that?"

"I don't, and going by the look in your eyes I suspect you'll try. Perhaps you'll succeed. You want me dead, and I deserve nothing less than your hate, your disgust and your rage." He shifts so that he's laying on his side with his head propped up on his hand as he stares down at me. "If I didn't think you were in danger from my brothers I would hand you my blade now and let you slit my throat for what I did to you."

I laugh bitterly. "This is all just another twisted game. Another trick. Another way to mess with my head, to keep me prisoner here. If you feel so guilty, why not let me go, huh? Why not do that?"

Across the room I hear Thirteen stir, she murmurs something in her sleep but it's too jumbled to make any sense of it. I clamp my mouth down on a scream of frustration, at myself for not attempting to run, at Thirteen for doing nothing more than stay by my side, at Leon for trying to fuck with my head.

I want out. I want to go home.

Yet, here I lay talking to the man who robbed me of my life.

"Let me go," I repeat, locking eyes with him.

He shakes his head. "I can't do that. Despite my need to protect you from my brothers, I *can't* let you go."

"Why?"

"Because I don't *want* to. Because you're the only thing that has made me feel more human than monster. Because... Because..." He brings his hand up to the centre of his chest, the heel of his palm rubbing up and down as though he feels pain. "Because I'm a selfish fuck."

"Then nothing's changed. You killed me, Thirteen brought me back to life, and I'm still a prisoner with the threat of death hanging over me. What am I supposed to do other than try and end this torment myself?"

Leon swallows hard as his gaze roves over me. "I don't know. I don't have the answer to that. All I know is that I can't... I *won't* let you go. I feel. I *feel*..." he laughs sadly, shaking his head. "You once told me that you were my *mirror*. That you would reflect every wrongdoing, every act of cruelty, debasement, pain, so that I would see who I am." He lowers his head, his face hovering over mine, his green eyes nothing more than swathes of nighttime. There's no colour, no light, just a bottomless void of sorrow.

"I also said I would never break no matter what you did to me. But I did break, didn't I? *You* broke me, and now all I have left are scattered pieces of who I was. I'm made up of broken shards that you caused. So tell me, Leon, how can I help you? Why would I help you after what you did, when all I feel towards you is *rage?*" I spit, angry tears leaking from my eyes now. "I want out. Do you understand me?"

Leon reaches for my face, tenderly brushing my tears away with his fingers that are shaking so badly I can feel the vibrations all the way to my bones. "The only way out of this life is death."

"Then so be it," I retort, gritting my teeth and turning my head away from him.

I can feel his warm breath feathering against my cheek as he lowers his mouth to my ear. "I won't let you take your life, Christy, and I certainly won't let my brothers try to do the same. I don't know what the future holds, but I do know that you're mine for however long I get to keep you."

For a moment all we are are two synchronised hearts beating the same staccato drum. A thump, thump, thump of quiet distrust, fear and uncertainty. The power play between us has shifted. I'm no longer just a prisoner or a victim. I'm as much the one wielding the ability to inflict pain as he is. He knows it, just as much as I do. With that knowledge I turn my head to meet his gaze.

"Then death it shall be. I'll kill you all," I reply quietly, ignoring the echo of my mother's voice as she begs me to remember who I am.

"*There is strength in compassion, bravery in tenderness, and hope in redemption,*" she had said.

I reject it. I reject him. I reject all of them.

"Then I ask one thing before you take our lives," he requests solemnly.

"And what's that?"

"That you remember this kiss before you slide the knife into my heart."

With that he breaks another promise and touches me with

his lips, with his broken heart, with his goddamn mutilated soul as he slides his tongue into my mouth and kisses me with a desperate kind of passion that surpasses anything I've ever felt before.

With every press of his lips, every stroke of his tongue, he pushes against the barriers of my hate, trying to reach the parts of me *he* broke. His fingers grip my face as though he's afraid I'll slip through them. His body presses against mine as he takes comfort from my beating heart and silent whimpers. He's kissing the girl who lay dying on the wet grass, the woman who, at one point, had felt more than hate for him, who'd felt empathy.

But I'm different now.

I'm only pieces.

I'm a sum of all the shattered parts that I can no longer glue together.

And those shattered parts are surrounded by an impenetrable wall that *he* put there, that The Masks built with their cruelty, their sadism, their abuse.

My walls are too thick now, so despite the heat from his body, despite the way his heart thrums against my chest and the passion I feel as he kisses me, my shattered heart remains protected.

I don't fight his kiss. I allow him to believe that I'm a willing participant. I kiss him back, knowing that as I do he believes I'm forgiving him whilst all I'm doing is building my defences.

The kiss deepens. My heart hardens as his softens, and with it the edges of another familiar feeling begins to seep into my consciousness. As we kiss a vision begins to unfold, the strength of it a weight that sits heavy on my soul...

.   .   .

"WHAT THE FUCK HAVE YOU DONE?" *The Collector accuses as he steps into the room.*

"It was a mistake," Konrad says, eying his father as he kneels beside a naked, pale-skinned woman dusted with bruises. She's unconscious. Unconscious, but breathing.

Behind him, Leon stands, his expression one of shock. The pair are no more than thirteen or fourteen. They're boys who've been forced to grow up under the brutal rule of a man.

"A mistake? She's supposed to be dead. I leave you both for one minute to take a phone call and this is what happens? You were supposed to remove the body, not fucking revive her."

"I d—didn't mean to do it. I wasn't thinking..." Konrad stutters, standing on shaky legs.

"You didn't mean to do it? You weren't thinking? Seems to me, son, all you've done is think. Feel..."

Konrad flinches as though slapped. "No. I don't—"

"It was my fault," Leon says, interrupting him.

The Collector's gaze snaps to Leon, eyes narrowing. "Your fault?"

"Yes, Sir." He nods, his gaze unwavering.

"Tell me how Konrad bringing this woman back to life is your fault." He folds his arms across his chest, raising a brow. "Did you possess his body? Did you step inside his skin and force him to do it?"

"I told him to do it," he replies, passing Konrad and stepping over the woman. "I can be very persuasive."

"You persuaded him to revive her...why?"

"Leon—" Konrad begins, his voice wavering.

"To see if he could," Leon replies with a shrug.

"To see if he could?" Their father repeats.

"Yeah. It was a bet. I bet he couldn't do it. Turns out he could."

"*And how the fuck do you know how to bring someone back to life?*" *Their father asks, turning his attention to Konrad.*

"*I read about it in a book. I figured it wouldn't be all that hard,*" *Konrad replies quickly, getting to his feet.*

"*In a book?*"

"*Yes. I—*"

"*He's been gagging to do it. Konrad has a fucking God complex or some shit. The twisted fuck,*" *Leon replies, laughing. He glances over his shoulder at Konrad, his eyes wide, imploring him to go with the story. Konrad swallows hard.*

"*Is this true, son?*"

"*I—*"

"*Oh, come on, Kon, don't be shy, you know you're a sick motherfucker,*" *Leon persists as he steps back over the woman, throws an arm around Konrad's shoulder and rubs his knuckles through Konrad's hair. Leon's act seems blasé, like he doesn't give a shit about the woman on the floor at his feet, but there's a shadow of fear around his eyes.*

"*Yeah, sick,*" *Konrad agrees, grinning widely, but that grin falters.*

Their father watches them both. Eyes narrowing. "*Quite the perversion you've got there, son.*" *He glances at the woman who's oblivious to what's happening around her.* "*But now we have a problem that needs cleaning up.*" *He looks between the pair, a sly smile pulling up his lips.*

"*W—what?*" *Konrad stutters.*

"*You brought her back. Except I don't want this piece of trash whore breathing. I want her dead. Kill her.*"

"*You want me to kill her?*" *he repeats, looking at Leon.*

"*Do you have a problem with that?*" *Their father asks, unbuckling his belt as he watches them both. When he pulls the* belt free, he holds the buckle in one hand and slaps the leather onto the palm of the other.

"There's no problem, Sir," Leon says, glaring at his brother.

"Oh I promise you, there will be if you don't do exactly what I say," Malik responds, crooking his finger at Leon. "Come here, son."

Leon obeys as Konrad watches with wide eyes. "What are you doing?"

"Leon is at fault, right? So he must pay for it."

"No!" Konrad shouts.

"He's not?" Their father asks, jerking his chin at Leon who removes his jumper and shirt, then gives his father his back.

"I am," Leon insists. "This is on me."

Their father releases the leather from his hand, snapping it against the wooden floor. The sound is like a gunshot going off. "You'll take the punishment?"

"I'll take whatever you give me," Leon replies.

"Good, because Konrad here is going to kill this woman and then revive her over and over again until I tell him to stop."

"You want me to kill her and revive her?" Konrad asks, eyes wide.

"Yes, you will do it until you can no longer bring her back, and whilst you do Leon here is going to be reminded of what happens when you do something that displeases me."

"Brother..." Konrad implores, staring at Leon who refuses to look back at him.

"Do it. Kill her. Bring her back. Then fucking kill her again. Do it, brother! Fucking do it!" Leon shouts.

Their father laughs.

He laughs and laughs and laughs.

He laughs when Konrad puts his hands around the woman's throat and strangles her.

He laughs when Leon's back begins to split, dripping blood from the lashes.

He laughs as Konrad presses his lips against the woman's mouth, then compresses her chest as he brings her back to life.

He laughs as Leon stumbles from the pain, righting himself again.

He laughs as one son loses himself to a sickness, and another to indescribable pain.

He laughs whilst Leon falls to his knees and Konrad rises to his feet, one son beaten down by a monster, the other forced to stand in the presence of one.

"If either of you lie to me again I won't be so lenient. Emotion has no place in this castle. Feelings are poisonous, they inflict pain. Kindness is a sin that will not be tolerated. Understood?"

"Yes, Sir," Leon bites out.

"Yes, Sir," Konrad replies, his hands trembling.

"Get rid of the body," Their father demands, before twisting on his feet and striding from the room.

Once he's gone, Leon rises slowly to his feet and turns to face Konrad who's staring at the woman's lifeless body, bruises upon bruises ringing her throat. "Brother?"

Konrad slowly drags his gaze upwards to meet Leon's. "I felt it."

"Felt what?"

"The power," he replies, holding his hands up as he stares at them.

"The power?" Leon asks, pain and concern etched across his face.

"You were right, Leon. I felt like God..."

. . .

SHOVING LEON OFF ME, I scramble backwards on the bed, my lips bruised from his kiss, what's left of my shattered heart pulverised by the vision.

"Christy?" he questions, chest heaving, cock pressing against the confines of his joggers. "Where did you go?"

"Don't. Don't come near me!" I shout, holding my hand up, warning him off me.

Across the room, Thirteen sits upright. "Christy?" she asks, moving her head to look over her shoulder.

"Don't!" I snap, "He's not wearing his mask."

She stills, not moving. "What's going on?" she asks.

What's going on? How can I tell her that we kissed, that I *let* him? How can I tell her that I had a vision of him and Konrad, that I witnessed the fierce love Leon had for his brother? How can I tell her that it tears me up inside to know how they've suffered? How can I tell her that despite those feelings I still want revenge, *vengeance*? How can I tell her that I can't forgive a man who was once an abused boy, broken over and over again? How can I tell her that I want to break him even more?

"Christy?" she prompts, as Leon stares at me.

Instead of answering her, I look into his eyes, swallowing the bile that burns my throat and say: "You might've been a boy who's suffered at the hands of an evil bastard, but that's no excuse for the actions of a man. You're not that boy anymore, so get the fuck away from me!"

Leon swipes a hand over his face, scrubbing at his skin before grasping his hair in fists. "*Fuck!* I don't want to be this man," he pleads, pulling at his hair so hard that strands of it come away in his hands.

"You can't change what you are," I retort, getting off the bed and backing away from him.

He comes after me like the predator he is.

Stalking me.

Teeth bared.

Eyes wide.

Fingers balled into fists.

In a blink of an eye he falls back into old habits.

Across the other side of the room, Thirteen glances at me over her shoulder, her eyes wide as she watches him approach me. I shake my head, urging her to look away.

"You're wrong, because I'm fighting with *everything* I am not to rip those clothes from your body and fuck you until I cut myself on every last broken part of your soul. I want to cover my dick in your cum, in your blood. I want to taste your tears. I want to bruise your skin. But I *won't* take what you're not willing to give. *That's* the difference between who I was and who I'm fighting to be," he says, pinning me against the wall with his body, his forearms pressed against the wall on either side of my head. Chest heaving, breaths frantic.

"Leon, back off!" Thirteen demands, but it falls on deaf ears.

Leon presses his forehead against mine. "Will you help me, Christy? Will you help me to be the man I was supposed to be before *The Collector* stole my innocence, my fucking kindness, my goddamn heart?"

Can I?

The honest answer is no. No, I can't.

But the answer I eventually give him is a whispered *yes*.

"Yes, I'll help you," I say, because whilst he might've shattered my heart, I intend to cut him with the shards and make him *feel*, just like I'll do to his brothers. Then, when they're at their most vulnerable, I'll have my revenge.

Konrad

"YOU NEED to raise your arm higher, bend your wrist back a little more. This is a blade-heavy knife, so throwing it by the handle is necessary," Five explains, placing her fingers beneath my bicep and lifting my arm higher as I focus on the target across the other side of the dungeon.

"Like this?"

"Exactly, Master. When you're ready, release the knife and remember to follow through with the movement."

Once she's satisfied that I'm gripping the knife correctly and in the proper stance, she steps back to give me space to throw. Drawing in two deep breaths, I pull back my arm, then throw as instructed. This time the knife lands exactly where it's supposed to: right in the centre of the Baron's severed head. The sound the knife makes as it slices through his bulbous nose is as satisfying as it is disgusting.

Five doesn't even blink. She's used to me and my...
perversions.

Don't get me wrong, I'm not turned on by a severed head,
particularly one that belonged to a sick fuck like the Baron, but
wielding a knife and using it correctly to cause the most amount
of harm as efficiently as possible? Sign me the fuck up.

Besides, it's a good distraction.

And fuck do I need one.

Rolling my head and shoulders, I attempt to let out some of
the tension in my muscles. I've been strung tight ever since the
night Zero died and Thirteen and Five brought her back to life.
Even now, a week later, I'm still fuming that I wasn't the one to
do that. I don't resent either Thirteen or Five, but I do fucking
resent Leon for preventing me from helping them.

"Again?" Five questions.

"Yes."

Five hands me another knife. It's smaller than the one I've
just thrown, but much more weighty. The surface of the blade is
covered in scratches, the black leather handle well worn. If you
look close enough, the sharp edge has tiny serrated teeth that
will tear at the skin rather than make a clean cut. I press the
very tip of the blade against the pad of my thumb. It barely
needs any pressure to slice through the skin. A tiny bead of
blood rises to the surface and I suck it off, smiling at the memory
it brings to the surface of Zero strapped to the St Andrew's cross
three cells over, her eyes rolling back in her head from the pleasure and the pain.

Just like her, this knife feels good in my hand. Like it *fits*.

"Most people believe that the bigger the knife the deadlier
the weapon, but that just isn't true," Five says. "Anything can be
used as a weapon to kill, you just have to know how to use it the
right way to get the job done."

"Is that so?" I ask, cutting a look at Five, knowing that she's not just talking about this knife.

"Yes." She jerks her chin at the knife clutched in my hand. "This is a handle-heavy knife so you should throw it by the blade. It'll strike the target better if you do. If your aim is true and you manage to sever one of the main arteries, it will kill a person. If you miss, the tiny teeth will tear through tendons and muscles as you pull it out. That type of wound is far harder to fix than one caused by a straight-edged blade."

"Like this?" I ask, pinching the flat edge of the blade between my fingers.

"Precisely. Position yourself as before, then when you're ready, throw."

Focussing on the Baron's gaping mouth still caught in a silent scream, I lift my arm over my throwing shoulder and keep my elbow tucked in so the knife is situated directly beside my ear, then throw. It slides right through his open lips.

"Better?" I ask, not particularly seeking her approval, but needing to strike up a conversation in order for me to get my mind off of wanting to simultaneously kill my brother for refusing to let me help bring Zero back, and thank him for doing precisely that. The two sides of me are at war with themselves. The part of me that has a modicum of decency left knows he was right to keep me away, the other part, the bigger and far more dominant part, is fuming.

Fucking *raging*.

"You're improving," Five replies before striding over to the Baron's head and pulling both knives out of his face. She reaches for a cloth tucked into the leather belt at her waist and cleans them before placing them on the table with the rest of her collection.

"Thanks to you."

She nods curtly, not certain how to react to my compliment. "You're a quick study."

"You're a good teacher."

"Thank you, Master."

Flicking her gaze away, she busies herself with wrapping up her collection of blades. I watch her with interest as her small hands slide over each lethal weapon as though they are more than just inanimate objects. I guess to her they are. These knives are the difference between her being fucked raw in every available hole whenever we have clients visiting the castle, to being a bodyguard to the Numbers.

Truthfully, of all the Numbers, I respect Five the most. Her skills far outweigh those of the others and whilst I appreciate their artistry, being able to sever an artery from thirty feet away by throwing a knife is far more impressive than being able to sing or play the piano. That shit might impress Jakub, but not me.

"Where did you learn how to do this?" I ask, aware that I've never actually bothered to find out despite the years we've lived under the same roof.

"I had a mentor in Calcutta. He died not long before your father collected me," she replies softly, continuing with her task.

"I see. Well, I'm sure he would be as impressed by your skills as I am if he were still alive to see them."

Five flicks her gaze at me, her skin creasing between her brows as she frowns. I'm aware that compliments from me are few and far between. It's not in my nature to be appreciative of anyone, let alone a Number.

I demand. I take. I fuck. I ruin. I hurt. I heal.

And then I do it all over again because I'm a sick fuck like that.

As much as it pains me to admit, Leon was right about my

intentions that night. I didn't want to bring Zero back solely because I cared enough to want her to live for my own selfish reasons. I wanted to bring her back because doing so would've been like a shot of heroin straight to my fucked-up heart. The high would've been like nothing else. Once upon a time Leon had referred to it as my *God complex*. I remember the moment well. I'd done something I shouldn't and he'd stepped in and taken a beating from our father because of it. Always taking a beating, always protecting us from ourselves. Being estranged from him is causing huge motherfucking problems. Not to mention that I miss the bastard.

It's all *her* fault.

Zero.

Zero with her fiery hair and courageous soul.

Zero with her scars that reflect my own.

Zero with her ghost eyes that I swear can see directly into both Heaven and Hell.

She's been playing on repeat in my mind; I've spent the last week thinking about her, about those eyes. I want to ask her if she saw Heaven when she died, whether it actually fucking exists because I sure as fuck know Hell exists. I spent the better part of my childhood living in it.

A lesser person wouldn't have survived such an experience. A lesser person would've ended up a dribbling, drooling shell of a human being after going through what me and my brothers have been through.

Only I'm *not* a lesser person. I'm not weak.

Instead of rejecting the darkness our father surrounded us in, I accepted it. I opened my arms and embraced it. You see, Leon is wrong when he says I've got a God complex, because God is good, right? I'm not good. I pretend that I am whilst knowing that I'm not. Jakub might be the heir to the Brov throne, Leon might be fucking Judas now, but me? I'm my father's son.

"Is there anything else I can help you with, Master?" Five asks me, drawing me out of my thoughts and back in the room.

I bark out a laugh and stride across the room, picking up a seven-inch Wharncliffe knife, turning it over in my hand. "I doubt it."

"Master?" she queries, stepping into my peripheral vision.

I glance down at her, paying more attention to what she's wearing now than I have the whole time we've been together. She's covered up today with her mid-thigh leather skirt and matching waistcoat. If any of the other Numbers, aside from Thirteen, dared to cover their bodies as much as Five has now they'd be sent to me in the dungeons for reformation. With Five, it's a little different. She has a somewhat elevated position, and whilst she performs in The Menagerie regularly, she doesn't fuck the clients. Well, that's not strictly true, she fucks one particular client who has claimed his right to her with a shit load of money and a steady supply of jewels from his diamond caves in South Africa. The Mole attends Ardelby Castle once a year on the night of The Brònach Masquerade Ball. Five will be reunited with him soon enough. I've no idea if she's looking forward to it or not and honestly, I don't give a shit besides her being fit enough to be able to fulfill her duties after he's gone. We've never had a problem in that respect, like I said, he's into vanilla sex with an exotic girl. I don't blame him, Five is uniquely stunning. Fortunately for her, the Numbers are off the menu for myself and my brothers, and vanilla really isn't our thing. Nor is *making love*.

That term is a foreign concept, and has never factored into our day to day lives, let alone our fantasies. Don't get me wrong, I'm down for giving all types of pleasure and am excellent at it, but there are never any feelings of love when I'm fucking a woman. More often than not, I'm imagining all the ways I can hurt them, and all the hours it will take to heal those wounds just so I can do it over again.

I'm incapable of love. More to the point, completely fucking averse to it.

I thought we all were, but when Leon had fallen to his knees at Zero's side, I'd seen a man broken by grief and destroyed by his actions. Those *emotions*, those *feelings*, they only happen when there is empathy, regret, kindness, fucking *love*.

He's been infected, and somehow we need to purge him of the disease.

"Tell me, Five," I say suddenly, cutting through the silence with my voice. "What is it about the human heart that makes a man like my brother want to destroy all that we've built here for one woman?"

I'm curious to know her opinion. I can't talk to Thirteen, given she's locked herself away with Leon and Zero, and I sure as fuck can't talk to Jakub who's so inside his own head right now that he can't even hold a conversation, much less talk about what happened.

"You believe Leon has turned his back on you?" she questions.

I frown, staring into her amber eyes that glow as brightly as any jewel I've ever seen. "I didn't say that."

"But isn't that what you meant?" she asks.

"Maybe," I shrug.

Five grips the handle of her favourite knife that is always holsted in the leather strap she wears across her chest. Pulling it free, she studies it closely before finally speaking. *"Your task is not to seek for love, but merely to seek and find all the barriers within yourself that you have built against it."*

"Plato?" I ask, thrown a little by her response. It's weighted and layered with meaning that I'm not in the frame of mind to pull apart right now. Especially not after everything that's happened. *Fuck love.*

"No, Rumi." She dips her head, tucking her knife back into it's holster. It's only then that I realise she was expecting my reaction to be one of anger, and that holding her knife in her hand guaranteed her safety.

She's not stupid, but really there was no need to be cautious. Five has earned her place as a trusted member of our household. She's invaluable to us and that's why we haven't already slit her throat for obeying Thirteen's orders to revive Zero. Her role, as much as anything, is to protect the Numbers, and that's what she did.

I can't blame her for it.

"So you believe in the legend of The Weeping Tree, is that what you're saying?" I ask her.

"I believe that there are many unexplainable things in this world that are beyond our comprehension. I also believe that truths can be twisted to suit another person's goals."

"Unexplainable things?" I shake my head. "We aren't ruled by some invisible force. We are the masters of our own fate."

"If I may talk freely?" Five questions.

I wave my hand. "Yes."

"Do you believe evil exists?"

"You're asking *me* that question? There's a fucking severed head nailed to the wall over there," I say, pointing to the Baron's head.

She nods. "I'm well aware. Please answer the question, do you believe evil exists?"

"I've seen the worst of what a human is capable of doing, experienced it myself. So, in answer to your question, yes, of course it exists."

"And do you believe you are evil, that your brothers are?"

"We are our father's sons. I don't deny it."

"This is true. Then let me ask you another question. Do you believe goodness exists?"

"It's not something I'm very familiar with."

"But you believe it exists."

"I guess it must if the opposite is true," I reply begrudgingly.

Five nods, folding her arms across her chest as she regards me. "Good and evil are social constructs. Dividing lines, if you will. They're designed so that a human being can more easily comprehend what is right and what is wrong by a certain set of rules they've been exposed to or choosen to live by.

"Okay, but what has this got to do with The Weeping Tree, with unexplainable forces, with fucking *fate*?"

"The Weeping Tree is a legend that's personal to your family, is it not?"

"True."

"And you believe that Marie's kindness all those years ago started a chain of events that led to you and your brothers being the men you are today?"

"Yes, that's common knowledge within the walls of the castle."

"You believe that Marie's kindness," Five continues, "Her *goodness*, eventually lead to a perpetual turn of events that has infected your family line for generations."

"You make it sound like a disease."

She sighs, but doesn't deny it. "You believe that kindness, goodness is wrong, abhorrent. *You* believe it's a disease," she repeats. "Why?"

"Because it is."

"No, because you've been exposed to one man's ideology where kindness, goodness, *love* are weaknesses, and cruelty, hatred and violence are strengths. You've been brought up beneath an entirely different set of rules based on a cycle of abuse that has occurred over countless generations."

"That began because a woman was *kind*."

Five shakes her head. "That began because a man feared a woman's ability to heal, to do good, and so he called her a witch and hung her from a tree to prove just how evil she was. Only the true evil was the man who used fear, hate and violence to intimidate and murder. Marie was never to blame."

"But that's your view based on what ideals and rules you were exposed to."

"Precisely."

"And your point?"

"And my point is, which is right and which is wrong? My views or yours?"

"Kindness started all of this," I say adamantly.

"And kindness will end it."

I fall silent for a moment, ruminating on what she's said, a sick kind of feeling brewing in my stomach. It's unfamiliar and I have the sudden, very desperate need to purge it from my fucking system. Five folds away her knives and ties up the leather pouch, securing it with a bow before tucking it under her arm and meeting my gaze.

"The way I see it, the question you should be asking isn't why the human heart has made your brother turn his back on you, but why a man with a heart so broken, so *evil*, so filled with endless darkness can save the very person he was supposed to destroy. Is it an invisible force called fate moving all the pieces?

Is it because of a legend written hundreds of years ago predicting it will happen?"

"I don't believe that, no—"

She dips her head, before locking her gaze with mine. "Then could it simply be because one man decided to embrace the feelings that he'd been forced to ignore his whole life? That after years of being indoctrinated, *trained* if you will, to behave a certain way, to believe another man's ideologies, that he was finally brave enough to go against all of that, and act with *kindness*?"

"I—" I begin, cut short by her continued frankness.

"Or perhaps you need to ask yourself this question: Why, if you are so completely your father's son, are you now having a conversation with me about the human heart, about good and evil, right and wrong? Perhaps it's not Leon's heart that you need to concern yourself with, but your own..." Her voice trails off as she regards me. Then with one final dip of her head, she says; "I shall see you at dinner this evening, Master. Good day to you."

I watch her walk away, my thoughts reeling.

CHAPTER NINE

Jakub

"DON'T!" I snap, holding up my hand as I shove past Konrad and stride into the Grand Hall, taking a seat at the head of the table.

Konrad follows me, his dress shoes clipping across the floor, echoing through the silence. "Jakub, we need to talk about this!" he says, sitting to my left.

I slam my fist against the dining table rattling the place settings and spilling wine from the glass Nala had already filled for me. She stands in the shadows, waiting for further instructions. "Nala, inform the cook and the Numbers that supper will be delayed by half an hour, Konrad and I need to talk."

"Yes, Sir," she replies softly, her voice wary as she scampers out of the hall, making her escape.

Like the rest of the staff and all of the Numbers, Nala is

shaken by the events that have unfolded over the last week. The legend of The Weeping Tree isn't a secret, and the news about it bleeding cut through the castle like wildfire. Even our guests, who have long since departed the estate, were intrigued by it, though knew better than to delve any deeper into what is clearly a story personal to our family, not to mention the watertight non-disclosure agreements they signed weeks before being allowed entrance to our home.

"Talk!"

"What are we going to do about Leon?" Konrad asks the moment she's gone.

"He made his choice," I point out.

"He made *a* choice."

"He made the wrong fucking one, Konrad. *I'm* the head of this family. It's my duty to ensure what we've built here remains intact."

"And it will," he protests.

Despite his sharp grey suit and teal mask that covers all of his face apart from an arch around his mouth and chin, Konrad isn't as put together as he wants me to believe. The truth is he's as fucked in the head over what happened as I am. I meet Konrad's gaze.

"He chose Nothing, and now there'll be consequences."

Konrad lifts his glass to his lips, taking a sip. "Look, I'm as pissed off with him as you are, but you cannot deny that he did what you asked. She *died*, Jakub."

"He broke our pact. He held a gun to us both so Thirteen and Five could bring her back," I counter.

"He's not himself."

"You don't need to tell me that. I fucking know."

Reaching for the steak knife lying on the table, I pick it up and press the serrated tip against the pad of my finger, drawing blood. The sharp sting instantly soothes me, and some of the stress leaves my shoulders. Lifting my finger to my mouth, I suck up the blood, watching Konrad as he stares off into the distance, lost to his own thoughts. Eventually, he turns his attention back to me.

"And are *you* yourself?"

"What the fuck is that supposed to mean?"

"Let me rephrase that, do you have your shit together, Jakub?"

"Do you?" I counter, pissed off that he can even question me given he's locked himself away in the dungeons this past week. "What exactly have you been up to, huh?"

He cuts his gaze at me, his eyes dropping to my chest. "Unlike you, I haven't been seeking relief from one of the Numbers. I've been focusing on keeping our family, our life we've built here, fucking safe."

"How I choose to deal with Leon's betrayal is of no concern to you, Konrad. Mind your place."

Konrad barks out a laugh. "My place? We are *brothers*."

"That hasn't stopped Leon from betraying us both."

"He has a history with Nothing. He met her as a child when he was only a few years older than she was. He saved her life before he knew her true identity. It stands to reason that he was changed by it, that the encounter left a lasting impression. He's *confused*," Konrad persists.

"Clearly," I retort, tired of this fucking conversation. Tired of feeling out of control. I only visited One a few days ago and already feelings of remorse, empathy and *guilt* have started to creep back in despite everything I've done to try and rid myself of them.

"Brother, tell me what you're thinking," Konrad says, flicking his gaze to the knife I'm still holding onto.

Without answering him, I score a line across the palm of my hand, the sharp pain only taking the edge off these emotions that refuse to fucking leave as blood seeps from the wound. But relief is short-lived. I need more than this temporary respite. Being with One wasn't enough. Hurting myself isn't enough. The way I'm feeling now is far worse than when I was a kid. At least back then the pain worked.

You need Nothing to soothe the pain, that's why, my internal voice scoffs.

"No, I need to inflict it," I grind out under my breath.

"What?" Konrad asks.

"Nothing."

He gives me a sharp look before narrowing his eyes at me. "What do you really think about the legend of The Weeping Tree?" he asks, changing tactics. He wants me to open up, to talk. But talking is dangerous, it's an outlet for emotions to run free and I cannot let him see how deeply affected I am by Christy's death and by Leon's betrayal, *and* the fact that she's still alive.

That she's still within my reach.

"It's a story. Nothing more," I'm quick to respond.

"So you're saying our family history is just a story, a fable?"

"No, that's not what I'm saying. Do I believe that kindness fucked our family over? Yes, yes I do. Do I think Christy is the one who'll fix us?" I laugh then, and it's bitter, full of dark and hateful things. "No. No, I don't."

You're lying to yourself. That's why you want her dead because you're afraid she can heal you. You're scared to be human because being human means you'll feel pain a thousand times worse than the lashes to your back and chest, and cuts to your fingers and hands.

I grit my jaw, balling my hands into fists on my lap and forcing the voice away.

"And the blood?" Konrad asks, completely unaware of my internal struggle.

"*Sap.* It isn't blood, Konrad."

"What about the letter from Nessa?"

"Bullshit."

"Bullshit?" he questions, taking another sip of wine.

"Too much of a coincidence. I've been thinking about it a lot. None of this adds up."

"You think Thirteen wrote the letter?"

I raise a brow at him. "You believe she didn't?"

His fingers drum against the table as he considers it. "She used her voice, Jakub. You and I both know what that means."

"It means she's gotten over her trauma."

"No," he shakes his head. "It means she felt strongly enough about saving Zero's life to find her voice to try and stop us. She didn't write the letter. What's more, she's convinced that everything within it is true."

"So who wrote it, if not her?" I ask him, knowing full well he's on the same wavelength as me, but needing to hear him say it.

Konrad meets my gaze. "It can only be The Deana-dhe."

"My thoughts exactly. They are purveyors of truth and lies. They have the ability to extract information out of *anyone.*"

"You think we have a traitor in our midst?"

I nod. "There's no other explanation. Someone here at the castle is giving The Deana-dhe the information that they need and they're using it to fuck with our heads."

"I agree, that's the only explanation, but what I don't understand is why push us towards Zero?"

"Isn't it obvious?" I ask, taking a sip of wine before continuing. "Arden knew we'd seek revenge for our father's death eventually. He knew we couldn't touch Grim or Beast without a blood bath, and that we would seek out someone close to them to exact our revenge. He made preparations to intervene. What better way to do that than to manipulate Thirteen into planting those seeds? Remember they deal in debts. No doubt Thirteen's grandmother owed them one. What's a little white lie from a dying woman to her granddaughter? Thirteen's the perfect Trojan Horse."

"You don't trust her?"

"Even if she's unaware of the web she's been caught in, she cares for Nothing. She will do what she can to protect her now. That has become abundantly clear and presents us with a huge problem."

"And Grim, do you think she knows that Zero's related to Arden?"

"Doubtful. Charles is our best hacker and even he couldn't turn up that information. Then again, it could all be lies to confuse and baffle. Perhaps Nothing isn't a Dálaigh after all."

"Yet our father travelled across the country personally..." Konrad's voice trails off as we come to the same conclusion.

"Indeed."

"Which makes me question his motives given the legend. Could he have believed it was true?"

"No. Our father didn't believe in fairytales anymore than I do. He wanted them dead because they're Dálaighs, not because of some bullshit legend.

"So you do believe she's a Dálaigh then?" Konrad asks.

I sigh. "Yes. Yes I do. It makes sense."

"But the legend?" he persists, his mouth pursing.

"Even if it were true, why her? There's nothing to suggest she was the one who'd somehow save us. Those cunts, The Deana-dhe, have weaved this whole fucking tale, garnering information then twisting it to suit their needs. That's all this is, manipulation at its finest. Though I must admit, writing a letter and using Thirteen to deliver it is genius in its simplicity."

Taking another sip of his wine, Konrad nods. "Then we have a war coming, brother."

"We had one coming anyway. It's just got more players than we initially anticipated."

ONE LEANS IN CLOSE, lowering her voice so that none of the other Numbers around the table hear what she has to say. "Should I expect to see you again?"

"Perhaps," I reply noncommittally.

"I wasn't to your satisfaction?" she asks, her gaze dropping to my hand. The blood has seeped through the linen, splotches of red stark against the crisp white, like droplets of blood on freshly fallen snow.

"You were exactly what I required," I lie, needing her off my back.

"Good. You know that for you I'm available any time day or night."

"I'm well aware, but you have a show to prepare for. The ball is coming up. Right now *that's* our priority."

"Even so..." she allows her voice to trail off, her offer thickening the air between us as she flicks her long black hair over her shoulder. She has beautiful hair, and once upon a time I had spent many nights with it wrapped around my fist as I fucked her mouth. Other men delight in such an experience, and pay thousands upon thousands to experience their cock deep-throating her pretty mouth. I abhorred it, only orgasming because I forced myself to imagine anyone else but her to get it over with.

Nothing was the first woman to ever make me come so hard I barely had the wherewithal to form a cohesive sentence, let alone stand upright. The way she'd sucked me off in my room of curiosities was unlike anything I'd experienced before.

She hadn't fought, she'd taken control.

She pleasured me like I meant something to her, and had touched herself whilst doing it. I'd intended to take, and whilst I did exactly that, she took, too. Her ability to mentally and emotionally guard herself is beyond anything I've ever witnessed before. Even though I was the one with my dick in her mouth, she was the one with all the power. She had me by the balls, literally, and the fact that I'm thinking about her now tells me that she *still* does.

God-fucking-damn it.

Fisting my hand, I press my fingers into the wound on my palm, chasing that memory away and any lingering thoughts of the woman who has no place living rent-free in my fucking head.

"Even so," I reply firmly, "I wish for you to do your job. The ball is of the utmost importance to me."

"I understand," she replies, nodding sharply. "The Numbers are ready to perform and have been for weeks. We are all very experienced at this, though I fear not everyone will be up to speed."

"Who?" I ask, placing my fork on my plate and casting my gaze around the table. I notice how the Numbers are quieter than usual. There is very little conversation going on and the atmosphere is tense. "Who?" I repeat, catching Six's eye. She looks away quickly.

"Zero of course. She hasn't attended any of the rehearsals since—"

"She's recovering right now."

"Recovering?" One questions, a little louder this time. Her voice draws the attention of Konrad, as well as the closest Numbers, Five, Six, Eight and Two.

"Yes, recovering," I reiterate, raising my own voice so everyone can hear.

"Jakub," Konrad warns, his gaze snapping to mine. Like me, he's barely touched his food. I ignore his concern and address the room.

"I want to put a few rumours to rest, right here and now. Firstly, Nothing had a reaction to the drug she was given the night of the show. She is recovering well. Thirteen is taking care of her." There's an audible sigh of relief from Three, Six and Seven. Konrad catches my gaze and a look passes between us. It's clear who her allies are in the group. Noted. "Secondly, I want to squash any rumours about the legend of The Weeping Tree. Trees do not bleed. *Humans* bleed, and if I hear one more conversation about what happened from any of you I will ensure you experience just how much blood a person can lose before the heart stops beating, but in case you're curious it's about forty percent."

The only Numbers who don't react in some way to my threat are One and Five. One because she thinks she's indispensable and Five because she knows she is.

"The staff like to gossip," One says, resting her fingers on my forearm. I grit my teeth, glaring at her hand. She removes it, folding her hands in her lap.

"Nala!"

"Yes, Sir," she replies, stepping out of the shadows and quickly moving to my side.

"Inform Renard of this conversation. Tell him to make it clear to every staff member that we will not tolerate idle gossip. No one is indispensable." Nala nods, her lips wobbling at the mention of her grandfather's name. "What is it?" I ask.

"Grandfather is unwell," she whispers.

"What do you mean he's unwell?" Konrad snaps, shifting in his seat so he can get a better look at her.

"He didn't want to concern you."

"Is Thirteen aware?" he asks.

"She knows, but Grandfather didn't want me to worry her further because she's been dealing with—"

"Go with Nala to fetch Thirteen, and take her to Renard. She's needed," I instruct Konrad, cutting her off.

"Leave this with me," Konrad says, giving me a look that only I can interpret before pushing back his chair and gripping Nala's elbow.

He's worried. Renard has been getting frail as of late. We've all noticed it, but have refused to acknowledge it. This is another problem we don't need right now. Renard knows everything about us, about Ardelby Castle and how to ensure everything runs smoothly. He stepped in as a carer when we were boys, and he took Nala under his wing when we asked him to. He knows *everything...*

Fuck!

Could he be the person who leaked information to The Deana-dhe? Could he be the one who's betrayed us? I watch Konrad and Nala leave, a weird kind of ache expanding in my chest whilst nausea churns my stomach at the thought.

"Master?" Three says gently, pulling my attention back to

her. The look she's giving me is one of both kindness and pity. It makes my throat tighten. "Are you okay?"

"Why the fuck wouldn't I be?" I ask, my voice low, lethal.

She blanches. Next to her Seven takes her hand, squeezing it. "She didn't mean to speak out of turn, Master," he says urgently. "It won't happen again."

I look between the two of them, a sudden burst of rage ripping through my chest as thoughts of betrayal, kindness, pity, fucking *love* bombard me. I need those feelings gone. I need a distraction. I need pain, and if my own isn't enough to do the job, then I'll take someone else's.

Three should never have opened her goddamn mouth.

"Fuck her," I demand glaring at Seven.

"What?"

"I said, *fuck her*. Do it. Now."

The room falls silent as I glare at Seven and Three, willing either of them to object so I can take some of my anger out on them. How dare she pity me. How dare he try to protect her.

"You want me to..."

"I said, bend her over the motherfucking table and fuck her in the arse!"

My fist pounds against the wood, rattling the plates and causing my wine glass to tip over and smash, spilling its contents and sending shards of glass scattering across the table.

Nine, Ten and Eleven's reaction is to giggle like the damaged women that they are. One sits back in her seat and takes a sip of her wine, a slow smile spreading across her face, and Six and Five keep their faces blank, free of emotion. Two claps with delight. Twelve remains distant and Four and Eight grin mercilessly.

"Since when did you feel that you are in a position to speak to me so frankly?" I ask Three, whose eyes are wide with shock.

"I didn't mean—"

"Don't say another word!" I roar. "Get up and bend over the fucking table!"

Three gets to her feet. She's trembling so hard that it takes her a few attempts to draw up her dress and bunch it around her waist revealing a thatch of neatly trimmed pubic hair and hips that would entice any warm-blooded man or woman. My anger brews as Seven strokes his hand up her arm and squeezes her shoulder gently before pressing his lips against her ear and whispering something. She swallows hard, blinking back tears that are pooling in her eyes, before nodding.

"Did I say you can speak to her?"

Seven locks eyes with me briefly, and in that moment I see a man who is willing to die for the woman he loves. Sensing his indecision, Three reaches around herself and grabs his cock, fisting him through the thin material of his trousers with one hand whilst she shoves aside the plates in front of her with the other. Seven lets out a moan that's filled with both pleasure and heartbreak as she makes him ready for her.

Further along the table Six attempts to hide her emotions, but fails as tears well in her pretty eyes. Next to her is Five, who locks gazes with me. I see her disapproval. It's the first time I've ever experienced such a reaction from her and it unsettles me to say the least, but I won't stop what's happening. To do so would be weak.

And right now I need them all to know how fucking strong I am.

That I'm not ruled by emotion. That I don't give a fuck about an old man dying or a woman who steals my thoughts every second of every fucking day.

"What are you waiting for?" I ask, relaxing back in my chair and folding my arm across my chest.

Seven presses his eyes shut then brings up his palm to his mouth, spitting into it.

"No!" I grind out. "Fuck her raw."

"What?" he has the gall to ask.

"I said fuck her raw. Every time she sits on her arse, I want her to remember her place, and every time you see her wince from the pain, I want you to remember that you're just as responsible for it as I am."

"And if I refuse?"

I pick up my steak knife, flip it in my hand then stab it into the table. "Then I kill you both. Right here, right now. Is that understood?"

He clamps his jaw tightly and nods, then removes Three's hand from his erection and places it flat on the table before leaning over and pressing a tender kiss against her tearstained cheek.

"I love you," he says, then impales himself balls deep into her arse.

Her scream echoes around the hall like a church bell notifying its parishioners of a death, and in that moment I don't know what I feel. There's no satisfaction in her tears. No relish in her pain. No gratification in his sorrow.

I don't feel better like I thought I would.

I feel fucking sick when I should be revelling in their torment.

What the fuck is wrong with me?

With every thrust my fucking stomach churns. With every tear shed my throat closes over. With every scream of pain I despise myself a little more.

I almost tell him to stop. Almost.

Then I remember who the fuck I am. Whose son I am and whose blood runs in my veins, and I remember that love is *cruel*.

Their *love* for each other is a cruel mistress.

It fabricates and lies. It steals hope and inflicts pain.

It forces you to do things you don't want to do.

No! Love isn't cruel. It's compassion, my internal voice sees fit to remind me just at that moment. *It's empathy. It's kindness. Seven has no choice, neither of them do. The only person who's cruel is you.*

I sneer, a laugh bursting from my lips. I ignore those thoughts and push them deep inside as I turn to the rest of the Numbers and say: "The ball is your priority and it is *crucial* the show is at its best. We have important people coming, all of whom are excited to experience first-hand the magic of The Menagerie. You will rehearse until the show is perfect. You will perform to the high standard I expect from you all, and you will fuck whoever pays the handsomest for the pleasure. Am I understood?"

"Yes, Master," comes the chorused reply.

"Good. If it's not perfect, there will be dire consequences." This I say to One, who acknowledges me with a nod.

"It's already perfect," she says with utmost certainty. "You have no reason to doubt us."

"Do not disappoint me," I say, before flicking my gaze back to the couple just at the moment Seven comes with a silent, almost pained groan. I watch as he pulls gently out of Three, his cock covered in her blood. She's trembling so hard she can barely stand as he helps ease her to her feet. Holding her upright, he pulls down her sheer dress before turning her in his arms and hauling her against his chest.

Neither say a word, they just cling to one another, both utterly oblivious to anyone else in the room. In that moment, when he cups her face and presses a tender kiss against her lips,

I am reminded of what it truly means to sacrifice yourself for love.

It's vulnerability.

It's pain.

It's *weakness*.

And I vow that I will never allow myself to fall into the same trap.

CHAPTER TEN

Leon

THE SOUND of a fist thumping against my living room door followed by Konrad's deep voice has me reaching for my gun as I stride across the bedroom. Thirteen and Christy look over at me, and I shake my head.

"Stay here."

Pulling open the door to my bedroom, I cross my living room, clicking off the safety. If Konrad thinks he can come here and take Christy from me, he can think again. The mother-fucker can't have her. I'll shoot him dead before I see him hurt her.

"Brother, open the door!" Konrad repeats, pounding his fist against the wood. The door rattles in its frame as I reach for the handle, curling my fingers around the cool brass.

"Leave before I put a bullet in your brain!" I grind out.

"I'm not here for Zero. It's Renard..." he pauses, and I hear a muffled sob. Is that Nala?

"What the fuck's wrong with Renard?" I ask, still refusing to open the door despite her tears and a sudden feeling of dread.

"He's... He's sick," comes Nala's quiet reply.

"Fuck!" I swear under my breath.

My fingers tighten around the doorknob. Turning it slowly, I step backwards and as the door swings open, I raise the gun and point it directly at Konrad's chest. "What do you mean, he's sick?" I ask her.

Nala looks between us then past me. I know without looking that Thirteen and Christy have entered the room. "Go back into the bedroom," I hiss, my muscles tensing as my finger presses against the trigger. One false move from Konrad and he's dead.

Leaning against the door frame, Konrad folds his arms across his chest. "Brother, there's no need for dramatics."

"Move one more inch towards her and I *will* kill you."

"Like I said, I'm not here for Zero," he replies, meeting my gaze before looking over my shoulder. I've no doubt where his attention is focussed. I can see how his eyes flare with interest, with lust, with fucking *need*. "But I will say good afternoon to you." His voice lowers as he dips his head respectfully then asks: "How are you feeling, Zero?"

Christy laughs sharply. "Like I was murdered then brought back to life."

Konrad chuckles in that lighthearted way of his, like this is just another conversation on another normal fucking day. For him, I suppose it must be, but for me, for Christy, for Nala and Thirteen, nothing about this is normal. It never was.

"What's going on with Renard?" Thirteen asks, approaching us. I glance over at her when she reaches my side.

Her expression is one of concern as she reaches for Nala, squeezing her arm.

"He's getting worse. None of the ointments or tonics that you gave him are working anymore. He's barely able to stand, let alone speak."

"He's that sick?" Konrad asks before I'm able to. If I didn't know any better, I'd say he cares about the old man.

Thirteen sighs. "He's been sick for some time now. From the symptoms, I believe it's pancreatic cancer, though I can't be certain," she explains.

"You've known this for *some time?*" Konrad asks, pushing off the door frame as he glares at her. It appears as though Thirteen has kept many secrets from us. A few days ago I might've been inclined to punish her for it. Not today. Not anymore.

"I have," she confirms, unruffled by his anger. "He asked me to keep it between us. Nala only found out recently and he swore her to secrecy," Thirteen explains quickly.

"What do you need, Nala?" I ask.

"Jakub asked me to fetch Thirteen." She looks between us both, then to Christy on the other side of the room, guilt shadowing her features. "He's *dying.*" Her voice cracks, and her face crumples as she sobs.

Thirteen gathers Nala in her arms and looks at me. I know she wants to help Renard, but she doesn't want to leave Christy alone with me either. She doesn't trust me yet. She's right not to. Being so close to Christy, wanting her so fucking desperately is forcing me to dig deep, to remain strong. I should never have kissed her, but now that I have, it's only compounded my feelings, making me want more than I have any right to. Despite that, I'm still a man who is used to taking what he wants, and I'm not sure how much longer I can hold myself back.

I'm fucked in the head. I know that.

"You should go," I say, gun still aimed at Konrad's chest as I address Thirteen.

She hesitates, chewing on her lip. "I want to help, but the only thing I can do now is make him comfortable so he isn't in any pain."

"Then go make Renard comfortable. I will not have his painful death on my conscience."

"Conscience?" Konrad remarks, shaking his head. "Says the man who has a gun pointing at his *brother's* chest."

'Yes, conscience," I snap. "That's *why* I'm pointing a gun at you, arsehole. I won't let you in here so you can do whatever the fuck you want to Christy. I'm protecting her from you."

"And who's protecting Zero from you, huh, brother?" he asks me, snorting back a laugh.

I fall silent knowing that he's right, that despite my promises not to hurt her, despite these feelings of empathy, care, fucking kindness, I'm still that man who cut her and smothered his cock with her blood. I'm still that man who wants to do the same all over again.

"Whatever it is you think I want to do to Zero, I *don't,*" Konrad continues. "Renard needs Thirteen. Perhaps Nala should stay here with you both. Would that work, Thirteen? Would you feel more comfortable if Nala were to remain here with Christy so that you can tend to Renard without fear that Leon will turn on her?"

"I won't turn on her!" I protest. Fucking arsehole playing good guy.

Thirteen looks over her shoulder at Christy. "How do you feel about that?"

"I have no issues with Nala," she says quietly, stepping into my peripheral vision. I feel the heat of her gaze but I refuse to take my eyes off of Konrad. "But I'm not comfortable with Thirteen going alone. Leon, you should go with her."

"No." I shake my head as Konrad looks between us, his gaze falling on the spot where Christy presses her fingers against my arm. His astonishment would be funny if I wasn't so utterly dumbfounded by her touch, so fucking *shocked* by it. I swallow hard. "I won't leave you vulnerable."

"Are you afraid that I'll run?" she asks softly.

"There's nowhere to run to," I remind her, forcing myself to concentrate on Konrad and not the way her touch burns my skin. "I know my brother. Jakub will seize the opportunity to get to you if I leave you alone."

"He's occupied with the Numbers right now. You don't need to be concerned about him," Konrad says.

"The hell I don't," I cut back. "Don't lie to me. I'm not a fool."

"Then we all go," Thirteen interjects. "I can treat Renard. You can watch over us both."

"Sounds like a solid plan," Konrad says with an easy smile. "At least Renard won't be alone when the time comes."

"How fucking noble of you," I scoff, launching forward and shoving him in the chest before slamming the door in his face. I only lower the gun once my back is pressed against the door. "Gather what you need, Thirteen."

She nods, rushing towards her bag and double-checking the contents whilst Christy opens her arms and Nala walks into them. "I'm so sorry," she whispers.

"It's me who should be saying that to you," Nala replies, hiccuping, her tears falling heavy now. "He hurt you."

Christy nods, meeting my gaze. "Yes, he did," she replies softly.

Unable to stand the way Christy's looking at me, I open the

door and step into the hallway where Konrad awaits with one foot propped up against the wall, the nonchalant fuck. "Don't pretend you actually give two shits about Renard. I know your game and it won't fucking work," I say.

"And you do give two shits?"

"Yes, motherfucker! It *hurts* to care. It fucking hurts like nothing else ever has. You don't look like a man in pain. In fact, you look very much like the man our father always wanted you to be. Relaxed, smug, fucking dangerous."

"You know jack shit. You're so caught up in your own little cloud of emotions that you see nothing beyond them. I hurt, too."

"Hurt?!" I bark out a laugh. "*Bullshit.* You wanted her dead."

"Need I remind you that *you* were the one who killed her!"

"It was a mistake. I thought..."

"You thought that strangling her wouldn't fucking end her life? Don't forget I was in the room, too. I witnessed everything that happened."

"And you did *nothing* to stop me." I look him up and down, sneering. "This is an act, and if you think for one fucking second I'm going to trust you with Christy, you've got another thing coming!"

"I wanted to help!" he bellows, pushing off the wall. I hold the gun up and he walks right into it, the barrel digging into his chest. "I wanted to bring her back!"

Fury fires through his blood, making the veins in his neck bulge beneath his skin. I match his fury with my own, remembering the time when we were just kids and he brought that nameless woman back to life only to kill her then bring her back to life so he could kill her over and over again. That day he went from the Konrad I knew to the Konrad our father moulded. It happened right before my eyes.

"Only so you could feel the way you did when we were kids. You're fucked in the head!"

Behind us the door opens and Thirteen steps out, Christy and Nala following closely behind. Konrad glares at me, his chest heaving. "We're all fucked in the head, brother. We're all fucked-up because of *her*," he says, his gaze flickering behind me briefly before he steps back, turns on his heel and strides along the hall.

THIRTEEN PULLS UP the thick blanket, covering Renard's chest, then looks over at me and shakes her head. "He has very little time left."

"No!" Nala sobs, her thin shoulders shaking with grief as she covers her face with her hands. She falls to his side, grasping his hands as he rolls his head towards her, lifting a frail hand to the top of her head. With immense effort, Renard strokes her hair.

"Hush, child. Don't cry for me," he croaks.

"Grandfather, *please* don't leave me."

"I have no choice." His hand falls back to the bed as she presses her tear-stained cheek against his.

"What will I do without you?"

"You will live, Nala. You will *live*."

Konrad stands in the corner of the room, his arms crossed over his chest. For the first time in my life, I wish he wasn't wearing a mask so that I could read him better. So I could see if he truly has the capacity to hurt, to *feel*.

Only he doesn't remove his mask and he keeps his gaze fixed

firmly on Christy who's watching the whole scene unfold. She hugs herself, her slight frame shivering despite the woollen dress she wears.

"Are you cold? Does this upset you?" I ask, offering her my jumper.

She shakes her head. "I've seen many people die."

"Of course. You worked in a hospice, isn't that right?" Konrad asks, cocking his head to the side.

"I did. I've looked into the face of death many times," she replies, meeting his gaze with a steely one of her own before turning them back on Renard.

"Those eyes..." he says, and she stiffens. "Tell me, Zero. What did you see when you died? Is there a heaven filled with angels sitting on fluffy white clouds and a God with a halo above his head? Or is death just darkness, empty, filled with... *Nothing?*"

"This is hardly the time for such a discussion," Thirteen says as she attempts to soothe Nala.

But Nala is oblivious, too wrapped up in her own grief to pay any attention to our conversation.

"It was a simple question. I'm curious," he states.

"I don't remember."

"So it was nothing. Interesting."

"I didn't say that," Christy retorts, her birthmark deepening in colour. "I just don't remember."

"Or you just don't want to tell us the truth," Konrad suggests, pushing off the wall. He places his hands on Thirteen's shoulders and moves her, taking her spot beside Nala. Crouching, he places one hand on Renard's arm, and one hand on Nala's back.

"There is a heaven, isn't there, Konrad?" Nala asks, forgetting to call him Sir in her moment of grief, and far more aware of our conversation than I'd thought. Tears slide down her cheeks as she looks to him for some kind of reassurance. She's searching for answers from the wrong person though. He no more believes in Heaven than I do.

"I believe everyone has a soul, and every soul has a destination," he replies quietly, the gap in his mask allowing him to give Nala a gentle smile. Fuck, he's good at this.

"Where will Grandfather's soul go?"

"That I don't know," Konrad replies evenly, glancing up at me.

I know what he's thinking though. Renard might never have killed a person, or hurt someone with his own bare hands, but he stood by as our father raped and murdered, clearing up his messes with little emotion and a clinical kind of detachment. He's softened somewhat over the years, and that's mainly due to Nala. Regardless, the old man won't be getting past the pearly gates, even if such a place did exist. Pretty sure he'd end up in Hell with the rest of us, or wherever the fuck the likes of us end up.

"Then how can I let him go if I don't know that I'll see him again?"

"You don't have a choice. Death is the end, Nala," Jakub says as he steps into the room. "Nothing more."

Christy draws in a jagged breath, her head snapping around as I draw my gun and point it at my brother. "Don't even think about it."

Jakub glances at me before his gaze falls to Christy briefly. He's wearing his silver mask, a half moon shape that curves around his nose and mouth.

"I'm not here to fight with you. I'm here to pay my respects. Lower your gun, Leon, or keep it aimed at me. Either way, I'm coming in."

"Leon, *please*," Nala says, her eyes wide and brimming with more tears. I'm hurting her with my actions. I look at Christy in that moment. I'm not sure why, for reassurance, guidance perhaps? She meets my gaze, unreadable.

"You so much as look at Christy the wrong way and Renard isn't the only one who'll die tonight," I warn Jakub, lowering my gun.

"Noted," Jakub retorts, striding towards the old man's side. He stands on the opposite side of the bed to Konrad and Nala. "Are you in pain?" he asks, his voice neutral, almost clinical.

"No more than you," Renard replies knowingly.

Jakub barks out a laugh. "I'm just fine, old man."

Renard draws in a ragged breath, wheezing as he tries to ward off death's pull, his cloudy eyes settling on Nala. "I must speak to The Masks alone, but before I do I have one last thing I want to say to you child."

"What is it, Grandfather?"

"You were a gift, and a perpetual comfort to an old man who didn't deserve it. My only wish is for your happiness. Everything I've ever done is with you in mind. Remember that when I'm gone."

"Grandfather," Nala whispers, sobbing now as she clings onto Renard, as though her determination alone will be enough to keep him in this world.

Jakub watches the interaction and despite his blank expression, I know he feels as uncomfortable by Nala's grief as Konrad and I do. For years our father's beliefs—*Malik's* beliefs, because I refuse to refer to him as my father for a moment longer—have been beaten into us, warping our views to match his. We've been taught that grief, love and empathy are weaknesses, *sins* even. Only now am I beginning to understand that isn't true. Don't get me wrong, these feelings hurt like a motherfucker, they make me want to turn on myself, on someone else. They make me want to inflict pain, wreak havoc, do damage, but I'm able to control those impulses just enough to not carry through with them. Why? Because of Christy. Because she makes me want to be better, do fucking better.

Renard pats Nala's back. "I don't want you here when I leave. Please, go now. There are things I must say, and you do not need to be burdened with them."

"I love you, Grandfather," Nala says between tear-swollen breaths as Thirteen gently peels her off him.

"As I love you." Renard coughs, his chest rattling as death clambers into every crevice and crack, filling his lungs like concrete. He looks up at Thirteen with a pained expression. "Thank you for what you've done for me, for them," he whispers.

Thirteen dips her head, squeezing his hand before gathering Nala in her arms. "It's time to go, Nala," she says gently.

"Thirteen, Three requires your attention this evening. Take Nala with you," Jakub instructs.

"What happened to her, brother?" Konrad asks.

Jakub scowls, shaking his head. "Not important."

"I won't leave Christy."

"You will do whatever the fuck I say, Thirteen! You're here for the Numbers. Three needs you, so do your fucking job."

Thirteen looks at Christy, her expression filled with concern.

"You should go."

"But—"

"Go!" Christy insists. "I have Leon."

I have Leon.

Who knew three simple words would have so much power.

Like an adrenaline shot straight into my veins, those words fuel my resolve to keep her safe from my brothers, *from me*.

Konrad's mouth drops open in shock and Jakub glares at Christy. I know that look. He wants her so fucking bad he's sick with it. Sick with fucking jealousy that he's refusing to acknowledge because that would mean admitting he feels, and that's something he's not ready to do. May never be ready to do.

"I'll be back as soon as I can," Thirteen says, squeezing Christy's arm as she passes by her.

Christy nods, wrapping her arms around herself as Thirteen guides Nala from the room, leaving her alone with a dying man and three feral wolves who could turn on her in an instant.

CHAPTER ELEVEN

Christy

"HELP ME TO SIT," Renard asks, patting his hands against the mattress as he looks from Konrad to Jakub who are standing on either side of him.

They do as he asks, sliding their hands beneath his armpits and gently pulling him upright, but they fail to adjust his pillows and he slumps forward, his head hanging awkwardly.

"Here, let me," I say, and without thinking I step towards the bed and reach behind Renard, adjusting his pillows with one hand and easing him back against them with the other.

Our eyes meet and his lips wobble. "Thank you."

I nod, my skin covering in goosebumps as I snatch my hands back, a familiar tingling sensation scattering down my spine from the touch. I don't want to lose myself to a vision, not now, not here alone with these men. Stepping back, I attempt to move around Konrad but he steps into my path, blocking my exit.

"You're a brave woman, Zero," he remarks. "Aren't you afraid I'm going to hurt you?"

"I've already died, what more can you possibly do to me?" I reply, straightening my spine and refusing to look away from his gaze.

"You'd be surprised," he replies, his eyes pensive.

I swallow hard, remembering the vision. "No, no I wouldn't."

Behind him Leon approaches, gun out. "I warned you, brother."

"I have no interest in dying tonight or any other night for that matter. Lower the fucking gun and let me speak to her," Konrad says, knowing without having to look that Leon has the gun aimed at his back.

"Say what you need to say, then let her pass," Leon insists.

Konrad lets out a bitter laugh. "He really will do anything to protect you. Tell me, Zero, do you honestly think *he's* your saviour after what he did?"

"What you *all* did," I remind him, flicking my gaze between the two men, acutely aware that Jakub's watching the scene unfold and Renard's chest is rattling even more now as death's grip tightens.

"Yes, you're right. We're all guilty of hurting you," he concedes, bringing his hand up to my face and brushing his knuckles over my birthmark, his touch exceedingly gentle. The look in his eyes is one of conflict, however. I don't trust him or his intentions. "Maybe that needs to change."

Leon snorts with derision and Konrad drops his hand.

"Right now, I think you need to listen to the words of a

dying man," I say, slipping around him, returning to my place at the back of the room and as far away from these men as possible.

"Thank you, Christy," Renard says, his chest heaving with exertion. "I have only moments left and my wish is to look upon the faces of the men I have known since they were boys. It's been quite some time."

Leon steps back from Konrad, holstering his gun. He's the first to remove his mask, laying it gently on the bed. "Renard," he says, dipping his head in acknowledgment.

"Hello, Leon. It's good to see *you* again," Renard replies, his eyes misting with tears.

"Likewise, old man," Leon mutters out.

Turning his attention to Konrad who is yet to remove his mask, Renard regards him. "I'm dying, Konrad. Does it matter if I look upon your face now?"

"I guess not," he replies, untying his mask and removing it.

"There you are," he says, searching for something as his gaze roves over his face. Eventually he appears to find what he's looking for and nods. "I see you haven't lost those boyish good looks."

Konrad lets out a quiet laugh, pointing to his cheek. "Do you not see the scar?"

"I see it, *and* I see you."

Slowly and with great effort, Renard turns to Jakub next, a tremulous smile pulling up his lips. "And you, Jakub? Will I get to look upon the man to see if the boy I once knew remains?"

Jakub grits his teeth, a muscle feathering in his jaw as he contemplates Renard's request. "That boy doesn't exist as you well know."

"If that's true, then it'll make no difference either way. This is my dying wish."

"And what makes you think I want to give you your dying wish?"

"Oh I know you don't, but it isn't for the reasons you want us to believe."

Jakub snorts. "I'll remove my mask for no other reason than out of respect for a man who has served us well over the years."

Pulling off his mask, Jakub chucks it carelessly onto the bed. It hits Renard on the thigh, bouncing off him. Anger suddenly wells within me, my gaze flicking to the gun Leon holds by his side. I could grab it and shoot the arsehole now for that alone. What a heartless prick.

"Jakub Brov," Renard mutters, stilling my fingers with the gravity of his voice.

Jakub folds his arms across his chest. "Yes?"

"Your father worked hard to mould you into his own form. I wonder, looking upon you now, whether he succeeded."

"You tell me, old man, given you helped him."

Renard's brows pull together as they stare at one another. Jakub a cold, unfeeling statue, Renard a crumbling husk of a man. "I deserved that. I deserve your anger."

"I'm not angry at you, Renard. I'm *grateful*. Strong men, powerful men like my father, were forged in pain, born from blood, honed with violence. I am my father's son."

Renard nods. "Perhaps, and perhaps your mother had more influence in who you are than even you're aware of."

"My mother?" Jakub blanches. "I don't even remember her."

Renard coughs, his frail hand barely able to cover his mouth as he hacks and hacks. Eventually he settles, his chest whistling and wheezing as he speaks. "That is a crying shame. She was a good woman."

Jakub raises a brow. "She was nothing but a whore. I'm glad I don't remember her."

"You really are a piece of work," I say, forgetting myself in the moment.

"And you are very strong-willed, Christy. Truly remarkable," Renard says, drawing my attention back to him. "You're very much like her."

"Like who?"

"*Your* mother, of course."

"*My mother?*" I ask, the question tumbling from my lips in a rush as The Masks stare at me in shock.

"What the fuck?" Konrad exclaims.

"Yes, I knew her as well."

"How?" I ask, ignoring the heated glares from the three men who right now are lost for words.

"I met your mother at the same time Malik did. They were teenagers at the time."

"My mother knew Malik before he..." My voice trails off as a disturbing thought crosses my mind. *No!*

"... Forced Leon to murder her? Yes. Your mother and your father first crossed paths many years ago," Renard explains, looking first at me then at Jakub as he continues.

"You're not fucking suggesting that *she's* my—" Jakub says, jabbing his finger in my general direction.

"No," Renard laughs, then coughs, the amusement bringing much needed colour back to his cheeks. "You're not related to one another."

I don't know whose sigh of relief is loudest, Jakub's or mine. Even Leon blows out a breath. Right now I don't even want to unravel *why* I feel so relieved, probably because no one wants a psychopath for a brother.

"I see that even in death you've still got a sense of humour," Konrad says with a wry grin.

Renard gives Konrad a quavering smile then focuses back

on Jakub. "Oldrick, your grandfather, took your father to Ireland to meet the O'Farrells when he was fifteen. That is where Malik and Niall, Thirteen's father, became... *acquaintances*. Malik didn't have the emotional capacity to have friends, but Niall was closest to a friend he ever got..." His voice trails off as he smacks his lips together.

"Water," I say. "He needs water."

Jakub nods, picking up the glass situated on the bedside table, bringing it to his lips. "Here," he says, helping him to take a sip. It's a simple action to ease suffering, and he doesn't even appear to realise how significant that act of *kindness* is.

"Thank you," Renard replies, patting Jakub with a shaking hand.

Jakub flinches at the touch, drawing his hand away as though burnt. Confusion, anger, fear, surprise, horror, it all slashes across his face. If I didn't know any better, there's *empathy* too.

"Continue," he snaps, shutting down.

"One evening Malik and Niall visited a travelling circus that was in the area. I was asked to accompany them. It was at the circus that Niall met and became instantly obsessed with Aoife, Thirteen's mother. Your mother, Nessa, was with her," Renard says to me. He draws in a few breaths, his collarbone stark against his paper-thin skin. "At the time Malik had no idea that Nessa was a Dálaigh, his family's bitter enemy. If he had, I've no doubt he would've tried to kill her then and there. Even at fifteen he was a brutal young man."

"Dálaigh?" I ask, my skin prickling with portent. "My mother's family name was *Brandon*."

Renard shakes his head. "No, you're a Dálaigh. Your family was once one of the most influential in Ireland. There are only a few of you left, however. Yourself, your cousin Arden and a few others who've long since gone into hiding."

"What? I don't believe you." I stumble backwards, my arse hitting the chest of drawers behind me, but despite my accusation something about this feels *right*. My mother never gave me much information about her family, now I understand why.

"It's true," Leon says, looking over his shoulder at me. "Your mother was a Dálaigh. You're a Dálaigh. Nessa said as much in the letter she wrote to us."

"Right, the letter," I mumble. Thirteen had told me about the letter my mother had written to The Masks but I haven't had much of a chance to talk to her about it, and Leon hasn't been very forthcoming either.

"She hid you from your family so that ours wouldn't find you," he continues.

"But he did. *You* did," I breathe out.

"Yes," Leon nods.

"So Malik killed my mother because of a feud between our families?"

"Partly," Renard confirms.

"Partly?" Jakub questions, frowning.

"Y—yes." Renard starts coughing, doubling over as he struggles for breath. It takes him longer to recover this time, his mottled skin turning greyer. His body is already corpse-like, sucked free of colour and vitality, but he loses the last pink tint of his cheeks with every hacking cough that leaves his chest. "That day at the circus when your parents were teenagers, the group visited a woman who read tea leaves. Everyone bar Malik took part, but the old woman saw fit to tell him something that would haunt him for years."

"What did she say?" Konrad asks, flicking his gaze to me, then to his brothers.

"She said that the Brov legacy will cease to exist when a woman with ghost eyes comes back from the dead and claims his sons for her own."

"What the fuck? Cease to exist?" Konrad says, his gaze darkening as he glances over at me. "As in dead?"

"Enough!" Jakub shouts, a dark laugh bursting from his lips as he bends over the dying man and grips his face roughly. "What did Arden promise you, huh? What fucking deal did you make with him in exchange for spinning this fucking story? It was you, wasn't it? You leaked private information about our family to that fucking cunt, didn't you? That letter from *Nessa*, using Thirteen to deliver it. All of it to fuck with our heads."

"No, Jakub. This has nothing to do with Arden," Renard says quietly, calm in the face of Jakub's anger. "I was there, remember. I heard what the old woman said." He coughs, his chest rattling now like a death knell. Jakub releases Renard, stepping back.

"So why not share this with us sooner?" Konrad asks.

"Because I believed the woman with the ghost eyes had died too, just like Malik had."

"My mother," I whisper.

Renard nods, his whole body shaking with the effort. "Yes."

He motions for me to come closer, barely able to lift his hand off the bed now. I shake my head, not willing to go anywhere near him or the men who are bound to me in ways I wish they weren't.

"At the time, Malik didn't understand what the old woman had meant," Renard continues. "By the time he found out what ghost eyes meant, we'd already returned to Ardelby Castle. He hunted your mother down for years believing she was the one who would end the Brov family line because she had different coloured eyes. When he finally found her, instead of sending his men to kill her, he took Leon. It was personal to him. You know the rest of the story. "

"Then why not make sure Nothing was dead, too?" Jakub asks, staring at me. "Father was there when Leon pulled her from the fire. He would've seen her eyes."

"It was dark," Leon says, glancing over at me. "Christy was in so much pain her pupils were blown wide. He didn't see. I didn't even see the differing colours."

"Regardless, my father never left any loose ends. You pulled her from the fire, you rescued her against his wishes. He would've killed her for that alone."

He's right, no matter how much I hate to admit that, Jakub's right. I should be dead. I'm not. Seems to be a recurring theme. I would laugh if it wasn't so horrifying.

"Leon?" Konrad questions.

"He told me to leave her," Leon explains. "He saw Christy's injuries and believed she would die anyway. I thought she would die. Her injuries were unsurvivable."

"And yet here she stands," Konrad remarks, a dash of awe passing over his face as he looks at me. I start to tremble, reading more into that look than what appears on the surface. He wants to see how many times I can die and come back. He's sick.

Jakub shakes his head. "No. You know father. He would've made *certain* that she was dead."

"We heard sirens. Help was approaching..." Leon says, swiping a hand over his face. "I left her barely breathing, she was *dying*..."

"But?" Jakub persists.

"But I told him she was already dead."

"And he believed you?" Konrad asks, shaking his head.

"He had no choice because by that time the fire engines were driving up the lane, and he couldn't go back to check. We cut across the fields behind their house to escape them. He never mentioned Christy again so I assumed she *had* died. Which is why, when Christy revealed her back to us I was so confused. I didn't know for certain Christy was the girl I pulled from the fire, but the coincidences were too hard to ignore. She was *supposed* to be dead. "

"Exactly," Renard says, focussing on me, "According to the obituary, you had died that night, too. Malik didn't know who Christy's father was and the lengths he would go to hide his daughter. And hide you he did. Malik believed he had wiped out any threat."

"Only he didn't look hard enough. If he had he would've found out who Christy was related to, and that she was Grim's half-sister and the same girl who survived the damn fire," Jakub says, approaching me. "So what do we do with this information?"

"Back the fuck off!" Leon grinds out, standing between us, and raising the gun once again.

"Stop!" Renard shouts, the effort leaving him doubled over and wheezing for breath. "You're missing... the... point."

"What point?" Jakub snaps.

"Your father didn't believe Nessa would end the Brov family line because she would murder you, he believed she would end the cycle of violence, hatred and abuse he perpetuated because she would kill that *part* of you. He believed in the legend of The Weeping Tree."

"Wait? What has the legend got to do with any of this?"

"You haven't told her?" Konrad asks.

Leon shakes his head. "The opportunity never arose."

"Tell me what?" I persist.

"When you died, The Weeping Tree bled," Leon says, gun still raised at his brothers.

"No." I shake my head not wanting to believe him despite that same feeling of *knowing* prickling my skin.

"Yes," Leon confirms, his voice filled with wonder and regret. "The cross you were strapped to was built from two branches from The Weeping Tree. You died. The Weeping Tree bled."

"I—" I begin, lost for words.

"Malik thought Nessa would be the one to die beneath the boughs of the tree," Renard continues. "That she would be the one to come back to life, that her kindness would infect you and in turn what you've built here would no longer exist. *That* is why he murdered her."

"He truly believed that?" Konrad asks, scrubbing a hand over his face.

"Yes. He truly believed that," Renard confirms, glancing at me. "Only it wasn't Nessa the old woman was talking about, it was Christy. I knew that the moment you brought her back to the castle."

"And you didn't say a word, why is that, Renard?" Jakub asks, his voice darkening.

"Because I watched your father strip the three of you of every last shred of goodness, and I did *nothing* to prevent him," he says with great effort. "I'm as guilty for who you've become as he is. So, when Christy arrived, and I saw how she was beginning to affect you, I knew she was the one the old woman was talking about. I had hoped I'd witness your transformation before I died, but alas it isn't meant to be."

Leon lowers his gun, looking from Jakub to Konrad. "Now do you believe?"

Konrad scrapes a hand over his ashen face and Jakub stares

at me, but it isn't either of them who breaks the silence, it's Renard. Meeting my gaze he gives me a small smile.

"Thank you."

"For what?" I whisper.

"For *surviving.* "

And with those final words, Renard takes his last breath.

CHAPTER TWELVE

Jakub

A FEW DAYS after Renard died, we finally buried him in the castle grounds. There's no official service, no vicar, no huge congregation of mourners, just myself, Nala, Thirteen, Konrad, Leon and her...

Nothing.

She hasn't spoken a word since we gathered in this meadow on the edge of the forest, merely folded her hands together and stared blindly at us all, seeing but not really seeing a thing. Her red hair is bright against her black jacket and matching skirt, the hem of which is covered in mud from our walk across the meadow. Every now and then her gaze flicks over to the forest, then back again.

"I wonder what she's thinking," Konrad mutters from behind his black mask, as bothered by her silent presence as I am.

"About the many ways she wants to murder us," I retort, not so quietly.

Her eyes shift upwards, landing on me. The heat of her gaze reminds me of Icarus flying too close to the sun, I feel the burn right to the marrow of my bones and I have the sudden urge to pull off my mask and feel the cold wind on my skin. I'm fucking suffocating.

"Yeah, probably," Konrad retorts, pulling a hip flask from inside his jacket pocket and taking a swig before offering me some.

"Not my poison," I say, shaking my head.

"Yeah, not mine usually either, she's standing over there," Konrad says with a laugh that's a little too fake for my liking.

"Brother?" I question.

He grips my shoulder briefly, then strides over to Leon and picks up another shovel, helping him to pile more dirt onto the casket and leaving me to contemplate why someone I've named Nothing could become every-fucking-thing. *To all of us.*

"She wouldn't you know," Nala murmurs, drawing my gaze away from Nothing and towards her. She's standing beside me now. I hadn't noticed her move away from the graveside, too engrossed with the woman who's here to destroy us.

"Wouldn't what?"

"Kill you. She couldn't do it, no matter how much she hates you all right now."

"She'd sink a knife in my back the moment it was turned," I say, feeling her anger spread over me like a second skin.

Nala shakes her head, her hazel eyes probing. "She reminds me of you."

"Me? Then I definitely know we're in trouble."

"You're not as bad as you want everyone to believe," Nala says softly, her fingertips brushing against my hand.

"No. I'm worse," I reply, drawing my hand away, flinching from her touch.

"I don't believe that."

I grit my jaw, looking away from Nala and back over at Christy who's staring into the grave now, deep in thought. Today her birthmark is a deep red, probably from the cold that has descended over the last couple of days. Autumn is slowly making way for winter, and with it the frosts have arrived covering everything in its path. "Believe what you want, Nala. I'm not in the mood to argue with you."

"See, you're not bad. If your father were here he would've thrown me into the grave alongside Renard and buried me alive for disagreeing with him."

"What makes you think I won't do that if you carry on?" I ask.

"Because we're family and you protect your family, you always have," she says, little white clouds escaping her lips.

"The only family you have is under six feet of freshly turned soil. You're a *servant*, nothing more. Don't elevate yourself to a position you've no business claiming."

Nala's lips wobble. I ignore the fucking tear rolling down her cheek and the stab of pain in the centre of my chest from causing it. "Well, thank you, anyway... *Sir*," she adds as an afterthought.

"For what?"

"For allowing me to bury him in this meadow. This was Grandfather's favourite spot. We spent hours here during summer together. He called this place our *piece of paradise...*" Her voice trails off as a sob releases from her lips and tears begin to fall freely from her eyes. I have to fight my instinct to wrap my arm around her shoulder and pull her close. Instead, I curl my fingers into fists and ignore it.

"He was efficient at his job," I reply tensely, disturbed by her emotions, unsettled by mine.

"I know he was just a butler to you," Nala sniffles, "But to me he was *everything*. Thank you for giving me to him."

She stares at the casket, more tears falling, her grief palpable. For a moment I'm struck dumb by her ability to show her emotions, to not be afraid of them. I guess growing up with Renard as her grandfather was a far better experience than growing up with The Collector as a father.

"If Malik were alive he would have you flogged for crying," I state.

"But he isn't here anymore. *You* are," she replies, letting her tears fall shamelessly.

Grunting, I nod, and for the thousandth time today I have to force myself to remain distant. The need to fold my arms around Nala and hold her like I had when she was a baby is getting stronger the longer I'm in her presence. But worse than that is being so close to Nothing and knowing I want her more than I want to breathe. It's fucking tearing me up inside.

She *needs* to fucking die.

"Do you have anything you wish to say?" Konrad asks, breaking the silence.

"No. You?"

He shakes his head, looking at Leon. "What about you, brother?"

"No," Leon says, swiping the back of his hand across his brow before dropping the shovel and glancing over at Nothing. Their eyes meet and she holds his gaze, something passing between them. Whatever it is, it's no longer just hate, there's more to it than that and it pisses me the fuck off.

"May I say something?" Thirteen asks. She's barely said a word all afternoon, and hasn't once made eye contact with me.

Though I can't say I'm surprised, she knows what I made Seven do to Three. I'm the villain here, at least *we're* in agreement about that.

"Please," Nala says, giving her a shaky smile.

"Make it quick. I have matters to discuss with One about the ball," I snap, needing to get as far away from this field and these fuckers as possible, even if it is back to the woman who takes as much pleasure in hurting me as I do in getting hurt.

Nothing snorts, giving me a disgusted look. Despite that, my bastard dick twitches. If I thought I could get away with fucking her mouth here and now without my cock getting bit off, I'd do it in a heartbeat. I'd have her kneeling in the damn dirt, my cock so far down her throat that her ghost eyes would brim with tears.

"When I was eight," Thirteen begins, "My father brought me here to Ardelby Castle for the first time. Renard was the member of staff who was tasked with introducing me to you three whilst our fathers talked business," she says, looking between us. "He took me to the parlour in the west wing, sat me down by the fire and gave me a cup of hot chocolate and an iced bun whilst we waited for you to join us. To pass the time he told me a story, a *fairytale*, he'd said." She pauses, smiling fondly at the memory.

"What was it about?" Nala asks, wrapping her arms around herself as she listens.

"He told me about this little boy, not much older than me at the time, who spent his days playing in an enchanted forest filled with fairies and pixies, unicorns and fauns. He said that the little boy had a big heart and a good soul, and that he was courageous and brave just like his mother once was..." Thirteen flicks her eyes to me briefly and my stomach ties into painful knots.

"Who was the boy's mother?" Nala asks.

"A fair maiden who died at the hands of an evil warlock not long after the little boy was born."

Nala frowns, looking at me and then back at Thirteen, catching on. "And the boy's father?"

"The warlock, of course."

"What else did Grandfather tell you in this story?" Nala whispers.

"That the warlock knew from the moment his son was born that he held too much kindness in his heart and that the only way to get it out of him was to treat him with cruelty. The warlock even stole two other little boys from their families and made them his own, treating them with cruelty too, just in case his own flesh and blood disappointed him. He was determined to make all three of them hateful, evil creatures like he was."

"Thirteen," I warn, wanting her to stop. To shut the fuck up. It's not as if we don't know who she's talking about. We all know how this story goes. There are no happy endings with this story.

But she shakes her head, pushing on. "Only he didn't count on those boys loving each other more fiercely than they loved themselves no matter how hard he tried to drive a wedge between them with all the awful things he made them witness, that he made them do."

"Enough!" I snap.

"Let her finish," Leon says, giving me a warning look, his fingertips running over the handle of his gun tucked into the holster at his waist.

"One day the warlock's birth son was playing in a field near the forest when he heard a startled cry," Thirteen continues on. "He thought one of the creatures he adored so much was hurt and his kind heart couldn't bear the thought. Without considering the consequences of his actions, he followed the cries and found a human baby tucked into the roots of a giant oak tree. She was cold and hungry and on the verge of death."

"This is about us, isn't it?" Nala whispers, reaching for my hand.

Her fingers wrap around mine and this time I can't bring myself to let go. Instead, I refuse to acknowledge what I'm doing and focus solely on Thirteen, despite Nothing's gaze burning right through me.

Fuck her.

Fuck her.

"The little boy took the baby back into the castle knowing the risk he was taking, and what his father would do to him and the child if he ever found out. Seeking help from his brothers, they made a pact to look after the baby, a little girl with the prettiest hazel eyes and golden hair," she says, smiling softly at Nala. "And for months they managed to do that until one day the evil warlock heard her crying and stormed into their room. He tried to kill the baby, but the warlock's servant managed to save her life by telling a story about how the child was *his* granddaughter. To everyone's surprise, the warlock allowed her to live but only if she was kept away from his three sons. So, with heavy hearts, they handed her over to the warlock's servant and closed their hearts off from her, hoping that one day, when the warlock died, they'd be able to care for her again—"

"And then the warlock died and they all lived happily ever after," Konrad interrupts, clapping his hands. "Great story, Thirteen. Cheers."

"Wait, I haven't finished yet," Thirteen says, as Nala grips my hand tightly in hers.

"Look, we all know how this story ends," I say, needing to get the fuck away from them all. I have enough trouble dealing with the memories of my childhood without being reminded of them here in this field where I fed the wildflowers my blood on a regular fucking basis.

"I said I haven't finished!" she says, her jaw set.

"Speak," I demand, losing my fucking patience.

"Renard was unable to finish his story because the three of you walked into the parlour and you demanded we play cards," Thirteen says, looking at Konrad. "Do you remember? You were better than all of us."

"Yeah, I remember," Konrad replies with a satisfied smile. "Still am."

"Anyway, just before it was time to leave and our fathers were saying goodbye, I asked Renard what happened to the little girl's mother and father. I remember frantically writing the question down in my childish scrawl, worried he wouldn't have time to tell me. As it happens, he didn't, but he did say that when the time was right, he'd tell me all about them."

"And did he ever tell you?" Nala asks, her voice barely audible.

"Yes, two nights before he passed away. He came to find me," Thirteen explains, glancing at Leon. "You and Christy were asleep at the time."

"So what did he say?" I ask sharply.

"He said that the little girl he called his granddaughter was in fact the *warlock's* child."

"What the fuck?" Konrad gasps.

"You're lying!" I grind out, the fucking ground tipping beneath me as a loud sob escapes Nala's mouth.

Thirteen shakes her head. "I wish I was, I truly do, but according to Renard, Nala is your half-sister from one of the servants your father had a *relationship* with."

Raped. She means raped, but is refusing to use that word in order to protect Nala from any more pain. "This is bullshit!"

"Renard asked me to wait to tell you until I thought the time was right..." Her voice trails off as she looks at our joined hands.

"Why didn't *he* tell me this? He had so many opportunities to do so over the years. He could've told me this on his fucking deathbed. Instead all he talked about was her," I say, glaring at Nothing as though all of this is her fault.

"He couldn't tell you whilst your father was alive, and once he was dead he still wasn't certain how you would take the news. The boy he knew, the one who saved a baby from dying in the forest, had grown up to be a very different man. He wanted to make sure you wouldn't hurt her. He was hoping he'd live to see the day when you'd finally become the man he'd always hoped you'd be and that he'd be able to tell you this himself."

"And by telling me this now, you think I *won't* hurt her?"

Nala gasps, but I refuse to look at her.

"You're *not* your father, Jakub," Thirteen insists, looking from my face to our joined hands. "No matter how hard you try to be. Nala is your sister, she's family, just like she's always been."

With great effort, I untangle my fingers from Nala's and take a step away from her. No one can know how close I am to giving up and letting that boy who held his baby sister in his arms come back to life.

No one.

"How did Nala end up in the forest?" I ask, forcing coldness into my voice, willing emptiness into my heart, accepting the darkness that touches my soul.

"When Renard found out Nala's mother was pregnant, he gave her money to start a new life somewhere far away from here. He knew she couldn't stay at the castle. Only she returned with Nala a few weeks after she was born in the hope your father would take responsibility for her."

Nala's lips wobble as understanding begins to dawn. "He killed her, didn't he? My father killed my mother."

"Yes," Thirteen says gently. "He killed your mother then asked another servant to take you into the forest. By the time Renard found out what had happened, you'd already been left for dead. The rest you know."

"Fuck! Fuck! FUCK!" Konrad exclaims, stumbling backwards. Leon reaches for him, hauling him upright. I don't understand his reaction given that Nala's *my* blood, not his.

"You're my brother," Nala whispers out, shaking her head in wonderment. Swiping at the tears streaking her face, she steps in front of me.

"Nothing's changed," I counter, taking a step away from her.

"You're my brother," she repeats, reaching up to touch my mask, "And I've never even seen your face."

"And you never fucking will," I snarl, slapping her hand away before twisting on my feet and striding away from her.

She calls after me, but I don't turn back. I keep walking away from my brothers, my sister, my friend, from fucking Nothing, until I'm inside the castle walls and heading towards One's bedroom and the hope of oblivion.

CHAPTER THIRTEEN

Christy

"HOW IS SHE?" I ask the moment Thirteen returns to Leon's room later that evening.

After Jakub's rejection, Thirteen had to guide a broken Nala back to her room. The poor girl had lost her grandfather and gained a brother... A *heartless* one.

"I gave Nala something to help soothe her heartache and help her sleep," Thirteen replies, swiping a loose tendril of hair back behind her ear. "She won't be awake for hours yet."

"That's good," Leon says, eyeing us both from his chair by the fire.

He's been thoughtful, quiet ever since we returned to the room, barely trying to engage in conversation, lost in thought. I know why. If Konrad's reaction was anything to go by, she was the woman I saw him kill and revive in my vision.

Nala's *mother*.

It's so unbelievably twisted.

"And Three?" Leon asks, adjusting his deep blue mask.

Thirteen chews on her lip as she stares into the flames. She looks haunted, troubled, and my stomach turns over with worry as she sits down on the chaise lounge next to me. It's late, but sleep is the last thing on my mind, though by the look of Thirteen that's exactly what she needs right now. Sleep. Rest.

"Thirteen, is she okay?" I ask. "What happened to her that night?"

"Seven hurt her," she replies softly.

My throat goes dry. "Hurt her? What do you mean? He lo—"

"—loves her?" Thirteen finishes for me. "Yes he does, very much."

"Then what happened?"

"Jakub happened," Leon says, and the look that passes between them makes my stomach bottom out. I know without even having to ask what went on.

Thirteen draws in a deep breath, letting it out slowly. "She's sore, bruised. I had to check the stitches that I gave her. I'm sorry I took so long."

"Stitches?" I whisper, waving away her apology.

"She had a tear in her perineum after what happened," she replies.

"Will she recover?" I ask curtly, pissed off that Thirteen saw fit to tell the man who could cause such pain that he has a younger sister. Renard was right not to tell him, what the hell was she thinking? Jakub will *never* change. None of them will.

"Physically, yes."

"And emotionally..." My voice trails off as I meet her eyes. We both know that recovering from such an act is a long, painful road. I just hope that their love for one another is enough.

"The alternative was both their deaths. They're a strong couple," she offers.

"Fuck," Leon exclaims, his jaw tight.

I snatch my head around, narrowing my eyes at him before I quickly settle my features into a neutral state. Not so long ago he was the one causing pain, relishing in it. Twelve's back and the scars that remain there are testament to that fact. We all know the damage Jakub is capable of inflicting, that *all* The Masks are capable of inflicting. I also know that Jakub taking his anger out on Three probably has a whole lot more to do with me than it does her. My stomach churns and the sudden urge to go to them forces me to my feet.

"I need to see them."

"I'm not sure now is a good time," Thirteen says, her face pinched, eyes troubled.

"They've been kind to me. I *need* to—"

"I'll take you," Leon says, cutting me off as he grabs the gun from the side table beside him, holstering it. "Come on."

"Thirteen?" I ask. She bites her lip, her hands shaking but she gets to her feet regardless. She's exhausted, her skin pale, her eyes sunken from night after night of poor sleep because she's been watching over me. Guilt climbs my throat. I grab her hand, squeezing it gently. "Stay here. Get some rest." I can't bring myself to say I'll be okay because, truthfully, I'm not sure that I will. It doesn't matter though, I have to see them.

"But—" she protests, glancing at Leon.

"We'll be back within the hour."

"Christy, I don't know if this is a good idea."

"Get some rest. It'll make me feel better. You're exhausted."

She nods, glancing at her watch. "If you're not back by midnight—"

"You'll turn me into a pumpkin?" Leon offers, a hint of a smile around his lips. Thirteen and I glance at one another, more shocked at his attempt at humor rather than the inappropriateness of it.

"I was going to say that I'll come find you, but actually I *have* been working on this elixir..." her voice trails off as she smiles softly. That smile drops when she focuses back on me. "You've been through enough trauma, Christy, I'm not sure witnessing theirs is going to help you."

"Staying here isn't either. I need to see them. *Please.*"

"Then let's do that," Leon says, cupping my elbow gently and steering me out of the room before Thirteen can protest further.

The castle is like some great slumbering beast as we walk the hallways side by side. The only sound I can hear is my long skirt swishing between my legs and Leon's shoes clipping over the tiled floor. The halls are dimly lit, the oil lamps turned down to a low flame, giving just enough light to illuminate the way. It's as though the castle is aware of the cruelty that has taken place within its walls and can't bring itself to brighten the hallways or rooms with more than a dull glow. When we step out into the courtyard that houses The Weeping Tree, I have the sudden, uncontrollable urge to stop and press my hand against the trunk.

Striding over to it, I trail my fingers against the rough bark, my eyes slowly lifting upwards as I search for the spot where it bled. It isn't long before my gaze falls on a streak of liquid leaking from a gap between the bark further up the trunk. It's too dark to tell what colour it is, the only light coming from the star-scattered sky above. Standing on my tiptoes, my fingertips graze over the liquid. Surprisingly, it's warm. When I lower myself back down, and raise my hand upwards, I can see that it is indeed the colour of blood.

"So it's true then?" I whisper.

A blast of cold air chooses that moment to rustle the remaining leaves of The Weeping Tree. One falls to the cobblestones at my feet, an answering message from a woman long since dead, the woman who's kindness changed the course of her family's life forever.

Yes.

I wrap my arms around myself, feeling cold to my very core. I sway on my feet and a sudden feeling of dizziness comes over me. The corner of my vision darkens and I know if I don't hold onto something, I'm going to fall.

"No," I whimper, pressing my body against the tree.

Vaguely I hear Leon call my name, feel him reach for me, but I can no longer see him as a vision barrels into my consciousness, knocking me out with such ferocity that I don't have time to ward it off...

"YOU MOTHERFUCKERS DESERVE *to be hanged for what you've done to Christy. Stealing her from her family and peddling her to your fucking sicko clients like a piece of meat. She should be dancing for the Royal fucking Ballet, not for you bastards at this motherfucking ball," Beast says, waving his knife in the direction of The Masks as Kate, and a man I don't recognise, tie them to the bolts embedded in the trunk of The Weeping Tree with cable ties. None of them are wearing masks and all three are beaten to within an inch of their lives. Bruises bloom across their swelling faces, blood drips from numerous cuts, the clothes they're wearing are dishevelled and torn in places.*

They've fought and it's clear who the victors are.

Of the three, Jakub looks to be the worst off. He's out cold, his head lolling between his shoulders, a deep gash running from his hairline to his right eyebrow.

Konrad isn't faring much better, the old scar on his cheek torn open and weeping blood. He coughs, and more blood releases from his mouth. "Do it. It's no less than we deserve," he mutters.

Kate grabs his face, her finger pressing into the newly open wound. "Get ready to say hello to your forefathers, prick, because they'll be seeing you very, very soon."

Konrad mutters something indistinguishable before his gaze lands on someone standing in the corner of the courtyard.

It's me.

Or rather my future self.

I'm standing beneath one of the stone archways watching this all unfold. My arms are wrapped around my chest, and I'm shivering uncontrollably as more punches are thrown. Beast lands one on Leon's stomach, making him double over and gag, his wrists pulling against the restraints. Kate raises her fist and hits Konrad on the cheek, the sound of bone breaking unmistakable, and the man I don't recognise punches Jakub in the kidney before spitting at his feet.

"Please," the future me whispers, holding her hand up for them to stop. There is pain in her eyes, such immense sadness that even though I'm yet to experience this moment, I feel what she feels.

It hurts to see them like this.

It's... confusing, the pain.

"Christy?" Kate questions, and that pain is quickly replaced with a cold, hard stare as the future version of myself strides across the courtyard, transforming with every step. She glides

across the cobblestones, her feet encased in gold ballet slippers that match the ribbons woven into her long hair and the gold dress that's encrusted with diamonds. She has an ethereal kind of beauty, otherworldly almost. Her birthmark is a stark red against the gold mask that covers the other side of her face. Like some fairytale creature, her dress floats about her body as she moves, but it's the look in her eyes that catches my breath. The intention to hurt glints just as much as the knife she's clutching tightly in her fist.

Kate steps back, glancing at the man with the dirty blonde hair. "Give her room, Ford," she says.

He gives Kate a quick nod before retreating. It's only then that I realise who he is. Kate's brother, mine. He's handsome, and I see the resemblance to Kate around his eyes and mouth even though I don't see any of me in him.

"Just let us shoot the fuckers and be done with it, Christy. It's time to go home," Beast says, rolling his head on his shoulders.

"We deserve to die," Konrad says, his voice gravelly, hoarse with pain. "I won't try to stop you."

"Dipshit, you're handcuffed to a tree," Beast retorts. "You couldn't stop us even if you wanted to."

Leon laughs, baring his bloodstained teeth as he does. "He's got a point, Kon."

Konrad ignores him, canting a look at Jakub before speaking. "If we wanted to stop you, we would've by now. We were expecting you."

"Are you trying to tell me that you don't deserve to die just because you 'allowed' us to beat the shit out of you," Beast says, making quote marks with his fingers, "Is that it? Cuz as far as I'm concerned, you three pricks couldn't fight your way out of a paper bag."

"No, that's not what I'm saying," Konrad replies firmly,

flicking his gaze back to the future me who seems to be having some kind of internal struggle given the way her features keep morphing from empathy to anger and back again.

"Then what? Because I dunno about everyone else here, but I'm over this shitstain of a night already. I wanna go home to my daughter with my family intact, knowing that you scum-buckets have been wiped off the face of the earth."

Konrad heaves out a shaky breath. "It was inevitable that men like us wouldn't survive in this world for long. I don't blame any of you for coming here tonight for Christy. I get it," he stresses, glancing at Leon then at Jakub, who begins to stir, before resting his eyes back on me. "But the only person here that has the right to kill us is you, Christy, the person we hurt the most. The woman we love."

"Love?" Kate spits the word out, her eyes narrowing. "You don't know the meaning of the word, you fucking psychopath."

"That's where you're wrong," Leon says, smiling despite the blood dripping into his mouth. "Christy taught us."

Beast, Kate and Ford all turn their attention to future me. But she doesn't acknowledge them, her focus remains on The Masks. "Stop talking," she whispers, her voice steady even though her hands are shaking.

Jakub stirs, his head lifting, puffy eyelids opening as he tries to focus. "End this," he mutters.

My future self sucks in a ragged breath, her expression faltering, the anger slipping. She wobbles on her feet, her body leaning forward as though pulled towards them. Kate notices, her brows pulling together in a frown.

"This is emotional warfare, Christy. They're trying to fuck with you. You don't need to do a damn thing."

"No. I'm the one who should do it. Me," my future self replies fiercely. "Jakub's right, I need to end this once and for all."

"Atta girl," Beast says, a grin pulling up his lips. "You're more like your sister than I've given you credit for."

Stepping towards the three of them, the future me holds the blade out in front of her. Without saying a word, she silently unbuttons Konrad's shirt and presses the blade against his skin. He groans, never once taking his eyes off her as she carves our name into his chest. Stepping back she looks at her handiwork then nods, before moving to Jakub. I suck in a shocked breath at the criss-cross of scars and scabs already decorating his chest as she carves more on top of them. When she reaches Leon, her expression falters as she traces her fingers over the scar already there.

"Do it," Leon urges.

She leans in close, and for a moment I think she's going to slide the blade up to the hilt into Leon's chest, instead she stills and I whilst I see his mouth moving I can't make out the words.

Eventually she pulls back, and placing the knife over the healed scars, my future self cuts into his skin until fresh blood drops from the parted flesh.

When she's finished, she steps back then says: "You told me that your hearts belong to me, that I brought them back to life. Well, I claim those hearts now. They're mine."

"Yours," all three respond as a blast of wind passes through the courtyard like a storm in a bottle.

"Look, Christy, as much as I love your flair for the dramatic and all that, these fuckers need to die. If you want their hearts, I'd gladly cut them out for you. It's a messy fucking job, but it's not like I ain't done it before," Beast says, looking about the courtyard as though he can't wait to get out of there.

"But they will die," future me replies softly, dropping the blade to the ground. It clatters to the cobblestones, The Masks *combined blood splattering over the stone at her feet and across her gold ballet slippers. "This blade is laced with poison..."*

"CHRISTY? FUCK, ARE YOU ALRIGHT?" Leon exclaims, leaning over me. His face only inches from mine, his thumb gently rubbing my cheek as he holds me in his arms. I blink up at him, the lingering after effects of the vision stealing my breath momentarily. Seeing him covered up in his mask, when only moments before he wasn't wearing one is even more disconcerting. "What happened?"

"I fainted," I reply quickly.

"I should take you back to my room."

"No," I say, pushing upwards, trying to shrug out of his hold as the sudden need to throw up burns my throat. "Let me go."

I shove him off me, stumbling to my feet, needing to get away from him so I can throw up in peace. In a few steps that's exactly what I do. I purge myself of the vision and of what I did. The shock and guilt releasing from me, splattering across the cobblestones.

I'm going to kill The Masks. I *saw* it.

That notion has turned from a thought into fact.

More bile burns my throat and I retch over and over again. I don't understand my physical reaction. This is what I wanted, wasn't it? They deserve nothing less.

"Christy, this was a bad idea." Leon rests his hand on my back, his hand sliding up and down as he tries to comfort me. It's a warm, kind gesture and in that moment I don't flinch from his touch, struck momentarily by the fact it doesn't hurt. Ever since I died and was brought back to life, the painful sensation no longer exists. His touch doesn't hurt. Right now, it doesn't even repulse me. I rise up, stepping away from him, wrapping my arms around myself as I try to understand why that is.

"Just leave me be."

"What happened, Christy?" he asks as I put space between us.

"I just fainted," I repeat. "It was nothing."

"It wasn't nothing." he pushes, his eyes pensive as he observes me from the other side of the courtyard just like he did that night Jakub handcuffed me to this tree. I've no doubt he's remembering our last time here together. I certainly can't forget it.

"You chained me to this tree..." I say, implying that I fainted from the memory when really the opposite was true. My voice trails off as I stare at The Weeping Tree, seeing not myself tied there, but Leon, Jakub and Konrad, their chests dripping with blood, my name carved into their skin, death only moments away.

"We did." He nods, his lips pressed into a hard line as he stares at me for long moments. "The damage is done. We can't take it back, can we?"

"No. You can't," I agree, swiping my hand across the back of my mouth.

Part of me wants to do violent things, wants to hurt him, is glad I'm going to get my vengeance. The other part of me, the part that sits within the impenetrable wall encasing my heart, wants him to get on his knees and grovel for my forgiveness, to allow him that opportunity to do so. To allow myself to forgive *him*. That part sickens me most of all.

"We should go," he says eventually, raking a hand through his hair. "Thirteen will come looking for us soon. I don't want to piss her off. That woman has skills beyond my comprehension. Pretty sure she's capable of killing us all. Honestly, I'm not sure why she hasn't tried already. It's not as if we don't fucking deserve it..." He gives me a wry smile, before turning on his heels and striding towards the door leading to the Numbers private wing of the castle.

"She's not the only one capable of killing you," I murmur back, my words lost beneath a gust of wind that sends goose-bumps scattering over my skin. The Weeping Tree creaks and groans, the ghost of years past mourning three deaths that are yet to unfold.

CHAPTER FOURTEEN

Christy

SEVEN OPENS the door to the room he shares with Three. As soon as our eyes meet, I know for certain what Jakub made him do. He wears his shame on his handsome face, a face that crumples with grief and guilt the moment he lays eyes on me. He's also fully dressed, and somehow that seems so at odds with how naked he is in the moment.

"I'm so sorry, Seven," I say, hugging him.

"I h—hurt her," he stutters, his fingers gripping the material of my dress as he presses his forehead against my shoulder and hugs me back.

Behind us Leon steps into the room, shutting the door with a firm shove. "You might want to let her go," he says, the nuances of his voice leaving no room for misunderstanding. He may be able to tolerate more things now but, clearly, another man touching me isn't one of them.

"Of course," Seven replies tightly, releasing me, a small muscle in his jaw ticking with anger.

"How are you?" I ask, regretting the question the moment it leaves my lips.

Seven swipes a hand through his hair. "I don't care about me—"

"Seven, who's there?" Three calls out from what must be their bedroom off of the small, but cosy living area we're currently standing in. It has teal and gold flock wallpaper, rich velvet curtains in a deep navy and a matching velvet suite.

"It's Zero, she's come to see you," he replies.

Three doesn't respond, and my heart sinks like a stone. "Is this okay?" I ask. "I could come back another time when she's had more rest."

"No, please stay. She..." he hesitates, dragging in a breath. "She needs someone to talk to and that person isn't the one who hurt her, that person isn't me."

"She didn't speak to Thirteen?" I ask, knowing she didn't but needing confirmation.

He shakes his head, eyes pained. "Barely. I just think she needs someone who..." He flicks his gaze over at Leon, rage passing over his features briefly before he shuts it down.

"Who *what*?" Leon questions, a scowl creasing his brow.

"Who understands what she's been through," Seven finishes. He drops his arms to the side, lifting his chin in a small act of defiance that a few days ago would've got him a session in the dungeon and a back ruined by a whip. I know he's expecting Leon to react like he always has, with violence and cruelty, but that reaction never comes.

There's only silence and a deep sense of guilt emanating from him.

"I'm *sorry*," Leon says, staring at me in such a way that makes me feel exposed, stripped bare, vulnerable.

Forcing my gaze away, I reach for Seven who's staring at Leon like he's grown another head, and gently squeeze his arm. "I'll try and help."

"Thank you. I'll wait out here with... *Master*." Seven says, swallowing hard, as though the very word itself tastes like bitter aloes, and for the first time since I've been here, I notice how Leon cringes at the title.

"Yes. Seven and I will have a drink," Leon says, jerking his chin to the liquor cabinet situated in the corner of the room. "Looks like we both could use one. I know I sure as fuck do."

Pushing open the door to their bedroom, I step into the dimly-lit room. A table lamp sits on a small table beside the bed, casting a soft glow about the space that should warm the room up if the atmosphere wasn't one of deep, soul-crushing sadness.

"Three?" I say hesitantly.

She shifts beneath the blankets, her slight frame pushing upwards as I close the bedroom door behind me. "Zero. It's so good to see you," she exclaims, plastering on a brave smile that breaks my heart.

"Don't do that," I say, rushing forward and taking her hand in mine as I perch on the side of the bed.

"Do what?"

"Pretend that you're okay."

"Are *you* okay?" she counters, deflecting the attention off of her and back onto me.

I squeeze her hands, nodding sharply. "I will be, and so will you."

"They hurt you," she whispers, a tear leaking from her long, dark lashes. I watch it track down her cheek and fall from her jaw. "I shouldn't have helped you to disobey them."

"That wasn't your fault. I knew what I was doing."

"And I know how The Masks work. I should've stopped you."

"You're not responsible for me," I say, trying to reassure her. "I was determined."

"But—" she protests.

"No. You're not responsible for what happened to me. *They are*," I press, not sure who I'm trying to convince more, her or me.

She nods, sniffing and wiping at her eyes, calming a little. "What happened after they killed The Baron? I've been so worried about you."

"That's not important right now."

"Zero... *Christy*," she whispers fiercely, shuffling closer to me on the bed, her bare arms prickling with goosebumps. "I'm *sorry*."

"I told you, it wasn't your fault. None of this is."

She chokes on a sob, her forehead falling against my shoulder as she cries quietly. "Seven didn't want to hurt me like he did. He would've tried to kill Jakub if he thought it was only his life at stake. I don't know if he'll ever get over the guilt..."

"It's still so fresh, but you can heal each other. You'll find a way."

"You don't understand. I've already forgiven Seven. I forgave him the moment it happened. I'm worried about the fact that he may never forgive himself. The guilt will eat away at him. It breaks my heart."

"Then you must tell him that. You *must* talk. Find a way to heal, together."

Three nods, her eyes welling with tears that she bravely blinks away. "Do you know, Seven's the only man who's ever treated me with respect, with *love?*"

I wrap my arms around her, pulling her close. "You've been through so much."

"I should never have asked him if he was okay..." she covers her mouth on another sob, clinging onto me tightly.

"Asked if who was okay?"

"Jakub. That's why he made Seven do what he did. He punished us both because I felt empathy towards him."

"God," I breathe.

"I'd never seen him like that. Jakub's usually so put together. So... *cold*, but he was distracted at dinner that night. Tense. Troubled. A couple nights before he'd been to the forest..." Three frowns, sighing heavily as her voice trails off.

"What does he do out there?"

"No one knows for sure, but every time he returns he's a mess."

"A mess?"

"Physically," she explains. "Though, usually, mentally calmer. A few weeks back, not long after you arrived actually, he went into the forest. I saw him a day later naked, covered in mud, twigs and..."

"And?"

"Blood. His back was covered in lashes."

"Someone beat him?"

"No. We think he beats himself. I thought that was his kink... You know, some people get off on that."

I nod. "Yes."

"But, I'm not so sure now. Whatever it once did for him, it doesn't anymore. He came back this time worse, not better. It's one of the reasons why I asked if he was okay. Then tonight..."

"Tonight?" I question, my throat drying.

"Thirteen was talking with Seven, trying to convince him to take a sleeping pill. I'd gotten out of bed wanting to look at anything other than these four walls and I saw Jakub outside on the grounds, bare chested and covered in bloody lashes, stumbling around and cursing the sky. I couldn't bring myself to look away. He was in agony, Christy. I know he saw me."

"What happened?"

She drags in a breath then blows it out. "He lifted his fist over his heart and bashed it against his chest. It was like he was apologising. Jakub never says sorry. Never. Half a minute later, One came outside to get him. They argued, and he tried to walk away but she grabbed his wrist and dragged him inside..." Her voice trails off as she swallows hard. "In that moment, I didn't see the man who was cruel to us, Christy, I saw a defeated *boy*."

My eyes widen, but I can't bring myself to say anything. I both *want* him to hurt, and feel sick at the thought. I swallow hard, holding onto the hate I feel for him with a tight, vicious grip. I fucking claw at it, pushing away everything else.

"Whatever One did to him, it's no more than he deserves," I say angrily.

She frowns, looking at me but not really registering my presence in that moment. "You don't understand. There are five rules we live by here at Ardelby Castle and we're *all* aware of them. But there's also a sixth rule that none of the Numbers say out loud but understand we *must* follow. I broke that rule last night."

"Who's rule?"

"The Collector's. It was his only one, and we were forbidden to share it with The Masks."

"What was his rule?" I ask, feeling a shiver track down my spine.

"To never show The Masks kindness or empathy. *Never*."

"And what would happen if you did?" I ask, feeling sick to my stomach.

"The Collector would kill us and torture them."

"Jesus. He was so *twisted*."

Three nods, her fingers curling into my forearms, her expression serious. "He was. The Collector was the devil incarnate. The Masks were shaped by him..." She sighs, fighting some internal battle that I recognise only too well.

"Don't!" I shake my head. "Don't make excuses for Jakub, for any of them," I add, reminding myself not to do the same, and clutching hold of that hate as tightly as I can.

"I'm not making excuses. I despise Jakub for what he did to Seven and me." She swipes at her eyes, brushing away more tears. "But I've lived in this castle for the best part of my adult life. I've witnessed many things, seen how they've suffered at The Collector's hands. When he died, we all breathed a sigh of relief. Even them, though I doubt they recognised that in themselves. It was like a weight had been lifted."

"What are you saying exactly?" I ask. "Because right now I don't want to hear that they're victims, too."

She gives me a sad smile. "Aren't they though?"

"By that same line of thinking, wasn't The Collector a victim of his father, like his father before him, and his father before him? We're *all* victims in one way or another, but how we choose to act in the face of violence and cruelty defines who we are as an individual... That's what counts."

My voice trails off as I realise what I've just said, and how much of a hypocrite I am because my intentions are no less violent towards The Masks. Does that make me the same as them, as their father? Am I just as evil for wanting revenge, for wanting to hurt them?

No. I tell myself. It doesn't, because after I've killed them this will all be over. I will go back home and work the rest of my life caring for people at the end of their lives. I won't perpetuate that violence over and over again like they have. The future me who cuts their skin with a poisoned blade will cease to exist the moment they die. This anger and rage I feel will end with their deaths. That's the difference between me and The Masks, with their forefathers. I won't carry it with me and infect the lives of others.

"A long time ago, I accepted my life here at Ardelby Castle. I accepted the rules and I lived by them. We all did. Believe it or not, I found a home here. But..."

"But?"

"When The Collector died things began to change. The Masks, they..."

"They what?"

"They became obsessed with seeking revenge for their father's death. It consumed them, but that obsession shifted when you arrived. I've seen the way they look at you. We all have. *You* affect them."

"I'm sorry you had to bear the brunt of that," I say, guilt slithering into my veins like a snake through grass.

"No," Three says, shaking her head. "That isn't what I meant."

"Then what did you mean?"

"There's something about you that they're fighting against with everything they have, to the point that Jakub is beating himself and Konrad is locking himself in the dungeons for days throwing knives at the severed head of the very man who hurt you."

"What?" My stomach rolls with nausea.

"Five has spent some time with him down there."

I shake my head, pushing that imagery out of my mind. "Are you saying I should feel bad for Jakub, for any of them? That *you* should?"

Three looks at her hands, picking at a loose bit of skin around her thumb nail. "Honestly, I don't know what I'm trying to say, or why I'm even saying it. All I know is that those men have endured great cruelty. The worst kind possible."

"And you haven't?" I counter.

"I didn't say that." Three swipes her hair behind her ears, then grips my hands in hers. "I'm just trying to understand how, even after The Collector's death, they're still not free."

"Are you free?" I counter.

She sighs. "No. I guess we never were."

"Then there's your answer. If they had any redeeming qualities they would've let you go the moment their father died. They wouldn't have kidnapped me. Leon wouldn't have whipped Twelve until she could barely stand. Konrad wouldn't have stuck his fingers inside of me whilst I was under the influence of a drug, unable to fight back, and Jakub wouldn't have forced Seven to hurt you."

Three flinches, but she doesn't try to argue. God knows I've had moments when I could see why these men are the way they are. I've felt pity and *empathy* despite their cruelty towards me. So I get where she's coming from. I really do. Except the difference is they had a choice when their father died. They had the chance to do better, to *be* better and they didn't take it.

"The fact you've suffered like them and haven't turned into a violent psychopath tells me all I need to know about the type of person you are compared to the men they *still* are."

"Then why did Jakub seek One out to beat him when doing it himself didn't work—?" Three gives me a sad look, and I know that whatever respect she still has for One, is now slowly trickling away as she begins to see the truth of this place and the woman who has helped to keep it and The Menagerie alive. "Konrad hasn't just been throwing knives at The Baron's head either," she continues. "Five said that he had a discussion with her about the human heart, about *love,* as though he was trying to understand the concept. Why do you think that is?"

I shrug my shoulders, refusing to answer her. Feeling sick at the implication.

"We all know that something happened to you that night we left you in the Room of Fantasies—"

"This isn't about me," I argue, cutting her off. "I came here for you."

"And whatever that was," she pushes on, "It has something to do with the fact that Leon hasn't left your side since. Leon, The Mask we fear above all the others, the most violent of all, is acting like someone who actually *cares.*"

"Don't do this, Three. If Jakub can punish you and Seven the way he did this evening because you showed him an ounce of kindness, imagine what he'll do if he ever heard about this conversation. Leave it alone, okay?" I begin to draw away, but Three grabs my hands, refusing to let me go.

"Wait..." Three's face pales, all colour draining from her skin as her thoughts run riot. "That night at dinner Jakub gave us this speech about The Weeping Tree. He warned us not to gossip, to speak of what happened. It bled..." Her eyes widen as she puts two and two together. "Did one of them...? Did you...?"

Did one of them kill me? Did I die?

I meet her gaze, refusing to cry about it, refusing to allow myself to feel anything other than anger. It feels like a lifetime ago, when in reality it's only been a little over a week.

"Oh God," she mutters, drawing her own conclusions from the look in my eyes as her tears fall freely now. "Oh God, I'm so sorry. You must hate me for trying to understand them. I'm a fool."

"I don't hate you, Three. You're a victim in all of this."

"What are you going to do?" She asks, pulling me into a fierce hug, so tight I can barely get my next words out. But through gritted teeth I do.

"I'm going to set us all free."

"How?" she asks.

"Don't worry. I find a way," I say, wondering whether she notices the subtle, but meaningful, turn of phrase.

CHAPTER FIFTEEN

Christy

"MY FATHER WAS right to fear you," Leon says, as he stares out of the window a couple of days later watching a storm gather over the mountains in the distance. It's raining heavily, thunder rumbling as lightning forks across the darkening sky.

"You regret pulling me from the fire?" I ask, resting on the chair beside the fireplace, acutely aware that keeping him talking is the only option I have until Thirteen returns from her visit to Three and Nala.

Turning around, he leans against the window frame, his fingers curling around the ledge. "Not now. No."

"But you did once?"

"Yes," he admits, swiping a hand over his face as another fork of lightning illuminates him in bright, white light. "Saving you resulted in Malik shooting Jakub's dog dead as punishment.

He also beat me so badly that without Renard's care I might've died."

His words hum with honesty, and a cloying feeling of pity churns my stomach. I shouldn't be surprised he was punished by his father or even care for that matter, but despite everything, I have empathy for the boy he *was*.

"Renard was a good man to you, to Nala," I observe.

"When he could be, yes." Leon, noticing my expression, swipes his tattooed hand through his hair. "He took care of all of us when he could, but aside from that one time when he stepped in to save Nala and spare Jakub another beating, he never stopped Malik from hurting us or any of the women he brought home."

"That must have been difficult to understand. Confusing," I concede.

"Renard was Malik's most loyal employee, but he did what he could for us. Our relationship with him is... *was* complicated. Besides, Nala was the one he cared about the most. Going against Malik would've put her in harm's way."

I nod, shivering as a cool breeze passes over my skin through the gaps around the window frame.

"You're cold?" Leon asks, striding across the room and grabbing some logs from the basket beside the fireplace.

"A little," I admit.

"You should've said something," he admonishes.

"We haven't really been in a position where I can ask things of you and you're willing to give them to me," I say, watching Leon as he arranges the logs, then reaches for some kindling and newspaper from another basket, placing them in the gaps between the wood. "You've only ever taken from me before."

"Things are different now, I had hoped you'd realise that,"

he replies, grabbing a box of matches from the mantle and lighting the stack of wood.

"How?" I ask, tucking my hair behind my ears as he shifts position, using an iron poker to ensure all the wood catches fire.

The warm glow flickers in his eyes as he turns to look at me. There's a softness to his gaze that just wasn't there before. It unnerves me. I'm not certain how to deal with this version of him.

"I thought I made that obvious. Don't I seem different to you?"

"If by different you mean you're not actively trying to hurt me, kill me, or fuck me, then I suppose, yes, you're different."

"You don't believe it will last?"

"I don't know what to believe," I say truthfully.

Even now when I look into his eyes, I feel the connection between us, some cosmic force that binds me to him even when all I want is to be free of it, unshackled from these chains that weigh so heavily on my heart. I just have to keep reminding myself that it will happen. That I'll be the one to sever those chains when the timing is right.

"And the legend, what Renard said? Do you believe in that?"

"My mother clearly believed we were destined for each other..." I say, my voice trailing off as I focus on the fire crackling in the hearth and not the dull ache in my chest at the thought of her.

"She was a seer," Leon states, watching me closely.

"Yes."

"And you?"

"And me what?"

"Do *you* see things? You have your mother's eyes after all."

"No," I lie, shaking my head. "I don't have any gifts."

"That isn't true," he remarks, grazing his fingers under my chin, urging me to look at him.

"You made *me* see, didn't you?"

"Not much of a gift if it doesn't work on all three of you," I murmur, the ache in my chest becoming painful for reasons I'd rather not delve too deeply into right now.

"I wouldn't be so certain about that."

His hand falls away as he grabs the armrest either side of me and shifts closer. I should be fearful. I should be on the defence. Instead I'm fighting off a headache and a deep sense of unease. I rub at my temples, willing it to go away. "You can't believe that, surely."

"I think they're fighting with everything they have *not* to remember who they were. They're lashing out, Jakub in particular."

"I see…"

"I don't think you do."

"You honestly think they can change?"

"I have, haven't I?"

My gaze snaps away as I contemplate that. Has he though? He isn't trying to actively rape me, that's true, and neither is he trying to kill me, but I still sense the darkness in him, the need to cause harm. To hurt. He gets a thrill out of that. *Pleasure.* I experienced it in the dungeon. That need is *still* there. It hasn't gone away, he's just able to suppress it better now that he has a little more control over his urges. But we all know that nothing good ever comes by suppressing who you truly are, it finds a way out eventually.

"Do you want to know what I honestly think?" I ask him.

"Yes," he breathes, searching my face.

"I think you're lying to yourself. I think that despite your ability to feel more, you still crave the same things you did before. You said as much yourself. You want to fuck me. *Hurt* me."

"I—"

"You want to cut me, smother yourself in my blood," I say, cutting him off. "There's a need in you. One that won't be satisfied no matter how much you try to pretend otherwise. So whilst you're not trying to force yourself on me right now, you still want to, don't you?"

Leon shifts closer, his firm abs pressing against my knees. The heat of his body seeping into mine. "Yes," he admits, and my spine tingles. "I want to do all those things to you. I think about the time in the dungeon every second of every fucking day. I replay it over and over again. I see my cock covered in your blood and the look of ecstasy on your face, and I want it so fucking bad. *So fucking bad*. And yet..."

"And yet?" I swallow hard, my voice painfully quiet.

"I want you to want it, too. I want you to crave that part of me like I crave all of you."

Caustic anger flares in my veins. "I *never* wanted that." I shake my head, trying to compose myself, but as sick as it is, there's this tiny, miniscule part of me that found pleasure in what happened. The balance between pleasure and pain was so carefully played between the two men that the orgasm I had was intense. Confusing. Mind-altering.

"What *do* you want then?" he asks me, capturing me in his gaze, his eyes begging for something, *anything*, to soothe his soul. As I look into them I'm reminded once again of the boy who saved me and my heart squeezes painfully at the memory.

No, I tell myself forcefully. I owe him nothing.

"I'm not playing this game anymore."

"This isn't a game. This is a man trying to claw his way back to humanity. You said you'd help me. Talk to me. Give me something to cling on to."

"I didn't agree to this..." I say, pressing myself back against the seat, hating the way my skin flushes at his nearness. My heart and soul might remember the damage he caused, the pain he inflicted, the life he took, but my body? My body only remembers how he *felt* when he touched and caressed me in the library, how he kissed me after cutting me in the dungeons, how I kissed *him* after I beat him brutally. It doesn't remember how it felt to be strangled, given I was so totally under the influence of the elixir I was forced to drink. My body can't hold onto *that* feeling of violence because I simply didn't feel it. Instead, it yearns for the softness I experienced after the pain and it *sickens* me.

"Don't you feel that?" he asks, his fingers gently hovering over my forearm.

"No." I lie, even when the hairs on my arms lift as his fingers pass over them. The energy between us practically crackles. Of course I feel it. That pull, that need, the connection. It's dangerous. *Wrong.*

"I don't *want* to hurt you beyond repair," he whispers, as he takes my hands in his and tracks his thumbs back and forth over my knuckles. There's a silent 'but' that hangs in the air between us. We both sense it, understand it for what it is. "You have to understand..." He heaves out a sigh as he continues to caress my hands, but I don't want to feel the warmth of his fingers, the gentleness. I need his roughness to remind me of who he truly is beneath this temporary facade, to remind me of what I must do.

"He's *lying.*"

I drag in a shocked breath, my head snapping around as I watch Jakub enter the room, locking the door behind him. Leon releases me, rushing to his feet, but Jakub grabs the gun carelessly left lying on the bureau and points it at him. It doesn't stop him though, Leon keeps moving towards Jakub. So he changes tactics and points the gun at me instead.

Oh God.

"Don't!" Leon snarls, stopping in his tracks.

Jakub ignores him, concentrating on me. The mirrored mask he's now wearing glints as another flash of lightning brightens the room. It's unnerving to see myself reflected within it. "He *wants* to hurt you."

Leon shakes his head "*No.*"

"The things he's done with those hands. I've seen him strip a man of his skin—peeling it like someone would an orange—without an ounce of regret. He learnt that trick from our father."

"My God," I whisper, my stomach roiling.

"I'm not that man anymore," Leon counters, begging me with his eyes to believe him.

"We both know that's a lie. You're still that man. You might want to strip yourself of that part like a snake would its skin, but it still exists within you. You. Live. For. Violence." Jakub says, punctuating each word with a jerk of the gun, before looking at me intently. "He wants to hurt you. He gets off on it."

"No, not like before." Leon argues.

"You don't *want* to cut her?"

Leon grits his jaw, refusing to answer Jakub. It doesn't matter though, we both know that he does, he admitted it only moments before.

"You don't *want* to squeeze her neck with your hands and feel the fear racing in her pulse?"

Leon flashes a look at my throat, at the fading marks there. His skin flushes.

"You don't *want* to mark her skin with your handprint, your teeth marks? You don't *want* to fist her hair and angle her head back so you can fuck her throat raw? You don't *want* to cover yourself in her virginal blood? You don't *want* to fuck her tight arsehole?" Jakub laughs at Leon's silence, removing his mirrored mask and dropping it to the floor. It cracks with the impact. "That's who we are. That's *what* we are."

"That isn't all I am," Leon replies, backing up slowly towards me. "I just don't know how to be any other way. I've never been shown *how* to be any other way. *We've* never been shown."

"And *she's* going to be the one to do that, is she?"

"Yes, if Christy's willing to help us."

"Us?" Jakub shakes his head. "No. We can't change who we are. We feed off of pain. We feast on violence. We're damaged, deranged. We're fucking monsters."

"He's *wrong*, Christy," Leon says, shaking his head emphatically.

"Prove it," he says. "Prove to me you can control your *true* desires and maybe I'll buy into this bullshit that Nothing is the one who has the power to change us."

"And how do you propose I do that?" he asks.

"Make *love* to her," Jakub sneers, spitting out the word like it's poison.

"What? No!" I shake my head, panic rippling through my blood as I stand, ready to bolt.

Jakub flicks off the safety. "Make love to her and I'll let her live."

Leon passes his hand through his hair, contemplating Jakub's demand as he glances at me.

"You can't be serious?!" I bite out, refusing to believe this is happening again.

"Do you want to die?"

"That's a habit I can't seem to break," I bite out sarcastically, acid burning my stomach with every word.

"Then so be it," Jakub snaps, his finger tightening over the trigger.

"STOP!" Leon shouts, holding his hands up. "Fucking Christ, Jakub. Just stop."

"Make love to her then. Do it. You're a changed man aren't you? So fucking prove it."

He shakes his head. "She doesn't want that."

"When has that stopped you before? You do whatever the fuck you want and damn the consequences," Jakub says, his eyes flashing with anger, but also with pain. He truly believes he's lost his brother to me. I wish I was so certain.

"I promised Christy. I *won't* hurt her like that."

"Okay," Jakub nods, pulling the trigger.

The sound of the bullet releasing from the gun is deafening and I squeeze my eyes shut, waiting for it to pierce my chest.

It doesn't.

Peeling open my eyes, I let out a shaky breath, my whole body trembling. I expect to be bleeding, I'm not. No one is. The wall behind me, however, has a new hole.

"Next time I won't miss," Jakub warns.

"What is it with you, Jakub?" Leon asks, glaring at his brother. "First you wanted me to prove Christy meant *nothing* to me, forcing me to strangle her to death—"

"I didn't force a damn thing and you know it," Jakub snaps back, a bitter laugh escaping his lips.

"And now," Leon continues, "you want me to prove I'm a changed man to satisfy your own twisted desires. Just admit how *you* feel about Christy. It's about time you man the fuck up. God knows I've been saving your arse for years now, and we both know why that is."

"What did you just say to me?" Jakub hisses, livid with anger.

"You heard me. I *know* you, Jakub. I know how hard you fight who you truly are. You've been fighting it for years, so don't you dare fucking turn this on me to ease your warped sense of loyalty to a man who doesn't fucking deserve it. You were *never* truly emotionless, not like Malik wanted you to be. You were *always* the one who had to fight the hardest to maintain the darkness he was hell bent on inflicting on you, on *us*. Malik beat you, forced you to fuck and degrade One because he *knew* there was no destroying that tiny glimmer of goodness within you, and when that didn't work he took you to the cabin and did far worse. You *feel*. You always have."

"I don't feel anything," Jakub roars, grabbing the lapel of his black shirt and ripping it open.

I gasp at his shredded, bloodied chest, at the weeping wounds criss-crossing his skin, the violence inflicted on his body.

"She did that to you?" I whisper, bile burning my throat.

Jakub's eyes narrow at me. "It didn't fucking work."

"Precisely!" Leon shouts. "You don't find any release with One because she isn't the one who can give it to you. Don't you see, Jakub, we're doing this right now because you'd rather hurt the people who have a chance at helping you climb out of the fucking hell you've been living in than face the truth."

"I'm doing this for you!" he shouts, pain etched across his face. "I'm trying to show you that this temporary personality transplant is just that, *temporary*."

"It isn't."

"Then *prove* it, motherfucker." Jakub reaches into his pocket and pulls out a knife and throws it. It lands equidistant between me and Leon. "Look familiar?" Jakub asks, pointing to the knife.

I nod. "Yes." It's the knife he had displayed in his room of curiosities.

"That butterfly tattoo is a symbol of the Dálaigh family, they're all marked with one. This tattoo right here once belonged to your uncle. My father murdered him, then cut out this section of skin and used it to fashion the handle as a reminder to everyone who fucks with the Brovs just what we're capable of."

My hand flies upwards to cover my mouth as I gag. "No."

"*Yes.* Our families have been bitter enemies for *years,* so whatever bullshit Renard heard, whatever your mother thought was true, and despite what my father believed, there is no changing the fact you are our enemy. You. Are. Our. Enemy."

"Why are you telling me this...?" I ask, clasping my hands together to stop them from shaking.

"Because whatever the fuck you've done to Leon, to *us,* doesn't change the fact that we cannot, *ever,* belong to one another..." Jakub realises his mistake the second those words leave his lips, his admission as telling as it is damning.

"Do you want her to belong to us, Jakub? Do you want Christy like I want her?" Leon asks.

Jakub's jaw grits. He refuses to answer. "Jakub. Fuck, this is important. Do you want her like I want her? Do you hope like I do that the legend is true? Do you *feel* it, too?" Leon asks, slamming his palm over his chest.

With a look of determination in his eyes, Jakub's grip tightens on the gun. "I offered you the chance to convince me not to kill her. Instead you only reminded me why she *must* die. Dálaighs have a habit of fucking things up for us Brovs, as you well know."

Leon rushes forward, pressing his chest against the barrel of the gun. "No. I'll do it. I'll fucking do it, okay?" he says, twisting on his feet as he faces me, eyes pleading.

I shake my head. "Don't."

"What am I supposed to do? I can't let him hurt you."

My eyes flick to the knife on the floor and I launch myself forward, grabbing it before he's able to. Holding it aloft, I square my shoulders, ready to fight. "You think stealing my virginity won't hurt me?" I spit.

"I'll be gentle," he promises, but I see the monster in his gaze despite his need to protect me. It craves my blood, my pain, just like it always did. He can't stop it. He *will* hurt me.

"You're a *liar!*" I accuse, my hands shaking. "I'd rather Jakub shoot me dead than be subjected to *this*."

Leon grits his jaw, looking over his shoulder at Jakub. "I have your word that if I do this you won't kill her?"

"You have my word."

Leon nods. "Christy..." he begins, stepping towards me.

"I *will* fight," I hiss, jabbing the knife in his direction as I back away from him and the predatory look in his eyes.

"Please don't do that," he begs quietly, unbuttoning his shirt as moves closer towards me. "Don't fight me. It'll only make this harder."

"For who, *you?*" I laugh hysterically now.

"Yes," he hisses. "Yes for me, but for you, too."

"I don't care. I'm capable of causing pain. You *know* I am," I warn, waving the knife in front of me in an attempt to fend him off.

"I do. Fuck, I do." He shucks off his t-shirt, dropping it to the floor. Kicking off his shoes, he reaches for the hem of his joggers and pushes them over his waist. He's naked beneath, his cock erect as he bares himself to me. He's turned on by this, just like I knew he would be.

"I will cut you!" I shout as he kicks his joggers away.

Leon's cock jerks at my threat and Jakub tips his head back and laughs darkly, a knowing look in his eyes. "Don't you see, Leon? She's nothing more than an animal herself. A violent, treacherous, lustful creature. She pretends to be kind, caring, pure, *good* but she wears a mask just like us. She craves violence, as well. I see it in her eyes."

"I am *nothing* like you. I'm just trying to protect myself!"

"No?" Jakub questions, licking his lips as his gaze roves over me. "I remember how you fucked my face with your pussy, how you took my dick in your pretty little mouth and swallowed my cum. You wanted my darkness then. It made you feel alive, didn't it?"

I shake my head. "No. That is *not* what happened. It wasn't like that."

Jakub smirks, eying us both as I back away and Leon prowls towards me. "Leon, you're drawn to Christy not because she's the one who'll smother the darkness within you, but because she's the one who can make it grow. A fucking *Dálaigh* of all people." He shakes his head, laughing at the thought. Then, as though the idea has just occurred to him, he says: "I tell you what, fuck her like you *really* want to, and not only will I *not* kill her, I will carve our names into her skin and we'll keep her chained up in our tower of sin *forever*," he says, changing tactics. Twisting this interaction to suit his needs, to fuck with Leon's head, with mine, and I know in that moment that this was his game all along. He never wanted Leon to make love to me, he wanted him to *hurt* me, to be the monster we all know he's capable of being. He wants to drag that part of him out into the open, tempting him with violence and sin. He wants his brother back.

Leon stills, his hands balling at his sides as confusion rolls across his features. "I don't want to hurt—"

"Yes. You. Do. Use her like you truly want to and you'll *never* have to be confused again," Jakub continues, capitalising on Leon's moment of confusion. "That pain you felt when she died wasn't because you cared for her, but because you didn't get a chance to steal her innocence and feed off her *pain*. You mourned what you lost. Now you can take it. Fucking take it."

"No. Don't listen to him. He's *scared* to feel. You were right, Leon, Jakub's fighting it."

"I'm not," Jakub replies, but his gaze flickers, revealing the truth of his mangled heart.

It shocks me.

"Oh my God, you are," I whisper.

"Just remember how it felt to press your fingers against her throat," Jakub presses on, cutting me an ugly look, and shutting down that glimmer of humanity. "Remember how her life ebbed away beneath your touch. Remember when you cut her and watched her bleed. It made you feel powerful, didn't it?"

"Yes," Leon admits in a whisper, narrowing his gaze at me as he fists his cock, the veins in his hands popping beneath his skin as slides his fist up and down the length of his shaft.

"Leon, don't..." I beg, fear creeping over my skin. Sheer terror makes my limbs feel heavy, burdensome as I shuffle backwards.

"You've lost your way, brother. She's fucked with your head, *our* heads, but I'm going to help you return to who you truly are. You crave pain and violence. It turns you on. *She* turns you on because her fire, her fight, it matches *yours* and there's nothing better than a worthy foe," Jakub says, goading him, manipulating him, continuing to twist his thoughts. "Think about how it will feel when you fuck her. The power of it as you smother your cock with her blood and take what's owed. Think about all the times you'll be able to use her to satisfy your needs, just like I promised. *Fuck* making love. If you do all the dirty, debased, violent things you want to her, right here and now, she'll be our toy *forever*. I will never let anyone take her from us, least of all me."

"You're heartless," I accuse.

"NO! I'M. A. BROV!" he roars back, thumping his chest with every word. "That's who I am. Who you are, Leon, and *nothing* can change that. Nothing. Our father chose *you* to be my brother. Show me I haven't lost you, too."

Horrified, I shake my head, wishing that the Leon who pulled me from the bathtub and begged me to stay with him would fight back, but with every step towards me that person slowly disappears and the monster within returns. He feeds off my fear, seeking out violence, and in that moment I realise something fundamental.

Jakub may have flipped the switch inside Leon, but only *I* have the power to flip it back.

I've done it once before and I'll do it again.

And that ability, *that* is what will help me to destroy these men once and for all.

So this time, when Leon launches himself at me, instead of fighting back, instead of sliding the knife I'm holding into his chest, I allow it to slip from my fingers. I accept his darkness knowing only I can draw out the light, knowing that someday very soon I will have my revenge.

Leon

MY HEAD IS FILLED with white noise. It deafens me, blinds me, stops me from thinking straight. It's loud, consuming, it takes over, the edges turning black as the white fills with bleakness.

Inside my monster howls in satisfaction, free from its constraints, unlocked by Jakub's provocation. My mental wall was weak. Jakub knew it. He fucking picked the rusty lock that had barely gained any strength and demolished it with a few choice words and a reminder of what resides inside my chest.

I'm a Brov. I'm a *monster*.

Launching forward, I rip at her dress, shredding it with my bare hands. The sound of the material splitting is louder than the fucking storm outside, but no match for the growl that rips out of my throat as I lose myself to the monster within and the violent need to take, to inflict pain.

The angry, rushing pulse of my blood forces a dangerous concoction of adrenaline, testosterone, dopamine and serotonin within my body. A volatile mixture that fills my cock painfully.

I want to *fuck*.

I want to fuck her tight cunt and make her bleed. I want to consume and annihilate.

"Mine!" I snarl, my frantic eyes falling to the pretty pink buds of her tits that peep out at me from behind the torn material of her dress. I swipe it aside, shoving it off her shoulders then grasp her greedily, roughly. She stumbles back from the force, her back hitting the wall as I maul her with my lips, teeth and tongue. My slick mouth covers her skin, tasting the fear in her perspiration, hearing it in her whimpers, feeling it as she fucking trembles from my touch.

"Fucking mine!"

Bowing over her, I scrape my teeth against her skin, leaving indents on the fleshy globes of her tits, her stomach and her hip bones as I bite and taste her. Her pussy is covered with a pair of cotton knickers, and I rip at those too, the elastic biting into her skin and leaving a red mark as I tear them off.

Her scent fills my nostrils, and I nearly go blind with the feral need to impale her on my cock, but first I want to feast on her pussy. My fingers curl into her thighs, bruising as I force them apart roughly. Ducking my head, I lick her from hole to clit. Her taste explodes on my tongue and I growl into her heat, panting and snarling, frustrated that I can't get close enough. Instinctively, I haul her legs over my shoulders, pinning her chest against the wall with my forearm as I grasp her arse with one hand and eat her the fuck out.

I'm ravenous, frenzied, *feral*.

I'm a fucking animal as I lap and lick at her, sucking her

folds into my mouth, scraping my teeth over her clit, spearing my tongue into her hole. But still it isn't enough. It isn't enough.

My hand drops from her arse and two fingers slide roughly into her pussy, punching through the thin barrier of her virginity. Tearing her wide open.

"Fuck yes!" I hiss, surging with power, with possession, as I take what belongs to me.

She cries out, pain etched with a huge gasping sob, her fingers curling into my shoulders. Something deep down inside of me pulls up sharp at the sound.

My hand stills. My head pulls back. I cock my head to the side as I strain to listen over the rushing of my pulse. It's so loud I can barely hear anything else.

Then I hear *her*.

"L—Leon," she whispers, her whole body trembling, shaking. Her tears fall onto my upturned face, each one of them a sobering reminder of what I've just done.

Wait.

Why don't I have a blade buried in my chest? Why isn't she fighting me? Why aren't I dead?

I shake my head, trying to stitch the last few minutes back together. Then it comes back to me in a nightmarish rush. Jakub's words, my needs, her pleas.

What. I've. Done.

"Fuck. No. No!"

I forcibly push the monster back into the makeshift cage within me, mentally locking it up with more bars, and several padlocks as my fingers pull out of her, scarlet with her blood. A bright red droplet slips from my finger and drops to the floor between my parted knees, falling onto the blade of the knife she was holding onto only moments ago. I shake my head, easing her legs off my shoulders. Picking up the knife, I stand, my free hand gently sliding over her thighs, smearing her blood as I notice the teeth indents I've left in her skin. I bit her?

"I hurt you... *again*." Her sob is the only answer I get as tears spill from her eyes. "Why didn't you stab me?"

She shakes her head, unable to articulate her thoughts. I crowd against her, cupping her face with my hands. My body presses against hers as I hem her in, aware that Jakub is still in the room with us, that he could shoot her still. I'm also aware that my bastard cock is still hard, that feral, dark, deranged part of me could still cause damage, still wants to.

"I could've killed you. Why didn't you stop me?" I repeat more forcefully.

"Because..." She trembles, her lips wobbling as she grasps for words. "B—because right now my pain is the only way to draw out the g—good in you."

Her words hit me like a juggernaut and my knees buckle at the truth.

I'm so messed up. I'm so, so fucked-up.

I'm beyond help, beyond redemption.

"I don't want your pain..." I mutter, gutted by her words, by the truth, even though she's right.

I saved her from the fire only when the sounds of her screams tore at me. I kissed her gently, tenderly, called her Christy in the dungeon only once she'd bled for me. I've stopped now, only because her cry of pain, her tears, had pulled me out of my trance.

"Fuck. *Fuck!*" I lament, forcing my legs to straighten and place the knife into her hand as I wrap my fingers around hers and press the blade against my throat. "Do it!"

"No," she shakes her head, trying to pull her hand back.

I press the blade harder against my throat, crushing her fingers in mine. "Do it. I don't fucking deserve to live."

"Leon, enough!" Jakub commands.

"Fuck you, *brother*," I snarl, twisting my head to look at him. "Don't you fucking get it? I'm fighting to be a better man. I don't want to hurt her anymore. I. Don't. Want. To."

"Then d—don't," Christy whispers, her breath feathering over my heated skin. With her free hand she twines her shaking fingers in my hair, forcing me to look back at her. "Don't hurt me anymore."

"I don't understand," I whisper.

"Make the pain go away."

"How? How can *I* do that?"

"You've done it before."

"What?" My hand jerks and I feel the sharp sting as the blade slices my skin, opening up the wound Konrad gave me only days before.

"*Kiss* me, Leon."

"Kiss you?"

"Show Jakub the side of you he truly fears," she continues, hiccuping against my lips. "Show him that there *is* more to you. Help *us*."

"Us?" I press my forehead against hers, my stomach bottoming out and my chest squeezing tightly at her generosity, her spirit, her fucking heart. "You would do that, after *everything*?"

"Yes."

Now it's my turn to be confused. "Why?"

She sighs, and with it I feel a loosening, a release of something. Is it acceptance? I'm not able to unravel that right now, too caught up in the whirlwind of my own feelings. "Because we were always supposed to get to this point. God knows I've fought hard against it," she says quietly, her lips edging along my cheek as she presses her mouth against my ear. "Earlier you asked me if I was a seer. I lied when I said I wasn't. I *am* my mother's daughter. I knew you were coming before you even found me."

My hand drops from hers as I drag in a sharp breath. She removes the knife from my neck, dropping it to the floor. She could have killed me. She didn't.

"You knew about us and you didn't run?"

"At the last minute I wanted to, but by that time it was already too late."

"I'm sorry."

She nods. "You have to promise me something, Leon."

"Anything. Fuck, *anything*," I mutter against her mouth.

"You must help me to help you, to help *him*."

"What can I do?" I ask, knowing that I'd burn the whole world down for this woman if she asked me to. "I'll do anything you ask except let you go."

She presses her eyes shut briefly. "Show me the tenderness I've seen glimpses of. Show Jakub that there is more freedom in kindness than there is in hate. Help him. Kiss me. Make *love* to me."

On the other side of the room Jakub sucks in a breath at her words, and in my periphery I see him drop to his knees, collapsing under the weight of her compassion.

"Yes," I mutter, pressing my mouth against hers. "I will kiss you every day for the rest of my motherfucking life. I will make love to you always, for as long as the world keeps turning."

My lips brush against hers gently, softly, with care and tenderness, and with every second that passes the need for violence abates and my desire to cause pain lessens. This kiss makes me more vulnerable than I've ever been and, conversely, the strongest. My blood pumps faster, my pulse beats louder, my heart fucking comes alive. It fills with emotion, with feeling, and as the seconds pass I can feel it slowly stitching back together piece by ragged piece. It enlarges and grows powerful, fucking indestructable, until it's no longer this pathetic, mutilated organ still poisoned with all the bad in me.

It begins to mend, for her, for my brothers, for me.

My fingers push into her hair as my mouth slants over hers. I want to slide my tongue past her lips, but I wait for her to open up, refusing to take something else from her. Waiting for her to kiss me back.

Then she does. She opens her mouth and lets me in.

"Christy. Christy. Christy," I mutter, grasping her cheeks as we kiss, and kiss and kiss. Her fingers curl into my hair, her body presses against mine, slick with perspiration, vibrating with an unexplainable need that matches my own.

It's like fucking magic, this energy between us, this *belonging*.

I can't explain it any other way.

"You're my home," I say, needing her to understand the full extent of what's happening to me.

She gasps, her eyes widening, her birthmark darkening. There's a glimmer in her eyes of some deeply hidden emotion that I can't even begin to unravel right now, too distracted by her beauty, her energy, *her*.

"Will you let me come home?"

"Yes," she breathes, her lips and tongue seeking mine.

The kiss evolves, and there's this frenetic energy between us snapping and crackling just like the lightning that continues to carve the night sky with forks and slashes. The palms of my hands tingle as I slide them down her body, my lips following their trail. I stop at every spot I bit her, pressing wet kisses against the teeth marks I made on her breasts, stomach and hip bones, my tongue laving over her skin in an attempt to soothe

the pain I inflicted until I'm on my knees between her legs. Cupping her pussy gently, I look up at her, acutely aware that Jakub is watching this all unfold.

Silent. Unmoving.

"I'm going to kiss the pain away. I'm going to soothe every place that I hurt. Can I?" I ask her, knowing that even though I want her badly, I can and *will* walk away if she refuses me. That I'm strong enough to do that now. That I will *always* be strong enough now because of her.

She flicks her eyes at Jakub and I follow her gaze. He's staring at us both, utterly stunned by the turn of events. Right now, he's trapped within his own tumultuous cyclone of emotions, he's a prisoner to them. Jakub couldn't hurt either of us even if he wanted to.

"*Please*," Christy murmurs, drawing my attention back to her as she stares down at me, her fingers snaking through my hair as her long tresses fall around her face in a tumble of waves. The kindness in her eyes, the compassion, and the willingness to accept this moment takes my breath momentarily. She takes my breath and at the same time feeds me precious oxygen. My heart thump, thump, thumps in my chest as we stare at one another.

I'm captivated, caught, enraptured by her.

"Take the pain away," she whispers, and I know she isn't just talking about hers, but *mine*, Jakub's too.

I nod. "Yes." Then with the utmost care, I press a gentle kiss against her mound, my mouth lingering over the junction where her pussy lips meet. I barely graze her there, acutely aware that right now I need to be gentle, reverent. I need to give, not take. She rocks her hips slightly, her fingers flexing against my skull and I take my cue, already understanding her body, her needs, as I slide my hands up her freckled thighs. She parts her legs, showing me without words that she welcomes this. Me. She's giving me the chance to do this over, and I won't fail her this time.

A streak of blood against her inner thigh reminds me of what I've done and the pain I caused, and without hesitating, I press my tongue against it, licking her clean, tasting her essence.

She gasps, her fingernails scraping my scalp as I trail my lips up, up, up until my mouth is pressed gently against her pussy lips once more. Slowly, I slide the tip of my tongue between her folds and over her clit, pressing it against the nub, tasting her.

She moans, rocking gently against my face.

My cock jerks, weeping precum at that simple gesture of *want*.

Bringing my hands to her pussy, I gently spread her outer lips then lick her again, this time using the flat of my tongue. She shudders, so responsive. Her legs part, giving me better access and I duck down further, tipping my head back, lifting my eyes to meet hers as I taste her, blood and all.

"Oh!" Her eyes widen, her nostrils flare, and a rumble of possession rises up my throat as I lap at every last drop of blood, consuming her pain and replacing it with pleasure. "Leon," she whimpers, her fingers tightening, her hips rocking, her mouth parting as she spreads her juices over my face and I breathe her in, worshipping her with my mouth and tongue.

When she picks up her pace, rocking and gripping and fucking my face in earnest, I keep my licks steady relinquishing all power to her, allowing her to take her pleasure, all the while learning the right spots to lick, to suck, to kiss, to press with my tongue. *Memorising* them.

As Christy nears the pinnacle, her movements become more jerky, her body taking over as she acts on instinct. My cock strains against my abdomen, bobbing with every jerk of her hips as I drink her in, smothering my face with her juices and when she starts to jerk against me, I hold her steady, my fingers gripping her waist as she explodes on my tongue with a cry of pleasure that rips out of the very centre of her chest.

I don't pull away as she slowly comes down.

I let her suffocate me with her pussy, willing to die from asphyxiation just to make sure I wring every last drop of pleasure from her.

"Leon," she whimpers, her body liquefying, her knees buckling.

The old me would've impaled her on his cock way before now. He would've been selfish and fucked her hard, fast and violently. He would've picked up the knife and cut her skin whilst he rammed his dick so deep inside that she would've felt him in her stomach. He wouldn't have cared if he hurt her, he would've been selfish and taken from her.

Instead, I capture her in my arms and let her fold herself over me, her arms around my back, her legs wrapped around my waist as she trembles with the after effects of her orgasm, content for the moment to just hold her.

Between us my cock twitches, blood rushing to the head as it grows painfully bigger pressed up against her abdomen, sandwiched between us. I want so badly to flip her over and take, so fucking badly, but I wait. I wait with a mental fist wrapped around my dick and iron chains securing the monster who still lives within me, who still wants to take, take, take.

But I have control now, and I will never, ever, do anything against her wishes again.

Never.

Christy's sweaty forehead presses against the curve of my neck, her long hair trailing over my shoulder as she shudders against me. For long moments I stroke my fingers up and down her back allowing her to pull the pieces of herself back together again until, achingly slowly, she sits back, her pupils blown wide as she looks at me.

"You okay?" I ask. A stupid question perhaps, but I ask it anyway.

There's a moment where all I see is confusion in her eyes, like she doesn't quite understand what has just passed between us, but it disappears the moment she grasps my face in her hands and kisses me passionately, answering my question with actions and not words. I groan into her mouth, my tongue dancing with hers. When I feel her hand slide between us and her fingers stroking the head of my cock, I almost come on the spot.

"Show him. Show me," she murmurs, grasping the base of my dick and shifting in my lap so that her knees are resting on the floor on either side of my thighs.

"You want my dick?" I mutter, unable to stop the crass words from parting my lips.

"I want your heart," she replies, positioning herself above me, the wetness of her pussy sliding over the head of my cock as she hovers so temptingly, achingly close. "Make love to me, Leon."

I don't need to be asked twice.

With my gaze focused on hers, and with painstaking care, I ease her down over my cock, inch by inch until I'm seated inside of her. She's tight, her internal walls fisting me in a vice-like grip that momentarily stuns me, adles my fucking brain. I have to take several deep breaths to stop myself from coming inside of her prematurely.

"You feel like fucking heaven," I say once I've gathered myself enough to speak.

"You feel like you belong inside of me," she murmurs back,

her voice pitted with wonder and perhaps the tiniest amount of regret. That regret pulls me up sharp, focussing my attention.

"Christy, I can stop. Fuck, I'll stop if I have to," I grind out, willing to show her I'm capable of doing just that no matter how much it would kill me to pull my dick from the warmth of her pussy.

"No," she shakes her head. "Don't stop."

"Then I'll give it to you, slow and steady. I won't hurt you if I can help it."

Christy nods, biting on her bottom lip as I slowly lift her up and down my cock, trembling with the effort to not come. Her hands find my shoulders, her fingers curl into my flesh as she holds on tight and trusts me to take care of her. I want to, so fucking bad.

I will.

She's slick, wet, and after a while she finds a rhythm with me, her breaths coming in tiny pants as she rides my cock, relaxing around my girth, her body accommodating mine.

"You're so tight," I say. Her perfect tits bounce up and down as she throws her head back and fucks me harder, faster. I duck my head, grasping her hips to keep her seated, still for the moment, so I can suck her nipple into my mouth and calm the building orgasm.

She moans, her back arching, pressing her tits into my face, her stomach against my abs, her pubic bone against mine. Held there, she moves her hips in tiny circles conjuring up more sensation in the base of my spine. My balls tingle as I release her from my mouth and palm her tits before grasping her face in mine.

"That's it, Christy, take what you need. Fuck me slow," I say, brushing my lips against hers.

She rides me like that, her forehead pressed against mine,

her lips brushing my lips, her breaths matching my own, my fingers tangled in her fiery hair, our gazes locked on one another. Her eyes blaze with intensity, with fire and passion, as she grinds on me. The slippery, wet sound of her arousal dripping over my balls, making my dick grow impossibly large.

"Leon," she whispers, her lips trembling as her hands slide up my neck and into my hair. She holds on tight and I can feel her internal walls squeezing tighter as her breathing hastens, an orgasm blooming deep inside of her that's mirrored inside of me.

With immense concentration and the possessive need to own her, to stake my motherfucking claim on this woman, I wrap my arm around her lower back and push up onto my knees, laying her down flat on the floor. Her eyes widen, her lips part, her brow creases with a question but I shut it down with a kiss, my hand reaching between us as I press my finger against her clit, holding it there as I seat myself deep inside of her.

"From this moment on you're mine. My brothers can either fight me or fight *for you*. Either way, I refuse to let go of the woman who's held up the motherfucking mirror and made me see."

Christy responds by wrapping her legs around my waist and clawing at my back, pressing up to meet me as I bear down to meet her, that collision setting off her orgasm that rips out of her mouth in a sound that's fucking music to my ears. Her internal walls contract and expand, tightening and loosening and I feel my own orgasm set aflame deep in the base of my spine, rush outwards, upwards. Just when I'm about to blow my cum deep inside of her, I pull out, fist my cock and cover her belly and tits with my release, the thready, white liquid marking her beautiful skin as I bellow out my own orgasm.

I don't give a fuck who hears.

Let the whole castle know I've taken Christy's virginity, that

I'm the first to claim this woman, *our* woman, the girl with ghost eyes who'll set us free.

Panting, my fist squeezes my cock, the veins in my hand and arms pronounced beneath my skin as I look down at Christy covered in my cum and give up the words only my newly formed heart can deliver.

"You own me, Christy. Not my brothers. Not Malik. Not my dark past. Not the ghosts that haunt me. Not the walls of this castle and the memories within them, nor the monster that still lingers inside my chest. You. Own. Me. My heart is yours. You can carve it out of my chest right here and now, and I wouldn't stop you. Just know that it's yours to do what you want with. *It's yours.*"

"You're mine?" she whispers, pushing up onto her elbows, the ends of her hair sticking to my cum, her thighs wet with her arousal, totally oblivious to my cum trickling down her chest and stomach as she sits up. My chest expands, something about seeing her birthmark so deeply flushed, her body so thoroughly fucked and covered in my cum, makes me want to flip her on her stomach and fuck her again. If Jakub didn't take that exact moment to let out a broken moan, I might've done it.

"Fuck!" he exclaims, falling forward onto his hands, his head bowed like a beaten dog, body shaking.

He's hurting, and I know exactly what that feels like because only a few days ago, I felt that way too. I felt the confusion, the desperate need to cling onto the past despite it slipping through my fingers, the absolute horror at realising you've lived a lie, the guilt, the fucking remorse, the desire to set things right but not knowing how to, the self-disgust and, finally, that glimmer of fucking hope, knowing that there's finally someone worth being a better version of yourself for.

I get it.

But that's his battle, not mine.

Right now, Christy is my sole focus.

Reaching for the discarded knife, I hold it out to her. "Cut me," I demand.

"W—what?" she stammers.

"I said, cut me. I want you to carve your name into my chest, right here over my heart." She hesitates and I grasp her wrist, forcing her to press the tip of the blade against my skin. I feel the sharp sting of it and let out a harsh breath as a drop of blood gathers, then slides down my chest. "Cut me. Make me yours."

For a moment Christy just stares at my chest, her eyes wide, shocked. Then she swallows hard, her gaze slowly lifting to meet mine as she nods.

"Make sure it's deep enough. It needs to scar," I tell her when she barely grazes the surface.

With shaking fingers, she presses harder, one hand flat against my pec as she begins to carve her name into my skin. I hiss with the pain and her hand stills.

"Leon—" she exclaims, pulling the tip away from my skin. She's trembling, her teeth chattering.

"Don't stop."

Her eyes glisten with emotion as she shakes her head. "I'm hurting you."

"You're not. I *need* you to do this... *Please*," I beg, placing my hand over hers.

Swallowing hard, she blows out a tremulous breath then presses the blade against my skin once more, slicing me open with a quiet kind of determination. She does it not because she wants to, but because *I* want her too. Once she's finished, I run my hand over the cuts, smothering my palm and fingers with my blood then press it against her chest, mixing my cum with my blood as I hold my hand over the thumping beat of her heart.

"Why did you want me to do that?" she whispers.

"Because I want everyone to know the name of the woman who's claimed my heart."

"No," Jakub cries, his voice hoarse, fucking broken. He lifts his head, his troubled eyes meeting mine.

"Yes, brother. It ends now."

Jakub gets to his feet, stumbling backwards. He falls against the bureau, righting himself before ripping open the door and running from the room.

"Leon, shouldn't you..."

"Go after him?" I finish for her.

"Yes," her skin has paled, her cheeks suddenly losing their colour.

"No. Jakub has to face his demons on his own. It's the only way."

She nods her head, then curls against my body, and this time I don't abandon her for a Brov, I hold her for my brothers, until they're ready to hold her themselves.

CHAPTER SEVENTEEN

Christy

"WE SHOULD TAKE A WALK OUTSIDE," Leon says a couple of mornings later whilst we're eating breakfast.

My hand stills, a heaped forkful of egg balancing precariously on the tines as I look over at him. "A walk?"

"You've not seen much of the grounds, or even the castle. I thought perhaps..." His voice trails off as he realises *why* that is. I'm still a prisoner despite how he feels towards me.

"Are you sure you want to risk it?" I ask with a heavy dose of sarcasm, lowering my fork and abandoning the fluffy eggs. "I might make a dash for it."

His gaze darkens. "If you run, I'll only chase you."

"Even now that you've got me out of your system and we've fu—"

"Made *love*," he interrupts, bristling, clearly offended by the off-handed way I described what happened between us. It was more than that, I know it as much as he does, but playing it down helps me not analyse my feelings too much. I don't want to go there. He grits his jaw, searching my gaze. "Do you honestly think now that we've slept together that I'm going to just let you go? If I wasn't going to before, then I sure as fuck won't now."

"Isn't that what you did after *breaking in* the other Numbers?" I counter evenly. "You fucked them, broke them, then cast them aside for others to do the same."

"You're no longer a Number, Christy, and you know it," he says, swiping a hand through his thick, black hair. It's still wet from the bath he took earlier, and a droplet slides down the side of his face, dripping from his jaw. I watch it splash onto his white t-shirt that's spotted with blood from where the newly formed scab has been aggravated by the material.

"Do I?" I cross my arms across my chest, picking a fight for no good reason other than I have to put him back inside the box labelled *the man I must kill* rather than the alternative which I can't even voice out loud, let alone think about. I've spent a lot of time going over everything that happened between us earlier in the week, and each time I've tried to convince myself it was nothing more than a means to an end, part of my plan.

Only it *wasn't*.

It was so much more than that.

"You have to understand something. I've only ever fucked women. I've *never* made love," he says earnestly. "That night with you I tasted heaven and I finally understood what those words meant. I felt..." He shakes his head in wonder.

"Wait!" I snap, pushing my chair back and standing. "Don't! Just don't say anymore."

Leon gets to his feet, circling the table as he stalks me. I back away from him, shaking my head, but still he comes for me, pinning me against the wall. My hands fly up to his chest and he winces from the sting as my palms rest against the cuts I made in his skin. "Why not?"

"It's too... I don't..." I stutter, unable to articulate how I'm feeling because, honestly, all I am is confused, and I should be completely clear headed and certain of my intentions towards him. He watches me struggle to respond, until eventually I blurt out the only thing I can say in the moment. "A walk outside in the fresh air would be welcome."

For a beat we just stare at each other and I expect him to push the point, instead he nods, shoving off from the wall and giving me much needed space. "Okay."

"Okay?"

"Let's go for that walk."

"And your brothers? Should I be worrying about them?" I ask, forcing myself to relax and reminding him and myself that just because he's changed his tune, doesn't mean either of them have.

"Five is keeping an eye on Konrad for me. He's hiding away in the dungeons right now."

"Hiding? From whom?"

Leon tips his head to the side. "From you, of course."

I give him a sceptical look. "And Jakub?"

"Occupied right now."

A flash of worry crosses his features but he hides it by grabbing his teal mask that's resting beside his plate and putting it on.

"You're not concerned he'll try and finish what he started?"

Leon checks his gun before reholstering it. "No. I know Jakub, he'll be trying to find a way to hurt himself some more so he doesn't have to face his feelings."

"You're not concerned about that?"

"We all have our way of dealing with things. Jakub's is to inflict pain on himself. I don't have to like it to accept that's what he needs." He meets my gaze. "We don't have to worry about him, at least not today."

"You're not filling me with much confidence."

Leon reaches for me, pressing his fingers onto my forearm as he steps into my personal space once again. He can't seem to help himself. "I will do everything in my power to protect you. Anything. Do you understand me, Christy? *Anything*," he says fiercely.

I chew on my lip, frowning as I drop my gaze and stare at his fingers squeezing my arm. My cheeks flood with heat at his nearness, and my body sways towards him, betraying me. I know he would, what happened between us the other night proved that.

"I want to believe you," I say, swallowing hard and forcing myself to take a step away from him. It isn't a lie, or even a half-truth. I do want to believe he's a changed man, but equally part of me hopes that he isn't so that when it comes to the point when I poison him, I can do so without a shred of guilt. "I want to believe that I'm safe with you now..."

My voice trails off as I try to make sense of the tumultuous feelings wreaking havoc within me. A few days ago my need for vengeance had been my driving force. It's what got me through to that point. This morning, however, things are a little less clear, and a hell of a lot murkier. Common sense tells me that just because we fucked, just because Leon fought against his true nature and won in that moment, doesn't mean he's a reformed character, and it certainly doesn't mean I should forgive and forget. Getting outside to clear my head should do me some good. I need fresh air and space.

I need to *think*.

Stepping out from his hold, I grab the long woollen cardigan Thirteen left for me to wear and pull it on over the jumper and leggings I borrowed from her. It's the most clothing I've worn since arriving here and whilst I know it doesn't give me any real protection, wearing clothes makes me feel better about myself and my situation. It gives me a modicum of power back, however tenuous that might be.

"You're safe with me. I won't hurt you ever again."

"You're hurting me just by keeping me here," I say softly, reminding him that I'm still a prisoner no matter how he pretends otherwise.

"You have to understand that I can't let you go. Despite how I feel towards you, I meant what I said before, I won't let you leave. You're *mine*, Christy."

My cheeks heat at the possessiveness in his voice and the intense way he looks at me, but despite that his words still anger me and I can't help but bite back. "Only if I allow myself to be, Leon. You might've made love to me, but I just *fucked* you," I say, twisting on my feet and striding towards the door, pulling it open, only for his palm to hit the wood and slam it shut.

"Don't do that," he growls, his length pressed against mine as he pushes me against the door.

"Do what?" I ask, forcing my voice to hold steady so it doesn't give away the frantic beat of my heart. My cheek rests against the smooth wood as he runs his lips against my birthmark gently. It takes every ounce of control not to shudder from his touch.

"Lie to yourself," he breathes against my skin. "I may have control of my monster, but that doesn't mean to say I'm not willing to put you over my knee and show you what I do to pretty little liars..."

"You said you'd never hurt me again," I whisper, forcing my body to stiffen and not melt into his touch.

"And I won't. You'll only ever feel pleasure from these hands, from my lips, my cock, but that doesn't mean to say that a spanking is off the menu, now does it?" Leon asks with a soft chuckle as he steps back taking both his heat and his promise with him. "Now, should we take that walk?"

WE CIRCLE the castle on our walk, passing through well-tended gardens that teem with plants, trees and shrubs. Even though it's nearing winter there's still plenty of foliage, flowers and berries brightening the gardens. I've no idea what any of the plants are called, but I appreciate their beauty and the crisp frost that clings to their leaves and branches.

"Do you have gardeners?" I ask, contemplating for the first time how a place like this is run. Aside from the male servant Jakub and I bumped into in the hallway leading to the Room of Curiosities, and the odd glimpse of maids going about their business, I've rarely seen anyone.

"Yes, we do. I don't have much to do with the staff. Jakub tends to oversee all of that, and until recently Renard managed all the staff on his behalf," Leon explains.

"Who will be taking over that role now?"

Leon shrugs, pulling out a flip knife and cutting a pretty pink and white flower from a nearby bush. His fingers brush over the velvety petals, before he lifts it to his nose and draws in a deep breath. "That's something we need to discuss soon, but right now the staff are managing just fine."

"How many staff do you have exactly?" I ask, watching as Leon carefully cuts off every thorn on the stem before handing it to me and pocketing his knife. I take it wordlessly, running the soft petals under my nose and inhaling the scent.

"At a guess, around fifty. Though it could be more..." His voice trails off and I feel the heat of his gaze warming my skin. "That's a Christmas rose, otherwise known as a hellebore. Pretty, isn't it?"

"I didn't take you for a botanist," I say, running my finger over the soft petals, side-eying him as we stroll along.

He chuckles and his face transforms with a wry grin. Swallowing hard, I look away. "I'm not, I just pay attention when, on the odd occasion, Thirteen talks about the plants she uses in her work."

"I see," I reply, following Leon through an archway cut through a very prickly looking bush. On the other side is a huge allotment with rows and rows of soil, turned and covered for winter, and some winter herbs growing in raised beds. At the back of the allotment is a small wooden shed. The door is open and inside I can see the faint outline of someone moving about.

"This is where Thirteen grows all her plants, herbs and flowers that she uses in her potions and lotions. She's been out here all morning harvesting what's left of her crop, she said she wanted to work on some more elixirs."

"She's truly gifted, isn't she?" I say.

"Yes. She's a rare find, one I'm glad my father never had the chance to exploit."

"You were good friends growing up?"

"Like Renard explained, Malik and Niall were acquaintances. Over the years we spent time with Thirteen. We were friends as much as we could be given the trauma we'd all endured..." His voice trails off as he stares off into the distance.

"What was she like as a child?"

"Much like she is now. Sweet. Cautious. Thoughtful. Kind. Strong."

"Do you care about her?"

"That's a difficult question to answer," he says, frowning.

"How so?"

"Well, up until recently I didn't care about anyone or anything other than my brothers, and even then those feelings were complicated," he acknowledges. "I know I love my brothers. I've always known that, but I was never able to express that love in the right way, in a healthy way."

"Do you want to be able to do that now?"

"I want to do many things, but I'm not sure how," he answers honestly. "My default setting is violence and distrust, but I don't want it to be."

We fall into silence for a moment as we both contemplate that. Deciding that I have no advice to offer him, I change the subject. "Who is Thirteen running from?" I ask.

"What makes you think she's running from anyone?"

"Just something my mother said in the letter she wrote to me."

"Your mother wrote you a letter, too?" Leon stills, turning to face me.

"Yes. Thirteen gave it to me that day I came looking for you..." I wince at the memory, and what I did, the violence *I* acted upon in a moment of blind rage.

Leon's eyes widen with surprise. "She never said."

"And if she had, what would you have done?" I ask, knowing full well that they would've punished her in some way and tortured me for answers.

"That's a fair point," he acknowledges. "What did the letter say?"

"Many things, but most of all my mother told me not to

ignore fate, that I was destined to cross paths with you all and that I shouldn't run from it, that if I did it would only cause more pain," I pause, plucking at the rose petals, watching them float to the floor one by one. "She said she'd seen parts of my future, that you were bad men, cruel and wicked."

"She wasn't wrong," Leon admits.

"But she also said that wasn't all you were, that I'd been put into your paths for a reason and I should embrace that."

"She told you to embrace *us*?"

"Yes. She believed that running away from my fate would be detrimental. She asked me not to make the same mistakes that she did."

"What do you mean?"

"She never told me everything, but she said that she ran from her own fate and fell in love with someone she shouldn't have."

"Your father?"

"Yes, she believed she was punished because of it, and that denying her true destiny was what led to her eventual death."

"I don't understand."

"She knew she was going to die that night when you set the fire. She saw it in her future, and rather than run from fate again, she took the punishment instead."

"Fuck," he exclaims, shaking his head.

"The letter she wrote to me was penned when I was four years old," I continue, unable to stop now that I've started. "I remember her writing it. I stood in the doorway of her bedroom and watched her writing the letter that wouldn't find it's way to me until years later. She'd known then that she only had four years left with me."

"I'm sorry," he says, gripping my wrist and pulling me around to face him. Tears form in my eyes at the memory of my mother and the loss I feel so acutely. "I'm sorry for your pain, for what I did. *I'm sorry.*"

"I believe you," I whisper, blinking back the tears and forcing myself to be strong. "She also said in her letter that Thirteen has run from her fate too, that it will catch up with her, and when it does I should be a friend to her."

"Do you know what your mother meant by that?" he asks me.

"I don't. I thought you might."

He shakes his head, his gaze flicking towards the shed as Thirteen walks out of it carrying a wicker basket filled with herbs and flowers. She lifts her hand and gives a small wave, oblivious to our conversation. Her expression is one of surprise, perhaps even a little relief as she looks at our conjoined hands. I hadn't even realised that Leon had entwined his fingers with mine until this very moment. I move to pull away, but he just grabs my hand tighter.

"When Thirteen arrived here a year ago she said that she'd had a disagreement with her father and that she needed somewhere to stay. We had no reason to disbelieve her."

"But the letters?" I ask. "It's not coincidental."

"No, it's not. She may have argued with Niall about something, but she also came here because of those letters. There's a lot that Thirteen isn't telling us."

"You don't trust her?" I ask.

"When she first gave us the letter from your mother, I was very distrustful of her motives. We all were."

"And you're not now?"

"I'm not. Thirteen has proven herself a loyal friend over and over again. Whatever she's hiding, it's probably for a good reason," Leon says, schooling his features and shutting the conversation down as Thirteen approaches.

"I'm glad you took my advice and got some fresh air," she says, shifting the basket of herbs in her arms. "Is everything okay?" she asks, her soft grey eyes focussing on me.

Is it?

Right now I'm holding hands with the man who killed me. Two nights ago he took my virginity harshly with his fingers then made love to me with a gentle kind of reverence. He'd kissed me, lavished me with affection and care, made me come, then asked me to carve my name into his chest, offering up his heart in the process. There's no denying that I'd felt a connection between us, and yet I'm still filled with distrust and anger towards him despite all of that. So the answer to Thirteen's question isn't a simple yes or no. Nothing is straightforward when it comes to these men. Nothing.

"We're working on making it okay," Leon answers when I'm unable to.

He squeezes my hand in his and I don't try to correct him because it doesn't matter anyway. Fate has plans for us all and none of us can do a damn thing to change it. I've learnt as much from my mother.

CHAPTER EIGHTEEN

Konrad

"AH, FUCK THIS," I groan, pushing myself up onto drunken legs. The room spins and I reach out to the closest thing to me which happens to be the putrefied head of the Baron. My fingers slide into his rotting flesh and I gag. "Fuck!"

Yanking my hand back, I swipe my palm over my filthy trousers. I'm still wearing the same clothes I was the day of the funeral, and in my drunken state I know that was at least four days ago. Maybe more. I should go back to my suite, shower, eat a proper meal rather than the sandwiches Five has been bringing me, and drink some fucking water, but that would mean going back up into the land of the living and facing my brothers, Nala, *her*.

Nope. I'll stay right where I am. Fuck you very much.

Swiping up the almost empty bottle of whisky from the table, I glug back the last swig, revelling in the burn. "Cheers,"

I slur, smacking my lips and wiping the back of my hand across my mouth before raising the empty bottle to the Baron's head.

If I didn't know any better, I could swear he smiles back. *Fuck.*

The room spins, but the distant sound of someone knocking on the metal door forces me to move as I stumble towards it. The knock gets louder, and I reach up to my face, checking to see that I've got my Mask on. I do.

Well that's something at least.

"Who the fuck is it?" I call out, rocking on my feet as the room tilts sideways. I try to focus on the metal door on the other side of the cell, but it's like I'm on a fucking boat and I can't seem to steady myself enough to get to it. Not that it matters because the door creaks open, and I find myself blinking at the silhouette of a woman standing before me.

"Zero?" I mumble, trying and failing to stop the room from spinning.

"No, Master. It's *me*, Twelve."

"Twelve? What are *you* doing here?" I ask, forcing myself to straighten my spine and take steady steps towards her. I fail fucking miserably, and would've ended up on my arse if she hadn't reached for me.

"Hey," she says, her arm around my waist, her shoulder beneath my armpit as she takes my weight. "You're drunk."

"Fucking blasted," I reply, not disagreeing with her. I wish I would just pass the fuck out already. I don't want to be left with my thoughts one moment longer. I've been too in my head. Too caught up in the events of the past few weeks. Too wrapped up in her.

Zero.

"This is all because of her, isn't it?" Twelve snaps, her

fingers digging into my side as I wobble on my feet. Looks like I've let the cat out of the bag. *Oops.*

"Yeah, her," I reply, not giving a shit about how that sounds or makes me look. I'm past the point of caring. "Just leave me to my fucking drink, alright?"

"No," she mutters, huffing as she struggles to hold my considerable weight. She's stronger than she looks, and right now through my drunken haze she looks almost enticing.

"You know I'm so out of it, even you look tempting in this light."

She stiffens at my backhanded compliment, but instead of leaving me to wallow in my own shit, she stays. I'm not surprised, she's so needy for any kind of attention from me that she'll take all the bad shit I say if it means spending even a few minutes in my company.

"You like my outfit?" she asks, holding me steady so that my drunk-arse gaze can take it's fill of her tight little body covered in nothing but a sheer, pale pink dress. She's hot, there's no denying that, and she sings like a fucking angel, but when I look into her eyes there's only me staring back. I don't see her. I don't feel anything. Twelve doesn't churn me up inside, she doesn't make me question every fucking thing I've ever known. She doesn't make me want to fuck her until I go blind. Doesn't she fucking get that I don't want *her.*

"I don't much care about your outfit..." I slur, the room choosing that moment to tip sideways. I stumble, taking her with me, expecting to end up in a heap on the floor but find myself slumped in a chair instead.

"You know if you need to let off steam, I can always help..." she says, ignoring my obvious distaste whilst she moves my limbs and settles me back onto the only chair I have in this room: my bondage chair.

It's been a long time since I've used it, and even longer since I've sat in it myself. I had hoped that by now Zero would be strapped to it screaming in pain and pleasure as I coaxed out her orgasm, her ghost eyes begging me to fuck the virginity out of her. I groan, feeling my booze addled dick sparking to life at the thought.

"Fuck me," I mutter, because who knew I could still get hard after three bottles of whisky and spending days with a rotting, severed head only six feet away from me.

It's a fucking miracle. No, Zero's the fucking miracle.

Thoughts of our fiery mistress flow into my mind like a hurricane ripping through a forest. Every memory I have of her makes my cock grow harder until I'm rock fucking solid.

I remember the way her silky hair felt between my finger and thumb as I cut a length from it that first day she arrived here.

I remember how she parted her lips on a moan as I felt between her legs on the table in the Grand Hall the night we introduced her to the Numbers.

I remember the scent of her fear whilst Leon cut her, and the groan of her pleasure when I sucked her pretty nipples into my mouth three cells over.

I remember her scarred and ruined back that I thought I'd be disgusted by, but instead only long to kiss, lick and *soothe*.

I remember her pretty birthmark that I would do anything to make darken with bliss.

I remember her smart mouth and wonder how it would feel to shove my dick into it and have her suck me off like she did Jakub.

I remember the way she danced in the library, and the way she moved across the stage during the show.

Every bit of her, every little nuance, calls to me. It fucking *calls* to me.

All I see, hear and smell is her. *Zero.*

My woman. *Our* woman.

Jakub can pretend all he likes, but she *is* ours. She's already brought Leon to his knees, and Jakub is so messed-up over her, he's losing his head day by day. I've never seen him so unhinged. The man has barely eaten in weeks. He hardly sleeps, and his body is covered head to toe in wounds both self-inflicted and given. I bet One fucking *loved* that. She's been waiting for the moment to sink her claws in. I just hope to fuck he knows what he's doing.

Wait, what the fuck am I saying? He hasn't got a clue what he's doing, that's the whole point.

And now look at me, drunk as a vagrant trying to numb the feelings Zero evokes in me and failing miserably. *Me*, a man who can only feel something, *anything* when he's either feeding off the pain of someone else or fixing the wounds he made so he can do it all over again.

I'm feeling all this shit and I don't know what the fuck to do with it. I don't know what to do other than drown myself in a whisky bottle or five, or throw knives at the head of the cunt who touched what belongs to *us*.

"Jesus, fuck," I mutter, feeling a sharp stab in my thigh that pulls me out of my thoughts momentarily. I peel my eyes open to find Twelve giving me an odd look, but before I can question what the fuck's up with her or why a warm feeling spreads out from my thigh, my eyes drift shut and my thoughts splinter once again until I'm back in Thirteen's room with Zero that day I'd stitched the wounds Leon carved into her ruined back. She'd been so still, barely making a sound as I sewed her back together, and with every stitch, I'd grown impossibly hard. God knows I had wanted to impale her with my cock. Instead, I'd gripped my dick and wanked off, coming all over her pretty tits.

Maybe it was that day when it happened.

Maybe that was the moment my damaged, fucked-up heart knew she was really, truly mine. Or perhaps it was when I stepped into the Room of Fantasies and saw the Baron abusing her.

No. I *know* when it happened.

It was the moment she died.

I fucking *felt* it.

I laugh, the room spinning like one of those rides at a carnival I was never allowed to go on as a kid because that would've given me a moment of fucking joy, and joy wasn't something our father ever let us experience unless it was from hurting someone.

Randomly, more laughter bubbles up my chest.

It's freeing.

Cathartic in a way I've never experienced before.

It's *honest*.

I laugh, and laugh, and laugh as the truth of what this means unravels in my chest.

I've been trying to block it out for days now.

But I can't do that anymore.

I don't fucking want to.

Leon was *right* to protect her. Jakub is *wrong* to want her dead.

My laughter fades and with it a strange kind of calm settles over me, a peacefulness. I know what to do now.

"That's it, just relax," Twelve croons, and I force my eyes open, focussing on Twelve despite wanting to return to my memories of Zero and sober up there.

"What are you doing?" I frown, as Twelve rests her small

hands on my thighs. I hadn't even noticed that she's kneeling between my parted legs until now. I'm so fucking out of it.

"Shh, just let me take care of you," she whispers, licking her scarlet lips, her fingers brushing over my dick. I'm surprised that it jerks against her touch rather than shrivel up from the contact.

"No! That isn't for you," I hiss, moving my hand to shove her off me only to find that I can't. My wrists, ankles, chest and thighs are restrained by leather straps. "You've strapped me to this motherfucking chair! Untie me! Right the fuck now!"

She bites her scarlet lip, her white teeth sinking into the soft flesh. "I just wanted to help you to relax," she says, pressing the heel of her palm against my dick. It shouldn't be pleasant because I do not want her like that, but fuck, my cock has other ideas.

"We've been dancing around each other for over two years now, Konrad," she whispers, her scent wrapping around me like weeds around flowers. It's choking, suffocating.

"It's all in your head," I protest.

"No," she replies firmly, giving my cock a quick squeeze through my trousers before she stands and removes her dress. Naked before me, she runs her fingers between her chest, over her stomach and slides them between her bare pussy lips.

"What the fuck are you doing?"

"What does it look like, Konrad?"

"That's *Master* to you," I bite back.

She just smiles and fingers herself. Anger burns my blood and fucking nausea churns my stomach, but my cock? It punches against my zipper as she pulls her glistening fingers from her cunt and places them into her mouth. I snatch my head away, refusing to look at the delight in her eyes as she focuses on my bastard dick.

"You want me," she says, gripping my jaw and forcing me to look at her as she reaches for my zipper, unzips it and pulls my cock free, grasping it at the base. "You don't have to deny yourself anymore. The Collector's gone. Leon has Zero locked up in his room and Jakub's screwing around with One. We can be together. It's okay now. You're free to choose me."

"GET YOUR MOTHERFUCKING HANDS OFF ME! I DON'T WANT YOU!" I seethe, struggling against the restraints tying me down. Only I know that once you're strapped into this chair there's no getting out until someone sets you free.

"Your cock begs to differ," she replies, her tongue edging between her lips as she wets them.

"Let me go, right the fuck now and I won't slit your throat for disobeying our rules. *Do not covet what isn't yours!*" I remind her.

"But you *are* mine. Look," she says, canting her head downwards.

I follow her gaze and stare at my engorged dick, thick veins running beneath the skin. It weeps precum as she slides her fist up and down it's length, her small hands barely able to fit around its girth.

"You fucking drugged me!" I exclaim, understanding what that sharp pain was a moment ago.

"Shh, it's okay," she murmurs, stroking me.

"Did Thirteen help you? Is this her way of getting back at us?" I ask, mostly to myself.

"No, Thirteen is distracted with Nala. I snuck into her room, helped myself to what I needed."

"You bitch."

"Don't you see, Konrad, the Quickening and my touch will

make all the pain go away. Just relax, let me heal you. I'll make it good, I promise."

"Heal me?! *You* can't heal me. I DON'T WANT YOUR TOUCH!"

She squeezes me hard, her fingers choking my dick as her top lip curls upwards. Madness glints in her eyes as a slow smile spreads across her face. "That's exactly what I thought when you first touched my pussy, now look at it, all dripping wet for *you*."

Her reply makes me gag, bile burning my throat as I swallow it down. Yet still my cock remains as hard as stone. I don't like this. I don't like this feeling of having no control over my own motherfucking desire. "UNTIE ME NOW!"

"Hush," she croons, jerking me off, her thumb sliding over the slit of my cock. "Don't make this harder for yourself because I intend on fucking you over, and over, and over again until there's no cum left in your body. I'm claiming it all. It's *mine*. You are mine."

"No."

"Yes," she insists, before reaching up and removing my mask.

I don't know why, but I press my eyes shut, like that's somehow going to stop her from being able to see my true face. I can't be bare before her. I can't be anything other than one of The Masks in a situation such as this. It's the only motherfucking thing giving me strength.

"You're more beautiful than I thought," she exclaims. "Open your eyes for me, let me look at you."

"Fuck you," I reply.

She laughs. "Oh Konrad, I intend to," she says before dropping to her knees and taking my dick in her mouth. I try to jerk her free, but with my chest and thighs strapped down, I can't.

She slurps and sucks on my cock, making these god awful noises that make me want to rip her head from her shoulders and nail her to the wall alongside the Baron.

Except I can't fucking do that.

So I let out a bloodcurdling roar instead.

I roar until my fucking lungs are gasping for breath and my throat is hoarse.

It makes no difference.

In fact it only seems to turn her on more as she bobs up and down my cock, sucking me hard and fast. When I finally quieten, when I stop struggling, she lets my dick fall from her lips with a pop, and looks me dead in the eye.

"Your efforts are a waste of energy, *Master*, no one will hear your screams."

Then she places her hands on the back of the chair, straddles my thighs and sinks down onto my cock. Despite the drug's attempt at doing its damndest to keep me in the present, I detach myself from the horror of this moment.

Maybe it's the booze that's dampened its effect, maybe it's the thought of Zero's judgement. Maybe it's the guilt that I've hurt Zero in the same way Twelve hurts me now by taking something that wasn't given. Either way it doesn't matter, because I retreat to the furthest corners of my mind and disappear.

Twelve rapes me, and I check the fuck out.

Just like I used to do as a kid.

CHAPTER NINETEEN

Jakub

I RUN BLINDLY, arms outstretched in front of me as I stumble over a fallen log. A sharp pain registers as a branch, snapped off by my fall, slices through my bicep. Blood slides from the gash but I don't stop moving. Pushing upwards, I swipe at the mud caking my face, rubbing at my eyes and blinking away the tears that fall. But it's no use. I can't fucking stop them.

Being with One hasn't helped, flogging myself hasn't helped. Watching Seven fuck Three against her wishes hasn't helped. Forcing Leon to act on his violence, and failing, hasn't fucking helped.

Watching him hold her, kiss her, make *love* to her has fucked me up more than I thought possible. My brother, who has stripped men of their skin and muscle with a cold detachment, had made love to Nothing with such tenderness that it had brought me to my goddamn knees.

Together they'd opened the floodgates and now I feel *everything*.

Guilt. Remorse. Lust. Hate. Pain. Fear. Empathy. Regret.

And I can't turn it off.

Like a dam that's burst its banks, all these feelings pour into me as my tears pour out. Every single salty drop makes me feel... I can't fucking deal with it.

You're weak! My father's voice snarls, taunting me from beyond the grave as I push on deeper into the forest. *You're a weak, feeble excuse for a man. I'm ashamed to call you my son.*

"SHUT UP!" I shout, my jumper snagging on another branch and yanking me backwards. I whirl around, lashing out at the ghost of my father, my fists slamming into the trunk of the nearest tree. My bones crack from the force, but I keep throwing punches, my skin splitting, my bones cracking, my knuckles swelling. With every punch I let out a bellow that sounds more like an animal caught in a trap than a man.

I should've drowned you as a baby when I had the chance... His voice taunts, an echo from the past, another reminder of all the things he used to say to me constantly growing up. Even after death his presence hasn't left me. He's all around me. He's in this forest, in the castle. He's in every scar that litters my skin. He's in my motherfucking head. I have no respite. He's a constant reminder of everything I'm supposed to be, was born to be. He's the Black Plague, a mutilator of hearts, a ruiner of souls.

Unlike her. Unlike Nothing who is everything he is not.

She's the speck of light in all this darkness. She's the warmth in the cold absence of feelings. She's our fucking salvation. I know it. Leon sure as fuck knows it, and Konrad? He's fighting against it as much as I am. But he'll lose. We all will.

Look at you, brought to your knees by a woman. You're pathetic!

"ENOUGH!" I cover my ears with my hands, spinning around on the spot as I search for his ghost in the darkening forest. If he were here now in the flesh I don't know whether I would beg for his special kind of punishment or wrap my arms around his throat and squeeze the life from him. I both hate him and have a twisted kind of respect for him. He's kept me free of feelings. He's beaten them from me. He's kept me cold, hard, unyielding.

Without him, there is nothing to stop those feelings from creeping back in. There's nothing stopping my mangled heart from slowly coming back to life.

She's got to you. She's stuck her claws into Leon and you did nothing to stop it. You're allowing her to ruin you, ruin what I built. You're a fucking disappointment!

"I tried! I fucking tried!" I roar into the forest, sending a flock of crows up into the air above me as I spin on my feet, with the forest spinning alongside me in a rush of greens, browns and blacks before I stumble, crashing into a bush.

I lie there, panting, my skin torn from the lashes One gave me, from the wounds I've spent the last few days inflicting on myself right here in the forest. My clothes are ripped, torn, and covered in mud and dried blood, but still I can't rid myself of these feelings I have for her. No matter how hard I try to bleed them from me, I can't. They've embedded themselves into the very marrow of my bones, and attached themselves to the cells within my blood. There's no respite. I can't numb myself to them anymore.

All I do is *feel* and it's killing me.

She's killing me.

No, she's bringing you back to life, another voice says. It's the same voice who forcefully shoves my father's hateful words away, the same voice who has tried to get me to change my mind about Nothing. *Feeling is pain, it's freedom. Embrace it.*

"It hurts," I argue, my voice hoarse, my body sore, my heart aching, my soul fucking tormented. "It hurts so fucking much."

Get up. Go to her. Go to her now. She will ease your suffering, just like she did for Leon. Just like she'll do for Konrad.

"No!" I shake my head, forcing my battered and abused body to move. I pull myself upright, grabbing the nearest branch as I get to my feet. "I can't."

My gaze focuses on a familiar tree in the distance, the bark of its trunk rough and a deep brown. It's circumference is huge, its roots growing up and out of the ground. At the base of the trunk is a mossy mound, scattered with leaves. Focussing on the great oak tree, I stumble towards it, falling to my knees when I reach the spot where I found Nala all those years ago.

Nala.

My sister.

I have a sister. A girl unmarked by the Brov legacy.

She's good and kind. Sweet and trusting.

She's brave, pure, untarnished by our father's darkness.

She's everything I am not.

She's everything you could be.

"No!" I shake my head, pushing upwards.

Twisting on my feet I run towards the only place I know will force me back into the darkness for good. It's a last resort, and my only fucking hope, but If I'm to continue my father's legacy then I have no choice but to go to the cabin and relive every moment of my time there.

I need to drown myself in pure, undiluted evil.

And I have to do it now.

CHAPTER TWENTY

Christy

"HOW LONG HAS he been like this?" Leon asks as we follow Five through the castle.

"It's hard to say," she replies, glancing over her shoulder at him. "I checked in on Konrad yesterday at about midday, brought him food and water. Then when I went back this afternoon, I found him like..." Her voice trails off as she flicks her gaze to Thirteen who's accompanying us. "It's like he isn't there anymore."

"What do you mean?" I ask as we descend the stairs into the dungeon. My skin scatters with goosebumps at the memory of this place. I've only been here twice, the first time when I arrived and was locked in a dark cell for hours and hours, and the second time when Leon and Konrad had me strapped to a wooden cross and took more than just an orgasm from me.

"Like he's just—"

"Switched off?" Leon finishes, a worried look on his face.

"Yes, exactly," Five agrees. "I couldn't wake him up. He's... *vacant.*"

"Fuck!" Leon's fingers tighten around mine, reminding me that he'd grabbed my hand the moment Five had come to tell us the news, and hasn't let it go since. The warmth of his palm seeping into mine and the way he hangs onto me as though I'm his anchor, combined with the fact that he's kept a respectful distance since he took my virginity, is just... *confusing.*

It's been days since I woke up from my coma, and longer since that night he killed me, and even though my anger and need for revenge is still as strong as it was, there's this slow creep of sympathy, pity, *empathy* towards him that's messing with my head. It's like the constant drip of rainwater onto limestone, no matter how hard the stone, over time it gets worn away. I don't want my anger to be worn away.

I *need* it.

But then I just remind myself of what I saw in my vision and I know that whatever fleeting feelings these are, they're not powerful enough to stop me seeking revenge. It's inevitable.

"What happened to him?" I ask, forcing those thoughts away.

"Trauma is usually the culprit of such a psychological reaction," Thirteen replies as we head towards the cell.

"Psychological reaction to what?" Leon asks.

He looks lost, confused, and honestly I'm right there with him. Konrad has always seemed so impenetrable, unbothered by anything. Christ knows these men have committed terrible acts, so what could possibly have caused such a reaction in him? Or is this just another game, another act just to fuck with me further?

"To his past, to Renard's death..." Thirteen replies, her voice trailing off as she looks at me. "To *your* death and subsequent resurrection."

"Mine?" I ask as we stop in front of an iron door that's been left slightly ajar. The smell coming from the room is horrific and I try not to gag. Why does it smell like death? Then I remember what Three told me and bile burns my throat. Konrad's been down here throwing knives into the Baron's severed head.

Oh, God.

Five focusses her golden eyes on me. "Yes, but there's more to this than that."

"What haven't you told us Five?" Leon asks, tensing.

"When I found Konrad he was tied to the chair, his mask was discarded."

"You looked at his face?" Leon snaps.

Five nods. "I had no choice. It's okay, I put the Mask back on him."

Leon nods sharply. We all know what that means for Five. "And?"

She blows out a sharp breath. "And his cock was out."

"The fuck?" Leon's skin pales.

"Without going into too much detail it looked... *well used,*" Five explains, her gaze flicking to me then back to Leon. He drops my hand and moves to push past Five who's blocking the door.

"Wait, there's more. He wasn't the only one I found in the cell."

"*Who?*" Leon demands.

"Twelve."

"Twelve?"

Five frowns. "She's dead, Leon."

"He wouldn't fuck her!" he grinds out, fury coating his words.

"No, you misunderstand me," Five says, eyes widening.

"What do you mean?" I ask, my gaze pinballing between the pair, confused by the mixed signals I'm getting. Konrad *wants* to fuck, to hurt and heal, then do it all over again. He said as much to me that day he sewed me up. That's his kink, so why is Five implying that *he's* the victim here. This was obviously some sex game gone wrong.

"I don't believe Konrad is at fault here," Five goes on to say.

"Of course he wasn't!" Leon retorts angrily, shocking me further. "Do you think he would've retreated to the furthest parts of his mind if he *wanted* to fuck Twelve?"

Thirteen gasps but I just feel numb, uncertain how to react. Is he suggesting she raped him? My head spins and I wobble on my feet. Thirteen reaches for me, placing her arm around my shoulder as we silently follow Five and Leon into the room.

The first thing I notice is Twelve hanging from a rope tied through a hook that's embedded into the stone ceiling. She's naked, her eyes bloodshot, her tongue hanging out of her mouth, her face swollen and dark purple. There's dried semen between her legs and even a little blood. I gag, my gaze flicking away from her face only to land on the severed head of the Baron. His skin is mottled, tinged green and brown, and filled with holes. A knife is embedded in his forehead, and one is wedged into the weeping socket of his eye.

"No. Oh Jesus," I whimper, the stale scent of sex and rotting flesh permeating the air, poisoning it. Too traumatised to move, I simply stand and stare at the carnage before me.

"Five, cut her down!" Leon demands making me jump.

He reaches for me, twisting me in his arms and ducking his head so he can look me in the eyes. "Konrad didn't do this. I *know* him," he says fiercely before crushing me against his chest in a hug that squeezes the air from my lungs.

It's true, he does, and that means he also knows that Konrad is capable of doing exactly what Twelve did to him, and *has* done to her in the past no doubt. When Leon lets me go, I know he reads that truth on my face. Regret, pain, *shame*, it all registers on his face as he swipes a hand through his hair. "Will you be okay for a moment?"

"Yes," I nod. *No*, I think.

My gaze tracks Leon as he strides over to his brother on the other side of the cell. Konrad's strapped to a chair, black leather restraints pinning him in place. He's still wearing the same clothes that he wore the day of Renard's funeral, a black suit with a white shirt that is no longer white but dirtied by sweat, and dried vomit. His trousers fare no better, covered in the white stain of their arousal, and his flaccid cock rests against his thigh. But none of that is more disturbing than the way he stares off into the distance behind the cover of his mask. His blue eyes are blank of emotion, of feeling, of any kind of life.

It's like he isn't even there any more.

"She did this to him," Leon says, gently resting his hand against Konrad's cheek, cupping his face and the mask Five had the wherewithal to put back on him, saving Thirteen, if not herself from a life sentence within these castle walls.

"Yes. Then killed herself because she knew what the consequences would be," Five finishes quietly. I glance over my shoulder as she lays Twelve on the ground, gently untying the rope from her neck. "She loved him in all the wrong ways." Her golden eyes find mine and a thousand words are spoken. I flick my gaze away from her, refusing to acknowledge them.

"*Fuck!*" Leon exclaims, pressing his forehead against Konrad's. "What have we done?"

That unanswered question hangs in the putrid air as Leon struggles to comprehend what's happened and how their actions have led to this point. Twelve was in love with Konrad, so much so that her love twisted into something dark and obsessive, *poisonous*. The Masks fucked with her mind, twisted her up inside so much that when she couldn't get the attention she craved from the man who abused and manipulated her, she took it for herself. She became the assailant, their violence perpetuating more violence, just like their father would've wanted.

That thought terrifies me because I *know* what that looks like for me.

"I can't," I mumble, shaking my head as I stumble backwards, emptying the contents of my stomach in the corner of the cell. I heave until there's nothing left and even then I don't feel any better. I feel like I'm losing myself to this place, to these men and the way they twist me up inside. It's a sickness that infects and destroys.

"Christy?" Leon questions. I hear the concern in his voice, and it only makes me feel worse, not better.

"Just give me a moment," I mutter, leaning my back against the wall.

He nods, focussing his attention on Thirteen. "Help me untie him."

"We should get him back to my room. I think I have some tonics that might help," Thirteen says, swallowing back her own emotions and pushing them aside as she helps Leon to untie him.

"No," Leon says, shaking his head. "We both know that your tonics and ointments can only heal physical wounds. I know what I need to do. I've done it before to get him back."

"This has happened before?" I whisper, staring at Konrad who is lost to some place far, far away from here.

"This isn't the first time Konrad has retreated into himself."

"What are you going to do?" I ask, forcing strength into my

jelly legs as I push off the wall and walk back towards them both.

"There's a place I go to get clean again," he replies, flicking his gaze to me before gently tucking Konrad's cock back into his trousers, covering him back up. It's such an intimate place to touch, and such a kind thing to do that I'm rocked by it. Leon doesn't notice my inner turmoil as he crouches before Konrad, and squeezes his thighs. "It's going to be alright, brother," he says.

"Can we do anything to help?" Five asks.

"I can't move Konrad on my own. I need Jakub."

Five shakes her head. "He's gone."

"Into the forest?" Leon's head snaps up as he looks at her.

"Yes..." Her voice trails off as she turns her attention back to Twelve.

"Fuck!" he exclaims, glancing at me, worry scattering across his features. He shakes his head, as though trying to clear it.

"Master?" Five questions, waiting for further instructions.

"First I'll deal with Konrad, then I'll go find Jakub. Will you help me to move him?" he asks her.

"Of course." Five steps forward as Leon wraps an arm around Konrad's back and lifts his arm over his shoulder, hauling him to his feet. Surprisingly Konrad manages to stand as Five ducks under his other arm. Despite her slight frame, she's strong.

"What can I do to help?" Thirteen asks.

"Get Konrad's room ready. He'll need something to help him sleep, and his fire will need to be lit. Can I leave you to do that?"

"Yes, of course." She flicks her gaze to me.

"Christy, go with her," Leon says.

"No. I want to help him." Those words leave my mouth before I can even comprehend them.

I do?

Leon thinks for a moment, then nods his head. "Okay."

"WHAT IS THIS PLACE EXACTLY?" I ask, momentarily stunned by the crystal clear water that seems to sink endlessly into the depths of this huge cave that sits beneath the castle.

"It's an underground lake. It's been here for centuries, way longer than Ardelby Castle," Leon responds as he and Five ease Konrad onto a sunlounger situated by the water's edge. It seems an odd piece of furniture to have given this cave is illuminated by a run of lights drilled into the cave floor and not the sun. In fact, as I look up at the ceiling of the cave I see thick tree roots growing downwards, a canopy of them. Some of the roots have grown down the wall and reach below the surface of the water, drifting there.

"Is that...?" My voice trails off as my eyes widen.

"The Weeping Tree? Yes. The courtyard is directly above us," Leon confirms as he struggles to remove Konrad's shirt.

"Do you need help undressing him?" Five asks, flicking her gaze between us.

"We can manage, but I'd appreciate it if you locked up the cell with Twelve's body in it," Leon says, searching Konrad's pocket and pulling out a key before passing it to Five.

"And One?" she asks.

"Not a word to One for now, or the Numbers. I need to deal with Konrad then we'll decide how to handle what's happened."

"Of course, Master." Five dips her head respectfully, then turns on her heel. Before she leaves I reach for her, pressing my fingers into the bare skin of her arm. She feels like silk even though I know she's as deadly as the knives she wears strapped to her chest.

"Thank you," I whisper.

Her gaze meets mine, understanding that I'm not thanking her for helping Leon to move Konrad, but because she helped save my life. "You're welcome, Mistress."

"No, I'm not your—" I say, shaking my head.

Her eyes warm with the smile she gives me. "Yes, you are," she says before stepping around me and leaving.

By the time I've gathered my faculties enough to turn around and face Leon, he has already undressed Konrad down to his boxer shorts and is helping him to sit up. Konrad groans, his broad shoulders hunching as his head falls between them. He's not so lost inside his mind that he's unable to move physically because we would never have gotten him down here, but he is completely absent otherwise.

An empty shell of a man.

Something about that pricks tiny little holes in the walls I've built up around my heart, and through those holes I feel more empathy sliding into my blood, churning me up inside. I shouldn't feel sympathy for a man who has done so many terrible deeds to so many people.

Yet, I do.

I do.

"I'm going to get him into the water. There's a ledge I can rest him on whilst I bathe him."

"Bathe him?" I ask, my gaze flicking between the two men.

"Yes. If anything can bring him back from where he's disappeared to, this place can..."

"Where has he gone?"

He looks at me with untold stories dwelling in his eyes,

stories I suspect he's never shared with anyone other than his brothers. There's so much he wants to say, but in the end he simply asks me one question.

"Will you help me bring him back?"

The immediate answer I want to give is held hostage by a host of emotions. Emotions that run rampant inside of me. This whole situation should be seen as a gift, a way for me to easily crawl into their hearts so that I can ruin them later, and yet knowing that's my aim makes me feel sick to my stomach. I should be happy about this opportunity, but all I feel is pity for a man so obviously broken by a woman who hurt him in the worst way possible, and empathy for his brother who only a few days ago ended my life.

"I shouldn't have asked," Leon says quickly, noticing the expression on my face. He stands, one hand resting on Konrad's shoulder whilst he quickly unbuckles his own jeans, awkwardly trying to shimmy out of them whilst ensuring Konrad doesn't fall head-first onto the hard rock.

"Wait, let me," I say, rushing forward.

Kneeling between Konrad's parted legs, I rest my hands on his shoulders, peering up at his face that's still partly covered by his mask. I remove it with a gentle tug and lay it on the ground next to Leon's discarded mask. Konrad lifts his head, and for the briefest of moments his eyes meet mine beneath a flop of dark hair. My stomach bottoms out. He's not there. He's gone.

"Thank you," Leon murmurs, stripping down to his t-shirt and boxers before lifting up Konrad's arm and ducking beneath it. He hooks it over his shoulder then hauls Konrad to his feet, an arm wrapped around his back as he manoeuvres him to the water's edge.

Konrad stumbles over a small rock and they both pitch side-ways. Without thinking about it, I rush forward to help and take

Konrad's left arm, ducking beneath it. Across his broad chest Leon glances at me, the gratefulness in his eyes causing another host of unwanted emotions to burn in my blood.

"Once we've got him into the lake it will be easier to support his weight."

"How is this even here?"

"Ardelby Castle is full of surprises," Leon replies, stepping onto the ledge and helping Konrad into the water with my assistance. His green eyes flick to mine and he gives me the tiniest hint of a smile, a smile I know would devastate me if he ever unleashed it fully.

"I'm beginning to see that," I reply, stepping into the water then sucking in a shocked breath. "It's so cold!"

"It is. Thank you for your help. I've got this now," he says, taking most of Konrad's weight and walking him deep into the water.

I watch as Leon gently urges Konrad to sit on the edge of the ledge, before he sits down beside him, his arm wrapped around his shoulder. Their legs dangle into the depths, the water lapping around their upper chests. For a moment Leon doesn't move, he simply stares out into the lake as though taking strength from this stillness of the water before he turns his attention back to his brother.

"Kon, you need to wake up now," he says before cupping some water in his palms and pouring it over his brother's head and shoulders.

With one ankle deep in the water, I debate whether to join them. A part of me is inexplicably and undeniably connected to these men, like magnets we're drawn to one another. The other part, the more sensible part, wants nothing to do with them other than tasting revenge.

It's a battle that wages a constant war within me, but in the end it's Konrad's sudden violent shivers and a cry of utter heart-break that forces my other foot into the water until I'm kneeling beside him on the ledge, my arms circling his body as my dress billows out around me, a dark cloud within the crystal blue-green. He continues to scream and those screams tear at my resolve to remain guarded, to maintain hatred, to segregate his pain from mine, to keep my distance.

I don't speak. I don't do anything other than press my body against his side and hold him whilst he evicts all his pain. It pours from him in a torrent of noise that echoes around this cavernous space like thunder rippling across a stormy sky.

He doesn't relent.

Minute after minute he disembowels himself of the pain, the veins on his neck straining against his skin as he lets it go. Throughout it all, Leon keeps pouring the water over his body, whispering words of empathy, kindness, and *love*. If it hadn't been for everything I'd been through at the hands of these men, I might've lost my heart to them at this moment.

Instead, I hold onto it as fiercely as I hold onto Konrad, refusing to let it soften further until the man who hurt me eventually, finally, calms.

"Leon? *Zero?*" he says, blinking rapidly as he looks from me to Leon and back again.

"Thank fuck!" Leon exclaims as my arms drop from around Konrad's body and I shift backwards in the water, the ripples disturbing the stillness.

"Why are *you* here?" Konrad asks me, his question coming out harshly as he twists to face me, grasping my shoulders.

Behind him Leon pushes up onto his knees on the ledge as he edges around Konrad, his hand clamping on his wrist. "I asked for Christy's help. Don't take your pain out on her," he urges.

Konrad's nostrils flare, and my teeth begin to chatter, my whole body vibrating with the cold as all the adrenaline that was keeping me warm, or at least oblivious to the cold, starts to wear off. "This place is sacred," he counters, his fingers digging deeper into my skin. I can feel the swell of the water lap against my breasts as he shifts his body to face me. "You don't belong here."

"She belongs wherever we are," Leon says as Konrad looks at him. "But you already know that, don't you?"

"It's okay. I'll go and wait over there," I say, trying to edge backwards, out of his hold whilst the brothers continue to stare at one another in some silent conversation I can't decipher.

"No!" They both say in unison, Konrad's grip tightening as he returns his attention to me and Leon moves to sit behind me, trapping me between the two of them.

"You're not going anywhere," Leon says.

Fear slithers up my spine at his tone of voice, and the feelings of warmth I'd begun to feel towards these men begin to ice over. "Don't," I warn.

"You misunderstand me. I don't want to hurt you. *We* don't, do we Konrad?" Leon lifts me into his lap, and wraps his arms around my waist, his mouth pressing against the curve of my neck. His fingers caressing the bare skin of my arm gently. My body shudders from his touch.

Konrad blows out a long breath, his broad chest shuddering with the effort. "No."

We fall silent as Konrad's admission sinks in. I should feel relieved, but I only feel dazed. I'm fighting so hard to hate, knowing that I can't be weakened by their softness, their gentleness, their past.

"She raped you," I whisper. I don't know why I chose this moment to remind him of what so obviously hurt him, but I do.

My gaze falls to our reflection in the water. It ripples with our movements, distorting what I see, echoing how I feel. My head is all over the place.

"Yes," he replies, forcing me to look at him again as he pinches my chin between his finger and thumb. "The last thing I remember is her sliding onto my cock. Then I blacked out. Where is she now?"

"Dead," Leon says.

Konrad clenches his jaw then looks out over the water, but he's not quick enough to hide the flash of pain, the regret, the anger. "How?"

"She hung herself..." I say, filling in the silence. Feeling sick at the thought.

"Why?" he asks.

"Because she knew what the repercussions would be," Leon says heavily, as though it pains him to admit that truth. Perhaps it does now.

"When will it end?" I whisper, knowing the answer to that question only too well. *Soon.*

I find no joy in that, only a strange kind of emptiness.

"This lake has never seen an ounce of violence, and we don't intend on changing that now," Leon says, misunderstanding my question. "This is the one place our father's influence never tarnished. There is no death here, only peace."

My teeth chatter in earnest now as I shift position. My dress ripples underwater, the hem gently caressing Konrad's knees now that he's facing me fully.

"How did you find this place?" I ask.

"Leon found it when we were small, not long after the first time Malik forced us both to suck him off before he raped and killed a woman in front of our eyes," Konrad says quietly.

"He forced you both to...?" My gut churns with nausea and bile burns my throat but I swallow it back down.

"Yes," Konrad nods. "We were eight at the time."

"I'm sorry," I whisper.

Konrad looks out over the water, quiet for a moment. He drags his thick fingers through his wet hair then turns back to face me. "We ran from him and found this place, hid here for days. Only hunger forced us to return to the castle, and back into the viper's pit."

"What happened to you?" I ask, knowing the moment Leon's fingers dig into my flesh that I'm not going to like the answer.

"He locked us in a cell in the dungeon and beat us to the brink of death," Konrad explains.

"You were just children..." My voice trails off as I contemplate the horror they've been through.

"When he left us for dead, we vowed to never share this place with him. Over the years, as Malik began to imbue his darkness into our hearts, Konrad and Jakub eventually stopped coming here, but I never did," Leon says, his fingers loosening their hold, his lips caressing the tender spot of skin where my neck and shoulder meet. "It was the only place I could feel free... even when I wasn't."

I can feel Leon's warm breaths feathering over my skin, and the heat of his chest sinking into my back as he inches us closer together until I have no choice but to wrap my legs around Konrad's waist, caught between them both.

"Brother," Konrad mutters, his gaze moving from mine to Leon's behind me. I see the love in his eyes. It's fierce. It burns brightly, and when he looks back at me, the heat of it scorches my skin until I don't feel the cold anymore. Until all I feel is fire.

Fire is pain. It's death.

It's also life and warmth. It's hope.

It's a contradiction, just like these men. Just like my feelings for them.

The constant push and pull, the heat and the ice.

Soon The Masks will die at my hands, yet here I am sandwiched between them, my body warmed by their presence. Leon's heat seeping into my back, Konrad's hands cupping my knees. I feel my icy heart thawing out because of their stories of abuse. Those stories, their trauma, it doesn't excuse them for what they've done. It doesn't. But it explains who they are, and why they do what they do. It's a truth that I don't really know how to deal with.

Can men so twisted, so messed-up by their past, who've inflicted pain and cruelty, ever be forgiven? Can they truly change?

I drill down into that thought as Konrad reaches for me, his palm cupping my face. His thumb gently caressing my cheek. When he leans in and presses a kiss against my mouth, I don't stop him. When he pushes his tongue between my lips and slides his fingers into my hair I don't shove him away. I let him steal a kiss, hoping that it will be enough to remind me that he *can't* change. That the evil his father infected him with is too ingrained in his cells, that no matter what he does he'll never be rid of it.

I expect him to go further. Only he doesn't. He pulls back, brushing his lips over mine before saying: "You're everything we've been taught to fear our whole life. You have the power to demolish all that we've built here. You have the ability to end the Brov legacy just like that woman predicted. Will you?"

He searches my face, waiting. Behind me Leon tenses. I debate lying to them both, but in the end all I can give them is the truth.

"Yes, very soon all of this will cease to exist."

Behind me Leon lets out a long breath, as though he's breathing air for the first time in years. Konrad's reaction is no different. His shoulders relax, his muscles soften, relief brims in his eyes. "Good. We won't stop you."

"You won't," I say. It's received as a question but is meant as a statement of truth.

Konrad grasps my hand, placing it over the centre of his chest. "You've already claimed Leon's heart, and for what it's worth, now you've added mine to the collection. All I ask of you, before you raze this place to the ground is one thing."

"And what's that?" I whisper, already knowing what he's about to say.

"That you free Jakub, too."

My throat tightens. "What if I can't do that?"

"But what if you can?" Konrad smiles gently, echoing the very words my mother had said before he presses a chaste kiss to my lips and stands, diving into the water.

CHAPTER TWENTY-ONE

Konrad

MY HEAD EMERGES from the surface of the water, icy droplets spilling over my brow and down my chest as I pull myself up onto the ledge carved into the cave wall on the other side of the underground lake.

For the first time in a very, very long time, I feel at peace.

Ironic, given what happened to get me here.

A mixture of guilt and anger burns in my gut. I push those emotions away, not wanting to fall back into the depths of my mind. I need to have a clear head. I need to think.

Edging back onto the ledge, I rest my hand against the root nearest me. Its bark is smoother than the rough trunk we're used to seeing above ground, softened by the water that runs in rivulets down the wall. This tree has seen so much violence. A history of death and bloodshed handed down through the generations, absorbed into its roots that spread out over this cavernous space.

The Brov family legacy is coming to its end.

Because of her, because of Christy Dálaigh.

The woman with ghost eyes.

The woman who is standing on the other side of the lake, my brother at her feet. Her dress is glued to her frame, showing off every curve, hinting at the beauty of her body hidden beneath the dark material, because it is beautiful, every scarred and damaged part of it.

The ends of her hair are wet tendrils, darkened by the water. Her face is free of makeup, her birthmark bright red from the cold, her lips turning blue at the edges.

She's a vision.

God, she's everything.

She's dangerous.

I knew it the moment I first laid eyes on her. I knew she'd ruin us.

Back then that had scared me. A man who fears nothing, had feared her.

And now? Now, I'm glad of it.

Let her ruin us. Let her demolish this place. Let her end the Brov legacy once and for all.

It's time.

Time to let it all go.

Not just the past, but the future, too. I'm not fool enough to believe she'll be a part of it. Leon might think he can keep her here forever, but I know better. As much as I want that too, I also know that Grim will come for her. That we will pay for our sins the way all our forefathers have, in blood and death. Then and only then will she be free of us.

All I can hope for is the here and now. This day, this moment.

All I can do is live in the present and hope that my actions from this second on are worthy of this woman. It's why I didn't take more than a kiss. It's why I didn't act on the impulses that still run through my veins because whilst she's shone a light on my darkness, weakened it, it still resides within me. Just like Leon's does, just like Jakub's will.

It's a part of who I am, who we are. It's our ball and chain, the rope around our throats, the knife buried in our hearts, the poison swimming in our souls. The darkness lives in the memories which haunt us, its scars both visible and hidden.

It will never leave us.

So all I can do is leave her. Give us space. Distance.

I suspect that's what Jakub is doing right now, although he covers that up with the need to inflict pain on himself to block those feelings of desire, need, empathy, kindness, *love*. It's a destructive skill our father trained him with. A painful cycle that has no ending.

A gentle splash in the water draws my attention back across the lake and from my thoughts. This time Leon is standing alone on the ledge, Christy swims towards me.

"No!" I shout, shaking my head, drawing my knees up to my chest.

She can't hear me though as she swims front crawl, her body strong, her strokes sure. She's no longer wearing her dress and all I can see is her red hair fanning out over her back, her legs and arms kicking through the surface, bringing her to me.

I look up at Leon, eyes wide.

"I'm coming, brother," he says, diving into the water after her.

She reaches me first, her slim fingers curving around the

edge of the rock as she pulls herself up onto the ledge. Droplets of water cascades down her body, and her perfectly proportioned tits wobble as she stands upright.

My mouth dries and I force myself to look away, gripping hold of the root of The Weeping Tree as though it's a lifeline. "You shouldn't be here right now. Go back. Stay with Leon."

"I can't," she whispers, and I get the distinct feeling she isn't talking about returning to the other side of the lake and safety, but what I'd asked her to do moments before I swam across here.

"You can. You did it for Leon. For me."

"Have I though?" she asks, getting to her feet and taking two steps towards me.

Her presence makes me skittish and my fingers flex and bend around the root of the tree. I swear I can feel it pulse beneath my fingers as though it's trying to tell me something important, but perhaps that's just hypothermia setting in. This lake isn't freezing, but it is cold and our bodies can only cope with the lowered temperature for so long.

"Yes, you have," Leon reassures her, pulling himself out of the water behind her. Knowing he's with us gives me enough strength to look at her.

With a slow sweep, my gaze lifts from her bare feet and ankles all the way up her shapely legs that are scattered with freckles, her strong muscles curving towards the apex of her thighs. My eyes linger on her mound, covered by simple white cotton knickers, soaked from the water and sticking to the curve of her pussy lips.

God, how I want to taste her.

I swallow hard, my hand gripping tighter to the root as I continue my slow perusal. My gaze slips over her stomach, to the curve of her waist and the slight jut of her ribcage. She's breathing heavily, her pale skin dusted with goosebumps and more freckles, her nipples puckered into rosy points delectable enough to feast upon. Tendrils of hair stick against her chest like ropes, only fuelling my need for darker things.

For a moment my mind drifts to our room above the library and all the sex toys locked up in the armoire. I imagine her wrists and ankles bound by rope, spreading her wide open so I can see her pretty cunt glistening with arousal.

Fuck!

How can Leon be so close to her like this and not want to ruin her for himself? I force myself to look at him and not lift my gaze to meet her eyes, knowing what she'll see in them. Only when my gaze falls on him, I notice how his t-shirt is now completely stuck to his skin and I see his scabbed chest beneath, her name carved into his flesh.

"What the fuck?!" I exclaim, eyes widening.

"I asked her to do it," he replies, knowing exactly what I'm thinking.

"When?" I bite out.

"When I—"

"When he took my virginity," Christy finishes for him.

Her voice is soft, gentle, but it still guts me like a knife. My fingers squeeze so hard around the root that my knuckles crack from the force.

"He *took* it?" I glare at my brother, unable to hide the jealousy or my need to fucking *kill* him.

"Jakub held a gun to her," he says, guilt climbing across his face, heat rushing to his dick. Christy is standing in front of him so she can't see what I see. She can't see his cock growing larger, pressing against his cotton boxers at the memory. She can't see the lust in his eyes, or the love.

It's *fierce*.

He loves her.

As I do.

As. I. Do.

"That shouldn't have happened," I say, forcing myself to my feet. My muscles groan, my bones ache, my blood boils and my heart...? That fucking pumps louder and faster than ever before.

"It happened," she whispers, her eyes meeting mine.

There's a flicker of something in her gaze, an internal battle that she can't hide from me. She's fighting her feelings, just like I have tried so hard to do. I see them swimming in her ghost eyes. Those fucking eyes that bewitch me. A sharp blue next to a brown so dark it's almost as black as my heart.

Light and dark... They remind me of the conversation I had with Five.

Good versus bad.

Right versus wrong.

I'm still bad, I know that, but then I look at my brother and see he's found a way to straddle the line. I wonder if I can do that too?

I know I want to. I *want* to.

"Jakub ran because of it," Leon continues. "He wanted me to hurt her... and I did."

"You did?" I growl, furious, *jealous*.

He nods tightly, his fingers seeking out Christy's as he entwines them with hers. "But I stopped. I stopped because of Christy, because she pulled me back from the brink."

"No," Christy shakes her head, glancing at him as he steps to her side. "You did that yourself. You made a choice to do better, to be better. Only you can do that. Only you."

"And you let me," he whispers, dropping a kiss against her bare shoulder before looking back up at me. "I made love for the first motherfucking time in my life," Leon admits, shaking his head in wonder. "Jakub watched every moment. He couldn't deal with it. He ran, Kon."

"To the forest?" I ask, worry coursing through my veins as jealousy rips through my heart.

"Worse. I think he's gone to the cabin," Leon replies, gritting his teeth.

"Fuck!"

"The cabin?" Christy asks, her gaze shifting from me to Leon and back again.

He nods. "Malik took him to the cabin in the woods when spending time with One didn't work. Jakub never told us what happened there but we both knew it wasn't good. He came back a little darker and more broken every time."

"Oh God." Her hand flies to her mouth and she presses her eyes shut as though that alone will prevent her from imagining the atrocities he would've suffered, is probably suffering now just being there with his memories, with the ghost of our father.

"He's fighting his feelings towards you with everything he has," I explain.

"And you?" she asks, opening her eyes slowly, staring right into the depths of my very being.

"I'm fighting, too. I'm fighting hard not to take you here and now, to fuck you into oblivion."

"Even after what happened to you today?"

"Even then."

She flinches and I see the disgust, the pity in her eyes. A normal person wouldn't want to fuck so quickly after what happened, but I'm not normal. None of us are. "You have to understand, sex is a weapon our father wielded against us time and time again. I found a way to cope with what happened..."

"You disappear."

"Yes," I nod. "I also *embrace*. It's fucked-up, but it's who I am. I look at you now and all I want to do is fuck you until I've purged all the darkness within me. I want to bleed it from my soul, so you'll accept me, not reject me..."

"But?" she questions, her teeth chattering now. I don't know if it's from fear or from the cold. Either way, Leon releases her hand and wraps his arms around her stomach, hauling her back against his chest, warming her up as much as he's protecting her from me. His gaze is as fierce as hers, and for a moment I'm struck by it. Even now he believes I could hurt her, and he'd be right.

"But I'm not sure that would happen even if you were willing. This darkness still lives within me. It won't let go," I admit, pressing a hand against my chest and rubbing at the pain I feel there. "I'm past saving."

"Tell me what you want from me," she says brazenly, her cheeks flushing.

I swallow hard, the words falling from my lips in a rush of heat, fire and lust. "I want to take you to our room above the library and tie you to our bed. I want to fuck you with every single dildo in the armoire and make you come so hard you won't know what day it is. Then I want to whip you, paddle your arse until it's as red as your birthmark, then soothe those marks with my lips and tongue. I want to taste your pussy, feast on it. I want to make you bleed. I want your mouth around my cock. I want my hands around your throat whilst I fuck you. I want to watch my brothers do the same. I want... I want... *Fuck!*"

I curl my fingers into fists, and force my mouth shut. Fuck, this is hard. Harder than anything I've ever had to do. I'm shaking now. My whole body is trembling like hers as I fight the need to impale her on my cock and take her against the wall of this cave like some ravenous beast.

"Brother," Leon warns, easing himself in front of Christy. Sensing I'm about to let go of my restraint.

"No," she says, pressing her hand over the name she carved into his chest, holding him back. "I need to understand what I'm dealing with. I need to look Konrad's monster in the eyes and see *it*. Let him finish."

Leon grits his jaw but he does as she asks, and I know in that moment he always will. I'm glad of it.

"My *monster* wants to ruin you, Christy," I admit, staring at her with my honesty.

"And what you've described is your monster's way of doing that?"

"No. That's sex. That isn't the monster. That's my desire. *Mine*. They're not the same."

"Explain," she urges. "I want to understand."

"Everything I've described, I want that with you and I *need* you to want it, too. I want you to walk into that room with us knowing what will happen and *desiring* it. I want you to trust us, the men who've hurt you." I laugh bitterly. "Fucking stupid right, to want that from you after what we've done?"

She drags in a surprised breath, her eyes widening. I can see the distrust in them. She thinks I'm a liar, but I'm not lying about this. It's why we haven't taken her to that room already. There is a fine line between what we want as men, and what the monsters our father cultivated need to feed the darkness. Sometimes they've blurred and that's when we lose our grip on sanity. In order for her to survive us, we have to keep those things separate. Always.

"I've been abused so many times over the years," I continue. "Too many times to count; I always, *always* made sure that the Numbers wanted what I gave them, even when they weren't ready to admit that to themselves. I know them better than they know themselves."

"And Twelve? Did you know her better than she knew herself?" There's an edge of anger in her voice, and I understand it. From her point of view, all she sees is a woman who's been kidnapped, imprisoned in this castle and then hired out for sex. A woman who was pushed to her limits and sought her revenge, taking what she wanted before killing herself, and whilst there's truth in that, there is also so much more she doesn't see, doesn't understand.

I sigh heavily. "When Twelve first arrived here, she fought her true desires. I coaxed them out of her because that's what I was trained to do, we were trained to do. It's why the Numbers have stayed, why they continue to perform, because they can be who they are without restraint. We've never lied about that."

"And you truly believe that?"

"I know it," I reply adamantly.

"Then how come Twelve did what she did to you? Explain that to me, Konrad."

"For a time, Twelve was everything we knew she could be. She was free to be herself, free to fuck the way she wanted, free to sing, free to bloom. She was beautiful, talented, a perfect addition to The Menagerie." I sigh, scraping a hand over my face. "Only I drew out more than her desires, I drew out her demon too, and she's been carrying it with her ever since. The moment I realised what I'd done I tried to reverse it, and when that didn't work, I kept her at arm's length. Only my absence had the opposite effect..."

Christy's gaze pricks with tears as she tries to comprehend what I've just said. "If that's true. If you truly believe you never took what wasn't given, wanted or desired, even if it was buried deep, then how do you explain what happened to me in the

Grand Hall, in the dungeon? I *never* consented to that. You stole from me."

My head hangs in shame. "We did."

"Then why do it?"

"Because we lost control with you. The lines were so fucking blurred we couldn't see straight. We were hyped up on revenge, fucked up with new feelings that we didn't know what to do with. We stole your orgasm on both occasions. We hurt you. It was wrong. We were wrong. I'm *sorry*."

I fall to my knees at her feet knowing that I should've done so the night Leon took her life. I should've been brave enough then to show what I truly felt beneath the layers and layers of darkness Malik had forced us to ingest over the years. I should've let those true feelings out like Leon had.

I was a coward.

I'm not anymore.

She tips her head to the side, watching me closely. "You regret kidnapping me?"

"No," I admit. "I don't regret that because we wouldn't have you here with us now."

"Can you control the monster within you?" she asks, stepping closer. I can feel her warmth, her strength, her courage. It moves into my personal space, wrapping around me, heating me up.

"I don't know. I want to, but I'm not as strong as Leon is."

"You are, brother. You *are*," he insists.

She reaches for me then, her fingers surprisingly warm as they press against my cheek and slide along my jaw. Her fingers tip my chin up as she urges me to stand. I follow the movement, captivated by her. She pushes against my chest, and my back hits the stone wall as her fingers gently wrap around my throat. Her touch makes my whole body shudder. My cock punching through the gap in my boxer shorts, straining to reach her. I *want* her. Yet still I retain the threads of my restraint.

"Will you hurt me again?" she asks, pressing her body against mine, her curves soft against my hardness.

"I might..."

She nods, her lips running across the sharp edge of my jaw, reaching for my ear as she whispers a question that shocks me to my core, "Do you want to kill me then bring me back to life over and over again like you did to Nala's mother?"

I gasp, my monster roaring to life as I reach up and grab her by the throat, flipping her around and slamming her against the cave wall. Air whooshes from her lungs as my body crushes hers. "How did you know about that, did he tell you?" I growl, my cock growing thicker as my monster bares his teeth at her.

"Brother!" I hear Leon snap, but I ignore him and he wraps his arm around my throat, cutting off my airway. "Let. Her. Go."

My fingers release around her throat slightly, if only so I can hear her answer.

"No. I saw it," she says.

"*Saw* it?" My voice a low growl that rumbles up my chest and into hers.

"Yes. I'm a seer too, just like my mother was. I saw what you did to her. I saw your monster come alive. I see it right now, inside of you. Can you control it?" she asks once again.

No. It says.

"I want to," I choke out. "I want to so fucking bad."

"Show me you can. Do it now," she urges.

"Christy..." Leon warns from over my shoulder. I can feel the heat from his body seeping into mine and the hard length of his cock resting against the crack of my arse, his desire for this unbelievably brave woman reflecting my own.

"This has to happen," she whispers, more to herself than anyone else as she stares right into the pit of my soul and into the depths of my monster. "This has to happen the right way, on *my* terms."

"Are you certain?" Leon questions.

"Yes." She nods her head with a determined look. "Yes, I'm certain."

Leon releases me, stepping back and taking his warmth with him. "What do you need me to do?" he asks her.

"Stay with us. Don't run like Jakub did..."

Her voice trails off and we all understand what she doesn't say. Leon is her protector now. He's proven himself, and she trusts him not to allow me to hurt her. He must nod his agreement because Christy focusses back on me.

"Purge your darkness, Konrad. Bleed for me," she says softly.

"How?"

"You know how. Put a leash on your monster and give me what's left of your heart," she says, placing her palm over the centre of my chest, waiting. Her words hang in the air between us. It's a lifeline barbed in danger, salvation wrapped up in vulnerability. It's *hope*. "Take me. Do it now."

"Yes!" I hiss, slamming my lips against hers, knowing that whatever's left of my heart now belongs to her.

CHAPTER TWENTY-TWO

Christy

KONRAD TASTES of fire and smoke, iron and metal, blood and carnage.

He tastes of pain, agony, danger, rage, *suffering*.

He's a dichotomy.

A victim, and an assailant.

Fear bubbles inside my chest as we kiss, but I force it aside and let his monster *take*. I open myself up to him, knowing it's the only way to get him to heal, and that fear inside of me... It makes way for a growing sense of empowerment.

It flows through my blood. It tingles beneath my skin. It gives me strength.

Me...

A girl who once hid from the world and all the people within it.

A girl who covered her scars and her birthmark so others

could feel comfortable.

A girl who cowered from life.

That girl slowly disappears as another stronger version of herself steps forward in the face of this monster...

Christy Dálaigh.

I kiss Konrad with the same intensity as he kisses me. I push off the wall and clamber up his body, my fingers sliding into his hair, my legs wrapping around his waist.

I take what he gives.

I inhale him into my lungs. I breathe him in.

"Zero," he grinds out, the violence of his kiss splitting my lip from the force.

The metallic taste of blood bursts over my tastebuds, but I don't whimper in pain, I growl in challenge. Then I bite him back. Hard. A roar rips out of his mouth as he yanks his head away, blood seeping from his split lip. Nostrils flaring, chest heaving, eyes blazing, we face off.

"*Monster*," I retort, meeting his gaze head on, refusing to back down in the face of it.

Pressing his body even harder against mine, he pushes me into the cave wall, pinning me there. I see the battle raging in his eyes, and the way he fights to hold back. I feel the heat of his passion, his need in every quivering inch of his body. I hear the indecision in every shaky breath he takes. I taste it in our kiss, in our combined blood that sits on my tongue.

We're on the cusp of something destructive or life-changing.

Either I tame the monster or it destroys us both.

"Kon," Leon warns from somewhere behind him.

"No, don't," I bite out because whilst Leon sees danger, I see a turning point.

You see, Konrad is a different beast to his brother. With Leon his monster was tamed by my pain, my tears, because our bond was forged the very same way all those years ago when we were kids. It was the key to unlocking the man, so he could lock up the monster, but that's not something that will work with Konrad.

I understand that instinctively.

Konrad needs someone who's willing to face his monster. He needs someone who will live and breathe and fight back in the face of it, *despite* it. If the vision of Konrad as a kid has taught me anything, it's this: his true nature is the boy who saved a woman, not the monster he became that day. So I face the very same monster his father brought to life in order to find the boy buried beneath, to show Leon that he still lives within Konrad and to heal a wound between them that was inflicted purposefully by a man who was evil, manipulative and cruel.

I do this without any thought to my safety because I *know* I'll survive what happens between us. I will survive it and I will survive them.

And because a tiny part of you wants to help him, a small voice inside my head says.

And maybe because of that, too.

We remain glued to each other, his cock pressed against my pussy, nothing but a thin layer of material separating us. In this moment, it's just us.

I'm fearless against his hostility. He's raging against my courage.

Without even saying a word, I dare him to do his worst.

"You want the monster?" he grinds out.

"No," I reply, shaking my head. "I want the man. Give *him* to me. Now."

Konrad's breathing becomes harsh, his hand finds my throat, his cock pushes against the feeble barrier between us as a slow sneer pulls up his lip. "I could kill you now."

"Do it then, *monster*. Fucking do it!" I scream into his face, my fingernails scoring down his chest, drawing blood.

"Do you know what happens to little girls who play with fire?" he asks, his fingers tightening around my throat, venom leaching into his voice as he lowers his head and locks his teeth onto my shoulder.

I let out a bitter laugh, then reach between us and yank my knickers to the side, a smile drawing up my lips. "Yeah, they get burnt," I reply, sheathing him inside of me in one quick downward thrust.

Pain lances through me as his teeth pierce my skin, drawing blood. His cock fills every millimetre of my pussy and I draw in a sharp breath at the fullness. With his fingers at my throat, I bare myself to him, expecting him to crush my windpipe.

He doesn't. Instead, he tips his head back and roars.

The sound is like the ground opening up beneath us. It's so very different from the cry he let out on the other side of the lake.

It's a war cry. He means to fight.

Well, guess what? So do I.

When he lowers his head back down, the briefest moment of shock registers across his face as I meet his threat and flip it on its head, squeezing him tightly within me, daring him to do his worst. I taunt his monster with one goal in mind, to own it, *him*.

He smiles slowly. "I warned you," he says, then the monster comes out to play just like I knew it would.

Konrad fucks me hard.

He fucks me like he wants to rip me open and feast on my innards. He fucks me with a dangerous kind of passion, and all the while I fuck him back. I take and I give. I battle and I rage, just the same as he.

In this moment, there's no room for tenderness, no space for gentleness, no capacity for kindness. This is us uncovering the layers and layers of abuse, years of violence, a lifetime of pain, hurt, and suffering. We both rip at it. We tear at the darkness. We fight against it with bared teeth and bloodied nails until it begins to pour out of him.

He bleeds his darkness just like I asked him to.

He bleeds it into *me*.

With every brutal thrust, with every harsh kiss from his lips, every savage grasp of his hand, he purges the monster.

We fuck. We kiss. We hurt. We fight.

The intensity between us grows, the passion ignites, the fire burns.

And bit by bit my hate recedes.

I grip at him, my fingernails scoring marks down his back as my hips slam against his and the tip of his cock hits my cervix. Crying out, I hold on for dear life, not because I'm in pain, but because an orgasm barrels out of nowhere. It rushes up my spine, exploding outwards in a display of noise and grunts and animalistic fucking as he pumps harder and I scream louder.

Our combined voices echo around the cave. My internal walls fist his cock, squeezing his dick in a vice-like grip, but still he pumps his hips.

Faster.

Deeper.

He buries himself within me—the monster *and* the man—as I come hard, clawing at him and screaming his name over and over, and over again. It's a lament, a portent, a warning to myself and my battered heart as both my body and my heart weep for him.

But if I thought this battle would end with my orgasm, I was sorely mistaken.

Konrad keeps pumping balls deep within me. He kisses me as hard as he fucks me, and I don't get a chance to come down from my orgasm and dwell in the satiated bliss that follows because he's not done with me yet. Konrad's large hands squeeze my tits, my arse, my hips, my arms, bruising me with his touch, marking me with his grip.

This is a purging of all the horror he's endured.

Every thrust tears at my walls.

Every kiss punches a hole in the solid foundation of my hate.

Yet, despite the brutal fucking, there's a vulnerability that I see within him. It batters at my defences as the boy fights against the monster who has grabbed hold of him so fiercely. It claws into his muscle and bone, desperately trying to hold on, but Konrad is stronger than he gives himself credit for.

With taut muscles and veins bulging beneath his skin. With sweat pouring from his body and eyes rolled back in his head. With teeth bared and my name on his lips. With every inch of his body, Konrad fights.

My God, he fights.

Everyone had warned me that Leon was the most danger-ous, the one to fear, but I know now as Konrad tries to extricate himself from his monster, that it was always him.

Back and forth they battle, and all I can do is fight *with* him.

At this moment, all I can do is help him.

It's not a position I ever thought I'd find myself in, but here we are.

Grasping his cheeks in mine, I force Konrad to look at me. I stare into the face of all his darkness as he rams into me and say; "I'm strong enough. Let it go."

"Fuccckkkkkkkk!" he roars, tears pouring from his eyes as he bruises me with the force of his pain, his whole body shuddering and shaking as he comes, the last dregs of his suffering leaking from him into me.

Leon steps up behind him, tears streaming from his eyes as his own feelings of love and empathy for his brother show themselves. I don't even think he realises that he's crying too, these men who've never been allowed to feel are doing so now, and it hurts.

It *hurts* them.

"Brother, let it go. Let it go," Leon says, circling Konrad's waist with his arm, pressing his cheek against his cheek.

Konrad shivers and shakes, his cock pulsating inside of me, his hips jerking against mine as he slowly calms, until finally something slips from his eyes and a long breath of air whooshes from his chest.

Everything stills.

His body. Mine. Leon's. Our mingled breaths. The beads of sweat covering our skin.

It all stops.

Time ceases to exist, and a strange kind of sensation begins to unravel inside of me. In that moment I realise that it isn't just Konrad who lets go of something poisonous, it's me too.

It's me too.

"Konrad, Leon, I need to tell you both some—"

Konrad raises his finger to my lips, shaking his head as he transforms before me. The expression on his face softens, his lips part and his eyes spark with... *hope*. That hope is like a sharp knife to my gut. It twists my innards, tearing me up. It cuts me deeper than I ever thought it could because I know what's coming.

There is no hope, only death.

And that realisation, it *hurts*.

CHAPTER TWENTY-THREE

Christy

"YOU'RE HERE," Thirteen says, frowning as I enter her bedroom on unsteady legs. "I was just about to head back to Leon's suite. Konrad's room is ready for him."

"I know, Leon's there with him now," I murmur.

"Is everything okay...?"

Her voice trails off as she takes a good look at me. Shock widens her eyes as her gaze rakes over the bruises scattered across the bare skin of my arms, finally resting on my split and swollen lip. I haven't seen the state of my back, and right now my dress is covering the worst of it, but I'm pretty sure it's covered in cuts and grazes from the rough stone of the cave wall despite the water washing away all of the blood in our swim back to the other side of the lake.

"What happened?!"

I shake my head, the words on my lips lost beneath the

sudden, overwhelming emotions that flood my system and force my knees to buckle beneath me just as Six steps out of Thirteen's bathroom.

"That tonic has really helped to ease my period pains, thanks Thir— *What on Earth?*" she exclaims, rushing forward at the same time Thirteen does.

Six is cursing under her breath as they both help me to my feet and guide me to Thirteen's bed. I fall into the warmth of Six's body, grateful for her softness as she eases me onto the mattress.

"Did Konrad do this? Was it Leon? What hurts the most?" Thirteen asks in quick succession, her eyes wild with worry as she crouches before me, her fingers skimming over my skin.

"No. It wasn't like that," I mutter, shaking my head.

She huffs out a breath, giving me a concerned look as she rushes over to her potions lined up across the counter on the other side of the room. She picks up bottle after bottle, placing them back down as she searches for something specific. Half a minute later she finds what she's looking for and grabs a clear bottle filled with a pale pink, sparkling liquid. I watch her in a daze as she pours it into a mug then adds a pinch of herbs from one jar and a dash of crushed petals from another before striding back over to me and placing it into my shaking hands.

"Drink this. It'll help with the pain," she says, before grabbing a jar of skin cream from the table beside the bed.

"I don't feel any pain," I reply, watching her as she unscrews the lid and starts applying the cream to my bruises.

"Perhaps not yet, but you will," she says quietly, jerking her chin to the mug I'm holding. "It has a sedative effect, too. You need sleep."

I follow her instructions robotically and take a sip of the drink, tasting elderberries and something flowery that I can't quite put my finger on as she applies the cream to the bruises on my arms before wiping the excess on her pinafore and screwing the lid back on the jar. She places it on the floor by her feet, looking up at me.

"What happened?" she asks, resting her hands on my knee.

"We fucked," I blurt out.

"You fucked?" Six asks. I hear the doubt in her voice, the concern. She sees a victim, not someone who is capable of murder, even if that's something that hasn't actually happened yet.

"Yes. I just fucked Konrad."

"Was that something you wanted?" Thirteen asks softly.

"Yes..."

My voice trails off as I contemplate the truth of that fact. It was so much more than fucking, so much more. I'd started out wanting to find a way into their hearts so I could break them like they broke me, but after what I witnessed tonight, the love Leon has for his brother, the way Konrad fought so hard against his demons made something inside of me shift. I felt it happen, and honestly, I don't know what to do with that, especially knowing what's coming. What I *can't* change.

I'm going to kill them.

Thirteen chews on her lip before tucking a stray strand of hair behind my ear and gently tipping my chin up. "Did you use protection?"

I shake my head, it hadn't even occurred to me. Not before I offered myself up to Konrad, not during and certainly not after. "No, I..." My voice trails off as I give her a helpless look. "The last thing I need is a baby."

Thirteen squeezes my hand and gets to her feet once more. "I have something that can help with that," she says as she grabs a little silver tin from the shelf above the counter and takes out a small brown pill. "It works similarly to the morning after pill. It's potent, and you will get cramps and bleed for the next couple of days, but it's perfectly safe, okay?"

"Okay," I say, taking it from her and using the last mouthful of the drink to wash it down. "Thank you."

"I also have something that I can give you to stop you getting pregnant. All of the Numbers take it," Thirteen says, flicking her gaze to Six.

"Yes, that's right," Six confirms. "It acts like the pill, preventing pregnancy."

"I see," I reply, nodding my approval. Thirteen grabs another small tin, gold this time, and passes it to me.

"When you start to bleed, take a pill. Then continue to take one each day."

"I will," I mutter, my cheeks flushing.

"The Masks are very meticulous with regards to our sexual health," Six says, whilst I gather my thoughts. "Every client who attends the castle has to provide proof of excellent sexual health. As you can imagine condoms are not used on the nights we entertain."

"I hadn't really thought about it," I admit, falling back into heavy silence once more.

Taking the mug from me, Thirteen places it on the floor by my feet. "Do you want to talk about what happened?"

"It's complicated."

"When is anything with these men not?" Six says, laughing softly.

I still don't know Six's story about how she came to be here, or what happened between her and Leon. She said that she thought she was in love with him once, and I want to understand what changed, why she still remains here, why she hasn't run.

"How did you come to be here, Six?" I ask, wanting more than anything to think about something other than these tumultuous feelings churning my stomach and making my head ache. "Tell me your story, so I can understand why you never tried to leave this place."

Six shifts around to face me, tucking her auburn hair behind her ear. "You truly want to know?"

"Yes. Please help me to understand."

She nods. "My real name is Nina Ricci. I was born in Northumberland, but I grew up in Florence, Italy. My father is, *was,* a British Diplomat. He loved his job, was good at it. When I was eighteen, he passed away six weeks after my mother died of cancer. Massive heart attack..."

"I'm sorry," I whisper. "Losing both your parents in such a short space of time must've been hard."

"It was..." Her voice trails off as tears prick at her eyes. She blinks them back and gives me a tremulous smile. "When they performed the autopsy on my father they said that his arteries were so blocked that it was a miracle he hadn't had a heart attack earlier. Honestly, though, I think he died of a broken heart."

"Losing people you love can do that," Thirteen says, a faraway look in her eyes that speaks of her own secrets and heartbreak.

"Thirteen?" I ask, pressing my fingers against her arm.

She shakes her head and gives me a small smile. "Ignore me. It's nothing. Go on, Six," she urges.

"I'd just been accepted to a prestigious opera academy in Milan when my father died," Six continues. "I bought a flat in the city with the money my parents left for me in their will and threw myself into my music. One night when I was singing in a bar to earn some extra cash and to gain more experience, I met Alonzo Ricci. He was handsome, charming, rich, and the son of the biggest mafia don in all of Italy. Of course, I didn't know that at the time, and by the time I'd found out how dangerous his family was, I'd already fallen deeply in love with him."

"Didn't he ever come looking for you?" I ask.

Six laughs, shaking her head. "We were married after a whirlwind courtship, but after a couple of months of marriage I knew I'd made a mistake. Alonzo loved the idea of me, and how I looked on his arm or on stage when I performed, but he never loved the true me. In fact, he had very little time for me outside of public functions. Most of the time he'd drink and fuck prostitutes rather than share a bed with his wife..." Her voice trails off as she sighs heavily. "Anyway, two years into our sham of a marriage, I sang for a private audience at the Ricci family estate. That same night Alonzo lost a game of cards to The Collector who was invited into their home for business. He'd heard me sing..."

"Your husband sold you?" I ask.

"He made a bet with The Collector. He lost. I was the prize."

"That's horrible."

Six shakes her head. "It felt that way at the time, but truthfully, despite what you might think, it was the best thing to happen to me. I couldn't divorce him because no one divorces a Ricci. Looking back, it was the only way out."

"You were trapped?"

"Yes, and now I'm free. I've found peace in this castle. A family. A purpose. I'm happy here. I know that's difficult to understand, but it's the truth nonetheless."

"So the Collector brought you back here after he won you in a game of cards, and gave you to Leon to break in," I say, remembering how Three had described what The Masks did to every Number when they first arrived at the castle.

"Exactly. Leon broke me down, he stripped back the layers of protection I'd built up as the wife of a man who never loved her, and made me into the woman you see before you now. I'm no longer Nina Ricci. I'm *Six*, and I'm stronger for it."

"But you're a *Number*."

"Yes, and that won't change. Not now. Not ever."

"I see."

"I don't think you do. I'm not a fool, Christy. I'm not under any illusions about this place, or about The Masks and the kind of men they are. I don't have Stockholm Syndrome. I choose to be here because I want to be, not because I'm forced to stay. Ardelby Castle isn't a prison. It's my home."

"Have you ever tried to leave?" I ask.

"No."

"Then how do you know that? If you've never tried to leave, how do you know that this isn't just a beautiful gilded cage?" I ask her.

Six heaves out a sigh. "Because I don't *feel* trapped. That's how I know."

"And Leon? You told me that you thought you were in love with him once. Are you?"

She squeezes my hand. "No, but he taught me how to be strong, and I will always be grateful to him for that."

"Okay," I reply, absentmindedly reaching for the spot where Konrad bit me, my fingers running over the little indents made by his teeth. I can only believe her, because what else can I do? My feelings towards these men are changing rapidly, and the more time I spend here, the more complicated they become.

"He hurt you," Six says, drawing my attention back to her.

My hand falls back into my lap. "I hurt him as well."

"You did?"

"Yes. Just like Twelve," I whisper, guilt about how I handled things suddenly pulling me up sharp. At the lake he'd swam away from me, but I'd chased him down. I'd sensed his weakness and I capitalised on it. I might feel differently now about Konrad, but I can't deny the truth that I wanted to bury myself in his heart so that I could break it later. My feelings, my emotions are so messed up by them that I couldn't see clearly, or think straight when I was around them. It's only now, with space and distance, that I see what I did.

"What?" Six asks.

"No," Thirteen says, shaking her head furiously. "Not like Twelve."

Six frowns. "What has Twelve got to do with this?"

"Everything." A sob breaks free from my lips at the memory of her hanging from the ceiling of that cell.

"Listen to me, Christy," Thirteen implores. "What happened between you and Konrad wasn't the same."

"You weren't there, you didn't see what went on between us. What I *did*," I argue.

What I'm going to do.

"Did you strap him down?"

"No," I shake my head.

"Did you drug him to make him hard?"

"No."

"Wait, what are you saying?" Six asks, looking between us both.

"Did you take something he didn't want to give?" Thirteen continues, ignoring her.

"He wanted to fuck me, but..."

"No buts. It's not the same," Thirteen says, firmly. "You didn't rape Konrad."

"Oh, God. Please tell me she *didn't*!" Six whispers.

Thirteen nods. "She did."

"Where is she now?"

Thirteen looks at Six, shaking her head. "I'm so sorry, Six, she's dead."

"They killed her?"

"No. Twelve hung herself."

Six visibly pales, the colour in her cheeks draining from her skin as tears pool in her eyes and fall from her lashes. My stomach churns, twisting in pain as Six gets up and rushes to the bathroom. I can hear her retching. I want to be sick too. Nausea rises up my throat and I double over, clamping a hand over my mouth.

"Don't do this. Don't punish yourself like this. It's *not* the same," Thirteen insists, rubbing my back gently.

"He'd just been through trauma, Thirteen," I manage to say.

"You *helped* him."

"No," I admit, shaking my head and fighting off the heavy pull of sleep that's beginning to creep up my spine. "I didn't set out to do that."

"What do you mean?" she asks, her voice low, soft.

I look at her and she moves in and out of focus as the sedative effects of the drink she gave me begin to take hold. I feel the familiar pull of oblivion just out of reach as it swarms at the edges of my consciousness.

"They hurt me so badly," I choke out, my eyelids drooping and my muscles beginning to relax. "I wanted to find a way to hurt them, too. I used sex like a weapon, just like his father used to do."

Thirteen presses her eyes shut briefly, when she opens them again they're brimming with tears. "Oh, Christy..."

"But what started out as a way to get revenge..." I slur, my body slumping into hers, "Ended up with me fighting *with* him. Konrad fought so hard against the darkness inside of him. I couldn't let him do it alone. I couldn't let him fail, even after everything he put me through. What kind of person does that make me?"

"A *good* person, Christy. A *kind* person. A *courageous* one," Thirteen says, her voice sounding far away. "You're nothing like Malik."

"I clung on so tight. So tight," I mutter, thinking about how desperately I tried to hold on to all that hate. "I failed."

"You didn't. You're healing them," Thirteen replies, misunderstanding me.

"You don't know anything," I mumble.

"But I do, Christy. I believe in the legend of The Weeping Tree. I believe in your mother's words and the truth of your heart. I believe that you're the one who'll love them the way they deserve to be loved, that they'll love you in return the right way with your help. Please don't give up on them, on yourself."

"It doesn't matter if I do end up loving them," I whisper, sleep pulling me under as my next words barely form. "Because they're going to die anyway. I'm going to kill them."

And with those last gut-wrenching words I fall into a deep, dreamless sleep.

AN ARM over my waist and warm breaths over my cheek wake me from my slumber as I blink back the heavy fog of sedation. Reaching down, I press my fingers against Thirteen's arm, only to draw back my hand quickly when I realise that it's far too masculine to be hers.

"Thirteen?" I whisper, wondering if we're back in Leon's

room and she's sleeping on the chaise lounge just a few feet away.

"Shh, you'll wake him," a deep voice says from the other side of the room.

"Leon?"

"Yes," he replies, stepping closer. I feel the mattress dip as he slides under the covers and I catch his outline in the strip of muted light coming through the gap in the curtains. "I didn't think you'd be awake for hours yet."

"What time is it?"

"Still early. Sun's coming up. I was about to leave, to go and find Jakub."

"You know where the cabin is?"

"Vaguely. He mentioned its location once. I'll find him."

"Okay," I nod, my stomach tightening in knots at the thought of Jakub returning to the castle. "Where are we?"

"In Konrad's bedroom. I figured Thirteen could do with a night in her own bed without any of us taking up her space, so I carried you back here. How are you feeling?"

Behind me, Konrad shifts restlessly, muttering nonsensical words in his sleep. "I feel okay," I lie, feeling far from it. My stomach is cramping from the pill Thirteen gave me and my heart is bruised from everything that's happened over the past few days.

Leon smiles, resting his head on the cushion next to me, his minty breaths mingling with mine. Running a finger over my birthmark, he pushes a few strands of hair behind my ear. "You're a very pretty liar," he says with a soft chuckle.

"I'm not," I protest.

"What, pretty or a liar? Because you've always been pretty —beautiful in fact—and right now you're lying."

"This isn't easy for me."

"Want to tell us how you really feel?"

"Us?"

"Sleep is for the dead," Konrad says from behind me, as he presses his nose into my neck and inhales deeply. "You smell like all the things a man like me doesn't deserve."

My heart pitter-patters inside my chest, betraying me. "I thought you were asleep?"

"I was. I'm not now."

There's a note of promise in his voice, and despite everything, my traitorous clit flutters right at the same time that my stomach cramps. Looks like my body has the same reaction to these men as my emotions.

Pain and pleasure. Love and hate.

Love...

Do I love these men?

Of course I don't. I wouldn't be willing to poison them if I did. I force that thought away, unwilling to face it or the future that's hurtling towards us all at a brutal pace.

"Are you in pain?" Konrad asks me as I let out a small moan, partly caused by another cramp and partly just from despair.

"Thirteen gave me something to prevent an unwanted pregnancy..."

"Shit!" Konrad exclaims, burying his face in my hair and pressing his hand against my belly as he rubs it gently, his warmth seeping into my skin. "I'm sorry."

"We'll do better. Be better," Leon says, as he brushes his lips against mine in a sweet, loving kiss.

"Are you bleeding?" Konrad asks, his lips trailing over my neck, along my jaw. My skin covers in goosebumps with every hot press of his mouth. The air between us thickens with undeniable lust and despite the confusion in my heart, my body reacts to them both.

I nod, feeling the telltale wetness between my legs. "I should take a bath..."

He growls into my ear, nipping it gently with his teeth. "Don't go... I need to taste you," he says, his mouth hovering over my ear as his hand skims over my stomach, towards my pussy.

"Taste me?" I blurt out, squirming beneath his hand.

"Yes, let me make you feel better. Let me show you I can be gentle too."

"But I'm..." Heat floods my cheeks at the thought.

"You think a little blood scares me, Christy? I'd happily drown in it."

"I don't—" I begin, my hand squeezing his, halting its descent to my pussy.

"Want this, me, *us*?" Konrad asks, trying to hide his hurt but failing.

"No, that's not it," I whisper, twisting my head so I can look at him.

"Then what?"

"I should hate you still. I should hate you both."

"You'd be right to," he counters, brushing his lips gently against mine.

"Perhaps." I sigh, releasing his hand, cupping his face instead. I run my finger over the scar on his cheek wishing I didn't see what I had coming in our future. "Right now, I don't want to remember all of that. I don't want to hate."

"I've marked you, *hurt* you." Konrad says, his fingers trailing over the bite marks and the bruises he inflicted. "I'm sorry."

"Me too," I whisper, running my fingers over the marks I made on his back.

"What do you need from us?" Leon asks, rubbing the tip of his nose against my cheek, kissing me gently.

"Help me to forget the past. Help me to be present in this moment, right now," I say.

"That we can do," Konrad says, pressing an opened-mouth kiss against my collarbone. "Let me taste you."

I nod, giving him permission to do just that.

"Fuck yes," Leon hisses as Konrad rears upwards, lifting my dress up and over my hips with the movement. He eases my legs apart, settling himself between them, his large frame edged in soft oranges and pinks as dawn rises and sunlight filters through the gap in the curtain.

"Look at you. You're fucking beautiful," he says, removing my knickers and trailing his thick finger through my folds. I jerk beneath his touch, heat flooding my sex at the carnal way he looks at me. "I'm going to kiss your pussy better and Leon is going to worship those pretty tits of yours whilst I do it. We're going to make you come so fucking hard, Christy."

"Show her, Kon. Show her how good it can be with us," Leon urges, resting his palm against my bare stomach as he gives me an open-mouthed kiss over the teeth marks on my neck Konrad had inflicted yesterday, soothing them with his lips and tongue.

"Every day for as long as she remains here," Konrad replies, lowering his face to my pussy and licking me from crack to slit before I can even question what he meant by that.

All conscious thought escapes me as Konrad delivers what he promised and fucks me with his tongue. He laps at me, his tongue swirling over my clit, alternating between licking, flicking and sucking as he slides one, then two thick digits inside of me.

"You taste just like I imagined," he growls, the deep rumble of his voice vibrating through my core.

"Oh god." I let out a moan of pleasure that Leon captures

with his mouth in a kiss that leaves me breathless. My stomach cramps combined with his expert touch make for a confusing mixture of pleasure and pain. I don't hate it.

"No, not him. God can't make you feel this sinful, Christy. Only us," Leon mutters against my skin, trailing his lips down my neck, kissing and sucking at the tender flesh just above my pulse as Konrad scrapes his teeth gently over my clit. I let out another moan, my body melting beneath their combined touch as Leon draws up my dress then pinches my nipple between his finger and thumb. The sharp pain added to Konrad's relentless licking has my back arching off the bed.

"Keep still," Konrad demands gruffly, reaching up and pressing my hips into the bed with his hands as he plunges his tongue into my core. The scent of my arousal mixed with the distinct metallic tang of menstrual blood fills the air and my cheeks heat at the carnality.

"Ohhh," I call out, embarrassment and lust fighting for dominance.

Half of me wants to scramble away from him, the other half wants to open my legs wider and grasp them both closer to me. Either way, I'm not going anywhere because both men have me spread open and pinned to the bed like one of the butterflies on display in Jakub's room of curiosities, its beauty captured within a moment of time, destined to be admired but long since dead.

Except I'm not dead. I'm very much alive.

I'm *alive*.

Leon massages my breasts in his hands, moving between one nipple then the other as he sucks, licks and nips at me, whilst Konrad crooks his fingers and presses against a spot deep inside of me, rubbing gently.

"Please," I cry, my fingers curling into the sheet as I whimper in pleasure at their combined torture. Sensation builds deep inside of me as these men play with my body as much as they fuck with my head. I writhe beneath them, losing a part of myself to their touch, to their mouths, to the pleasure they give me. Konrad rears backwards, the loss of his mouth on my pussy making me cry out loud.

"Don't worry, I've got you, Christy," he says, grasping my hips and dragging me to the end of the bed. He kneels on the floor, his hands cupping my arse as he lifts my legs over his shoulders then dives back into my pussy.

Licking.

Sucking.

Fucking me with his tounge.

My eyes roll back in my head as I let my senses take over. I push all thoughts out of my head, refusing to think about anything other than how they're making me feel right now, here in this moment. Leon moves down the bed too, his hands, lips and mouth finding my breasts as he continues to suck, nip and lick my nipples.

"Christy," they mutter in unison.

This fire between us builds, it takes over. It breaks down every wall between us. It devours all the wrongs, burning them to ash whilst conjuring a sensation deep within my core. It builds, wild and fierce, powerful and strong until I'm coming hard. With my eyes pressed shut, my back arching, my mouth open wide on a passionate scream, I come. I come, tears sliding down my temple as I shudder, my body jerking against Konrad's face.

"That's it, Christy, sing for us," Leon says, capturing my cry with his lips, plunging his tongue into my mouth and kissing me with the edges of his soul until my orgasm ebbs away leaving me relaxed, satiated, calm, *content*.

When the final tendrils of my orgasm disperse, Leon slides

off the bed as Konrad climbs back in, pulling me into his chest and curving around my body.

We both watch him as he gets dressed. "Rest, I'll be back as soon as I can."

"Bring him home," Konrad says.

"I will." Leon nods, flicking his gaze to me. "Jakub's going to be at his worst, Christy, this won't be easy."

"When has it ever been easy," I murmur, watching him leave as my skin breaks out in goosebumps and another vision pulls me under.

CHAPTER TWENTY-FOUR

Christy

BEFORE I'VE EVEN OPENED my eyes, I know that this vision is going to damage me deeply. I can sense it. There's an age-old darkness that pulls at my ghostlike limbs, its sharp claws trying to find purchase, and when it can't do that, it simply wraps around me, smothering me in years of vile gloom. Something tells me that this is another vision from the past, the edges feel worn and torn like that of an old letter. I fight the pull, wishing I could fall into the arms of sleep like normal people. I'd even take a nightmare over this, but I know there is nothing I can do but to open my eyes and accept what the universe deems fit to show me...

. . .

"YOU THINK *that just because my blood runs in your veins that you're immune to my wrath?"* Malik snarls, his bloodied fingers swiping a scarlet trail down Jakub's cheek.

"No, Sir," he replies, flinching from his touch, his teeth chattering as he folds his skinny arms around himself into a tight ball, trying and failing to stave off the cold that creeps into the wooden cabin, covering the bare wood in a light dusting of frost.

Jakub's reaction only serves to anger his father further. Malik raises his hand, slapping him so hard across the back of the head that Jakub falls forward onto the floorboards, his forehead cracking against the wood.

"Get up!" Malik roars, gripping his hair and yanking him upright before he's even had the chance to right himself.

"F—father, please!"

"Please, father. Stop it, father. I'll do better, father. Ugh, you simpering fool."

Malik lets him go, but not before pulling out a clump of hair. The strands fall to the floor like the tiny flakes of snow drifting outside the open door, a few finding their way into the cabin and landing on Jakub's naked skin.

Trying to hold back his tears, Jakub uncurls his body and pushes upwards on shaky legs. Around his ankles are iron manacles and a long chain fixed to the cabin wall. He's so thin that his ribcage is visible beneath his skin and his stomach is concave. It's hard to tell given he's so malnourished, but he looks to be about sixteen years old.

"That's it, stand like a man!" Malik says, cracking his neck as he trails his fingers along a row of rusty torture implements. They look well-used.

If I could throw up, I would.

"Father, I will accept my punishment like a man. I won't disappoint you again."

Malik barks out a laugh, his black eyes wild with insanity as he regards his son. "I have a feeling you'll still disappoint me long after death comes to claim me," he replies with a sneer, picking up a chisel and a small wooden mallet.

"I won't," Jakub retorts, swallowing hard. His Adam's apple bobs up and down as his father approaches, but despite the fear written across his face, he manages to maintain eye contact. Something tells me that if he looks away now, his father will drive that chisel into his heart.

"You know I really should've drowned you the moment you were born, and I would've done that if I didn't think your whore of a mother would miscarry even more of my children. Ironic that you were strong enough to survive her inhospitable womb, but turned out to be weak as shit. Such a fucking disappointment."

Jakub's eyes flash with pain, but he remains tall despite such hateful words, showing strength even when he's covered head to toe in bruises, lashes and cuts. The sections of his skin unmarred by such cruel hands are mottled with cold. There's no doubt he's suffering from hypothermia.

"Do what you need to do," Jakub says, lifting his chin defiantly.

Malik sneers, a cruel smile pulling up his lips. "I don't need your permission to do whatever the fuck I want to you. You're my flesh and blood, I own you. Now bend your arm and give me your elbow," he demands. "But I warn you, if you scream, cry or even fucking puke I'll leave you out here in the cold to die."

Jakub nods, gritting his teeth as he does what his father instructs. With the bony point of his elbow raised, Jakub watches as his father places the rusty, blood-caked chisel against the tip of the bone then slams the mallet against the handle, shearing off skin and a slither of bone.

Jakub screams. It rips out of him in a cry so filled with pain and despair that I feel every inch of what he's feeling. We both fall to our knees, me grabbing my stomach, him clutching his bloody elbow.

Malik laughs, dropping the torture implements on the floor before twisting on his feet and striding towards the door, Jakub's desolate cries of pain following him out. When he reaches the porch just beyond, Malik turns on his heel and looks back at Jakub.

"I want the demon that I know lives within you. Only he is worthy of the Brov legacy. If you survive three days and nights out here in the cold then I will give you one last chance to prove yourself to me. Let's see how you fare against Mother Nature, shall we?"

And with that, Malik strides off into the forest leaving his abused son naked and curled up in a ball in the corner of the cabin.

The sobs that follow are heartbreaking, and even though this is a vision of something that's already happened, I can't help but crawl towards Jakub so that I can rest my ghostly hand on his shoulder and will him to feel the empathy that pours from me in a torrent of salty tears.

"Please, help me," he whispers, staring right into my eyes as though he can see me, as clearly as I see him now. Except this time he isn't a malnourished sixteen year old boy half dead with hypothermia and covered in bruises, he's a man. I'm staring into the face of the man I've come to know these past weeks and he's utterly broken...

"*JAKUB!*" I scream, waking up with a start, my whole body shaking as bile burns my throat. The after effects of such a harrowing vision disturbing my equilibrium as the bed seems to undulate beneath me.

"Christy, what is it?" Konrad asks, snapping awake. He reaches for me in the dark, his hand finding my thigh which is covered in a sheen of sweat just like the rest of me is.

Konrad moves away from me briefly, flicking on the bedside lamp, before capturing my face in his hands. "Are you sick?"

I shake my head. "We need to go to him. We need to go to him now," I say, tears falling unbidden down my cheek.

"To who?"

"Jakub. He needs us."

"What?"

"He needs us. We have to go. Now!"

"I CAN'T GET ANY SERVICE," Konrad says with frustration as he tucks his phone back into his pocket. "The forest is too dense and we're too far from the castle."

We've been walking for an hour, and every so often Konrad tries to call Leon but with no luck. Every minute it takes to get to them is another minute too long. I have this sense of impending doom that just won't leave me. "How far into the forest is the cabin situated? Leon left a while ago," I say, trying and failing to hide my increasing concern.

"I'm not certain. Malik only ever took Jakub to the cabin. What I do know is that it's built on a meadow somewhere near the centre of the forest. If we keep walking in this direction we should get to it soon," Konrad replies, taking my hand as he helps me over a fallen tree. But despite his assistance I still manage to stumble, my jumper snagging on a branch as I tip forward. Konrad steadies me, his large hands finding my hips as

I slam into his chest, knocking the air from my lungs. I gasp, the world spinning for a moment. The side effects of the vision still linger like a bad smell and makes me want to throw up.

"Shit, sorry," I mumble, placing a shaking hand against his broad chest.

"I got you." He looks down at me, his blue eyes shrouded by dark hair, his face free from his mask that he removed and tucked into his backpack the moment we were deep enough into the forest. "Your cheeks are flushed. Should I be worrying?"

"No," I say softly, easing myself out of his arms as I breathe in deeply. "This is normal after I experience a vision."

Brushing a strand of hair off my face, his fingers trail over my cheeks as he stares into my eyes. "I knew from the moment I looked into your eyes that there was something special about you. You have an incredible gift."

"More of a curse," I mutter, a chill running down my spine at the memory of what I saw in my vision.

"What did you see exactly?" he asks, tucking my hand in his, as we continue to make our way through the forest.

"Jakub in the cabin as a child. Malik had him chained to the wall. He was naked, malnourished, beaten black and blue, covered in cuts and scrapes." I blow out a steady breath, willing strength into my voice. Konrad remains eerily quiet as I speak, and when I glance up at him his features are tight, a muscle in his jaw jumping from how hard he grits his teeth. "Malik took a chisel to his elbow, slicing off the skin and some bone."

"Fuck!" Konrad shouts, sending a squirrel that had been sitting on a low branch watching our approach scurrying up the tree.

"I'm so sorry for everything you've been through," I say, guilt climbing up my throat at the thought of what's to come. "Konrad, I *must* tell you something. I saw—"

He glances at me, then shakes his head. "Whatever it is, I don't want to know. It was hard enough surviving the past, I don't want to relive it again," he admits.

"But this isn't about your past," I say, stopping and tugging on his hand. He chews on the inside of his cheek, flicking his gaze from my face to the dense forest beyond.

"Then it's about our future?"

"Yes. Something happens—"

"Did your mother ever tell you what was coming in your future?"

"No," I say, shaking my head. "At least not whilst she was alive."

"You received a letter, too?"

"Yes." *And a visit from beyond the grave.*

"What did it say?"

"Mostly what I already knew. She also reminded me of what I'd forgotten."

"Forgotten?"

"About the fire, and Leon saving me..."

"You beat the shit out of him because you remembered what he did, didn't you?"

"Yes," I admit.

"She's sneaky, your mum, a true Dálaigh. What a way to get revenge," he says with a wry grin.

"No," I shake my head. "She wasn't like that. All that anger was my own and had nothing to do with her. In fact, in the letter she asked me to remember who *saved* me, not who killed her. She was trying to help me remember the boy who pulled me from the fire, not the one who lit it."

He observes me for a moment, thinking. "And in our letter she told us our paths were always destined to cross. That our fates are intertwined," he explains, cupping my hands in his and pressing a kiss against my knuckles. "She said that every action has a reaction, and every decision a consequence. She asked us to let you live, Christy..." His voice trails off as he bows his head in shame, his forehead pressing against my fists. "Your mother has been guiding us together, but at no point has she told us what our future will be. There has to be a reason for that."

"There is. My mother feared that if she told me what she saw in my future that there would be repercussions for me, and she didn't want to risk Fate's wrath."

Konrad nods. "Then that's a good enough reason not to tell me what you saw. I've already hurt you, I refuse to hurt you further by being selfish."

"But I—"

"No. I don't want to know what's coming, Christy. I just want to live in this moment with you for as long as I am granted the pleasure," he says, cupping my cheek gently. "Christ knows I don't deserve it, but I will take whatever time there is left apologising for every wrongdoing I've committed against you." Leaning down, he presses a gentle kiss against my mouth. "I'm sorry for hurting you. There won't be a moment that I don't feel guilt, regret. I'm sorry. Truly." His thumb finds my bottom lip as he pulls back. "I don't need to see the future to know I need to be with you here in the present."

"You don't know what you're saying," I mutter as he gently slides his thumb against my parted lips, silencing me.

"I know exactly what I'm saying, Christy. I'm not a fool, Leon might be burying his head in the sand and avoiding the very real fact that your family will come for you, but I'm not. They will come, and we will pay, I have no doubts about that. So please, let me take whatever time we have left and savour every moment of it."

With a heavy heart, I nod my head. "Okay."

After another half an hour of silent reflection, the forest begins to thin out and more sunlight streams through the canopy overhead, covering the forest floor with dappled light.

"We're here," Konrad says, pointing to a gap in the trees further ahead which sits a wooden cabin in a small clearing. "This is the place."

The cabin is made of dark wood and has a low-pitched roof covered in ivy that creeps across its entirety. Long grass grows up the sides of the building, and what once was a deck is now just broken wood overtaken by weeds. There are no windows, and the door is hanging off its hinges as though someone has kicked it in. It's everything nightmares are made of.

No, it's where nightmares were endured.

My skin instantly covers in goosebumps as my stomach churns violently at the oppressive darkness that emanates from within the cabin. My body's reaction is instant and brutal.

"I'm going to be sick," I say, twisting my body away from Konrad before projectile vomiting.

"Christy, what is it? Is this your period or the vision?" Konrad asks, rubbing my back as I empty the contents of my stomach.

"Neither," I manage to choke out, my eyes watering as I slowly find the strength to stand upright. "Don't you feel that?"

"Feel what?"

"The evil that seeps from that place. It's so strong, so overwhelming," I whisper.

He reaches for me, pulling me against his chest and hugging me tightly, his hand cupping the back of my head. "Not anymore, not now when I have you."

CHAPTER TWENTY-FIVE

Jakub

A FEW HOURS *earlier*

EVERY INCH of skin on my chest and back is torn and weeping blood from the whippings One gave me and the lashings I gave myself. Deep purple bruises bloom on my stomach, thighs and upper chest from my own fists and the paddle One used at my request. There isn't a single part of my body that's left unmarked in some way.

Pulling aside my shirt, I press my finger into one of the tears on my pec, watching the newly formed scab open and weep more blood, and even though I should feel pain, I don't. Overwhelmed and unable to take any more, my mind has switched off the link to my pain receptors.

Physically I'm numb.

But there's no release for me here, none, because without pain distracting me all I can do is *feel*.

I'm sick with emotion. Tortured by feelings.

I'm ruined by empathy and fucking compassion.

I'm bound. I'm chained. I'm a fucking prisoner to it all.

There is no light, no end to my misery, no fucking escape. All these feelings are holding me hostage. So all I can do is hope that my father's ghost and all of the memories inside of the cabin will set me straight once and for all. It's the last thing I can think of doing. If this doesn't work, then nothing will, and death is all I have left.

Stepping into the clearing, I breathe out little white clouds as I stare at the ramshackle cabin that has no windows and only one way in and out. When I was a kid, this place was the antithesis of hope. It was helplessness, hopelessness. It was agony, misery and suffering. My father brought me here to beat and torture every last shred of kindness, empathy, and love out of me and each time he did, it had worked. For a time at least. But, eventually, I'd slip back into my old habits and he'd have to do it all over again.

The last time I was here was when I was sixteen. Konrad had been busy with Three, breaking her in, and Leon was out of the castle on a business errand for my father. I had taken a walk in the grounds and came across a rabbit that had been caught in one of the numerous traps my father had placed around the estate gardens. The wire snare was wrapped around its hind leg as it struggled to get away, but with every movement the wire cut deeper into its flesh. By the time I'd found it, the rabbit's leg was almost severed.

My first mistake was cutting it free.

My second mistake was wrapping it in my jumper and taking it back to my room.

My third, being caught by my father crying over its lifeless form an hour later.

Tears weren't tolerated in our household. Empathy and kindness were treated like a sickness to be bled out of us. I'm covered in hundreds and hundreds of silvery scars all over my body from sessions with my father and his knife. Most of them have been obliterated by new scars inflicted by my own hand and One's whip, but the thing with scars is that it doesn't matter how many are on the surface, the worst ones are those that you can't see. I'm riddled with them both externally and internally. I have scars upon scars upon scars, and every single one has a horrifying memory to accompany it.

"You're pathetic!" My father had said. *"Weak for crying over a fucking rodent."*

But I wasn't crying over the rabbit. Not really. I'd seen hundreds of rabbits snared in traps before, either dead or dying, but I'd never had the urge to set them free like I had that day. Maybe it was because my true impulses were beginning to show themselves again after being repressed for so long, or maybe it was because on that day, in that moment, the rabbit had reminded me of myself. Trapped and desperate to escape with absolutely no hope of ever being able to.

I'd cried at the futility of it all, for the fight that rabbit had to endure, and for the life it had lost so brutally. I'd cried because everything seemed so fucking hopeless. That no matter what I did, or how many times my father would beat me I'd still *feel*.

I think he'd known that too. So after a session with One, he dragged me to the cabin kicking and fucking screaming. It was the first time I'd genuinely fought him, and boy did he make me pay.

For two weeks, he kept me in the cabin. He beat me until I passed out. Whipped me until the walls of the cabin were painted with my blood. He called me names, then spat on me. He starved me. He watched me shit myself and forced me to sit in it. Then, just when I thought I'd survived the worst of it, he took a chisel to my elbow and sliced off skin and bone and left me for dead. He took every last shred of humanity I had left and decimated it with his abuse.

He expected me to be a corpse on his return. He didn't expect me to survive.

Only I did, or at least a part of me had.

That boy who'd cried over the lifeless body of a rabbit had died on the cabin floor, and in his place the demon my father had always wanted was born. If I hadn't brought Nothing into our home, that boy would have remained dead and buried.

You and I both know that boy never really died, he just disappeared for a while.

"Shut the fuck up!" I shout, striding towards the cabin.

With every step that voice inside my head gets louder. The boy I once was desperately trying to make me change my mind and turn back around. He wants no part of this torture. He doesn't want to step inside the place that broke him. He doesn't want to sit within its bitter gloom and suffocate on the vile defecation of his past.

He wants the woman I call Nothing. *He* wants Christy.

But neither of us can have her. Not the boy, and certainly not the demon I am.

We don't deserve kindness, happiness, empathy, fucking love.

We're useless, weak, pathetic, a piece of fucking shit.

And the only way to rid myself of every feeling I'm suffering from is to step back inside the cabin and into the pits of Hell.

"BROTHER?" A familiar voice says.

I ignore it. I ignore everything other than my father's voice.

"No son of mine will be some animal loving, spluttering cry-baby. Płacz, a dam ci powód do płakania, ty draniu!"

He always said that; "Cry and I'll give you something to cry about, you little bastard."

It was his favourite saying, and he always followed up his threat with the promise of pain.

Every time, with no exceptions.

My ruined back scrapes against the rough wood of the wall as I relive the punches and the kicks, the slaps and whippings, the slashes of his knife as he cuts my skin. My stomach churns as I recall the stinging warmth of his piss on my open sores and the feeling of gratefulness because I'd been so fucking cold and at least it had warmed me up.

"Worthless. Fucking. Cunt," he'd said whilst emptying his bladder all over my abused body.

I remember clutching my knees to my chest, just like I'm doing now, hoping that eventually he'd tire of beating me. He never did. I think the fact I stayed alive both impressed him and pissed him off. Either way, he took his rage and disappointment out on me over and over again.

I relive the shame and the horror, the self-disgust and the embarrassment as memory after memory scatters around me like dead leaves falling to the forest floor. Each one is just as painful as the next. I wish I had the strength to crush them under my feet, to pulverise them into dust but I don't, and that's just as well because I need these memories. I need them to turn me back into the demon my father moulded with bloodied fists, harsh words and rage.

So I remain huddled in the corner of the cabin, naked and vulnerable as old scars are rubbed at and sliced open. I bleed out, new blood on top of old. It dribbles through the self-inflicted crevices and cracks as I paint the wall scarlet with every shudder and shake until I'm drowning beneath memories so painful, so violent, that I withdraw deep inside. I sink back into oblivion under the weight of it all.

Coming here hasn't made me stronger. It's broken me once and for all.

I have nothing left to give. No strength left to fight.

There is only horror. Pain. Regret. Sadness. *Guilt*.

I wish I could be angry, but any anger I have is aimed at myself and the things I've done.

God, the people I've hurt. The pain *I've* caused. It sits like a mountain on my shoulders, crushing me into the ground and pulverising my bones. My shoulders are no longer strong enough to carry the weight of my sins. I can't be the man my father wanted me to be, and I can't be the man the boy I once was wished I could be. I'm just a tormented soul that has lived too long, and fought too hard.

I've carried the weight of my sins for an eternity.

I'm exhausted.

I'm done.

With one last ragged breath, I allow my body to slip to the floor. Any lingering warmth seeps out of me as my soul begins to untether, freeing itself from the confines of the cage I've kept it locked up in. I feel as though I'm floating, carried on a gentle current away from this mutilated body that could no longer house a soul that was both manufactured villain and inherently good. With every second that passes, I welcome the cold hands of oblivion and *peace*...

Only oblivion comes in the form of warmth and heat, gentleness and sympathy, kindness and empathy. It's tentative at first, a light dusting that flutters over my skin. Then that feather touch becomes gentle strokes, and I feel the warmth seeping into my skin, gliding through my veins as it reaches for the last tendrils of my soul and holds on tight.

It wants me to stay alive.

But I don't want to live like this anymore.

No! I protest. *No. I want to die. Let me go.*

A battle rages within me behind sightless eyes, as I try to leave my body behind, but the warmth keeps coming. It tugs on my soul as it roams over my skin, gently imbuing heat and life back into my cold, broken body. It urges me to stay alive. It moves from my shoulder, down my arm before squeezing my hand, willing me to hold on.

But I don't want to. I don't want to.

"I came. I'm here," she says softly.

She.

Her.

The girl we stole.

The girl we imprisoned.

The girl I hurt.

Nothing...

Christy.

She offers sanctuary with her touch, a home in her arms that I don't deserve, but one I've longed for my whole pitiful existence. I've been so cruel to her and yet, here she is, comforting me in this fucking place filled to the brim with pure, undiluted evil.

She shouldn't be here.

My body jerks, electrical currents building beneath my skin, snapping and crackling, forcing life into my pulse as it pounds loudly in my ears.

Thump. Thump. Thump.

I fight hard to let go but she fights harder to hold on.

One minute I'm slipping back under, the next hauled towards the surface.

Back and forth I'm pulled between life and death.

She doesn't give up, she doesn't let go, and like the currents of the sea I feel myself returning to the shore, drawn to her just like I have been since the moment we stole her.

Warm breath hovers over my cheek as she whispers in my ear, "This isn't the day you die."

The words are given softly, spoken gently. There's no hate, no intent to harm, just honesty.

Just the truth.

This isn't the day I die.

And just like that my soul reattaches, locking into place.

Click. Click. Click.

With consciousness comes pain. It thunders through every inch of me and forces a scream to rip out of my throat as the world and everything in it comes crashing back in full, agonising technicolour. I feel it all at once. Everything that my body had turned off is suddenly and irreversibly switched back on.

It hurts.

It motherfucking hurts.

Every cut, slash, bruise and break rips me open. Every memory. Every act of violence and cruelty. I relive it all in one single rush of pain that arches my spine, lifting me off the floor, sending my legs and arms flying outwards like a baby slipping from its mother's arms.

I'm on fire. I'm a mass of agony, misery and torment.

My teeth grind together. My knuckles threaten to break free from my skin from how hard my hands are fisted. My elbows, arse and heels press into the hardwood floor, reminding me of injuries inflicted on the boy who crawls towards her through the mire of our past, desperate for comfort, for love, for a drop of human kindness. He writhes beneath my skin, desperate to shake free from the man he grew into. But it's no use because he's pushed back by the hurricane of pain whipping up old wounds and merging them with recent ones.

There's no release. Not this time.

This is my penance. This is retribution for all the bad *I've* done, all the sins I've committed because I wasn't brave enough to say fucking no.

"It hurts. God it hurts," I grind out, my head tipped back against the wooden floorboards, my neck strained, my muscles taught. My blood is like acid in my veins, burning it's way through my body and sliding from the newly-scabbed wounds that rip open from all the writhing.

"Brother, easy now," Leon placates.

I don't question how he's here. I have no recollection of when he arrived, but as he moves into my peripheral vision, I'm grateful for his presence. We've always shared our pain, and this time is no different. Another scream rips out of me and my body shudders violently.

Leon grasps my shoulders, pinning me to the floor. "Hold him down. He'll hurt himself more if we don't restrain him."

Another pair of hands wrap around my ankles as I judder and shake, twist and turn. I recognise his touch. Konrad.

"We're here, just ride it out," he says, his voice thick with emotion, with *love*.

And I feel it. I feel their love for me. It floats around me, uncertain but there. Tentative but hopeful. As kids we forged a deep bond through mutual suffering and a desperate need to belong, to find affection even if it wasn't readily given. We buried that love deep inside, holding it close to our hearts so our father wouldn't pry it away from feeble hands that weren't strong enough to fight him off. I'm grateful for their presence, but it's not their touch that forces my eyes open, that pulls me back from the brink, that soothes the boy *and* the man, that comforts my soul.

It's *hers*.

"Shh, it's okay now. We're here," she whispers, her fingers trembling as she cups my cheek in her hands, stroking my skin with a tenderness I've no right to receive. "Just listen to my voice. Concentrate on my touch. Okay?"

My heart thumps painfully as a groan releases from my mouth, the electric current of my pain ebbing away with every gentle stroke of her fingers. She caresses my skin like a mother would her sick child and I so want to curl into her touch, seek warmth and safety in her hold.

But I've no right. I've no right to want such things, so I flinch away instead.

"Don't fight this. Just let me do this for you, *please*," she begs, her voice trailing off as she chokes on the words, like it's as hard for her to offer up her kindness as it is for me to receive it.

My eyes refocus, muted light creeping into the darkness as she leans over me, her long hair falling in a curtain around us both. We lock gazes as guilt and gratitude fight for my attention. I don't know how to form the words to apologise, to beg for forgiveness, so I do nothing but stare at the woman who's turned my whole world inside out, and who's saved me from death when I only granted hers.

"Let him go," she orders softly, a host of emotions passing over her features as she looks up at my brothers.

I feel the absence of their touch as the warmth of their fingers is replaced with cool air. Without them pinning me down, I turn on my side and clutch my legs to my chest in self-comfort, because even though my soul may have found its way back into my body, I don't have the strength to stand, to do anything other than lie here, utterly vulnerable and at her mercy. She could kill me now and I wouldn't have the strength to fight her off. Not that I would. It's the least I deserve.

Except there's no violence, there's only kindness as she lays down beside me on this disgusting, dirty floor and wraps her body around mine, her arms circling my back, her thighs pressing against my shins, her nose brushing the tip of mine.

I don't move.

I barely breathe.

A bone-weary tiredness washes over me, drawing me into a different kind of oblivion. My eyelids begin to droop and I don't fight the pull of sleep, too exhausted to stay awake.

"I'm sorry," she whispers.

"For what?" I murmur, fighting to stay conscious because it should be me who's apologising, not her. Seconds tick by as she stares right into the very depths of me.

"For what's to come..." she replies sadly, just as I'm dragged into a deep, dreamless sleep.

CHAPTER TWENTY-SIX

Konrad

"FIVE, SIX, SEVEN, EIGHT," One calls, her voice keeping to the beat she plays on the grand piano.

Two twirls across the stage beside her, then misses a step, stumbling over her feet. "Shit!" she exclaims, righting herself.

One slams her hands onto the keys. "There will be no mistakes!"

"I'm doing the best I can, One. This isn't exactly my forte," Two replies, swiping a hand over her sweaty forehead as the two women glare at each other.

"I don't care. We need a dancer, and you're the closest we have to one given Three is out of action and Zero is nowhere to be seen."

"I perform aerial acrobatics, I'm not a miracle worker."

"Again goddammit!"

Beside me, Christy shifts uncomfortably. She's been distant, troubled, and hasn't wanted to leave Jakub's side. She's barely slept since we brought him back to the castle last night, so I thought a change of scenery might help. Then again, bringing her here probably wasn't the best decision I've ever made. In fact, given I've called all the Numbers to the studio to tell them about Twelve, it's the fucking worst. But we're here now, and this has to happen. It's time to face the music and, selfishly, I'd rather do it with Christy by my side, given Leon's making arrangements for Twelve's burial and can't be here.

"Her timing is off, she just needs to concentrate when counting the beats," Christy says quietly from the darkened corner we're standing in.

"Is that right?" I reply, failing at finding any words, much less ones that will reassure her. Watching her and what she did for Jakub yesterday will forever be ingrained in my soul. Without her kindness and empathy, I've no doubt we'd have lost him for good. Thirteen might be able to heal his wounds, but only Christy can heal his heart and soothe his soul.

Only her.

At least I have to believe that's what she's been able to do because he is yet to wake up and tell us for himself.

"Two has the ability and the grace needed for what One's trying to achieve, she just needs practice and time," Christy murmurs.

"Is a couple of weeks enough time?" I ask, adjusting my mask so that it sits more comfortably on my face.

"A couple of weeks?" she repeats sharply, and I know at that moment that whatever she's seen in our future has something to do with the night of the ball.

"Yes, The Brònach Masquerade Ball is in a little over two weeks."

Her gaze flicks to mine and she swallows hard. I see the

agony in her eyes and I want so much to relieve her of it that I almost, almost, ask her to give up her burden and share it with me, but then I remember what she said, that it'll only harm her in the long run, and shake my head free of the thought.

"Konrad, I wish that I could change the—" she begins, but I cut her off by grabbing her hand and pulling her against my chest.

"No, don't torture yourself. Stay in the present with me. Right now I need you by my side whilst I break the news to the Numbers. One thing at a time, okay?"

She curls her fingers into my shirt, as she allows me to comfort her. It feels good that I'm the one able to give her a tiny moment of reprieve. *Me*, a certified psychopath.

Tipping her head back, she looks up at me, her expression is one of resignation that quickly morphs into determination. "Okay, let's do this," she says, straightening her spine as she slides her hand into mine.

As we step out of our hiding place, Two takes a tumble, missing her steps and earning her another glare from One that I'm sure would've turned into another tirade had Christy not distracted her.

"You have all the steps in place, Two, just listen to the beat of the music and you'll get there eventually," Christy says.

One's head snaps up, her eyes narrowing on Christy. Her expression changes from one of blatant dislike to guarded suspicion as she glances at our linked hands. "Master, I didn't know you were standing there," she says, looking between us, her lips pursed as she ignores Christy completely. "What can I do for you?"

"Why is it only the pair of you? Where are the others?" I counter, irritated that they've not arrived despite my specific instructions for them to be here at nine am on the dot.

"On their way. I thought it would be advantageous to spend a little more time rehearsing this dance given Three is still... *recuperating*, and can't partake. I see you're better," she remarks, cutting Christy an unimpressed look. "Perhaps you could perform this dance instead of Two?"

"No!" I snap. "She won't be performing at the ball."

One's mouth presses into a hard line and I know she wants to question my decision, but she holds her tongue, plastering on a fake smile instead. "As you wish," she says, before motioning at Two. "I'm sure Master would like to see how hard you've been working on perfecting this dance for the ball. Shall we start from the top? No mistakes this time."

"Fine." Striding over to the centre of the floor, Two takes up her starting position and waits for One to count her in.

"Five, six, seven, eight." One's fingers fly over the piano keys as Two begins to dance, and whilst she starts off well, it isn't long before she stumbles over her steps, cursing as she hits the floor once again.

One slams her hands onto the keys in disgust, the sound reverberating around the hall. "What is wrong with you, Two? You need to get your shit together and step up until Three decides to drag her arse back to work instead of moping about."

"Three has stitches. She *isn't* moping about," Christy snaps, her eyes flashing with anger.

One blows out a breath then stands, pushing back from the piano. "I really don't know what all the fuss is about, it's not as if the rest of us haven't experienced a few stitches in our vaginas before. I've seen clients fuck her harder than Seven did at the dining table. Anyone would think—"

"That's enough!" I shout, cutting One off.

She nods tightly, hiding the blaze of anger that flashes across her face behind another fake smile. Which is just as well because behind us, the door to the studio opens and the rest of the Numbers, including Three and Seven, enter.

"Master," they each murmur in turn.

I can't help but notice how Four and Eight give Christy a disparaging look, taking their place beside One and Two. Clearly there's no love lost there. Three, Five, Six and Seven, however, react completely differently towards her. They each give her a warm smile that she returns in kind. Last to arrive are the triplets; Nine, Ten and Eleven. As usual they bring a childish vibe with them, giggling behind their hands as they enter the room, but instead of finding it mildly irritating like I usually do, it just makes me feel uncomfortable. I've turned a blind eye to their damage over the years, but that's not something I can do anymore. There are many things that need fixing, but first this.

Coughing to clear my throat, I squeeze Christy's hand, then let it go and walk into the centre of the room. "I asked you here today because—"

"Where's Twelve?" Four asks, cutting me off and earning her a scowl that immediately silences her. I may have fought and gained control of my monster for Christy, but I'll be fucked if I let Four disrepect me in such a manner, or any of the Numbers for that matter. She has the good grace to mumble her apology and I accept it way more graciously than I ever would've in the past. She's got Christy to thank for that.

"Twelve is the reason I've brought you all here this morning," I say, glancing around the room. My gaze falls on Five whose eyes flicker with acknowledgement. She dips her head giving me her silent support.

"How long will she be receiving punishment?" One asks, picking at her nails as though bored. "I really need her in good enough health so she can perform at the ball. I can't afford to lose another Number."

"Twelve isn't receiving punishment," I reply, locking eyes with her.

"Well if she hasn't been in the dungeons with you, then where the hell has she been? We have a show to prepare for and she's the first act, she *knows* this!"

"Twelve is dead."

The room descends into a deathly silence, punctuated by quiet sobs from Six.

"W—what do you mean, she's dead?" One stutters, her face paling. I see her thoughts running rampant through her head.

"Leon is arranging her burial. She will be laid to rest in the formal gardens the day after tomorrow."

"You killed her—?"

"No. Twelve hung herself. She took her *own* life."

"But why?"

I grit my jaw, pushing away the memory of that night. "She took something that didn't belong to her and she knew what the consequences would be, so instead of facing them she hung herself."

"What did she *take* exactly?" One's gaze falls onto Christy with suspicion, as though this is all her fault. It gets my back up, and I can feel my temper fraying.

"Something that belonged to *me*. Something she coveted," I reply, unwilling to give her the full story. I don't need to explain myself to One, to any of the Numbers. Not about this.

"This has something to do with you, doesn't it?" One accuses, focusing her attention back onto Christy, her dislike flaring.

"This has *nothing* to do with Christy," I interject.

"*Christy?*" One hisses, and the look she gives her is one of pure hate. Jealousy too. That is plain for everyone to see.

"Be very, very careful how you choose to continue, One."

Christy reaches for me, her fingers tightening around mine. She's afraid I'll let my monster run rampant. I won't. For her I'll keep it chained, but that doesn't mean I will allow her to be attacked so blatantly. One is pushing her fucking luck and I don't have the same ties to her as Jakub does.

Did. Like he *did*.

Because if that arsehole wakes up the same as he was before he took off to that fucking cabin, we're going to have an issue. One is not a part of his present or his fucking future, however brief. *Christy* is.

"I will repeat this one more time. Twelve's death had nothing to do with Christy. Is that understood?"

One blinks rapidly as she tries to regain some equilibrium. "Apologies, Master. This is all such a shock," she says, her hand fluttering to her chest. If she thinks for one second I believe her little act, she can think again.

The tension in the room rises as One struggles to figure out the best way to act in this situation, whilst the rest of Numbers deal with their genuine shock and sadness at the news. Three leans into Seven's embrace, Six is comforted by Five. The triplets huddle together, soundlessly crying. Even Four and Eight hold each other's hands, shock and fear plastering them to the spot. Two reacts much the same as One with disbelief and suspicion, and I can't help but wonder when she lost the ability to feel compassion. Was it before she arrived here like One, or did we strip it from her over the course of her life with us? Eventually One pulls herself together and gestures at Six who is sobbing quietly.

"Six will take Twelve's place, she can learn the aria. That is if the ball is still to go ahead of course?"

"Yes, it's still going ahead," I confirm.

"Good. But we still have the issue of Two underperforming and Three unable to perform. Without Twelve, we're stretched thin. I'm not positive we'll have a show worthy enough for the ball."

"Then I'll dance," Christy offers, her chin tipped up defiantly.

"No!"

"I *need* to do this."

"No," I repeat, glaring at her. "It's out of the question."

"You had no problem with me performing in the last show," she replies, folding her arms across her chest.

My anger flares, and I have the sudden inexplicable urge to put her over my knee and spank her arse for daring to fight me on this. "That was before!"

"Three can't perform," she says, calm in the face of my anger. She glances over at Three, giving her a supportive smile. "And she shouldn't be asked to until she's completely recovered. I can do this."

Shaking my head, I grip Christy's upper arm and walk her to the other side of the studio, backing her into the darkened archway we were standing in before. I don't give a fuck what the Numbers think.

"Out of the fucking question," I hiss, my anger uncorking. "You go up on that stage and you'll be the centre of attention. Do you know how fucking beautiful you are? How fucking alluring? Jesus, Christy, you turned our heads didn't you? The people who'll be attending this ball are not the kind of people you want attention from understand?"

"Konrad, this *has* to happen," she whispers, pressing her

palm against my chest and urging me to understand. Her ghost eyes blink up at me and I see the truth in them.

My fucking heart plummets. This has to happen because she's *seen* it.

"Fuck!" I exclaim, having the sudden urge to kiss her, to press her against the wall and ravage her mouth with mine and forget everything but us. Her fingers curl into my shirt and she meets my kiss half way. Drawn to me as much as I'm drawn to her.

I kiss her with fierce possession, grasping her hair and forcing her lips apart with my tongue. She kisses me back with apologies and secrets on her tongue. It's a desperate kiss that hardens my cock with desire, and I know if I don't pull away now I'll fuck her against this wall with the Numbers listening on. Stepping back abruptly, I let her go, and with one last lingering look, she steps around me and back in the room.

"I will learn Three's dance. I will perform at the ball in her place," she says, and my newly beating heart fucking chokes on its own blood.

CHAPTER TWENTY-SEVEN

Christy

JAKUB'S BEEN asleep for sixteen long hours. Thirteen and I have tended to his mutilated body, treating his wounds and bruises as best we can. Her potions and lotions are powerful and much of the redness around the cuts and lashes has paled, though it will be a long while before they've healed. His skin and wounds are clean and whilst the majority of his body is covered in bruises, there is some colour in his cheeks that wasn't there before.

"I'm concerned," Thirteen says, canting a look at me as she applies more ointment to a particularly stubborn wound that isn't reacting as well to the cream she's been applying religiously to it every hour on the hour.

"You think he needs antibiotics?" I ask.

"No," she replies, shaking her head. "These wounds will heal and he'll recover, I'm certain. I'm concerned about..." She sighs, wiping her hands on a handkerchief and reaching over to grab my hand. She squeezes it gently, our joined hands resting over the steady beat of Jakub's heart.

"What?"

"I'm concerned about you all. About your future."

"Our future?" I ask, feeling the thump of my pulse quickening.

"Do you remember what you said to me the other night?"

I look away, chewing on my bottom lip. "Yes, I do."

"And was that something you believed or something you saw?"

"I shouldn't have said anything..." My voice trails off as a thread of fear creeps up my spine. I squeeze her hands. "I *can't* say anything more."

"Why?"

"Because I don't want to tempt fate. I can't change what has to happen."

"*Has to?*" She cocks her head to the side, frowning.

"Yes, *has* to. Even if you try to run from Fate, it will catch up with you in the end. My mother learnt that the hard way."

"Then why have you been given a gift such as this if you can't use it to change the course of the future?" she whispers, even though there's no chance of waking Jakub up. He's completely oblivious to our conversation, so buried beneath fatigue that I'm starting to wonder whether he'll ever wake up.

"Because this isn't a gift," I reply. "It never was."

"But your mother sent the letters. She found a way to help," Thirteen protests.

"You're right, she did, but she never told me exactly what would happen, only that I can't fight what's written, that I mustn't make the same mistakes she did." I sigh, glancing at Jakub, at the dark shadows beneath his eyes and the tightness of his jaw even in sleep. "The only difference is now I'm no longer fighting it."

Thirteen nods in understanding. "I'm sorry it's such a burden knowing what's to come."

"Me too," I whisper, my voice trailing off as I look at Jakub's sleeping form.

I don't know what will happen when he wakes up, whether he'll be the same man who forced Seven to hurt Three or if he'll be someone different. All I know is that my mother was right, at least partially, because there *is* strength in forgiveness and bravery in compassion. I felt that acutely when I'd comforted Jakub whilst he fought his demons on the floor of that hellhole. He isn't a good man, but once upon a time he had the potential to become one. I saw that in the child he was. I felt that within the ruined boy still living inside of him as I wrapped my arms around Jakub and held them both, whilst he broke apart in my arms.

As he'd trembled beneath my touch, no more than a terrified animal past the point of lashing out, I couldn't help but wonder what kind of man he would've been if he'd been nurtured and loved the right way. Knowing that we'll never get the chance to find out fills me with a deep sorrow.

I don't understand the point of all of this. Why have our paths crossed in such a way if their journey comes to an abrupt end in the very near future? It makes no sense, and I've twisted myself up trying to unravel it all, trying to understand the point of all of this heartache.

The only thing I know to be certain is that Grim, Beast and Ford are coming, and soon. I'm going to carve my name in their chests with a poisoned knife. I'm going to kill them anyway. It doesn't matter that my feelings towards these men are changing. It doesn't matter that the thought of killing them turns me inside out. Our future is already written and all we can do is walk the path we were meant to walk right to the bitter end.

With a heavy sigh, I untangle my fingers from Thirteen's and take the pot of cream she offers me so that I can smother the wounds on Jakub's chest. I know he's resting, recovering from his recent injuries, but there's a listlessness about him, an enduring sadness that can't be disguised even in sleep. His suffering hasn't ended, it's just taken a different turn.

"I can't change the future," I say softly. "I can only do what feels right here and now in the present."

She nods her head. "I guess that's all we can do."

OVER ON THE other side of the room, Thirteen clutches a steaming mug of herbal tea as she looks out of the window watching the sun slowly lower towards the horizon. Since our talk a few hours ago, she's been quiet, her heart harbouring as many secrets as my own. I recognise the weight of them sitting on her shoulders.

"Thirteen, why don't you use your name? You're not a Number, not in the same way as the others."

"I'm not a fan of my name," she smiles, her gaze still fixed on the horizon.

"Why?" I ask, pulling the blanket up around Jakub as he sleeps. "Cynthia is pretty."

"Not when it's shortened to Cyn..." Her voice trails off as she loses herself to a memory which shadows her features and rounds her shoulders.

"Thirteen, there was something my mother said in her letter to me. I've been meaning to talk to you about it, but the opportunity never arose..."

"Oh yes? What was that?" she asks, placing her mug of tea on the table beside the window and sitting down in the chair on the opposite side of the bed.

"My mother said I should trust you."

She grins. "Thank goodness. I hope you do."

"To be honest, there was a moment that I wasn't one hundred percent sure about you or your intentions, but I am now. You're a good person."

"Well, thank you, I think."

"That wasn't the only thing my mother wrote about you in her letter."

Thirteen pulls the sleeve of her sweater over her hands. "This sounds ominous. Are you certain you should be telling me this?" she replies with a thin smile.

"She said you were running from your own fate, that it's going to catch up with you eventually and when it does I need to be a friend to you. Do you know what she meant by that?"

Jakub murmurs in his sleep, groaning as he shifts onto his side giving Thirteen a moment of respite. I readjust his blanket, tucking the thick material around his body to keep him warm. The fire in the hearth has almost burned out, and even though I'm wearing a thick pair of flannel pyjamas, I can feel the steady creep of cold as it passes through the gaps in the wooden floorboards. For a minute Thirteen picks at thread on her jumper, staring off into the distance. Eventually with a heavy sigh, she opens up.

"Your mother was right, I am running from something. Someone actually. Three someones to be precise."

"Who?"

"The Deana-dhe."

"The Deana-dhe?"

"Yes, it's the name given to a group of very powerful, very dangerous men."

"Wait..."

My voice trails off as I try to recall why I recognise that name. Then I remember the first vision I had of Grim and Beast speaking on the telephone to Arden and them mentioning the name.

"Arden Dálaigh is one third of The Deana-dhe. Lorcan Sheehan and Carrick O'Shea make up the other two thirds. Together they're the most feared men in Europe," Thirteen explains, confirming my suspicion.

"More feared than The Masks?" I can't help but ask.

"The Masks are well-known and respected by their clients for what they can provide them: an incredible show, beautiful men and women, fantasies, *sex*. The Masks will punish anyone who goes against them, so they have a reputation—"

"Kill you mean," I interrupt, remembering the Baron.

"But," she continues, "They're not feared in the same way as The Deana-dhe..."

My eyes widen in surprise. "So what makes The Deana-dhe so frightening?"

"Firstly, they're undefeated in the underground fight scene, and secondly, they deal in debts."

"Like loan sharks, you mean?"

Thirteen shakes her head. "No. Not like loan sharks. The kind of debts they deal with can't be paid with money."

"I don't understand?"

"The Deana-dhe deal in information, in *secrets*. Most of the time the debt a person has to pay in exchange for the information they've requested isn't of monetary value, it's *personal*."

"Like what?" A chill runs down my spine at the thought of what Grim and Beast will owe them in payment of their debts, but my skin positively turns icy when Thirteen meets my gaze.

"Like asking a woman gifted in the art of herbal medicine to avenge the death of a beloved family member."

"What?!" My heart seizes in my chest. "But I thought..."

"You thought I only came here to deliver the letters from your mother? I did, but I also came here to repay my debt."

"No!" I shake my head, my thoughts scatter as I try to piece together what the hell is going on.

"Why?"

"Because that's what I owe the Deana-dhe for giving me the name of the man who murdered my mother," she whispers. "I wanted revenge, only now the Deana-dhe have found a way to get theirs. They used me to do that. I would never have agreed to the debt if I'd known what they had planned."

"Then why did you?"

"The Deana-dhe don't tell you upfront what they want in exchange for the information you seek, they cash in at a later date. A year ago, a few days before my grandmother died, I bumped into Arden in Dublin when I was visiting a friend. Only it wasn't a coincidental meeting. It never is when it comes to those men."

"Thirteen, no," I say, shaking my head, my voice rising. "I don't understand. If you really hated The Masks, why persuade me to stay? Why give me my mother's letter? Why give her letter to them? Why tell me that you believe we belong together, that you believe in the legend, if all you want to do is kill them?"

"Who said anything about killing them?" she asks me, a slow smile pulling up her lip.

"What do you mean?"

"When they asked me to avenge the death of Michael, Arden's father, your uncle, I *knew* they meant for me to kill The

Masks, but your mother pointed out something very important to me in her letter. They didn't use the word *kill* specifically, Christy. I'm not about to become a murderer for those bastards. I won't."

A rush of air leaves my lungs as I sit back in my chair, relief flooding my veins. "Then what are you going to do?"

"Not me, Christy. *You.*"

My heart literally stops beating as she gives me a knowing smile. "The other night you said to me that it didn't matter if you loved The Masks because they're going to die anyway, that you were going to kill them. I was confused at first, given what your mother wrote in her letter to me, but I've finally understood how this is all going to play out," Thirteen explains, sliding her hand into her skirt pocket and pulling out a folded piece of paper, handing it to me. With my heart pounding in my throat, I unfold it and begin to read.

CHAPTER TWENTY-EIGHT

Christy

DEAR CYNTHIA,

I don't have much time to explain why you are so very important to me and my daughter, Christy, but I hope that this letter will be enough to convince you to help us both. To help all our families to heal, including yours.

Your mother and I grew up together. We were the best of friends and I loved her like a sister, but circumstance and hatred between men tore us apart.

When I heard of Aoife's death, we hadn't seen each other in years, not because we didn't want to but because we had no choice. It hadn't surprised me that she died protecting you in a war she couldn't prevent. Her love for you was like the ocean, vast and deep.

She was the most beautiful soul, and I miss her every single day.

I wish, more than anything, that I could've been present in your life. That you and Christy could've grown up together and become friends just like your mother and I had. Alas, it wasn't meant to be, but I hope more than anything that you will form a lasting friendship after all of this is over. I hope that old wounds between families can finally heal and that you won't be kept apart like your mother and I were.

I look up at Thirteen, my eyes welling with tears, unable to articulate how unutterably sad I feel for our mothers, for the both of us for losing the women we adored so much in such terrible circumstances.

"Keep going," she says softly.

Swiping at my tears, I carry on reading.

In this envelope you will find two letters. The first is for Christy. The second is for the men who call themselves The Masks, your old friends and my daughter's kidnappers.

I'm asking you to give the letter to my daughter exactly two weeks after she arrives at Ardelby Castle. The second letter you must give to The Masks on the night of the show when Christy wears the pink dress.

These letters have been kept safe for fifteen years by your grandmother who, like me and Aoife, was tired of seeing the people she cared about hurt by foolish men. She gave them to you on this night for the same reason I am writing this letter, to stop more bloodshed. She was a good woman, and I'm so terribly sorry for your loss.

Again I look up from the letter, confusion giving me pause.

"My grandmother gave me these letters the night she passed away. She asked me to read the one addressed to me, but not to open the others," Thirteen explains. "Your mother saw many things, and she has tried so hard to protect you from beyond the grave."

"I know," I say, dropping my gaze back to the letter. "I know."

You must be confused, so I hope this letter will go some way to explaining things. By now Arden Dálaigh, my nephew, will have asked you to pay your debt. I know this because I've seen it. Like my daughter I have the ability to see things that are yet to happen.

The Deana-dhe want revenge for my brother's death. They want you to kill the Masks.

You can't do that.

Not just because you are a good person and cannot, under any circumstances, darken your soul with murder. Not just because these men and my daughter's future are inexplicably entwined. But because I'm trying to prevent history from repeating itself.

There's been too many deaths, too much heartache, and if I can do one thing before I leave this world, it's to fix this mess our fathers and their fathers before them have inflicted on us all. Your parents' families have been at war for years, as have my family: the Dálaighs and the Brovs. Men have caused these wars, all of this pain, and it's time for the women to take back control and end the violence once and for all. It's what your mother wanted, what I wanted, but fate conspired against us. Your mother died trying to stop a war, and in a few years, I will die in the crossfire of another.

It wasn't our time to fix it, but it will be yours. Yours *and* Christy's.

This time the stars have aligned better than I could ever

have hoped for. There's a chance that peace can be found and lives saved if you help my daughter to fulfill her destiny, and trust me to help you to fulfill yours.

Tonight you must leave your home and revisit your old friends. Go to Ardelby Castle and find your place there. Tell them whatever you need to in order for them to allow you to stay.

You must wait until my daughter arrives and help her to fulfill her destiny. Guide her as best you can without telling her what you know. Not until the time is right. You'll know when the time comes for honesty. Whether I like it or not, she was meant for The Masks as they were meant for her. The Dálaigh's and the Brov's war will end with their love, it has to, otherwise all of this will be for nothing.

My gaze tracks across the letter to Jakub's sleeping form. He looks so vulnerable lying there, beaten and battered. Truthfully, I don't even like this man. I feel pity for him, empathy for the child he was, and there's a connection between us that is as confusing as it is frightening, but *love*...

Could I ever really love him?

Could I love any of them?

My feelings for Leon and Konrad have begun to change, that's true, but being *told* I'm destined to be with someone isn't the same as knowing it or *feeling* that love for myself. Surely, I have the right to choose? I know I don't want them dead, but do I want their love? Can I give them mine? I'm still uncertain.

She will fight against it, and there is a point in Christy's future that I can't see beyond, but I'm hoping that with your help it won't be the end of her journey, just the beginning. That is why you must deliver these letters. It's imperative that you do.

Then there is the not so small matter of the debt you need to repay. Your paths will cross with the Deana-dhe again on the night where everyone wears a mask. On this night, you must help Christy to convince everyone that The Masks are dead.

"The Brònach Masquerade Ball," I say when my eyes lift to meet hers. She doesn't need to say anything to confirm my guess, we both know I'm right.

I have every faith in your abilities to pull this off. You are gifted in the art of alchemy, just like your mother had been before you. You know what you must do.

Give The Masks the chance to prove themselves worthy of my daughter. Love can only blossom when it's given the space to do so.

They need time.

But time is something they do not have. Grim loves Christy, and she will not rest until The Masks are dead. Neither will the Deana-dhe.

So find a way to make this happen.

Do this, and you will help two families finally lay their pasts to rest.

Which leads me to your future...

I flip over the page, only to find it blank. "Where's the rest?" I ask, looking up at Thirteen who's staring off into the distance, lost to her thoughts.

"I have it, but that part is about me and doesn't concern you," she replies softly with a gentle smile.

"Thirteen... *Cynthia*."

"No, Christy. I can't. Please don't ask me to explain. All you need to know is that I'm okay with it. If you can do what you have for The Masks, then I can do what's asked of me, too."

"Okay," I nod, folding the letter up and passing it back to her, knowing all too well what kind of predicament she's in. Taking it from me, she tucks the letter back into her skirt pocket.

"When you said what you did the other night I thought perhaps your mother had got it wrong, that you would kill The Masks in vengeance. It only just dawned on me that you saw something in your future and interpreted it the wrong way, because whilst it might be me who makes the poison to stage their deaths, it's you that administers it. Am I right?"

"Can you do it?" I ask in response, refusing to answer her question but acknowledging her assumption.

"Yes. Leave it with me."

CHAPTER TWENTY-NINE

Jakub

PERFUME LINGERS BENEATH MY NOSE—A wisp of vanilla and a hint of musk. I breathe in deeply, drawn to the scent and forcing my eyes open.

Daylight streams through the window stinging my eyes as I blink back the remnants of the deepest sleep I've ever been under. I refuse to close them again, not whilst my heart is so utterly captivated by the most beautiful woman to ever grace my pitiful existence.

Christy's here.

She's standing by the window, her flame-red hair hanging down her back in gentle waves, the tips grazing against her arse as she gently rocks from side to side, her arms wrapped around Nala in comfort.

"He'll wake up. You'll see," Christy says, rubbing her hand gently up and down Nala's back.

"Are you certain? He looks like death," Nala replies, biting her wobbly bottom lip. Her eyes are pressed closed as she rests her cheek against Christy's shoulder.

"I feel like death, too," I say, my voice sounding like metal scraping over stone.

"Jakub!" Nala screeches, untangling herself from Christy's arms and hurtling towards me.

She throws herself across my body, her face buried in the crook of my neck as she sobs. I stiffen, not from the pain, although every-fucking-where hurts, but because I'm not used to such affection. It's alien to me, foreign. My arms slowly come up, wrapping around her body as she cries and laughs against my chest, and a warmth spreads in my veins despite the awkward way I hold her.

"You absolute idiot!" she shouts, pulling back and gripping my shoulders, shaking me a little. "You scared me. Don't ever do that again!"

I wince as her fingers curl into my flesh, pressing against the lashes and bruises that I know cover my skin like a patchwork blanket. Fuck, it hurts, but it's nothing in comparison to the pain I felt waking back up in that cabin.

"Hey, go easy," Christy chides softly. Her gaze is wary, as if she expects me to react with anger or spite.

"It's okay. I deserve much worse than a hug," I reply, shifting my gaze away from Christy and trying not to focus on how my motherfucking heart races in my chest just being in her presence.

Nala clicks her tongue, helping me to sit up. She arranges the pillows behind my back, swiping at her tear-stained cheeks once I'm settled. Perching on the edge of the bed, she shakes her head, her blonde hair whipping around her face as she moves.

"I'm your *sister*."

"My sister," I repeat in wonder.

I was an arsehole to her after Renard's funeral. I didn't know how to handle the news or the way she'd looked at me like I was her saviour, so I'd rejected her and searched out One like a bad fucking habit.

"Hey, big brother," she says softly, her fingers finding mine as she clutches my hand. Her gaze roves over my face and it's only then that I realise I'm not wearing a mask. Habit makes me want to hide myself from her. Not because I want to protect her from seeing me but because I want to protect myself from her judgement. Will she see our father in my features? The thought makes my stomach turn.

"My mask!" I snap.

"It's too late now." Nala grins, tipping her head to the side. That one crooked smile easing the sudden rush of shame at having any resemblance to our father. "You know, we have the same mouth and nose."

"I'm not sure that's a good thing," I retort, wiping a shaking hand over my face as I battle the need to cover myself up.

"What are you talking about? I'm glad I look like *you*. It's physical proof that I'm not alone, wondering who I belong to."

"You were never alone, Nala. Even if I might've made you feel like you were."

She nods solemnly. "I know that. I knew your father too, remember. *Our* father," she corrects herself. "I knew what kind of man he was and what would've happened if you'd tried to have a relationship with me even without knowing I was your sister."

"I'm *sorry*—"

She shakes her head, cutting me off. "For what, saving me? Don't be sorry for that."

"You know what I mean. I didn't know who you were."

"It's in the past, let's leave it there," she says with far more forgiveness than I've any right to hope for. Despite her youthful exuberance, Nala has a wise soul. An old soul.

"You've had us really, *really* worried."

"Us?" I ask, my eyes following Christy as she moves around the room. She purposely avoids eye contact with me, but I can tell by the way she holds herself how intently she's listening.

"Me, Leon, Konrad, Thirteen... *Christy*," Nala says, giving me a smile that brightens her eyes.

"Is that so?"

"Yep." Casting a quick look over her shoulder she scoots closer, whispering under her breath. "She's barely left your side since you've been out cold. *She's* been really worried about you."

"She has?" I whisper back, something close to a smile pulling up my lip. I don't think I've smiled in years, not like this, not because the thought of someone caring for me makes me feel good.

"Yes, applying ointments to your wounds that bitch inflicted." This time her voice rises and it earns her a sharp intake of breath from Christy.

"*Nala...*" Christy warns, her shoulders tensing, afraid of my reaction.

"I won't hurt her." I say firmly, my hoarse voice sounding far more gruff than I'd intended. "She needn't fear me."

Nala grins, pressing her hand over my heart. "I've never feared you. I always knew the real you was in there, somewhere. It just took the right person to draw you out."

Christy frowns, chewing on her lip. She doesn't trust me, and for good reason. I'm not sure I entirely trust myself either.

"You're different," I say, changing the subject and cocking

my head as I study Nala. Despite having lost Renard so recently, there's a lightness about her that wasn't there before.

"Are you sure it's me that's different?" she asks, studying me back, her nose wrinkling. "I mean you look like crap, there's no getting away from that, but..." She grasps my hand, and I'm reminded of the way her little fist had wrapped around my finger as a baby. The flood of warmth I felt earlier flares inside my chest. She's my blood, my family. The baby girl I'd saved from hypothermia sixteen years ago is my *sister*.

"But...?" I ask, swallowing back the lump of emotion in my throat. *Fuck.*

"Your eyes have changed. You always used to look like a caged animal either waiting to be beaten or ready to bite, and now..."

"And now?"

She squeezes my hand. "You don't anymore."

Christy coughs, interrupting with an apologetic smile. "I should go and get you something to eat. You must be hungry."

Unable to help myself, I allow my gaze to trail over her body as she waits for me to answer. She's wearing a long, chocolate brown jumper over black leggings, and thick socks. Nothing about what she's wearing is particularly sexy, but the blush of her cheeks, and the deepening colour of her birthmark sends a rush of blood to my cock. With immense effort, I pull my knees up so Nala can't see her big brother's growing hard-on.

"Jakub?" Nala prompts, failing to hide her grin as she flicks her gaze between us. "Do you want something to eat?"

My stomach takes that exact moment to growl in agreement. "I do, but first I need to..." My voice trails off as I glance down at my dick. I need to do more than piss, but I don't think I can stand on my own right now let alone temper my hard-on so that I can actually relieve my bladder. There's no fucking way I'm struggling out of this bed with my baby sister looking on. Not given the physical state I'm in, and I'm not talking about my bruises and cuts.

"Are Leon and Konrad about?" I can just about tolerate them helping me.

Christy frowns. "How desperate are you?"

I wince. "Desperate."

Nala pulls a face. "I'm not sure I want to see my brother piss himself," she says, giggling.

"Fuck no. Get out!" I retort sharply. She continues to laugh at my expense. It's both hugely irritating and kind of refreshing. Is this what having a younger sibling feels like? "Nala, go!"

"Okay, okay. Christy can help you," Nala says with a mischievous look in her eyes as she backs towards the door. "It's not as if she hasn't seen your dick before."

"Nala!" Christy's cheeks flare with embarrassment.

"Hey, no judgement here. I always knew you two were made for each other."

"I haven't seen his dick," Christy mutters.

Liar.

"Hey, I just meant because he's naked beneath that blanket and you've been looking after him. Stands to reason you'd have seen it."

"Can you stop talking about my dick?!" I exclaim, which only makes Nala have another fit of giggles.

"Would you mind asking the cook to make some chicken soup with lots of vegetables?" Christy asks, changing the subject expertly whilst ushering Nala out of the door. "Once you've done that, perhaps you could go and find Leon and Konrad, tell them Jakub is awake."

Nala waggles her eyebrows. "Sure thing, I'll give you some

alone time. Do you want me to tell Thirteen that Jakub's awake or should I wait a bit for you to, you know—?"

"She's busy right now," Christy says, cutting her off. "I'll go and fetch her once Jakub's eaten and Leon and Konrad are here."

"Okay, sure. Don't do anything I wouldn't do," Nala sing-songs, winking as she skips out of the door.

Christy pushes the door shut, breathing out slowly before turning to face me. She plasters a determined look on her face, but I see the hint of fear she tries to hide. "Okay, let's get you to the bathroom."

Shifting my body, I shuffle towards the edge of the bed and swing my legs over the side. Pins and needles prick my skin as blood rushes to my feet. I wiggle my toes, allowing my aching body to adjust to the new position. Despite the pain I feel, my dick is still determined to stay hard. It tents the sheet slung over my waist.

"I'm naked," I blurt out.

"Like Nala said, it's not like I haven't seen your dick before," she replies evenly, her gaze dropping to mine. If she notices my erection she doesn't acknowledge it.

"Right," I mutter, peeling back the bed sheet. Ignoring my bastard cock, I stare at the ruination of my body. Fuck, it's worse than I remember. I look like a piece of cracked marble. Bruises litter every inch of my skin, made worse by the criss-crossing of newly-formed scabs. However, most of the cuts and lashes are knitting together nicely and I know I have Thirteen to thank for that.

"Should I be worried?" Christy asks me.

"About my dick?"

She raises a brow. "No, not about your dick," she replies

dryly. "Should I be worried that you're going to try and kill me again?"

"You're here alone with me, so why don't you tell me?"

"I'm asking you."

She has every right to question my intentions. It's not as if I've given her any reason to trust me. I've done nothing but try to kill her since Thirteen brought her back to life. A million words spin through my head as I stare at her, none of which I can articulate. I want to know why she helped me, why she hasn't tried to murder me in my sleep, and why she's being so fucking *kind*. My brain scrambles to form an apology, and when it can't come up with one that is worthy of such an incredible woman, my mouth snaps out a crass reply instead.

"You don't need to be afraid of a man who's about to piss himself."

Christy nods, ignoring my rudeness and tucking a strand of hair behind her ear. Ducking down, she hooks my arm over her shoulder, hoisting me upright. I wobble on unsteady feet. Nausea churns my stomach, which in turn softens my cock. Thank fuck for small mercies.

Slowly, and without complaint, Christy guides me into the bathroom and over to the toilet. "I can take it from here," I bite out, male pride getting the better of me as I press my palm against the tiled wall and wait for her to leave.

"I think you should sit, rather than stand," she says. "I don't want you passing out."

"I've got this!" I say through gritted teeth, but my body proves me a liar and I fucking wobble on my feet.

"Sure you do." Ignoring my caustic behaviour, she helps me to sit. As soon as she's satisfied I'm safe, she walks to the other side of the room and fills up the bath. "Just let me know when you need help getting into the bath," she says before stepping back into the bedroom.

Five minutes later I'm chin deep in warm water, the soothing scent of lavender-imbued salts filling my lungs. Christy sits on a stool beside me, her ghost eyes watching my every move.

"How are you feeling now?"

I think about the question for a moment. It's innocent enough. It's the kind of question normal people ask each other all of the time. Except I'm not normal. We're not normal. This whole fucking situation isn't normal.

"Raw," is all I'm able to answer.

"It will take a while for all the bruises and cuts to heal," she says, tucking a strand of hair behind her ear. "Thirteen assured me the bath salts wouldn't sting..."

"Thirteen is exceptionally good at what she does. Whatever she's put in the water is soothing, not irritating. Besides, that's not what I meant. I know *these* wounds will heal."

"It will get easier," she says softly.

"Will it? How can you be so fucking sure?" I hiss, sudden anger bellowing inside my chest. I'm not angry at her, but at my father. He's still here in this room, in this castle lingering like a rank smell. He's in my fucking blood, staining my DNA with his darkness.

Squaring her shoulders she twists her body around. "Because Nala was right," she says firmly. "You don't look like a scared animal ready to bite, distrusting of everyone and waiting to be beaten. You look like a man willing to learn how to be human."

"Aren't you afraid I'll hurt you again?"

"Are you willing to learn?" she counters.

"I asked first."

"Yes," she replies. "I'm afraid of many things. Including you *and* your brothers."

"Then why are you still here?"

"Are you saying you're willing to let me go?" she asks, narrowing her eyes at me.

Fuck no.

When I don't respond, she rests her hand against the lip of the bath and moves to stand. I reach for her, grasping her wrist tightly. "Wait!"

She stiffens, her eyes moving from my hand to my face and back again. I can see the kindness seep from her gaze and a brittle hardness settle in its place. I hate that's what I do to her. I want to change that but I don't know if I can.

"Let me go."

"I wish I could," I reply, my fingers loosening despite my words. "But I knew the moment we took you that I would never be able to let you go, not willingly anyway."

She nods as if in acceptance of that fact. "I know."

Capturing her hand, my palm tingles, and I wonder if she feels it too, this electricity between us. It buzzes beneath my skin, swelling my cock. Thank fuck the water has turned opaque from the bath salts otherwise she'd see how fucking hard I am for her. *Again.*

"I can't promise I won't fuck this up."

"So don't."

I feel her pulling away, but I can't let her. I can't fucking let her. Tightening my fingers, I pull on her wrist until she's bending over me. Her hair falls forward, the tips dragging over the surface of the water, sticking to my wet chest. Our faces are a few inches apart, and I bring up my hand to cup her cheek, her birthmark darkening beneath my touch. "I'm still his son."

"You have a choice," she argues, pinning me with her ghost eyes.

"I want to be worthy of you—"

She shakes her head, pressing her fingers against my lips. "It isn't me you need to be worthy of, Jakub. It's the kid who was beaten and abused on the floor of that cabin, and it's the man who woke up inside of you and said no more. That's who you need to be worthy of," she says, and with that, she turns on her heel and leaves me with a raw heart and a cock made of stone.

CHAPTER THIRTY

Christy

TWELVE IS BURIED beneath a silver birch tree in the gardens of the castle the following afternoon. Much like Renard's burial, it's a quiet affair, but this time the Numbers are in attendance too. Everyone is solemn, thoughtful, including the Masks.

I glance over at Konrad. His arms are folded over his chest, his navy mask covering the entirety of his face, but he can't hide the look in his eyes from me. There's pain there. Guilt. Anger too.

Twelve raped him. It was wrong. The fact that he's here speaks volumes.

"Until very recently I hadn't understood what it felt like to lose someone you care about..." Jakub clears his throat, his gaze lifting from the coffin to the Numbers lined up on the opposite side of the grave. "But I get it now. I'm sorry for your loss."

Bending down, he picks up some soil, sprinkling it over the coffin before stepping back then glances at Six who begins to sing.

Her voice lifts into the air, whipped up by the freezing wind and carried off over the gardens and beyond. Goosebumps scatter across my skin at the haunting melody and I watch in turn as each of the Numbers takes a handful of soil and throws it onto the casket before heading back into the castle. One is the last to pay her respects, and as she lingers over the grave her eyes lift in search of Jakub. We haven't really talked since he woke up yesterday, and last night I went back to Thirteen's room whilst he, Konrad and Leon had a conversation that I wasn't privy to. I'm not sure what I was expecting, but being dismissed like that, wasn't it.

"We should head back," Jakub mutters, a muscle feathering in his jaw as he finally notices One staring. My gut twists as he motions for her to take a walk with him, her coy smile making my blood boil. She abused him. She hurt him. My lips thin into an angry line.

I'm not the only one who's pissed off.

"What the fuck's up with that?" Konrad snarls watching the exchange.

Leon shakes his head, putting his hand on Konrad's chest. "He knows what he's doing."

"The hell he does. She's not the woman he should be spending time with right now and we both know it."

"This needs to happen," Leon says, then catching me staring, steers Konrad through an arched hedgerow into the ornamental gardens beyond. Curiosity makes me want to follow them, pride makes me stay put.

Beside me Thirteen shivers, a frosty wind picking up her hair, the ends dancing over my cheek.

"I should get back," she says softly, her eyes telling me what she's unable to say out loud. We left the mixture brewing and according to Thirteen, there's a lot more to do before it'll be ready.

"Me too. I'm meeting with Three to go over the routine for the ball," I say, my eyes still fixed on One and Jakub who've stopped to talk far enough away that we're unable to hear what they're saying. Jakub's body language is closed, defensive, but One...? I grit my teeth as she leans in close, pressing her hand over his chest that she ruined with *her* whip.

"Don't let One wheedle her way back in, Christy," Thirteen says, squeezing my hand. "She isn't what he needs. She never was."

"They have a lot of history," I counter, unable to unscramble my confusing emotions when it comes to these men.

"Old habits are hard to break, especially when you've been trained to give and receive abuse like it's normal. She's all he knows. Show him that there's an alternative. I know you can do it, you've already proven you can."

"I'll try," I mumble, not entirely sure I'm capable given we've only just formed a tentative truce.

"Are you coming?" Thirteen asks after a beat.

With one last glance at Jakub and One, I thread my arm through Thirteen's and head back inside the castle, taking another step towards a future that's already been written.

"THANK you for doing this for me," Three says as I collapse next to her on the wooden floor of the studio.

"Of course," I reply, pulling off my dance shoes and rubbing my aching feet.

"You've picked up the steps really quickly. It's impressive." She gives me a half-smile that doesn't reach her eyes.

"Are you okay?"

It's a stupid question because of course she can't be. Twelve was buried this morning. Why on earth would she be okay?

"I just can't quite believe she's gone. We weren't the best of friends, but she was family. I cared about her."

"I'm so sorry. This must be so difficult."

"It just feels like everything is falling apart. I was so certain of my place here with Seven and performing in The Menagerie. Ardelby Castle has been my home for so long. Only now..."

"Only now?"

"My life before here wasn't good, Christy," she explains, staring off into the distance. "I've lived in this castle for eight years. At first it was hard. Not because I was desperate to return home, I wasn't, but because this place was so completely different to where I'd come from. I used to live paycheque to paycheque working as a stripper and a prostitute. When The Collector gave me the opportunity to live here at Ardelby Castle, I jumped at the chance. I wasn't taken against my will. I don't have any family looking for me. He didn't pay anyone for me."

"You came here voluntarily with *him*?"

She nods. "It was either I keep living in a dingy, flea-infested bedsit in East London and selling my body for a hot meal, or moving here. What would you have done in my position?"

"I'm sorry."

"Why? For making a decision to better my life?"

"No, for having to make that decision in the first place. I'm sorry you didn't have people to look out for you."

"I looked after myself the best I could. But one shitty decision led to another and I ended up trapped by my life. The only thing that made living bearable was my ability to dance. The Collector saw something in me that no one else had, and despite the fact I was scared shitless of him, that I knew he was a bad, *bad* man, I was more scared of growing old and dying a worthless whore beaten down by life. When he offered me the chance to perform in The Menagerie, I took it." She sighs, swiping a strand of hair behind her ear.

"I didn't know."

"Why would you? When we arrive here we're stripped of who we were. I was happy to do that. I had no ties to the girl I was. I didn't want to be her for a moment longer. This place is my home. I embraced it."

"I hear a *but* in there somewhere."

She swallows hard, swiping a tear from the corner of her eye. "I love belonging to The Menagerie. We may quarrel, and perhaps I'm closer to some of the Numbers than I am to the others, but we're a family, however dysfunctional. It's just that—"

"You're beginning to see things a little differently?"

"In a way, yes..." Her voice trails off as she looks over at Seven. He's sitting on the other side of the studio with a pair of headphones on studying a sheet of music in front of him. Apart from saying hello in greeting, he hasn't looked up once since I arrived here two hours ago.

"What's Seven's story?" I find myself asking.

"When Seven was brought here, he tried so hard to escape. His past is completely different to mine, and I know he has a family out there who love him, who *miss* him."

"But he said that—"

"That being here was a good life?" She shakes her head. "He stays for me. He's sacrificed everything for me."

"You make it sound like he had a choice to leave."

"Oh, we both understand that there is no choice. What I mean is that before he fell in love with me, he was willing to die rather than stay here. He would've fought to the death for his freedom, just like he would've fought Jakub instead of hurting me the other night. On both occasions he did neither because of me. I've kept him here."

"You've kept him alive," I counter.

"But at what cost? He can barely look at me now."

"Have you talked to him about what happened?"

"I've tried, over and over again. He just clams up or gets angry. Not at me," she says quickly. "He just can't forgive himself."

"What do you think will help?"

"Aside from killing Jakub, not much," Three laughs sadly. "He feels like a failure, that he should've stood up to him."

"If he had, Jakub would've killed him, killed you," I say, hating that it's the truth, but knowing that he wouldn't have hesitated. I'm hoping the man he is now would think twice about forcing Seven to commit such an act, let alone even consider killing them both for refusing. I have to believe that's the case, otherwise this path I'm following will all be for nothing.

"*I* know that. He does too. It doesn't make any difference though."

"Can I ask you something?" I ask.

"Sure."

"If there was a chance that you could live a happy, safe life outside of Ardelby Castle, would you take it?"

Three glances over at Seven, smiling sadly. "We both know that can't happen."

"But if there was a chance, would you leave with Seven?"

"You forget that I've lived out there in the real world, and it wasn't all that good to me." Three grasps my hand in hers and lets out a small laugh. "Not to mention the fact that none of us are going anywhere. The Masks would *never* allow it."

"But what if the Masks didn't have a choice?" I mutter, knowing that soon they'll be dead, at least long enough for the Numbers to make their escape should they wish to do so.

"What do you mean?"

"Nothing. Just ignore me. Let's go over the routine again," I say, standing and pulling her up with me.

A few minutes later, whilst Three is running through a particularly complicated sequence of steps, I catch Seven looking up from his sheet music. His gaze is focussed solely on her. It's clear that he loves her very much. It's also clear that he's sinking beneath the weight of his self-hatred and that there's really only one way to fix it. They need a chance to start over again, someplace far away from here, and I know just the person who can help.

Grim.

CHAPTER THIRTY-ONE

Christy

STEPPING OUT INTO THE COURTYARD, I look up at the Weeping Tree, it's doused in a silvery light from the star-scattered sky. The gnarled wood of its branches are bare, the thick trunk pitted with scars of its own. Above ground it stands like a silent sentinel, witnessing years of violence, bearing the weight of it. Below the surface its roots grow deep, reaching for the serenity of a cool lake, slaking its thirst in the peaceful quiet.

"Am I doing the right thing?" I whisper as an icy breeze lifts up my hair in answer. Twisting on the spot, I peer into the shadowed arches surrounding the courtyard. My sweat-slicked skin covers in goosebumps.

I'm not alone.

Instinct tells me it's one of The Masks.

But which one?

Is it Leon, an angel wrapped up in the sins of the devil?

Is it Konrad, a monster chained up by a man who's finally strong enough to imprison it?

Or is Jakub, an abused boy who's shed the skin of the demon his father moulded in his image?

Lifting my face to the sky, I breathe in deeply, refusing to fear these men. Willing to trust my mother, myself, even Fate. I've fought The Masks. I've struggled with my emotions.

I'm tired of the uncertainty of my feelings, and the certainty of fate.

Tonight I don't want to think. I don't want to fall into another troubled sleep. All I want to do is dance until I'm too tired to stand.

So that's what I do.

Lifting onto my tiptoes, I throw my arms out to the side and begin to dance.

Not the steps Three taught me, but my own. My movements aren't bound by routine, they don't conform to a sequence. I dance from my soul. I let out weeks of turmoil, pain, anger, shame, fear.

I release myself from the guilt. I let it all go.

Pirouetting across the cobblestones, my hair whips out around me as I spin and spin and spin, moving around the Weeping Tree fluidly.

There's no sense to my steps, just feeling. Just emotion.

I dance for Marie, for the woman whose kindness was turned into a lifetime of suffering.

I dance for the generations of Brovs who've suffered at the hands of their fathers.

I dance for Twelve who's love turned tortured, violent.

I dance for Renard who didn't live to see the men he hoped The Masks could be.

I dance for my mother, for Aoife.

I dance for the Numbers.

I dance for Thirteen, for myself.

I dance for The Masks.

Rain begins to pour, the freezing water dropping onto my skin, drenching me in seconds, but still I dance. I leap and twirl. I kick up the water pooling at my feet, sending silvery droplets scattering around me. I don't stop when thunder rumbles, not even as its angry boom shakes the ground beneath my feet. I don't halt my steps when lightning cracks directly above me, highlighting my masked observer. I don't even falter when he steps into the courtyard, the blade of a knife glinting in his hand.

Jakub.

For the first time in my life I'm glad I can see into the future because it makes me fearless in this moment. Instead of running away from the danger, I dance towards it. I embrace the present, trusting in our future.

Jakub stills as I pirouette around him. His knuckles are white from the tightness of his grip around the handle of the knife as thunder booms and rain pours down, drenching us both. Water runs in rivulets over us, sticking our clothing to our skin, but he doesn't move and I don't stop dancing. There's a freedom in my movements, a strength that cannot be tamed or caged. Not by fear, not by uncertainty, not by distrust.

Another crack of lightning illuminates the courtyard in stark white light revealing the two remaining Masks. They rush forward, but I don't need either of them to protect me. Not this time.

"Stop!" I command. Their feet still, obeying me. Stepping in front of Jakub, I lift my hand to his white mask, palming it in my hand. "You haven't come here to kill me," I say, my jaw chattering with cold as the rain continues to pour.

"You don't know that," he retorts, his hazel eyes locking onto mine then dropping lower as he raises the knife and presses the tip between my breasts.

"I do. You won't kill me," I say, *knowing* he doesn't want to.

"I could drive this into your heart and end this all now," he insists, the tip nicking my skin, drawing the tiniest drop of blood. "I've thought about it over and over again. Even after all the kindness you've shown me, I've thought about it."

"But you won't."

He stares at me, eyes blazing. "What if one day my father wins, and this barely human heart of mine turns to fucking stone again?"

"That's impossible," I say.

"It's not. It happened over and over again. Every time the goodness seeped back he poured cement over my heart, trapping it in a coffin of darkness."

I shake my head, the wet ropes of my hair flicking as I move. "On the floor of the cabin you fought against your past. I watched you claw your way back to humanity one painful memory at a time. You broke through all that stone encasing your heart. You're still fighting. If you weren't you would've driven that blade into my heart already. That counts for *everything.*"

"What if I'm not fucking strong enough."

"You are. If your brothers can do it, so can you," I say, placing my hand on his and urging him to lower the knife.

"But they don't have his DNA!' he exclaims, his hand dropping, the knife falling from his grasp.

"Nala does, and she's *good*, Jakub. She's kind, thoughtful, sweet."

The air cracks with electricity that lifts the tiny hairs on my arms, filling the courtyard with seismic energy. Behind us the

Weeping Tree creaks and groans in the wind that's funnelling around the courtyard, covering us both in goosebumps.

"Every time I look in the mirror I see him. Every time I speak I hear his motherfucking voice. He's in my blood like a fucking infection!" Jakub shouts as he claws at his shirt, tearing at his skin, ripping open barely knitted wounds. "He's in my head," he continues, ripping off his mask and tapping his temple. "He's everywhere I fucking look."

"Then together we'll find a way to help you drown his voice out until one day you won't hear him anymore. We'll show you another way to live so you won't feel his presence, or see him in your reflection. We'll do it together. "

"I don't deserve your help. I don't fucking deserve it. My God, the things I've done. FUUUUCKKK!" he roars, balling his hands and tilting his head back to the sky.

A stream of curse words fly free from his mouth as he lets out years of pent-up anger, frustration and disappointment. It floods out of him as he rages and rages until, eventually, he falls to his knees, panting and breathless.

Behind him, Konrad and Leon watch with pain in their eyes, unable to do anything but observe their brother fall apart again. Whilst Jakub might have faced his past in that cabin, and survived the trauma for a second time, he's still fighting the hold his father has over him. It's not as simple for him to separate himself from his father. This will take time, and like my mother had written in her letter to Thirteen, time is something he doesn't have.

Crouching down, I cup his face in my hands and remind him of what I said to him yesterday. "Be worthy of the little boy who saved that precious baby girl from dying. Do this for him, for Nala, for your brothers."

"For you," he chokes out.

"What you hear inside your mind are just echoes of your past. That's all they are. That's all they'll ever be. They don't hold any power over you."

"I could kill you. If not today, then tomorrow or the day after that."

"But you won't."

"I could hurt you."

"You could, but that's because you don't know how to be any other way."

"I don't trust myself around you."

"Then trust *me*," I say, swallowing hard and forcing thoughts of the night I'll carve my name into their chest right here in the courtyard out of my head. "Trust me to show you a better way."

His teeth grind together, a lifetime of conditioning battling with his need to give in to a new way of thinking. "I'm so fucking scared," he admits.

"I'm scared too, Jakub. I was scared when Leon claimed my virginity so brutally then made love to me like I was the other half of his soul. I was frightened when Konrad fought his monster whilst fucking me but more so when I fought alongside him, willing him to win. I'm terrified that I'm wrong and you'll never be free of your demons, that you'll end up hurting me despite wanting to be a better man. I'm afraid fate is fucking with us all and in the end everything we've been through will all be for nothing."

"Will you ever forgive me?" he asks, his voice pitted with sorrow, regret, remorse, *grief* as he presses his forehead against mine.

"Your redemption doesn't start and end with me, Jakub. It never has."

"Tell me what I should do, Christy."

"Learn a better way."

"Show me," he breathes. "I need you to please fucking show me."

"I've already promised you that I would," I say. "I just have to be certain you want it, too."

"I do. Fuck, I do. I'm so sorry for it all, Christy."

His apology whispers around the courtyard, carried off in the wind as the rain eases and the thunder moves off into the distance. With my heart battering against my rib cage, I brush my lips against his, then silently take his hand in mine, pulling him to his feet. "Come with me," I say, leading him across the courtyard and through the castle back to the Masks suite, with Konrad and Leon in tow.

"Could you light the fire?" I ask Konrad as we enter their communal living area. He removes his mask and swipes a hand through his wet hair, pushing it back off his face.

"Sure," he replies, setting to work. I think he's glad for something to do. There's a growing tension that sizzles between all of us that's becoming increasingly hard to ignore.

Leon removes his mask as well, dropping it onto the side table next to Konrad's. "What do you need from me, Christy?" he asks.

"Just be here."

"Always," he replies with a dip of his head.

"You've pulled open some of your wounds," I say, focusing my attention back on Jakub and running my fingers gently over his chest. "These will need more ointment."

"Don't," he whispers, as though my featherlight touch hurts him. "I need to feel the pain."

"No," I shake my head, continuing to gently stroke his skin, and use the cuff of my shirt to dab at the blood weeping from some of the wounds. "You think you need the pain to numb the feelings, but you don't, not anymore. *Feeling* is what makes you human, Jakub, it's what prevents your heart from turning into stone."

He trembles beneath my touch, his teeth chattering from the cold and perhaps with more than a little uncertainty. He's only ever been taught to fear kindness, empathy, compassion. I need to change that, but first I have to be honest with him, as honest I can be without revealing what's to come. "I know what your father did to you in that cabin, Jakub. I saw it."

Jakub draws in a sharp intake of breath, his skin paling. He stumbles a little, and Leon steps up behind him, steadying him.

"You saw what he did to me...?"

"Yes. I'm my mother's daughter after all."

"Fuck," he exclaims, his shoulders dropping with shame.

"I'm sorry for everything you've had to endure. No child should have to suffer such cruelty." Before I can change my mind, I wrap my arms around him, pressing my cheek against his chest and hugging him close. He stiffens from my touch, but I don't let him go. I want him to feel my compassion, to accept it, not push it away.

"Christy, what are you doing?" he asks on a shaky intake of breath.

"Holding you. Comforting you," I reply, willing him to relax.

"You want to fuck me?"

"I want to show you that human connection doesn't have to be painful," I reply, making a decision as I press a gentle kiss against his collarbone. Stepping back, I slowly undo the buttons of my shirt, the material parting and revealing a strip of flesh as my hands fall away. "I want you to know that giving and receiving kindness doesn't have to hurt." I shrug off the wet material, the warmth of the fire welcome on my cold skin.

"Jesus, fuck," Konrad exclaims, his voice gravelly as his gaze licks across my bare flesh, prickling my skin with goosebumps.

"Beautiful," Leon murmurs, his chest heaving and lips parting on a ragged breath.

"Christy," Jakub utters and despite his cock tenting his pants, he remains fearful. Terrified even.

"Don't be afraid," I whisper and with a deep, calming breath, I remove my ballet slippers, skirt and knickers until I'm completely naked before them.

Now I'm utterly vulnerable as I bare myself to them. They've all seen me naked before, but this is different. I'm no longer harbouring any ill will towards them. I don't wish them dead. I don't want to hurt them like they hurt me in the past. I don't want to perpetuate cruelty and hate. I want to put aside all of the wrongs and make this right. Fate has woven our story, the threads of our pasts pulling us closer and closer together, stitching together old wounds, new ones and healing our hurts. We're bound, the Masks and I. It's an undeniable truth that I have no desire to fight against.

For a moment I just stand with my hands hanging loosely at my sides, a deep sense of rightness filling me. Beyond the night of the masquerade ball, I've no idea how this is all going to play out. I've had no more visions, there aren't any further letters from my mother. Right now the future is unknown.

As it should be.

Taking a step towards Jakub, my flesh pricks with goose-bumps, my nipples puckering under their combined attention; the devil, the monster and the demon.

The angel, the man and the boy.

"When?" he whispers, his head ducking to meet my hand, his eyes pressing closed as I gently run my fingers over his face. I know what he's asking me: when did I stop hating them? I answer as truthfully as I can.

"When you saved my life," I say, catching Leon's eye as I brush my fingers over his hand. "When you fought your monster for me," I add, flicking my gaze to Konrad and giving him a warm smile before meeting Jakub's gaze. "When your soul cried out to mine for help."

"You're ours," Jakub whispers possessively.

"No, Jakub, you're *mine*," I reply, and with that truth the last wall between us crumbles to dust.

CHAPTER THIRTY-TWO

Jakub

HER MOUTH BRUSHES against mine in a featherlight kiss. It's tentative, searching, delicate in a way that makes my cock thicken and swell.

You're mine.

Nothing. Zero. Naught.

Christy Dálaigh. Grim's sister. Nessa's daughter. Arden's cousin. The girl with the ghost eyes. The woman our father feared above all else.

She has claimed us.

It was never about Christy being ours. It was always about us belonging to her.

Never has anything felt so right, so true, so *honest*.

When we'd kidnapped her, all I saw was a pretty girl who I could use to seek revenge. I dismissed her. I didn't care who she was. I didn't care about who loved her. I didn't care that she was a victim of a war that had nothing to do with her. I didn't care.

She was no more than a plaything. Someone to use and abuse as we saw fit.

She was *Nothing* to me.

Until slowly she began to creep under my skin. Her courage, her fight, her determination to make us see began to chip away at the facade I'd lived behind for years. That boy who I thought had died on the floor of the cabin began to awaken. He knew way before I did that she was far from nothing. That she was everything. *Is* everything.

Day by day she peeled back the layers, showing us the woman beneath the masks she wore, whilst all we did was continue to hide behind ours. Her courage. Her strength. Her fight. Her determination to make us *see,* slowly but surely had an impact.

She held up a mirror just like she promised and I didn't like what I fucking saw.

It hurt to look upon the man moulded in my father's image. I both wanted to shed him like a skin that no longer fit, and grasp hold of him and never fucking let go. The two sides of me waged a war until the beaten down boy clawed his way back and shoved the man he became into a padlocked corner of his mind. It hurt. It still hurts to feel so fucking exposed, so vulnerable, and yet, as her lips move against mine, the pain lessens.

Her fingers slide across my cheek replacing memories of being slapped about by my father with a tenderness I've never experienced before. My lips part as she strokes my tongue with hers, searching, gentle. I groan into her mouth, my cock instantly hardening from her softness.

Kissing One had always been a battle of wills. It was teeth clashing, biting, hands grasping, scratching. Either she would own me, or I would own her. There was no give or take. Kissing One was about possession, ownership, obsession. It was passionate for all the wrong reasons.

But this kiss...? Fuck, this kiss is passionate in all the right ways. It's like the sun rising on a summer's morning. It's warm, languid, life-affirming. It imbues compassion, heralds connection, it encourages kindness.

As she kisses me, her fingertips find the collar of my shirt and she pulls back the material, her bare breasts brushing against my ruined chest as she slowly peels it from my skin.

"If I hurt you, tell me, okay?" she says, brushing a tender kiss against my throat before slowly dropping to her knees. I watch in fascination, in awe, as she unbuckles my belt and unzips my trousers, pulling them and my underwear down my hips.

My cock springs free, precum beading on the tip. Christy looks up at me, a sweet smile on her lips as she kisses the head of my cock.

My brothers groan in appreciation, and whilst I know this is a turn-on for them, right now this isn't about them. This is about forging a connection and healing wounds between *us*. Me and the girl I once called Nothing, who's proven herself to be everything we needed.

When Christy pulls away, I don't grasp the back of her head and press my dick against her lips like I had in his room of curiosities. I give her the freedom to do what she wants, and right now that's removing my wet clothes.

Pulling off my shoes, she eases down my trousers and boxer shorts the rest of the way and I have an undisturbed view of her scarred back. My cock fucking aches at the sight, turned on by what others perceive to be ugly. But all I see is strength, courage, determination.

She's endured pain and survived it, and that's fucking beautiful.

Groaning, my hand grips my dick, squeezing the base as I try to temper the tingling in my balls. Discarding my clothes, Christy looks up at me from her kneeled position then presses her birth-marked cheek against the hard length of my cock. I watch how her birthmark blushes a deep red, and I swear I almost come.

"Who are you?" I whisper, my fingers trailing over her hair as she runs her lips up from the base of my cock to the tip, her tongue peeking out to lick my slit. Her pink lips glisten as she closes her mouth around the head of my cock and sucks me into her mouth. "Fuck!" I exclaim, my eyes rolling into the back of my head.

"She's our fucking saviour," Leon mutters in response, moving in my peripheral vision as he takes a seat by the open fire. Konrad joins him, sitting in the chair on the other side of the hearth.

"She's everything," he adds. "She's the lifeblood to our motherfucking souls."

"Yes," I breathe, curling over her, my hands running over her scarred back, my cock engorging with every lick and stroke. I press my finger into a whirl of knotted skin as she sucks me off slowly, her mouth and tongue pulling a mind-altering orgasm from deep within me. My balls tighten, the base of my spine tingles as I grasp her hair, holding on for dear life as I unfurl from around her, needing to see her choke on my cock. She looks up at me, her eyes watering as I press against the back of her throat. Pulling back slightly, I allow her to draw in a deep breath through her flared nostrils, relishing the way she suctions me into her mouth and swirls her tongue around my cock.

"Fuck!" I exclaim, my knees buckling.

I grip hold of her shoulder, steadying myself as she reaches up and grasps my hips, urging me deeper into her throat, never once taking her eyes off me. I fuck her mouth like that, staring into the abyss of her soul, wondering how a man like me could deserve a woman like her.

"You're beautiful," I exclaim, my toes curling as intense pleasure builds in my balls and the base of my spine. "I'm going to come, Christy. I'm going to come down your pretty little throat," I say, letting out a deep groan, my dick pulsing, my whole body shuddering as I spill my cum over her tongue. An instant well of gratification and gratefulness opens up inside my chest for this woman and her ability to drag me out of my head so that I can fall so deeply for her.

She's a miracle. A gift. One I'll never take for granted again.

Christy pulls back, licking her glistening lips as she looks up at me, her pupils blown wide. There's no fear in her eyes, no hatred, just acceptance of who she is, and what we are together.

My orgasm relaxes me, the tension I'd walked into this room with, disappearing as Christy climbs to her feet, and I take her proffered hand. She leads me to the sheepskin rug laid out on the floor in front of the hearth. The wool is soft beneath my feet as we stand before each other, the warmth of the fire heating our skin. She slowly circles me, her fingers blazing a trail of heat over my flesh as she moves.

"I want you to concentrate on my voice," she says.

Her exceedingly gentle touch instils both fear and a heavy dose of hope within me. Kindness has only ever brought me pain, and yet, her compassion has drawn me out of the darkness of my past giving me the strength to survive. I can't help but shudder, my whole body vibrating from her touch. I can't lie and say that part of me doesn't want to run from her compassion, that I don't want to take her roughly and fuck her with violence just like I did with One so many times over the years. Those parts of me are still there, but I'm fighting to control them, for her, for me.

It's a battle that rages deep within the confines of this ruined and ravaged skin I wear.

"I want you to breathe deeply," Christy continues, her voice a lullaby that soothes, not torments. "Allow your body to get used to my touch and your mind to understand that in this moment I *won't* hurt you. I'll never hurt you."

There's a crack in her voice that has me reaching for her, my hand sliding through her hair as I cup the back of her head in my hand. My own compassion flaring to life at her pain.

"What is it? What's wrong?"

Her fingers find an old scar on my chin, her thumb running over the length before she presses a soft kiss to it. Her lip trembles, her eyes brim with tears that she blinks away. Determined to remain strong, fierce in the face of my scars. "There isn't a part of you that isn't marked in some way. I see your suffering in every inch of your skin." Her head drops, as she presses her forehead laying against my chest. "I'm sorry."

"This isn't on you, Christy," I say, my fucking heart thundering behind my ribcage. It wants to rip out of my chest and fling itself into her hands, knowing that she's the only one who'll keep it pumping. Who'll keep it *safe*.

She lifts her head, swiping at her eyes. "I can't take away the memories that caused these scars but I can replace them with better ones. Will you let me?" she asks, trailing her gentle touch over another old scar that my father gave me when I couldn't stop crying after he forced me to fuck One.

"I don't know—" I say, my voice catching. My father has fucked with my head so much that her kindness makes me want to run. Fucking her mouth is one thing, but allowing her to soothe me, quite another.

"Brother, let her. Let her help you," Leon says, urging me to be brave, to face my fears. "It's time to let it all go."

Our gazes clash, and I'm reminded of the gentle way he'd loved her whilst I'd watched. He'd turned his back on the darkness and stepped into the warmth she'd offered him. He was fucking brave.

I need to be the same. "Yes," I whisper.

Her shoulders relax, a release of air parting her lips as I concede. Then, one by one she drops a gentle kiss to my scars. The old ones, the new ones. The ones inflicted by my father, by One, by myself. She kisses them all. She moves around me, pressing a kiss to my shoulder blade, to my lower back, to my right arse cheek, to my hip bone and knee, to my shin and calf, to the palm of my hand, to my lower stomach, my pec, the underside of my ribcage. To my elbow.

She kisses every last scar, soothing away every rotten memory with kindness and compassion, with empathy and care. My skin prickles with goosebumps, my body immobilised by her need to heal what's been broken over and over again, and with every kiss my cock jerks, hardening beneath her attention.

"What are you doing to me?" I whisper, a *motherfucking tear* rolling down my cheek. I don't swipe it away. I don't try to hide it. I just allow myself to feel safe in the knowledge that this time I won't be punished for it. I'm not weak because I'm crying. I'm not a fucking failure because I choose to accept kindness and compassion. I'm stronger for it. I'm stronger because of her.

"It's okay," she murmurs, her lips brushing over another scar, another bruise, another memory scored into my skin.

On and on she goes, kissing and caressing, soothing and

consoling, healing me with kindness and compassion. I would be lying if I said it didn't hurt. It does, but not in the same way as it did when these scars were inflicted. This kind of healing hurts because it forces me to *feel* when before all I ever sought was numbness, an escape from a world that was utterly cruel to a boy who never lived up to his father's twisted expectations. It's endless the way she heals me, every kiss unspooling the bitterness and pain, knitting together the wounds that have festered deep inside of me.

"Christy," I lament, my arms widening and as she steps into my arms I smother her with kisses, with fucking affection, with desire and heat and passion that is given lovingly and without an ounce of violence.

In her arms I'm free to be the man I always wanted to be. In her arms I'm no longer a sinner, I'm human. In her arms I'm given permission to *love*.

So I love.

I love with all my motherfucking heart.

"Brother," Leon says, distracting me briefly. I follow the sound of his voice as he strides towards me from the bureau in the corner of the room. I hadn't even noticed he'd moved, so engrossed in Christy. He holds out a condom, meeting my gaze. "We do this right."

"There's no need," Christy says, shaking her head. "Thirteen gave me something to prevent pregnancy just like the others. We don't need it."

"I haven't slept with anyone for years," I say. "Before that our father always insisted on making sure we were clean. It's a habit we haven't broken."

"I trust you."

Regardless, this time I need to know she's all in. I don't want to steal anything from her ever again. Cupping her cheeks, I press a soft kiss against her mouth. "Are you certain?"

"Yes."

"I will never, *ever*, take from you again. If I slip up, then make me *see*."

"I will," she whispers, before crushing her lips against mine and kissing me until my knees fucking weaken.

Grasping her hips I lift her up, continuing to kiss her as she wraps her legs around my waist. My cock jerks as it brushes between her soft folds, finding heat and a slippery wetness that makes my dick harder. A soft whimper parts her lips at that barest of touch where our bodies meet in the most private of places. I drop to my knees needing to sink myself inside her, needing to *feel*.

Right now there's no pain, there's no fear, there's no hesitation.

There's just us.

My entire focus is on Christy, on her deepening birthmark, on the way her ghost eyes watch me intently, on her kiss-bruised lips parting on a breath, at the compassion she imparts so selflessly.

"Lie back," she says, urging me backwards with a gentle touch.

Adjusting my position beneath her, I lie down and every now and then she drops her lips to my battered flesh, pressing more open kisses against my skin, lavishing my cuts and bruises with her tongue and sending jolts of pleasure to my cock. When her knees finally rest on either side of my hips, she leans over me, her arse rising up in the air and no doubt giving Konrad a clear view of her pussy. I almost, *almost* wish I was seeing what he was seeing, but then she gently grasps the base of my cock and slowly sinks onto me, and all rational thought is replaced with stars and fucking comets as a moan escapes my lips.

She moves slowly, rocking and sighing. Her skin flushes with pleasure, her nipples harden to points and her pussy slicks for me. Everything I am is hyperfocused on the way her internal muscles tighten around my dick. The way she feels so right, so perfectly made for me.

Look at us, a Dálaigh and a Brov.

Enemies who've become lovers.

Pleasure zips up and down my spine. I don't have to fight to keep an erection, it happens naturally. There's no wishing this moment would be over soon, only a longing for it to last a fucking lifetime. I could die a happy man buried deep inside of her.

"Open your eyes, look at me," she whispers.

I can't deny her anything. I open my eyes and look.

With her flame-doused skin highlighted in reds and golds, she's a nymph, a fairytale creature. She looks like she belongs in Renard's story, the one he told Thirteen all those years ago. She's a dream, a vision, a *legend* that has come to life. She's everything I've always wanted.

She's perfectly imperfect.

Her birthmark is a deep red that curves over her cheek and around her mouth in a permanent mask that should always be looked upon and never hidden. Her freckled chest and thighs are a constellation of stars that I could stare at forever. The warmth of her pussy is a dream brought to life, and when she lifts herself slowly, I can't help but lower my gaze to the part of our bodies that are joined together so intimately. I watch in fascination, in rapt attention, as her pussy hugs my cock, sliding up and down, up and down. Every single part of me is tingling, from the tips of my toes to the top of my head. Her ability to both soothe me and excite me is beyond anything I could ever have hoped for.

With her hands pressed against her thighs she picks up her pace, her pussy lips parting over my cock that's glistening with her juices. My gaze rises over her slightly rounded stomach, up the edges of her ribcage and over her pert breasts until I meet her gaze. She fucks me with tenderness, never once looking away, and I feel something powerful click into place.

Belonging.

I belong to her.

She owns me, every last damaged, fucked-up and broken part.

"You brought me back to life, Christy," I say, reaching for her hips and holding her steady as she rocks against me. "And my heart will be yours from this moment onwards. Do what you want to it, I'll hand it over willingly."

Christy presses her palm against the centre of my chest and nods. "Then I want you to listen. All of you," she says, even though her gaze remains fixed on mine. "One day I'll lay claim to your hearts and on that day, you have to trust me to take care of them. I won't break them, I *promise.*"

"I do trust you," I reply.

"Promise me," she insists, her expression serious, her eyes worried.

"I promise," I agree and she heaves out a sigh, her body relaxing even as her pussy tightens around my cock.

Grasping the globes of her arse, I gently guide her movements, helping her to find the right rhythm. She throws her head back, her mouth parting, her eyes pressed shut as she loses herself to sensation, to this moment here and now. She rocks over me, her pussy pressed against my abdomen as she hugs me tight, finding pleasure from me, giving pleasure back.

My brothers watch on, their hands around their cocks, their eyes fixed solely on her. She's a bright blaze of light that burns away the cold, lonely darkness we've existed in for years.

They're as hopelessly gone for her as I am, and a new kind of possessiveness rushes in my blood, a protectiveness that takes shape, building form with every slide of my cock inside of her.

I didn't lie when I said I wouldn't let her go, that's as true now as it was when we took her. The difference is I don't do it out of spite. I do it out of love.

Love.

I love Christy.

If she wasn't already so completely joined to me in the best possible way, I would've slid inside of her and shown her just how much I loved her. As it is, those three precious words stay locked inside my chest as she falls forward over me, arching her back, I lift up slightly so that I can take what she offers and suck on her nipple, groaning as she moans, her hips moving faster as my cock slides in and out of her dripping pussy. She's so wet for me.

So fucking wet.

Our movements become less controlled as I lick from one breast to the other and back again, my fingers flexing over her arse as I encourage her to pick up the pace. Instinctively she hugs me to her, hauling me up into a seated position as she tucks her forehead into the crook of my neck, pressing featherlight kisses against my skin and it only seems to intensify our connection as our bodies meld together. Her softness against my hardness. Her gentleness against my jagged edges.

This isn't fucking, it isn't even just sex, this is lovemaking.

She might not be able to acknowledge that yet, but I see it for what it is. I *feel* it, and it's as real and as tangible as her body pressed against mine. Christy isn't just claiming me. This is her owning me body, mind and soul. This is her making love to me, and it's the biggest gift she could ever bestow on me. So with our mouths pressed together, our skin slick with sweat, and our bodies joined, we come.

We come together, a Dálaigh and a Brov, my brothers watching on.

CHAPTER THIRTY-THREE

Christy

"HOW DO we know if it will work?" I ask, biting on my lip with worry as Thirteen stirs the off-white viscous liquid. Twenty-four hours have passed since I slept with Jakub and I've spent the majority of that time with Thirteen helping her with the poison.

"I have to test it out," Thirteen replies, pouring the liquid into a slim gold vial.

"Wait, I assumed you'd done this before," I reply, sniffing the air, surprised to find that it doesn't have a scent.

She shakes her head. "Not exactly."

"What do you mean, not exactly? How can you possibly know it will work?"

"The last time I made something similar, the person I used it on actually died."

"What?!"

"It's okay though, I managed to bring him back," she says quickly, waving her hand in the air and dismissing the issue like it's nothing.

"Thirteen, who are you exactly?"

"Aoife and Niall's daughter..."

"You know what I mean," I say. "What you can do it's not—"

"Normal?" she asks, cocking her head then rolling her eyes. "Coming from the woman who can see into the future."

"Good point," I mumble.

She grins. "I just have an affinity with herbs and plants, flowers and berries. It's not magic, just science, and a good scientist must always test her work. Which is precisely what I'm going to do this time. We can't actually give the Deana-dhe what they want, now can we?"

"Test it out? What, on an animal?" I ask, my stomach churning at the thought. "Where are we supposed to get one from?"

"No, not on an animal, on me."

"No! You *can't* do that!"

"Of course I can. It's not as if I'm willing to try it out on anyone else."

"Thirteen! What if it kills you?!"

She rolls her eyes. "It won't. Well, I mean it will at least give the impression that I'm dead because that's the whole point, but I'll wake up after a couple of hours. Promise."

"And if you don't?" I ask, my voice rising with panic.

"Then I guess I messed up." She shrugs, laughing.

"This isn't funny," I say.

"It kind of is..."

I pull a face, then start pacing up and down. "This is a bad idea. Could we not just order something in?"

"What, from Poisons 4 U?"

"You know what I mean!" I exclaim, wringing my hands.

"Even if we could somehow get into the black market and buy something, it'll have a permanent effect. Which defeats the point. Trust me. I know what I'm doing."

"Seriously, Thirteen, what the hell *are* we doing?"

"Saving their lives," she says, reaching for me and grasping my shoulders. "It's going to be alright."

"I feel sick."

"Don't throw up, Christy. I really just need to get this over and done with and you throwing up isn't going to be helpful," she replies, snatching the knife from the counter and dipping the tip of the blade into the vial. She extracts a droplet of the mixture, then hands me the bottle. "Could you cork that, please?"

I take it from her, and without giving me any warning she slices the palm of her hand, the poison mingling with her blood. "There, now we wait."

"Fuck!" I exclaim reaching for her as she rocks on her feet.

"I should probably lie down," she says with a small laugh, her cheeks flushing a furious red.

Gingerly taking the knife and placing it on the countertop next to the vial of poison, I help her onto her bed. "How long does it take to work?" I ask, getting her comfortable.

"A minute or two, give or take."

"What should I do?"

"Wrap up my hand then wait with me?" she asks as though there was any other option.

"Of course I'll wait with you. I'm not going anywhere."

"Good. Okay then."

"What should I expect?"

"My heart will begin to slow down," she explains, shuffling

to the centre of the bed. "It will get to a point where it will appear as though it's no longer beating. At that point, my lips will turn blue. Don't be scared, okay?"

"Are you kidding me? I'm terrified right now."

"It will have a similar effect of a bear going into hibernation. My body temperature will plummet and that will put me into a kind of sleep stasis. When the poison wears off, my normal bodily functions will kickstart and I'll begin to warm up. Once my body temperature regulates, I will just kind of wake up as though nothing happened. At least that's the idea."

"At what point should I worry?"

"I will be out for a few hours. If I don't wake up after three or four, then I guess it hasn't worked."

"Thirteen!" I shout, unable to help myself.

She smiles, her eyes glazing over. "Stop panicking, it'll be fine."

I lay down next to her, taking her hand in mine. "Please don't die," I say, brushing a strand of hair off her face.

"I'll do my best," she whispers.

"I mean it."

Her head falls to the side, her pupils dilating as she stares through me. She already feels cold. "If I don't wake up will you tell them that they were right..." she slurs, the blood draining from her face.

"Tell who they were right, The Masks?"

"Tell them that I lied," she gasps, her voice sounding raspy. "That it was always supposed to be..."

"Thirteen! Shit!" I grasp her face, my thumbs pressing against her cheek bones as her eyes roll back in her head and her lips turn a horrid shade of blue.

"Tell them what?" I ask, my body covering in a rash of

goosebumps as the familiar pull of a vision grasps at me. "Wait, no!"

But it's too late, she's gone and I'm pulled under.

BLINKING *back the fog that always accompanies a vision, I step into the ruins of an old castle. It's mid-winter, a frosting of snow covering the ground and stone walls. In front of me are a group of boys sitting around an open fire talking animatedly.*

No wait. Three boys and a girl.

A girl I recognise.

Thirteen.

She's wearing boy's clothing and a flat cap, her hair tucked up beneath it, but there's no mistaking who it is now that I can see her more clearly.

"Just take a drag and this will all be over, Cyn," one of the three teenage boys says, his voice melodic. The accent is southern Irish, thick and lyrical. He has dark hair that falls forward into his bright amber eyes that are almost the colour of the flickering flames. He's holding a joint, the tip sizzling as he drags in a lungful.

Thirteen shakes her head, folding her arms across her chest as he releases the smoke from his lungs. Her body language conveys everything her voice cannot as she draws up her jean clad legs and hugs her knees to her chest.

"You're seriously not going to get high with us? This is your recipe," the boy with the silver-blonde hair sitting next to her says. He too has haunting eyes, the shade not dissimilar to his hair. The fairness of his skin and unusual colouring would suggest that he may have Albinism.

Thirteen shakes her head, picking up her notepad and pen,

scribbling furiously: It messes with your head. I'm not making anymore. It's bad for you.

"Yeah, you are," the third boy retorts, his light brown hair cropped short to his head as his coal black eyes narrow at her. "We tell you to do something, you do it, Cyn. No fucking argument."

She scowls at him, her pen rushing over the paper before she turns it around and taps the pad furiously. Fuck you, Carrick!

She moves to stand, but the black-eyed boy, Carrick, grabs her wrist and tugs her into his lap. "Now, now, Cyn. Don't fucking tempt me," *he growls into her ear whilst simultaneously pulling off her flat cap. Her hair tumbles around her shoulders and he presses his nose into her tresses, breathing in deep. She wriggles in his lap, her elbows meeting his stomach, but he just laughs, gripping her tighter.*

"Stop fucking with her, Carrick. She'll only go blab to her father and we don't need that old shit on our backs," *the boy with the silver eyes says. Of the three, he looks the most uncomfortable with what's going on.*

"Fuck Niall O'Farrell, he's just the Collector's bitch." *Carrick replies, tightening his arm around Thirteen and clamping his teeth on her ear. She instantly stills, her eyes wide with pain and shock as he bites down hard enough to draw blood.*

"Which is precisely why she's off limits," *the boy with the amber eyes says. He looks between the two boys, a muscle feathering in his jaw. His shoulders are tense, his spine rigid.*

"But, Arden..." *Carrick replies, releasing her ear and licking at a spot of blood dripping from her lobe.* "You and I both know we always get what we want, and I happen to want Cynthia O'Farrell. Don't fucking lie and tell me you don't feel the same. We all do, don't we Lorcan?"

Lorcan looks away, refusing to answer him.

"I said, let her go," Arden replies, his amber eyes flashing with warning.

"You always did have a soft spot for Cyn. Shame her old man is in cahoots with your bitter enemy. Doesn't that make her guilty by association? Or maybe it's you who's guilty by association, huh?" Carrick taunts, trailing his tongue over Thirteen's cheek. "Your dad would turn over in his grave knowing you've made a deal with the devil's right hand man."

Thirteen stills, her wide eyes flaring with shock. Clearly she didn't know that her father was doing business with Arden.

"Yep, Arden here is working with your father, cailleach," Carrick says, running the tip of his nose over her jaw as he squeezes her breast. Rage flashes over Thirteen's face and she forces her head back, managing to crack Carrick's nose, forcing him to let her go. "Motherfucker!" he exclaims.

Lorcan laughs, taking the joint from Arden as Thirteen scrambles towards her pen and pad, her anger a blaze of words across the paper.

Don't touch me ever again! She writes. Next time you do, I'll be the witch you accuse me of being and turn you into a toad!

Lorcan tips his head back and laughs raucously, passing the joint to Carrick who swipes at the blood trickling from his nose. "You're feisty tonight. I fucking like it."

Thirteen narrows her eyes at Carrick before giving him the middle finger, then turns her back on them both and starts gathering her things.

"Where do you think you're going?" Arden asks, pushing to his feet. He takes the joint from Carrick and strides over to her. She shuffles backwards on her arse as he approaches, the pad and pen discarded as he crouches down in front of her.

She shakes her head. No!

"We call you cailleach because that's what you are, a witch.

It's a compliment, Cyn," he says, his hard eyes softening. "Come on, one toke. That's all I need."

She shakes her head again. No!

Ignoring her, he takes a deep pull of the joint and grasps a fistful of hair, roughly yanking her head back. The look she gives him is one of pure hatred, and whilst everything about his body language suggests he feels the same way, the look in his eyes as he lowers his mouth to hers speaks an entirely different story.

"Open wide, Cyn," Carrick drawls, watching Arden brush his lips over her mouth.

She shakes her head, tears glistening at the corners of her eyes.

"Just do it, Cyn, and this will all be over," Lorcan says, a heavy sigh on his lips. "You know we can't take the goods unless you've tried them out for yourself."

Thirteen glances his way, disappointment flickering in her eyes. A look passes between them and eventually, she parts her lips, a single tear sliding down her cheek that she roughly swipes away.

"There we go, cailleach," Carrick mutters as Arden presses his mouth against hers and she breathes in the smoke he slowly blows into her mouth. Releasing his tight grip on her hair, Arden inches back, allowing Thirteen to breathe out the remaining smoke. A cloud of grey dances between their faces.

"It's true, I'm working for your father. The old fool has no idea who I am," he says, "But don't get too comfortable, Cyn, he's still my enemy. As are you. If you speak of this. If you tell him who we are, who I am, I will make your life a living hell. Understood?"

She glares at him. Hate blazing in her eyes.

"It's a shame you hate us so much," he says, cupping her cheek almost reverently. "Given you're our soulmate."

Thirteen's eyes widen and she shakes her head furiously, pushing past him and grabbing her things. She picks up her pad and pen, and writes: We are NOT soulmates. I am NOT yours.

"Oh, you will be," Carrick mutters. "By hook or by crook."

"Just let her leave," Lorcan adds, swiping a hand through his silvery hair and kicking at the earth with the heel of his boot. "She doesn't want to be here."

Arden chuckles, his expression changing to one of distaste as he steps back. "Until we meet again, cailleach."

I WAKE UP WITH A START, blinking away the vision and reaching out to my side. My fingers hit warm skin.

Warm skin.

"Cynthia? Thirteen?" I shout, ignoring the dizziness that always follows a vision and twisting around to face her. I can go over what I saw later, right now making sure she's okay is my top priority. With utter relief, I notice that the blue hue to her lips has disappeared and there's colour in her cheeks once more. "Thirteen?" I repeat, pressing my fingers against the pulse in her neck. It beats. "Oh, thank God!"

Pushing myself upright, I check the time on the wall clock. We've been out for almost two and a half hours.

"Christy?"

Snatching my head back around, I look down at my friend who's swiping a shaking hand over her face. "You're alive. It worked!"

"I knew it would." She smiles, pushing upright.

I help her to sit, throwing my arms around her in a hug. "Thank God!"

"So what happened whilst I was out?" she asks.

"Erm..." I pull a face, my thoughts straying to the vision I had of her and the Deana-dhe.

"I didn't wet myself did I?" she asks, interpreting my facial expression the wrong way as she checks her crotch.

"No, I don't think so," I respond, smiling a little.

"Then what? It'd be useful to know what to expect so that I can make sure they're okay after you leave with your family."

"Leave?" I frown, my stomach flipping over at the thought.

Thirteen reaches for my hand, squeezing it gently. "You have to go with them, Christy. You know that, right?"

"Of course I do," I say, blinking rapidly. Truth be known I hadn't thought past the night when I poison them.

She nods, patting my hand. "So what happened to me?"

Heaving out a sigh, I shake my head. "I've no idea, I passed out alongside you."

"A vision?" she asks.

"Yes, one of you and the Deana-dhe."

Thirteen sucks in a sharp breath, her face paling. "What did you see?"

"You have a history with them that stretches beyond the debt you owe, don't you?"

She nods. "Yes."

"You grew up with them?"

Thirteen sighs, swiping a shaky hand through her hair. "I was sent to a boarding school when I was fifteen. My father thought the special unit for *troubled* kids would help me find my voice again." She laughs bitterly. "All it did was make me a target for three boys who had nothing better to do than torment a girl who couldn't scream."

"They hurt you?"

"They tried. I got them back good though..." A smile streaks across her face as she traces the cut on her palm.

"The poison you made before, the one that killed someone?"

"Yep." She shrugs. "He deserved it."

"Which one? Was it Arden?"

She shakes her head. "Carrick. He was always the most hateful."

"Ah," I nod, makes sense given how he behaved in the vision.

"What did you see?" she asks, chewing on her lip, her gaze wary. It makes me wonder what kind of things went on between them.

"You were sitting in an old ruin. Arden forced you to take a blow back of a spliff. Carrick bit your ear. They wanted you to test the hash you'd supplied."

She nods sharply. "That was the summer I left the boarding school. They were in town briefly. My father had no idea who Arden was, who they were. If he had, he would've no doubt informed the Collector. I didn't see them after that for two years..." Her voice trails off as she looks down at her hand, her fingers curling into her palm.

"That's what my mum was talking about, wasn't she. You're not running from them because of the debt you owe, you're running from them because they're your soulmates just like Arden had said."

Thirteen flinches. "I don't believe in soulmates," she replies.

"We both know that isn't true," I reply softly, and this time she doesn't argue.

CHAPTER THIRTY-FOUR

Christy

"CAN I BORROW CHRISTY FOR A WHILE?" Leon asks as he steps into Thirteen's room a few hours later. Behind his deep blue mask, his gaze scorches a trail of heat over my skin as he stares at me. I don't need to look in the mirror to know my birthmark is deepening in colour. It seems to do that a lot around The Masks.

Thirteen laughs. "Since when have you ever asked permission to do anything?"

"Since I learnt not to be an arsehole," he shrugs, glancing at her. "You can thank Christy for that."

"Believe me, I do," she winks at me as she surreptitiously pockets the vial of poison. "Besides, I've taken up enough of Christy's time today as it is."

"Are you sure you're okay with this? I could stay a while longer and help you to finish up?" I ask, more concerned about the fact she's just ingested poison and we have no real idea if there are any long-term side effects.

She shakes her head. "No. I'm good. I'm going to take a bath then check in on Three and Seven. See how they're doing."

"Okay, if you're sure?"

She nods. "Go. Have fun."

Have fun.

Until recently, spending time with The Masks wasn't exactly my idea of fun. How things have changed.

"So what have you been up to with Thirteen?" Leon asks, as he slides his hand in mine and we exit the Numbers' wing of the castle.

"She's been cooking up some more liquid foundation. Some of the Numbers have run out," I lie.

He side-eyes me, pulling a face. "Want to tell me what you've really been doing?"

"I kind of needed someone to talk to. Things have been pretty intense around here," I say. It's not a complete lie and the best I can come up with in the moment.

"And you can't do that with us?" he asks, holding a door open for me as we pass into the hallway that leads to the library.

"I don't know, can I?"

Pulling me around to face him, Leon dips his head so he can look me in the eyes. "Things are different now. I want you to talk to us."

"I want to do that, too," I reply, chewing on my lip and wishing I could open up and tell them everything.

"If it takes us a lifetime to gain your trust, then we'll spend every single day doing just that," he says, misunderstanding my apprehension and unaware that time is something we don't have. I've no real idea if my plan with Thirteen will work. I've not seen past the night of the ball and there are so many variables that could happen, that even thinking about it makes me want to throw up.

"I appreciate that," I say, unable to say anything more.

Like a gentleman, Leon holds the door open for me and I step into the library, my stomach instantly rumbling at the delicious smell rising from the platters of food set out on a table that Konrad and Jakub are already sitting at. Neither are wearing their masks, and Leon removes his as soon as he steps into the room.

"Good afternoon, Christy," Konrad says as they both rise to their feet. All three men are dressed smartly and my heart tightens at the effort they've made.

"What's all this?" I ask, smoothing my palms over my crinkled dress.

"Dinner," Leon replies, placing his hand on my lower back as he guides me into the room, closing the door behind us.

"I can see that." I smile, my skin heating at the way they stare so openly at me.

Jakub pulls out a chair for me to sit down on. "We wanted to do something... *nice*," he says, his hazel eyes cutting to his brothers as his cheeks heat. "Isn't this what normal people do?"

Konrad grins. "Brother, you're blushing."

"Leave him alone, Kon," Leon says with a smirk. "We all know he's not the only one blushing, except in your case it's your dick." Leon pointedly looks down at Konrad's crotch and I stifle a giggle at his erection tenting his trousers.

"Fair point." Konrad shrugs, leaning over to press a kiss against my cheek once I'm seated. "I can't help it if Christy has my dick rock fucking hard twenty-four seven.

"Ditto, brother, ditto," Leon agrees, adjusting himself, and this time it's my cheeks that are heating.

"Well, I appreciate it. This *is* nice. Thank you," I say,

picking up a roll from my side plate and breaking off a piece to eat, if only to give my hands something to do. I've suddenly become very nervous, and this time it's not from fear.

"What would you like to eat? I had the cook make us a selection of dishes because I wasn't sure what you liked," Jakub says.

I follow his hand as he lifts the lid off a large bowl of spaghetti tossed with chargrilled vegetables, garlic and parmesan. Next to it is a plate piled high with slices of meat. There's grilled fish, skewered prawns, all manner of vegetables, salads, soup and even fondue filled to the brim with bubbling cheese that smells divine.

"It all looks delicious. You choose," I say.

Jakub nods then glances over all of the items, finally settling on the pasta. He piles some onto my plate. "I think you'll like this."

Picking up my fork, I twirl it around and around in the pasta then place it in my mouth. The taste is delicious and I can't help but moan around the burst of flavour that hits my tongue. My eyes flutter shut as I chew. Swallowing, I open my eyes, my fingers coming up to my lips as I laugh, embarrassed. "It's delicious," I say.

"Fuck," Konrad mutters, licking his lips, his gaze hyperfocused on my mouth. "Watching you eat is so erotic."

Leon swallows a mouthful of red wine. "Fuck, yes it is," he agrees, his voice thick with approval.

I squirm in my seat, their combined attention making my skin heat. I look between the three of them, uncertain what to do. This is new territory for all of us. We don't exactly have a good record of spending time together at a dinner table.

Jakub coughs, sensing my hesitation. "Ignore my brothers. Eat, drink. Let's talk. Nothing bad is going to happen, I promise."

"I know," I nod, helping myself to another mouthful as the three of them dish up food onto their plates.

For a while we sit and eat in silence, the air thick with tension and an undercurrent of nerves. As much as I know these men, I don't really know them at all and that becomes more and more obvious as time passes. If these men are to be mine, and me theirs, then we have to know more about each other than just our painful pasts. Leon was right that we should talk, and this seems like the perfect opportunity to do that.

"That was heavenly," I say, placing my knife and fork on my empty plate and taking a sip of red wine. It has a deep, woodsy flavour with a sharp aftertaste that somehow reminds me of the three of them.

"There's plenty more," Leon says, eying up the remaining food.

"I'm full. Perhaps the staff might like to finish it?" I suggest.

Leon nods. "Give me a moment and I will call for the staff to come and clear the table," he says, getting up and striding over to a phone in the corner of the room. After requesting the table be cleared and dessert brought up, he returns, taking his seat. "Masks," he says, just as there is a light knock tap on the door a minute later.

"Come in," Konrad instructs as soon as they've covered their faces.

Half a dozen staff enter the room and within a couple of minutes have cleared the table and left behind a trolley loaded with numerous desserts, all of which look tempting.

Once we're alone, they reach up to remove their masks. "Wait," I say, a sudden idea popping into my head. "Will you keep them on for a moment?"

I can see the confusion in their eyes, but they nod in agreement. "What is it?" Leon asks, canting his head to the side as he looks at me.

"I wanted to tell you something about myself. Something that you don't already know about me, but I'm only going to do that once you've told me five things about yourself. Once you've done that, I want you to remove your mask and tell each other something you've kept secret."

"We don't keep secrets from each other," Jakub says.

"Yes you do," I reply, daring him to argue. "We all have secrets." They remain silent, each of them unsure. "Please, this is important to me," I say, realising in the moment that it is. I want to know the real men behind the masks, beneath the trauma.

"Okay. I'll go first," Leon says. He meets my gaze and blows out a breath. "So five things about me. I like classical music. Bach is my favourite composer. I prefer rain to sunshine. I hate coffee. I got this tattoo because it reminded me of you," he says, running his fingers over the black reeds on his forearm, his muscles flexing beneath his touch. "And finally, I still get turned on by blood and knife play. That hasn't changed despite the fact I have..."

That hasn't changed. It's not meant as a threat, just the honest truth.

Picking up a dessert knife from the trolley, Leon runs the blunt edge across his palm. A shiver tracks down my spine at the memory of what happened in the dungeons between us. Swallowing hard, I lift my gaze up to meet his. "And something about you nobody knows."

Reaching up Leon removes his mask and rests it on the table, before fixing his attention on me. "The night I pulled you from the fire, I broke in through the downstairs window of your cottage. It was thick with smoke, and the fire had already gutted your kitchen," he says, letting out a long slow breath. My skin turns cold, goosebumps rising across the surface of my arms as I listen. "I saw your mother. She was covered in flames, stumbling towards me."

"Oh my God," I say, bringing my hand up to my mouth. Tears prick my eyes, but I blink them back, forcing myself to stay strong.

"She said something to me. Something that haunted me for years afterwards, but it only made sense recently."

"What did she say?" Jakub asks when I'm unable to form any words.

"She said: *please, let her live.* Even back then she was trying to forewarn me of what was to come."

"Fuck," Konrad mutters before knocking back a mouthful of bourbon.

"You didn't try to help her?" I ask. It isn't an accusation, merely a question I need answering.

Leon shakes his head. "She died seconds after saying that to me, Christy. Honestly, I don't even know how she managed to speak. I had to make a choice, pull her from the fire, or you. I chose you."

I blink away the sting of tears. "Thank you," I say eventually.

"For what?" he asks, guilt shading his eyes.

"For telling me the truth." Picking up my glass of wine with shaking hands, I take a sip, needing the kick of alcohol to steady my already fraying nerves. "Who's next?"

"Me. I'll go," Konrad says instantly.

"Okay tell me five things about you," I say, forcing all thoughts of my mother out of my head.

"I hate classical music. Fuck Bach, give me Led Zeppelin any day."

"Fucking heathen," Leon mutters, rolling his eyes.

"I play the guitar."

"Electric or acoustic?" I ask, taken aback.

"Both."

"Wow."

"Is that so hard to believe?" he asks me.

"Yes," I shake my head, smiling a little. "Sorry, go on."

"I like the smell of freshly cooked bread. It reminds me of my past, though I don't have any recollection as to why. I have a fear of heights, and finally, there hasn't been a minute that's gone by when I haven't thought about taking you upstairs..." he says, glancing at the secret door hidden in the row of book-shelves across the other side of the library. "I want to strap you to that bed and make you come over and over again."

My skin heats at the gravel in his voice as he removes his mask. "And what don't Leon and Jakub know about you?" I ask, pressing my thighs together to ease the sudden throb between my legs.

"Just Jakub. Leon's aware."

"What the fuck?" Jakub exclaims, looking between the two men.

"I killed Nala's mum. It was me," he says quickly, as though ripping off a bandaid in an attempt to temper the pain.

Jakub's eyes widen. "You?"

"Malik had strangled Nala's mum. He'd sent me to clean up his mess, but instead of getting rid of her body I brought her back. He caught us."

"Us?" Jakub asks, looking between his brothers.

"Leon was with me. He took the fall for it. Malik punished Leon whilst I was forced to kill Nala's mum then give her CPR over and over again. It was only when I could no longer bring her back that Malik stopped whipping Leon. *I* killed

Nala's mum." He shakes his head, scraping a hand over his face.

"You tried to save her," I say gently. "Your intentions were good. *Malik* killed Nala's mum and then he turned your empathy and compassion against you both, just like he always did. You had no choice."

"How did you...?" Konrad asks, then his voice trails off as understanding dawns.

"I saw it. *All* of it."

"And you're still looking at me the way you are. How can you even bear to be in the same room as me?"

"Because you were a victim as much as Nala's mum was," I say softly.

His relief is palpable, but it's quickly overshadowed by panic. "How the fuck am I going to tell her? I don't want Nala to hate me, even though I deserve nothing less."

"Normally I believe in telling the truth, no matter how painful. But honestly, she's been through so much already. What would she gain knowing it was you who killed her mum, apart from more heartache? For now this stays between us," I say, reaching for his hand and squeezing it tightly.

Konrad sinks back in his chair, nodding.

With a tremulous breath, I turn to face Jakub. "Your turn," I say.

"Sure," he replies, and for a moment his attention is focused on his wine glass as he swirls the liquid around and around. When he lifts his gaze to meet mine, I see sorrow first and fore-most. It makes my throat dry and I have a very real need to reach for him and take away some of the pain he harbours so deeply. Instead I listen.

"Every year on the anniversary of Star's death I take the same walk that we used to do together when she was alive. She loved me unconditionally and I miss her," he says, picking up his glass of wine and taking a sip before continuing. "I don't drink tea or coffee, I prefer chamomile tea, it helps me to sleep because most nights I can't. That day when I first kissed you, the lotion you were covered in had the scent of patchouli. I love the smell, it reminds me of..."

"Of?" I prompt.

"My mother," he says, meeting my gaze.

"So you remember her?"

He shakes his head. "Not particularly, but that smell, it's like home."

"I understand, scent can be very powerful, especially when it comes to unlocking memories."

"I've been collecting obscure objects for years now," he continues with a nod. "I appreciate uniqueness, and find comfort in what others find unattractive."

"Why?" I ask, knowing this is an important part of his psyche.

"Because my father would bring home beautiful women to use and abuse, then when he didn't get what he wanted out of them he would take it out on me. Beautiful things only ever caused me pain."

"I'm sorry," I say, stroking my fingers briefly over his forearm. He grits his teeth at the memories, then continues.

"I have a telescope set up on the roof of the castle because I'm into astronomy."

"You study the stars?"

"Yeah, Jakub's got a thing about *Uranus*..." Konrad smirks, and Leon barks out a laugh. Even Jakub smiles.

"Hilarious," he replies, and the soft chuckle that parts his lips makes my stomach flip. That little spark of happiness changes his whole demeanour completely.

"Got you laughing didn't it?" Konrad retorts with a wink as Jakub removes his mask and places it on the table before focusing back on me, his expression serious once more.

"And something you've kept secret?" I prompt.

Jakub presses his mouth into a hard line, then pulls out a mobile phone from his pocket. "Charles, our hacker, intercepted a call between your sister, Beast, and Arden Dálaigh. It took him a while to unscramble the conversation—they've got a pretty good set-up—he only recently sent it to me."

"And you kept this from us because?" Konrad asks, his tone of voice one of annoyance.

"The conversation was an interesting one, but not surprising," Jakub continues, ignoring Konrad's question as he presses play on the message.

My skin turns ice cold at the sound of Kate's voice, not because of what she's saying, but because I've already heard it. It was the conversation she had about attending The Brònach Masquerade Ball. The one I'd seen in my vision.

"How long have you known?" I ask.

"Oh I've always known they'd come, Christy, but I received this information about a week ago," he adds. "Your sister protects the people she loves. It was inevitable. The difference now is how we're going to handle it." Jakub glances at his brothers. Leon frowns and Konrad drags a hand along his jaw.

"And how are you going to handle it?" I ask, feeling sick to my stomach, even though I know that whatever he chooses to do won't be successful. Beast, Ford and Kate will see to that.

"Brother?" Leon questions when Jakub doesn't answer straight away.

"I was ready to kill them all," he admits. "But I know that if we were to do that then we'd lose you forever. I'm not about to make the biggest mistake of my life. I've already made so many."

"So what are you suggesting instead?" Konrad asks.

"We're going to let Christy poison us just like she and Thirteen have planned."

"What?!" Leon exclaims, his eyes widening in shock as he looks from Jakub to me.

I rise to my feet, pushing back the chair as I back away from the table. "How did you...?"

"Five," Jakub replies, getting up slowly, stalking me.

Fear thumps inside my chest, rabid like a dog in its attempt to leap out of my chest and run away. He promised he'd never hurt me, and yet there's a tiny part of me that doesn't know for certain that he won't.

"I don't understand," I reply, flicking my gaze to Konrad and Leon who are watching us both with their mouths agape. Shock rendering them immobile.

"I sent Five to invite you to dinner a few hours ago. She found you both on Thirteen's bed and came to fetch me. You were out cold, dead asleep, and Thirteen looked like a corpse."

"The hell?" Konrad exclaims.

"I saw the cut on Thirteen's hand, the vial of liquid and discarded knife on the counter and for one horrible moment I thought you both committed suicide," he says, his hand shaking as he swipes it over his face, a brief flickering of grief glancing across his features. "But when I couldn't find any cut on you and realised you weren't cold like Thirteen, I understood what she'd done and recognised that you were under the influence of a vision. I witnessed it once before, but at the time I hadn't realised what was happening to you."

"What the fuck are you talking about, Jakub?" Leon asks, rising from his chair. He storms across the room standing beside me, ready to defend me.

"I spent a whole afternoon watching Christy sleep a couple

weeks after we kidnapped her. I was fascinated by how deeply she slept and the fact that I could place Star's collar around her neck and she never stirred. Only you weren't sleeping, were you?" Jakub asks.

"No," I admit.

"And Thirteen?" Leon snaps, confusion and worry making him short-tempered.

"Thirteen was always the Trojan horse." Jakub sighs. "I suspected her arrival here was more complicated than she'd let on, and whilst the Deana-dhe have every reason to come here to seek revenge just because we're Brovs, I think possibly it has as much to do with Thirteen as it does us."

"You think she's involved with the Deana-dhe? That she wants to hurt us?"

"Yes and no," he replies heavily.

"Fuck!" Konrad swears.

"Don't doubt her. Thirteen *is* your friend, a really good one," I say, willing him to believe that.

He nods. "I believe you," he reassures me. "Whilst I sat there watching you both debating what to do, I remembered what you said to me the other night. You said that one day you'll lay claim to our hearts and on that day we'd have to trust you to take care of them. You promised you wouldn't break them. I knew then what you were both trying to do. So I waited to see what would happen, and when Thirteen's lips started to return to their normal colour, I knew what you had planned. They're coming for us, but you've already *seen* that, haven't you?" he asks.

Tears prick my eyes but I refuse to answer him. Knowing I can't risk confirming his suspicions even though he's right about it all.

"She can't say," Konrad intervenes. "Don't make her."

Jakub nods. "I trust you. I trust Thirteen. Fuck knows we don't deserve your protection, but we will accept it, Christy," he says, reaching for me, his hands wrapping around mine. "I can't see into the future, but what I do know, what I've always known, is that your sister and the Deana-dhe won't rest until we're dead. I was ready to die for you. But when I saw there was a possibility that we could get a second chance..." his voice trails off as he pulls me against his chest, his lips brushing over mine. "I knew I'd do anything to have it. *Anything.*"

I can't respond, not just because he's pressing a kiss against my lips, but because I'm terrified that I'll change the course of the future somehow. Instead, I kiss him back. I answer him as best I can with my actions. That's all I can do in the moment. When we pull apart, we're both panting and Leon and Konrad are watching us intently.

"They'll take her," Leon says, his fingers curling into fists at the thought.

"But at least we'll all be alive to see if she returns," Jakub replies, glancing at me.

"No!" Leon exclaims, shaking his head.

"I've gone over it in my head so many times. It's the only way, brother," he insists.

Konrad swipes a hand through his hair. "This could all backfire..."

"How the fuck am I supposed to let you go?" Leon asks, shaking his head.

"You have to trust me, *please*," I beg, reaching for him. His jaw clenches, but he doesn't argue this time. "I can't tell you what you want to hear. I can't tell you what's going to happen, but I can share my truth, or at least part of it," I say, dragging in a steadying breath.

"Go on," Jakub says, a softness in his eyes that gives me the courage to continue.

"I've hated you all. I've wished you dead over and over again," I admit. "I was willing to use my body to gain your trust, and up until recently my plan had always been to seek vengeance. To hurt you the same way you hurt me. I *wanted* you all dead," I say, my voice trembling. "But now..."

"Now?" Konrad gently prompts, his blue eyes blazing with emotion.

"If I've learnt anything living with this gift is that I *have* to trust in it. I don't know what will happen past the night of the ball, but what I do know is this: I don't hate you anymore. I want you to be free from your past and the pain it's caused you. I want you to know what it feels like to live without violence, or the threat of it. I want you to be better men. I want you to learn from your past mistakes..." My voice trails off as I look at them each in turn. "I want you to *live*."

Konrad reaches for me, his palm cupping my cheek. "Then that's what we'll do, but if fate has other plans then I want to enjoy these last fews days together. If I'm going to hell, Christy, then I need to at least take a little bit of heaven with me."

"What do you want from me?" I ask, my voice breathy, a flush of heat climbing over my skin at their combined attention. I've asked them this question countless times before, but this time I mean it differently.

"Will you come upstairs with us? Will you allow us to worship your body the best way we know how? Will you trust us to take care of your pleasure in ways you've never experienced before?"

My skin heats at the thought. I've seen the secret room hidden above the library. I know what they keep locked away in the armoire. I'm well aware of their sexual predilections. The question is, am I ready to immerse myself in their world so completely?

"We want to love you, will you let us?" he continues, his blue eyes hooded with desire, with lust, with... *love*.

He steps back, allowing me the space to decide, to look upon the men who've so wholly and irrevocably changed me. I give them the only answer I can.

"Yes."

CHAPTER THIRTY-FIVE

Leon

MY HAND GRIPS around the handle of the knife as Christy lies back on the bed. She's naked, her skin cast in a golden glow from the fire Konrad lit in the hearth, her hair fanned out over the bed, a fiery mane bright against the white cotton sheets. Jakub leans over her, strapping the leather cuff to her wrists and ankles and pulling on the chains, spreading her wide open.

"Ohh," she exclaims, her skin covering in goosebumps, her nipples pebbling with anticipation. My gaze is immediately drawn to her ripe pussy, glistening like a peach, her excitement already creaming her ruby red core. I don't think I've ever seen anything more beautiful. Shaped in a perfect oval, her labia is fleshy and pink, her clit a tiny nub just waiting to be rubbed and licked, her opening tight. I see it contract with arousal, her feet sliding along the sheets as she tests the strength of the restraints. My already hard cock strains against my trousers as my gaze tracks lower still to the stretch of skin between her opening and arse.

Fuck, what I wouldn't do to take her virginal arse and make it stretch for me. Adjusting my dick, I approach the bed. My eyes lifting to meet Jakub's. I don't need to look at his dick tenting his trousers to know just how much he wants her, too.

It's going to be a long, long night.

"The sash, Kon," Jakub says, jerking his chin towards the armoire.

Konrad opens the doors and searches through the various lengths of silk until he finds the one he's looking for. Striding over to the bed, he passes it to Jakub who leans over and ties it around Christy's head, covering her eyes.

"What are you doing?" she asks, her voice breathy, filled with anticipation and a hint of fear.

In small doses fear can be an aphrodisiac, and tonight she'll learn that we're experts at walking the tightrope between fear that excites and fear that terrifies.

"Taking away one sense heightens the others," Konrad explains as Jakub lowers his mouth over Christy's nipple and gently scrapes his teeth against the tight bud.

"Jakub," Christy cries, her heels pressing against the mattress as her back arches.

Jakub smiles, pleased that she's turned on by him, by this, that her enjoyment is his pleasure. The change in him is remarkable.

"I've got you," he whispers, and I watch as he runs his tongue over her chest, giving the same attention to her other nipple, before blowing cool air over her skin. Rapt, I stare at them both, marvelling at how her skin flushes pink and her pussy weeps for him, for us.

Stepping towards the bed, I place the knife on the mattress

and undress, stripping naked. Jakub and Konrad following suit. This isn't the first time we've shared a woman, but it is the first time we've shared a woman we love. Konrad wasn't lying when he said we want to love her, we do, every last inch.

"Bring the peacock feather and the flogger," I say, never once taking my eyes off of Christy.

"Flogger?" Christy asks, her voice quaking as she twists her head to the side, straining to hear. She tries to bring her arms and legs closer to her body but Jakub reaches up and pulls the chain forcing her legs and arms open once again and locking them in place. He trails his fingers gently from her wrist, down her arm and over her rib cage, reassuring her with his touch.

"The flogger isn't just used to whip a person, Christy. Trust us," Jakub says as I take the flogger from Konrad.

He places the peacock feather on the mattress, keeping hold of a vibrator he selected from the armoire. Shifting around, Konrad takes my place at the foot of the bed as I stand beside Jakub. Slowly I lower the flogger over her mound, allowing the long leather straps to settle between her parted legs, dragging the straps upwards and over her stomach, then back down between her parted pussy lips.

"Oh!" she exclaims.

"The feather, Jakub," I instruct, loving the way her body reacts to the simplest stimulation.

He gives me a slow smile, his hand fisting his cock briefly before he climbs on the bed and reaches for the feather. Sitting on his heels, his scarred and bruised knees pressing against her rib cage, Jakub trails the peacock feather over her breasts whilst I drag the flogger up her pussy and over her stomach, repeating the action over and over again. She shudders beneath our touch, her mouth falling open as she moans.

"That's it, concentrate on how this feels," Konrad says,

dropping to his knees as he whispers the words over her inner thighs, the tip of his tongue edging towards her sex. She gasps as he presses the cool metal tip of the vibrator against her clit, her hips bucking at the vibration.

"What's that?" she asks breathily.

"A clit stimulator," Konrad responds, his voice thick with arousal as he stares at her pussy.

Little pants release from her mouth as she rocks against the vibrator. She's already relaxing in our presence and the difference in having her trust is plain for all of us to see. It's a gift, one I will never take advantage of.

"This is just the beginning," Jakub whispers as he leans over her and presses his mouth against hers, kissing her deeply.

"Touch is the first sense we're going to explore," I add, gently flicking the flogger over her stomach as Konrad slides his tongue into her opening, her stomach muscles flexing and contracting with our combined attention.

"Do you want more?" Konrad asks.

"Oh please, yes," she whispers, straining against the restraints as we continue to assault her senses with touch. She starts to roll her hips, her body undulating in a wave as we each simultaneously stroke her with the vibrator, flogger and feather. When I trace the path the leather straps have taken over her stomach with my mouth, and Jakub lavishes her nipples with his tongue, her skin flushes and her lips blush a deep pink. I could watch her like this for years and years and never get bored. Except we have just days until the course of our future is decided.

Fuck.

My heart does a somersault and my gut tightens. I don't want a future if Christy isn't in it.

I won't... I *can't* live without her.

Forcing that rogue thought out of my head, I trace my tongue over the mound of her stomach until I'm forehead to forehead with Konrad. He drops the vibrator to the bed, grinning as he gives me access to her clit.

"Tandem?" he asks,

"Of course," I agree.

"Jakub, give the chains some slack," I say, and Jakub quickly reaches up and releases the pulley a little, allowing Konrad to adjust her position.

"Bend your knees, Christy, and put your feet on the mattress, keeping your legs wide," Konrad instructs, sliding his large palms under her arse and lifting her up so I can place a firm cushion beneath her.

"L—like this?" she stutters, her body shaking from pleasure as my fingers slide through her pussy and swirl over her clit.

"Exactly like that," I say, my voice thick with arousal. "Such a good girl."

Konrad glances up at me, giving me a nod then lowers his mouth, tonguing her from her opening, down her perineum to her arse. She sucks in a surprised breath as he gently fucks her arse with his tongue, but when I add my lips to her clit and start tongue fucking her there, the sound she makes is far more beautiful than any Bach piece.

Oh how she sings for us.

Fuck my cock aches for her! It's experienced softness with her and now it wants to fuck. Hard.

But first we get her off.

Together Konrad and I lick, suck and fuck her pussy with our tongues. Occasionally, our tongues meet, but neither of us pull away, feasting on her pleasure that spills over our lips and into each other's mouths. We've always been close, the three of us, and living the kind of life we have, sexual contact is the only kind of affection we were ever allowed to indulge in. We've never fucked each other, but we've shared women, and if our cocks touch or mouths meet during those occasions, we never pull away.

Behind me, I'm aware of Jakub shifting higher up the bed. When I take a moment to look over my shoulder at him, I can see him rubbing the tip of his cock over Christy's lips. She gasps, and he slides the head of his dick past her parted lips, one hand fisting the base, the other bracing against the headboard. His attention is solely fixed on her mouth and I don't blame him. It's fucking beautiful.

"Eyes on the prize, brother," Konrad says, a deep chuckle vibrating up his throat as his hand disappears out of sight. I know he's gripping his dick. I'm doing the same. How can we not touch ourselves when we have such fucking perfection spread open beneath us.

Lowering my lips back to her pussy, Konrad and I pick up the pace. Both of us are drowning in her pleasure as she weeps for us. Her hips grind against our faces, her movements jerky, her legs shaking as her orgasm builds and builds. I imagine a white-hot ball centred deep in her womb, growing in size and power as we give her the best head of her life.

Fisting myself, I pump my cock, feeling the familiar feeling of an orgasm gathering in the base of my spine and knowing the moment she comes, I will too. Her cries of pleasure are the key to uncorking my own. Christy's moans intensify, her whimpers distorted by the slip and slide of Jakub's cock between her lips.

"Sing for us, beautiful," I say, my voice gruff as Konrad rears back.

I follow his gaze as it drops to the knife resting on the mattress a little ways over, our thoughts in sync as he grabs it, his fingers wrapping around the blunt blade. I nod, easing back, my fingers replacing my tongue on her clit as he slowly inserts the thick, ridged, wooden handle into her pussy. She shudders at the sudden intrusion, her spine pressing into the mattress as her fingers and toes curl into the sheets, her cries louder now that Jakub has pulled free from her lips. Fisting his dick, Jakub picks up the feather and traces it over her pebbled nipples whilst stroking his cock.

Taking his cue I grab the discarded flogger, gently trailing it over her pussy as Konrad fucks her with the handle of the knife, fisting his dick with his hand. With touch we bring her to the edge, but as Jakub begins to speak, it's the sound of his voice that heightens her pleasure.

"Look at your pussy, so pretty and wet," he says, the grip on his dick tight with want. "I want to spill my cum all over your birthmark. I want to mark you with my cum. I want to own your heart like you own mine. I want to take care of it. Fuck, Christy, I love you!"

And with that declaration Jakub tips his head back and roars, his dick jerking as he paints her birthmark and lips with thready white cum. I watch as she parts her mouth, her tongue snaking out to taste his cum. When Jakub bends over her and kisses her, tasting himself on her lips, Konrad orgasms, covering her thighs with his cum, all the while driving the handle deeper into her pussy, working her up into a frenzy.

"Come for us, Christy. I want to see your cunt quiver," I say, willing her to let go, needing her to come so that I can too, because I refuse to do it without her.

Jakub pulls back, allowing her to drag in a deep breath. Her back arches as her legs and arms tense, pulling against the restraints. She's so fucking close. Sensing her impending orgasm, Konrad pulls out the handle of the knife, his eyes locking with mine before he kneels between her legs once more and pinches her clit hard. Christy screams and her pussy contracts, a stream of cum squirting out of her and onto Konrad's parted lips as he drinks her down, pressing his mouth against her quivering hole and lapping at her wetness. I orgasm a second later covering her trembling stomach with my cum.

Twenty minutes later Christy is clean and lying on her side on the bed, her legs drawn up as she slumbers, the blindfold removed. The loosened restraints are still strapped to her wrists and ankles, and the pink slash of her pussy is plump and tempting as Jakub and I move silently about the room cleaning ourselves up and gathering more items from the armoire. I place the item I've chosen on the side table and slide in behind Christy as Konrad enters the room, carrying a tray piled high with the desserts we left in the library.

"Are you still hungry?" I ask, smirking.

Konrad grins, flicking his gaze to Christy. "Aren't you?"

"Ravenous," I agree, knowing I could feast on Christy forever and never get sick of the taste.

Konrad places the tray on the side table and climbs onto the bed. "Hey," he says, brushing a tendril of hair off her face, waking her up gently. She yawns, uncurling her body, stretching like a cat. I watch as the skin on her scarred back pulls taut as she moves and I have the urge to run the blunt edge of a knife through the whorls of healed skin. Instead I use my fingers, loving the feel of the ridges and grooves. Turned on by them.

"Hey," she whispers back, her voice soft, shy almost. She doesn't ask me to stop touching her this way, instead she kind of shifts a little so I can access more of her scarred skin, a long breath easing out of her parted lips as Konrad softly kisses her. My tongue chases my fingers, and I lick her scars the same way I would her pussy. Reverently.

"Did I fall asleep?" she asks when Konrad finally pulls back.

"Just for a short while," Jakub says, standing at the end of the bed and laying down three items.

"What have you got there?" she asks, pushing upwards onto her elbows, her bare breasts wobbling as she moves. My cock instantly thickens.

Jakub takes a moment to answer, unashamedly fisting his growing erection as his eyes rove all over her body. Her lips part at his attention, and the slow trail of kisses that Konrad presses against her arm. I mirror him, unable to stop touching her, kissing her, too.

"A tuning fork, anal beads and a bottle of perfume mixed by Thirteen," he says.

"Wow," Christy whispers, her cheeks flushing a deep pink. "Quite a selection. Are they for me?"

Jakub nods, picking up the anal beads, showing her the string of medium sized black orbs linked together with string, almost like a pearl necklace. He runs them over his palm, watching her intently. "If you're willing, one of us will insert these into you. At the point where you're ready to orgasm, they'll be removed."

Her mouth drops open, her chest heaving at the thought. "Will it hurt?" she asks.

He shakes his head. "On the contrary, you'll find the sensation very pleasurable. I promise you, there'll be no pain."

"I've never—"

"Are you willing?" he asks, fixated on her.

"I'm willing to try," she says, biting her lip as a cute flush of pink creeps up her neck and across her cheeks as he replaces the string of anal beads on the mattress and picks up the tuning fork.

"Is that what I think it is?" she asks, eyes wide.

"It is."

She squirms on the bed, pressing her thighs together. Konrad nips her breast. "Spread your legs, Christy," he demands.

"I'm not—"

Her sentence is cut off when Konrad smooths his hand over her stomach and cups her pussy, his middle finger dipping inwards. For a moment quiet descends and the only sound to be heard is Christy's soft pants and the slip and slide of Konrad's fingers moving through her parted folds. His attention has the desired effect and her legs drop open. Satisfied, Konrad removes his hand.

"What do you intend to do with that?" she asks after a moment, her gaze focused on the tuning fork.

"Both the sound and the vibrations are very... *Stimulating*," he replies by way of explanation.

"And the perfume?" Christy asks.

"Is designed to heighten pleasure through the sense of smell," he explains, lifting up the small glass vial and popping the cork. He places it under his nose and draws in a deep breath before passing it to me. I watch as his eyes roll back briefly and his skin flushes a deep pink in the places not marred with bruises. The hit is instant and obvious.

Taking the vial from him, I breathe in deeply. My nose tingles and my eyes water from the potency as a rush of sensation rips through my body and makes my balls tingle.

"Fuck!" I exclaim, the lingering notes of geranium, sage and grapefruit a pleasant after effect.

Passing it under Christy's nose, she breathes in, her skin breaking out in a rash of goosebumps as her eyelids flutter shut from the scent and her fingers curl into the bedspread.

"That smells incredible," she murmurs, pressing her thighs

together once again at the surge of pleasure endorphins that I know she's experiencing right now, because I am too.

"Thirteen could sell this and make billions," Konrad says, taking it from me. He tips the vial up onto the pad of his finger then swipes it down the centre of Christy's chest all the way down to her navel, chasing the scent with his nose like an addict taking a hit of cocaine. "Fuck, yes."

His hand lowers and he fingers her again, riding his own pleasure whilst stimulating hers. When I reach for the knife I'd placed on the side table, her breathing halts and she stiffens.

"And the knife?" she asks warily.

"For *my* pleasure," I say, pressing the blade against my palm, and dragging the tip through my flesh. The skin parts, blood beading, the drops falling onto her bare chest.

"Leon," she whispers, fear rounding her eyes, her chest heaving.

"I won't cut you without your permission, but I am going to paint your skin with my blood," I say, placing the knife on her stomach as my cock punches against her hip as the pain makes way for euphoria. Swiping my bleeding palm over her chest and up her neck, I wrap my fingers around her throat, my blood smearing across her porcelain skin. She turns her head to me, her gaze drinking me in as I gently squeeze, then release her throat. "Do you trust us?"

She nods.

"Good, because everything we do is with your pleasure in mind. Okay?"

"Okay." She licks her lips, nerves and excitement fighting for her attention as she squirms on the bed, the chains rattling.

"Keep still, Christy," Jakub orders gently as he picks up the tuning fork and a small leather drum. "There won't be a moment when you don't enjoy this. I *promise*. We have so much to make up for and it starts right now."

Lightly tapping the fork against the drum, he holds it upright. Combined with the stimulation the perfume has already evoked, the sound is not only pleasant to the ear but causes a visceral reaction in Christy.

She draws in a surprised breath, the hairs on her skin lifting as Jakub runs the still vibrating instrument slowly up from her ankle to her knee and down her thigh, holding it against the very top of her thigh just shy of her pussy lips.

"That feels... Ohhhhhhh," she cries.

"Good?" Jakub prompts, a smile on his lips as he taps the tuning fork against the drum once more, then lowers it to her pussy lips. Her whole body quakes as he rests the tines against her tender flesh, the sound and the vibrations rushing across the most sensitive part of her body.

Christy shudders from the contact. "That feels *so* good," she murmurs, rocking her hips.

"You won't be leaving this room until you've come multiple times, Christy. I want to erase every shitty thing we've done with pleasure. Let us love you the best way we know how," Jakub says, lifting his gaze to meet ours. "Leon, Konrad, you know what to do."

Whilst he continues to activate the vibrations, adjusting the position of the tines so that they oscillate against her pussy, making Christy writhe in pleasure, Konrad places a wedge of melon against her parted lips.

"Bite," Konrad says, and she obeys, her tongue snaking out, lapping at the juice before she takes a bite. He allows her to chew then swallow, then slides the rest of the melon between her parted lips.

"Now suck. Suck on it like you would suck my cock," he demands. "I want to see your pretty mouth at work."

Christy hums in agreement and closes her lips around the watermelon and does exactly that, her body jerking against the rapid and continual vibrations from the tuning fork. Her pussy is dripping now, her wetness sliding down the crack of her arse, lubing up her tight hole.

Not to be outdone, I trace the underside of her breasts with the blunt edge of the blade, following everywhere my knife has touched with my bloodied fingers, and then my tongue. Tasting my essence on her makes me as hard as rock. I'm so ready to fuck that it's taking every last ounce of control I have to prevent myself from shoving Jakub away and burying myself inside of her. He must sense my need, because a moment later he's calling my name.

"Leon," he says, jerking his chin at me, his gaze dropping to the anal beads as he moves around the bed to stand next to Konrad, giving me room to insert them.

Grabbing some lube from the armoire, I smother the anal beads then lower myself to the floor at the foot of the bed so I can get a better view of her tight hole. Shifting the position of the tuning fork over her pussy lips so that the tips of the prongs are facing downwards, Jakub gives me a nod.

"Easy does it, brother," he says, a note of warning in his voice as he slides the prongs over her clit. Christy moans, and I use the opportunity to swirl my lubed up finger over her hole.

Gritting my teeth to prevent myself from coming immediately, I gently insert my forefinger inside of her. She's so fucking tight and I have to suck in a deep, controlled breath as I watch a drop of wetness slide out of her pussy and over my finger. For the next minute or so, whilst Jakub rubs her clit and Konrad feeds her all sorts of desserts, kissing her between mouthfuls, I finger her arse, getting her ready. When her sphincter begins to relax I press a kiss against her thigh.

"Christy, I'm going to insert the anal beads now," I say, slowly removing my finger and pushing the first small bead inside of her. She moans, her head lifting off the mattress, her eyes blinking as she attempts to acknowledge me. Her pupils are blown wide with pleasure, her body simultaneously malleable and strung tight. "Just relax, okay? I will insert each bead slowly one by one. It shouldn't hurt, but if it does, tell me and I'll stop."

She nods.

Slowly, I press the second anal bead into her lubed up hole. She jerks at the sensation, her stomach muscles tensing, her core contracting and releasing, but the groan of pleasure she releases from her lips and the way her jaw slackens tells me she's enjoying every moment.

"Jakub, her clit," I say, urging him to continue touching her there because right now his jaw is slack and his fist is pumping his dick hard as he watches her pussy leak for us.

"Fuck," he mutters, shaking his head at just how fucking lucky we are before dropping the tuning fork to the bed and swirling his middle finger over her swollen clit. He fingers her whilst I insert the remaining beads until she's filled with them, the circular rubber hook on the end of the string of beads left flush against her skin.

"All done," I grind out, a rush of blood surging up my cock as I stand. Gripping the base of my dick, I temper the flow. Konrad notices, grinning at me.

"Alright, brother?" he asks, a smile in his voice.

"You?" I reply, noticing the precum beading on his own dick. I raise my brow, knowing how desperate he is to sink inside of her because I feel exactly the same way, too.

He follows my gaze, grinning before pressing his thumb

against the slit and swiping at the droplet, replacing the slice of melon with his thumb. She moans, sucking him into her mouth. Konrad swears under his breath and a chuckle escapes my throat. He's barely hanging on.

I know the feeling.

Shifting back to our original positions, we continue to arouse Christy. Time passes, the hands of the wall clock shifting as the last of the afternoon's light fades into darkness, stars lighting up the sky beyond the leaded window.

One by one Konrad feeds her a sample of each dessert, using his fingers to feed her, whilst I trace our names over her stomach with the blunt edge of the knife. My heart rate picks up as her skin pales briefly from the pressure of the knife, turning pink as the blood rushes to the surface once more. Jakub presses the vibrating tuning fork against every erogenous zone, and together we build her pleasure to impossible heights, but only ever keeping her on the edge of an orgasm. She cries and whimpers, begs and pleads; every time she comes close we draw back, never allowing her to come, keeping her on a knife-edge of pleasure. It's an exquisite kind of torture, and one she'll benefit from in the most incredible of ways when we do eventually allow her to come, but that won't be until we're all buried deep inside of her. *Deep* inside.

Her skin beads with sweat, her body undulating from our touch. Beneath us Christy is lost to sensation, to touch, taste, scent and sound. She reacts on instinct, allowing her body to take over as she writhes beneath our expert hands. We've all been trained in the art of pleasure, using it in the past along with pain to break the Numbers and reform them into stronger versions of themselves.

But this isn't about breaking, this is about *bonding*.

It's about forming a connection so intense, physically,

emotionally and spiritually, that no matter what happens in the future we will always be bound to one another with an attachment much stronger than the chains that keep her restrained now.

She will always be ours, as we will be hers, in this life or beyond.

I'm as certain of that fact as I am of my love for her.

Flicking my gaze back down her body, I slowly drag the blade over her skin, careful not to cut her. Her body rolls, following the movement as my cock swells painfully.

I need to be inside of her. Making love to her was the single most incredible experience of my life, but right now I want to fuck. I want to let go of all this pent-up anxiety and lose myself in her completely. I'm trembling with need for her. It's painful, and if I don't release some of the stress I fear I'll use this knife and cut her skin, and I promised I'd *never* hurt her again.

Jakub, sensing my need, removes the tuning fork from her pussy and lays it on the mattress again. She trembles, panting at the loss of such a unique sensation.

"Christy, I'm going to untie you," Jakub says. "Once you're free, I want you to get onto your knees in the centre of the bed."

Shifting to give her room, Jakub reaches up and unhooks the chains attached to her ankles and wrists. Trembling, Christy shifts onto her knees with the help of Konrad, then focuses on Jakub as he moves towards her.

"Spread your knees for me," he demands softly.

"Like this?" she whispers, her birthmark deepening as she slides her knees further apart.

"Just like that," he replies, climbing onto the bed and sliding his legs between her parted thighs, his erection bobbing against his abdomen as he moves.

"So fucking pretty," he says, swiping his palm down the

centre of her chest before cupping her pussy. "You're so wet. Look at you dripping for us."

"Yes," she breathes, rocking against his hand, her pussy sliding over his palm. "Please, I need to come. I can't take it anymore."

Jakub's eyes flare with his own need to impale her on his dick. "Yes, you'll come," Jakub bites out, licking his lips as he stares at her pussy soaking the palm of his hand. "You'll come all over our dicks. Are you ready to take us, Christy?"

Her only answer is a deep, guttural moan.

Jakub looks between Konrad and I, and we both know what he's asking without him having to say a word. He's claiming her pussy, and wants to know who'll be joining him.

Konrad chuckles. "You've all had the pleasure of Christy's beautiful mouth. Now it's my turn."

I can't help but release a breath. Good, because I was willing to fight him for her pussy.

Fisting Christy's hair, Konrad tugs her head back and licks the last traces of chocolate from the corner of her mouth before kissing her deeply. Pulling back and running the tip of his nose over her birthmark, he says, "I can smell your arousal, Christy. It's the sweetest scent."

She watches him, her skin flush and her eyes wide as he reaches between her legs and swipes his fingers through her folds, before raising them to his nose and breathing in deep.

"I don't need Thirteen's perfume when I've got you," he says, sucking her wetness from his fingers before stepping backwards, dick in hand.

"You're not joining in?" I ask, reaching out, my fingers tracing over Christy's scarred back as Jakub guides her over his dick. Straddling him, she rocks her hips, his cock sliding through her folds as she tips her head back, moaning.

"I'm happy to watch... *For now*," he adds, his hand sliding up and down his dick as Jakub grasps her hips, forcing her to keep still.

"Once you were Nothing to me," Jakub says, drawing her attention back to him. Christy drops her gaze, staring down at him through the curtain of her hair. "Now you're *everything* to us," he says, stroking his hand down the centre of her chest, his fingers splaying out over her stomach as she stares down at him. "But know this, we won't wait forever for you to return to us when you leave. We *will* come for you."

"You will?" she murmurs, hopefully.

"We will chase you to the ends of the Earth, Christy. How could we possibly not?" he replies, holding her steady as she slowly sinks down onto his cock, the expression on her face one of relief and desperate hunger.

"You've brought us back to life," I add, straddling Jakub's thighs, and positioning myself behind her. Swiping her hair over one shoulder, I reach for her chin, twisting her head to the side and dragging my lips across her cheek before resting them on her ear. "We will die for you, Christy, but we won't live without you, not now that you're our beating heart," I say as I pillage her mouth with my tongue and kiss her like she's the oxygen my heart needs to breathe.

"You own us. Body, mind and soul," Konrad continues, "And now for just a short while we'll own your pleasure."

Jakub adjusts his position beneath us, lying flat on his back, and I press my hand between Christy's shoulder blades, encouraging her to lean forward over him. She places her hands either side of Jakub's head and he groans as she shifts above him, holding her hips steady so he can temper the sensation I know he must be feeling. At the sight of his dick spreading her wide and her puckered hole contracting around the anal beads as she moves position, a rush of sensation zips up from my balls and my dick twitches, leaking precum.

Fuck, I need to take her arse, but not now, she's not ready. Not today, but soon.

Instead, I place the tip of my cock against the base of Jakub's dick, guiding it slowly upwards until it presses against her opening. She gasps, her spine arching as she realises what I'm about to do. With one hand on my dick and the other grasping her hip, I lean over and run my lips against her scarred back, kissing her.

"I'm going to slide inside of you. We're going to claim you, *together*," I say, my breath fluttering over her skin.

"Oh yes, please, *please*," she begs, pressing back against me.

With immense care and control, I hold my dick steady as I push inwards, my eyes focused on our conjoined bodies as hers stretches to accommodate us both. Christy releases a deep, guttural moan. The sound makes my cock grow harder, filling with blood as it rests against Jakub's dick, the veiny ridges heightening my own pleasure as Christy's inner muscles tighten around us. Even though I want nothing more than to rock my hips, I keep still, allowing her body to adjust to the thickness of us both.

"I'm so... So *full*," she exclaims in a breathy rush.

Fuck I know the feeling, because if anyone has penetrated our hearts and ripped us wide open it's her.

"Look at you. Fucking stunning," Konrad says, his deep voice rumbling up his chest. "Does it feel good? Do you weep for my brothers, Christy? Is your mouth as moist, as fucking wet as your pussy is now? Will you take my dick between your lips whilst my brothers fuck you?"

"Yes!" she exclaims, her body trembling as she looks up at him.

"Good, because I'm going to claim your mouth, Christy. I'm

going to spill my cum down your throat whilst you embrace us all," he grinds out, nodding to me.

Reaching for Christy's hair, I wrap it around my fist, gently tugging her head backwards as Konrad strides to the foot of the bed. Grasping the wooden post of the bed to steady himself, Konrad kneels either side of Jakub's head on the mattress then fists his dick, his thumb smoothing over the tip of his cock before he swipes it over Christy's lips.

"Open up for me," he demands. Christy drops her mouth open, her tongue sliding over the head of his cock as he slowly eases his way past her lips and into the heat of her mouth. "Fuu-uuuuucckkkk," he exclaims, head tipping back as she takes him.

My own arousal is heightened by the way his stomach muscles bunch and strain beneath his skin, reminding me of how my own body feels sunk so deep inside of her.

"Keep as still as you can, Christy. Let us do the work," Jakub says from beneath us as I grasp her hair tighter and keep her head angled and her throat open for Konrad.

She makes a soft whimper as Konrad palms her cheeks and begins to gently slide in and out of her mouth. He's barely moving, but it's enough to push her back down onto our cocks, taking us deeper.

Right at that moment, as I watch Konrad's thick length gently fuck her beautiful mouth, Jakub's dick slips against mine and for a second all I see are flashes of white light as pleasure takes over. Unable to do much else, I allow Jakub to set the pace. He starts with a slow thrust, his dick moving up and down the length of my dick, Christy's arousal slicking us both. Our balls touch as he moves, sending shockwaves of pleasure ripping up and down my spine. As much as I want to fuck hard, I'm well aware of how much we're stretching Christy, so with exceeding care I move in tandem with Jakub.

He pushes in, I pull out. He pulls out, I push in.

The hardness of his dick and the softness of her pussy is a heady fucking combination. I've never experienced anything as erotic, and when my heavy-lidded gaze drops to the curve of her arse and her tight hole, my balls tingle with my need to come.

I'm so fucking close.

Konrad groans and Jakub joins in, his fingers digging into Christy's creamy hips as he holds on for dear life. She's our anchor, the rock that holds us steady, the roots that have bound us all together, the lifeblood that has made our battered hearts beat.

Fucking Christy like this, together like this, is beyond anything I could've hoped for. The three of us have been lost for so long, wrapped up in our own living hell that there was no comfort in each other, let alone with anyone else. Now look at us, tethered to this woman. This beautiful, brave, courageous fucking woman who owns us all.

"Fuck, I'm going to come," Konrad says, his face flushed, his muscles rippling as he loses a little bit of control and thrusts deeper into her throat.

"Come, brother. Come down her throat. Fill her up with your cum just like we're about to," I say, knowing my words will push him over the edge.

He meets my gaze and for the briefest of moments, acknowledges the connection we share, the love we have for each other, and then, with his chin tucked into his chest and his eyes fixed on Christy, he comes hard, trembling and cursing and shaking and whispering words of love until he's spent.

"Fuck, fuck, fuck," Jakub curses, and I can feel his dick swelling with his impending orgasm just as Konrad pulls free from her throat. Grasping her face, he dips down, kissing Christy and tasting his cum on her lips as she moans into his mouth. Her inner walls tighten, clamping around us both, quivering with her own impending orgasm. Jakub's close too by the sounds he's making.

Thrusting deeper, harder, faster, Jakub and I fuck Christy.

All sense of control is lost as we move inside of her. Her beautiful body stretched for us, creaming our cocks, making us slip and slide with ease.

Whilst Konrad kisses her softly, we love her loudly, our cocks like pistons deep inside of her. Our groans a cry of ownership and relief. It feels like at any moment now we'll punch through her cervix and take up lodgings in her womb. Fuck knows I'd happily spend the rest of my days there.

"I'm going to come!" she screams.

When her back arches I reach down between us, pulling out the anal beads in a gentle, but steady movement, and like the pin of a grenade being released, Christy's orgasm explodes around us, detonating our own.

Throwing her head back, she screams, her nails digging into Jakub's chest, marking him with her pleasure. Seconds later Jakub follows suit, his dick jerking and pumping against mine, setting off my orgasm like a motherfucking freight train. It's so powerful that for a moment I'm blinded by it, blinded by *her;* our mirror, our light, our motherfucking beating heart.

CHAPTER THIRTY-SIX

Christy

"WE HAVE two days to go until the ball, *Christy*," One says, snarling around my name. "I need perfection, not mediocrity."

Beside her Two stretches, laughing smugly. You'd think she'd be grateful that I stepped up. Not a chance. She's as cold and self-centred as One is. There'll be no gratitude from either of them, despite rehearsing with the Numbers these past few days for hours and hours until my feet are covered in blisters and my toenails ripped and bloody.

"Christy is far from a mediocre dancer," Three interjects with a scowl. "She's picked up the routine quickly and is as good a dancer as I am. Better actually."

One snorts in derision, jerking her chin towards the centre of the room. "Again," she snaps. "We have just two days left until the ball. I want perfection. It *isn't* perfect."

I huff out a breath, getting into my starting position when all

I want to do is poke her damn eyes out for what she did to Jakub.

"Uh oh, One sure is pissed at you," Four says sweeping past me, her long blonde hair flowing out behind her as she moves. In her hands she holds her violin and bow, and I watch as she rests it beneath her chin and starts to play.

"Again!" One snaps, glaring at me.

Gritting my teeth and ignoring the giggles coming from the triplets I begin to dance. Pretty soon I'm lost to the movement and everyone in the room disappears. Dancing for me is cathartic, a way to express myself when worries, thoughts and fears make that impossible. It's a side of me that, until I arrived here, was kept secret.

Not anymore.

Moving across the floor I think about Grim and Beast and how I'm going to navigate my emotions around them. I think about my uncle and aunt who will be beside themselves with worry. I think about how much I've changed since arriving here, about the friends I've made and the relationships I've formed. I think about my mother and her letters. I think about The Masks, and my feelings towards them.

The other day when I had said that they were mine, I meant it. I *felt* it.

That hasn't changed. If anything it's strengthened. With every passing day my feelings have grown exponentially, and the bond I share with them is strengthening. Made stronger since that incredible night we shared in their room of pleasures. *Our* room of pleasures, because if I know one thing for certain: no other woman will set foot in there. No one but me.

A feeling of possessiveness fills my chest, and it makes my steps vigorous and angry as I imagine One's talons trying their best to sink into Jakub. I've seen the looks she's been giving him, the obsession in her eyes, the *jealousy*. She's a problem, and I have no desire to leave this castle knowing she'll be left behind with them. But what choice do I have?

I have to leave in order to save their lives.

"Okay, I've seen enough!" One snaps, dragging me mentally back into the room.

I pant, my chest heaving, sweat sliding over my skin as I glare at her and she glares back. I'm fully aware of the rest of the Numbers watching us face off, but I don't care.

She wants Jakub, but she *can't* have him.

"Is there something you want to say, One?" I ask, my voice icy.

One stands, pushing back the piano stool. It clatters to the floor, the sound making the triplets jump and Six shake her head at me in warning.

"Christy, don't," she says.

"Everyone out!" One snaps, glaring at the Numbers.

"Christy?" Three asks, hesitating as the triplets, Four, Eight and Two leave the room.

"I'll be fine. One and I need to talk."

Three gives Five a look of concern, a silent conversation passing between them before Five flicks her amber eyes to me. "I'll be just outside if you need me, *Mistress*," she stresses, fingering a small blade strapped to her chest as she walks out with Six.

"*Mistress?!*" One questions, her eyes widening at Five's choice of address.

"Indeed. The Masks have chosen *Christy*. I respect that choice as should you," Five says calmly, before following the rest of the Numbers out.

One waits for the door to shut before rounding on me. "You

really think you've changed them, don't you?" she asks, shaking her head in disbelief.

"I don't think, I know."

"Do you *really*? You've been here what, a couple of months, and suddenly you're our mistress? I think not," she exclaims, grabbing a bottle of water and downing half of it.

"I don't want to be anyone's mistress, One. That was Five's choice to refer to me that way, not mine."

"And it's not their choice either. The Masks do not have a mistress, *they* are the masters."

"If that's the case then why do you look at Jakub the way you do? Like *you* own him."

"Because I do!" she snaps, spittle flying out of her mouth in anger.

"No," I shake my head. "You don't."

"I was here first! I left my old life behind to become One. I endured those first few months with his father. I fucking *survived* them. I shaped Jakub from a boy into the man he is. *Me*, not you. So despite what they call you now, you're still Zero. You're still Nought, fucking Nothing!"

"Shaped him?" I laugh, shaking my head at the absurdity of it all. "You *abused* a child. You hurt him over and over again in some twisted, fucked-up mind game alongside his sick father."

One's eyes narrow at me. "I gave him what he needed. I still give him what he needs and don't you fucking forget it!" "

"Needed?" I snarl, taking a few steps towards her. "What he needed was someone to protect him. Someone to get him, Leon and Konrad away from here, and out of that evil bastard's clutches. You perpetuated abuse. You helped to *make* him into a monster!"

"No. I did what I had to do to survive!" she screams back, panting now.

Our breaths fall in angry puffs but her outburst reminds me that no matter how much I dislike her, she was a victim of the Collector's too, and for a moment it tempers my anger.

"I understand that," I say with a heavy sigh, hating that I have to concede that point. "I can see the damage that man has done to you all, but perpetuating it? He's been dead for two years, One."

"You don't know anything," she spits, taking my olive branch and crushing it beneath her foot. "You haven't been through what we have together. Jakub and I have a connection, a bond, and no one else can break that."

"Perhaps that was once true, but not anymore."

"Oh, you think you can break it? Only I can give him what he needs," she argues.

"It's already broken, One. He doesn't need pain. He *never* did."

"Bullshit. It wasn't that long ago that he came to me begging me to whip him, and why do you think that was, Christy?"

"Because he was hurting. Because he was twisted-up inside, confused, *scared—*"

"Exactly," she cuts in. "*You* did that to him. Not me. I just helped him to find peace."

"No!" I snap. "You only added to his pain. You reinforced everything that bastard taught him to believe. You made him think that pain is the only thing he deserves. That affection, kindness, compassion is a sin, is weak. Do you have any idea of the damage you've caused?"

One narrows her eyes at me, folding her arms across her chest. "I am well aware of what and who I am. I am also acutely aware of what you are."

"And that is?" I ask, wishing I wasn't so easily baited.

"You're a phase, an infatuation, a new piece of arse, and a

fucking ugly one at that. You're nothing but a damaged piece of pussy that they'll tire of in a few weeks. *That* is all you are," she replies, sneering, her beauty twisted into an ugly mask.

"You're so wrong," I say, feeling nothing but pity for her.

"It won't be long until you're yesterday's news," she continues, "And we'll be back to how we were before you came here and screwed it all up!"

"I didn't come here. I was brought here against my will and now—"

"And now you think you can save them, I suppose? Perhaps you've even convinced yourself that you love them? God you're so transparent. Ever heard of Stockholm Syndrome? You're the perfect example. Fucking textbook case."

"You don't know what you're talking about," I argue.

"Don't I? What do you think will happen when you leave here?"

"Leave?"

She smirks. "You think I don't know who you are? Who your sister is? I'm not a fool. I survived the Collector because I wasn't just talented and beautiful, but because I was also *smart*. Your sister will come for you and you will return to your life just like you've wanted ever since arriving here. You'll forget about the men you claim to care about."

"You don't know anything," I retort, stepping into her space and pressing my finger roughly against her chest, refusing to acknowledge that she's right, at least partly. "Back off from Jakub. From all of them."

"Don't threaten me. You've no idea what I'm capable of."

"Oh I know exactly what you're capable of," I retort with disgust. "You're a sadistic bitch with a sick obsession."

She smirks, looking me up and down as though I'm nothing

but a mere pile of shit beneath her shoe. "But at least I'm *loyal* to The Masks. I know a turncoat when I see one."

"What do you mean?" I ask.

"We both know that when it comes down to it, you'll choose your family over The Masks. All this bullshit about you caring for them ends when your sister arrives and tries to put a bullet in their chests."

"That *isn't* going to happen," I reply firmly.

"You're right, it isn't, because the difference between me and you is this: *my* family is here within the walls of this castle and I will *always* choose them," she says, her fingers finding the ends of my hair as she leans in close and presses her mouth against my ear. "I will protect them and what we've built here, don't think I won't." Pulling back she gives me one last lingering look before striding toward the door.

"When it comes to the people we love, we're not so different, One," I call after her.

With her hands wrapped around the handle, she turns to look at me. "Watch your back," she warns, before pulling open the door and striding from the room.

"Mistress?" Five asks, stepping into the room and closing the door behind her. "Are you okay?"

My shoulders drop as I let out an anxious breath. I'm not afraid of One, but I am afraid of what she's capable of doing. "How much do you know?" I ask Five, cutting to the chase.

"All of it," she replies with a sharp nod of her head. I suspected as much, but I need her to spell it out to me.

"And that is?"

"I know about what you and Thirteen have been doing, about what you have to do on the night of the ball. The Masks trust me, as should you."

"*Can* I trust you?" I ask.

"Of course," she replies instantly. "As far as I'm concerned you have earned my loyalty by giving them yours. You can trust me."

"Then I need to ask you a favour."

"Anything, Mistress."

"Please, just call me Christy."

"Okay, Christy," she replies, smiling a little.

I breathe a little lighter knowing that I have her on my side, and some of the tension in my chest releases. "One has threatened my family. She knows they're coming for me but she doesn't know anything other than that. I need her out of the way—"

"You want me to kill her?" Five asks, frowning. "I have been entrusted to protect you, and I have promised to do that, but she is still..."

"Your family?" I ask.

"Yes. I do not agree with her ways, but she is the glue that has held us all together these past years and I can't turn my back on that."

"I understand and I don't want you to kill her, I just need you to keep her out of the way on the night of the ball, because if she hurts my family I will have no choice but to act, and there's been enough blood spilt within the walls of this castle. For this plan to work, she can't get in the way. Will you help me?"

"You have my word."

"Thank you."

"And Mistress. I mean, *Christy*..." Five says.

"Yes?"

"What about after you leave?"

"I'll need you to keep an eye on her and take care of The Masks until I return. I'll figure out what to do about One then."

"When will that be? I'm not sure they'll survive without you for long."

"As soon as I possibly can. I *promise...*" My voice trails off as I look at her. She's worried, I am too. There's so much I don't know. I used to despise my gift, now I just want to be able to see how this all pans out. I need to know we'll all be okay. "Will you watch over them?"

"Of course I will," she agrees, pressing her hand to her heart and giving me a warm smile.

"Thank you."

"No, it is me who should be thanking you," she argues.

"What for?"

"For healing the hearts of three men that I care about."

She moves to leave but I reach for her, my fingers curling around her hand. "Wait, can I ask you something?"

"Yes."

"When this is over, will you tell me your story?"

"When this is over I will gladly do that. I would even like to be a part of a new chapter in your own story if you'll allow me."

"You mean to stay here?"

"This is my home, but I would never assume it will remain that way when you return."

"Of course this is your home. I would be glad of your company, and your friendship, but don't you want to find your family?"

She shakes her head. "My family sold me. I have no desire to ever see them again."

"I'm sorry," I say.

"I'm not..." Her voice trails off as she regards me. "What will become of the rest of the Numbers?" she asks.

I sigh. "I guess that's up to them."

"You mean to free them?"

"I know my sister, she will give them a choice to leave here. It's more than they've been given in the past," I say gently.

Five presses her lips together in a firm line. "I understand. Is that all?"

"There is one more thing."

"And what's that?" she asks, tipping her head to the side, her long black plait falling over her shoulder.

"What's your real name?"

"Raksha," she answers immediately.

"Raksha? That's beautiful. What does it mean?"

"It means *she who protects*, and I promise to do that," she replies with a gentle bob of her head, before spinning on her heels and striding from the room.

CHAPTER THIRTY-SEVEN

Christy

OVER THE NEXT two days Ardelby Castle becomes a hive of activity in preparation for the ball and I've seen more staff milling about the castle than I have since arriving here. Seeing all these new faces leaves me with a feeling of dread, reminding me that in a few short hours my sister will be here and once again my life will be flipped upside down.

"What do you think?" Jakub asks me, dragging me free from my thoughts.

"I think it's exquisite," I reply, taking in the incredible transformation before us and forcing a smile on my face. "Is it always this extravagant?"

"Of course. The Brònach Masquerade Ball is quite the event. People from around the world travel to the castle to attend. It has to be extravagant. It's expected."

My head tips back as I stare up at the vaulted ceiling now

hidden behind huge swathes of black silk that are hanging from a central point and draped to the cornices circling the room. They're fixed in place with a row of gold tulle that circles the room. The layered material falls to the floor in a shroud of gilded darkness with pretty, twinkling white lights interwoven into the fabric, making the backdrop appear like the night sky. High above a trapeze hangs from the most central point of the roof where Two will perform over the circular stage situated in the centre of the hall below it. Placed around the stage area are twenty round tables covered in black tablecloths, ten gold chairs surrounding each one. In the centre of every table there is a beautiful flower arrangement of calla lilies dripping with lengths of white pearls, gold chains and tiny black-laced masks.

"And the sex, is that an expectation too?" I ask, side-eying him. "How does that work exactly? There are two hundred seats here."

"We have a bidding system in place," he replies. "The highest bidders get the Number of their choice to spend the night with. The winners stay and the rest of our guests leave at two am."

"Have the bids already taken place?"

"Yes. Each Number, apart from Three and Seven have been bought for the night. Given their situation I've removed them from the bid."

"Situation?" I frown, chewing on my lip. It was more than a situation and we both know it.

"I mean to make amends," he says softly, scraping a hand through his hair. "What I made Seven do to Three, it was wrong. I won't force Seven to entertain on his own. They fuck together or they don't at all."

"It was inexcusable..." I agree, my voice trailing off.

Jakub heaves out a sigh, and I hear the agony in it. "I know what I did and I will live with the damage I caused them both for the rest of my life—"

"But?" I cut in.

"No buts," he shakes his head, grasping my hand. "Look, Christy, I know how you feel about our business. I know how uncomfortable it makes you, but I can't change what's going to happen tonight anymore than you can. The bids have already been received and the winners notified. Our clients are not men and women you disappoint. Tonight must go ahead. You know that, as well as I."

"It does," I agree reluctantly, my gaze drifting to Konrad and Leon who are on the other side of the room directing a group of staff as they place One's baby grand piano onto the stage.

"Believe it or not, the colour scheme was Konrad's idea," Jakub says, bringing my hands up to his lips and kissing my knuckles, trying in his own way to alleviate the sudden tension between us.

"Is that so?"

"Yes. He has quite the eye for it, wouldn't you agree?" I can hear the smile in his voice and would appreciate the lightness if I weren't so preoccupied with what's to come this evening.

"He does..." I reply, my words trailing off as anxiety churns my stomach. I've felt sick all day, and nothing Thirteen has given me has been able to stop this feeling of dread growing larger.

"You're scared, aren't you?" Jakub asks, his gaze fixed on me as I try, and fail, to pull myself together.

"Terrified," I admit.

"Me too," he says quietly, so quiet that I almost think I'm mistaken until I see the expression on his face, despite the fact that half of it is hidden by a tan, leather mask.

"I wish I could reassure you, Jakub, but I can't."

"Still no more visions since the last one?" he asks, placing my hand against his chest and covering it with his own. It comforts me, feeling the steady beat of his heart.

"No," I reply, hoping that he doesn't notice the lie. Jakub is referring to the vision I had of him in the cabin and not the vision where I saw Thirteen and the Deana-dhe as teenagers. I haven't told them about it because that's her story to tell, not mine.

"It isn't all that unusual. I've gone weeks before without having a vision. It's just..."

"Just?"

I frown, trying to explain how I feel. "It's just that I feel empty somehow."

"Empty?" he questions, flinching from my words.

"Oh no, please don't misunderstand me," I rush to say. "I'm not talking about the way I feel about the three of you. It's just that something has shifted. I *feel* different."

His fingers trace the back of my hand that's still pressed against the steady beat of his heart as he stares at me, his hazel eyes more brown than green today. "How *do* you feel about us?" he asks.

"Certain," I reply immediately.

"Certain?"

"Yes. I'm certain that all the hate I felt is gone. All the pain has disappeared, the distrust, the doubt and suspicion."

"We don't deserve you," he replies, briefly pressing a kiss against my lips.

"Stop saying that. We're past that now. I want to be with you. Not because of some legend, or because of what a woman said years ago way before we were even born. Not because Fate has deemed it her wish, or because some people believe I'm suffering from Stockholm Syndrome—"

"What? Who said that?" he demands, cutting me off with a scowl.

"It's not important, what's important is that *I* want you, all three of you. It took me a while to understand that," I say with a smile, *knowing* it's true.

"For all of us to understand that," he reminds me. "But Christy, *who* said you have Stockholm Syndrome?"

I sigh. "One, who else?"

"She has no fucking right," he seethes. "I'll speak with her."

"Stop," I say, grabbing his arm as he moves to walk away.

"She's overstepped. I need to remind her of her place," he argues.

"How?"

"What?"

"How will you remind her of her place, Jakub? Will you punish her like you made Leon punish Twelve? Will you beat her, whip her, chain her in the dungeons?" I ask, uncertain why I'm defending her when she wouldn't do the same for me.

"She's disrespected you, *us*, our relationship. I won't tolerate it!" His voice rises, and on the other side of the room Konrad and Leon look over at us. I shake my head, waving away their concern. They make their way over anyway.

"I'm a big girl. I can deal with a few spiteful words, Jakub."

"This is my fault. I should never have gone to her when I did. I knew it was foolish. I have to fix this now. I won't let her treat you like that, Christy. I won't."

"What's up?" Leon asks, looking between us both.

"One," Jakub grinds out.

"Is she going to be a problem?" Konrad asks, though it's less of a question and more of a statement.

Jakub opens his mouth to speak, but I shake my head. "No.

She won't," I say, attempting to reassure them despite my own concerns.

"And you know she won't be a problem because...?" Leon inquires, eying me carefully, assuming I've had a vision.

"Not because I've seen anything in our future," I sigh, "But because when it comes to the point that I have to..." I swallow hard, another well of nausea rising up my throat at the thought of poisoning them. "I've asked Five to keep One out of the way."

"Why would you need to ask Five to do that?" Jakub asks, his voice low, lethal.

"Aside from the fact that she'll try to stop me. One knows who I am, who my sister is. She knows they're coming for me and she'll try to intervene," I explain.

"She threatened you, didn't she?" Jakub asks, his voice deadly.

"She's willing to do anything to keep you safe, Jakub. In her own, messed up way, she loves you."

"I'm going to fucking kill her!" he snaps as a look of agreement passes between Konrad and Leon.

I grip his arm. "No!"

"Christy," he warns, glaring at me. "I won't have anyone threaten your life."

"I said no. There'll be no more deaths. Five has promised to keep her out of the way until it's done. I trust her to do that, as should you."

"She won't stop, Jakub. You know that as well as I do," Konrad says to him.

"Please. Whatever you're thinking, *don't*. We'll figure out another way that doesn't include violence."

"Why are you protecting her?" Jakub asks.

"I'm not protecting her. I'm protecting you. You've all fought too hard to be where you are now. Don't you understand? I can't risk losing you to the darkness again so soon. I *refuse*," I say firmly.

"And I won't lose you to her jealousy either. So what do we do?" Leon asks stubbornly. "We might be changed men for *you*, Christy, but that doesn't mean to say we'll allow her to hurt you. *I refuse*."

"Look, I *know* she won't be there when I do what I have to do. So I can only assume that Five does what I ask and keeps her away, or that it's at a point in the night when she's otherwise engaged. Please. Just let this go for now and we'll figure out how to deal with One when I return. Okay?"

"Jakub, think about this," Leon warns.

"I'm with Leon. One is volatile right now. Dangerous. Look what happened with Twelve," Konrad adds.

Jakub looks from me to his brothers and back again, a muscle feathering in his jaw with the stress. "Tonight we do this Christy's way."

"Jakub—" Leon begins, but Jakub cuts him off.

"One will be onstage most of the night and after The Menagerie performs she'll be with the Wolf. If at any point she manages to get away from him, we have Five as back-up."

"Has it slipped your mind that Five will also be busy tonight? She has her yearly date with the Mole,' Konrad points out.

"And have you forgotten stamina really isn't his speciality? Half an hour with Five and he'll be passed out. We do this Christy's way, but with one exception."

"And what's that?" I ask.

"If any of us catch One trying to hurt you, she'll be dealt with instantly. No second chances."

"Five will make sure that doesn't happen," I say, more to reassure myself than them.

"Then that's settled. Let's have lunch in our suite before the madness starts. I've asked Thirteen and Nala to join us," Jakub says, taking my hand in his.

"Shit, Nala! She won't understand. She'll *hate* me," I exclaim. I hadn't even considered how she's going to react to what I'm going to do, let alone the pain it will cause her. I'm a terrible person.

"She won't know. I've asked Thirteen to give her a tonic. She'll be asleep through it all," Jakub says.

"Thank God." My shoulders drop and Jakub releases my hand, pulling me into his arms as I murmur my thanks into the warmth of his neck. "I couldn't bear to think of her distress. She's been through enough."

With his arms wrapped around me, Jakub hauls me closer, and for the briefest of moments I allow myself to hope that maybe everything will work out and we'll get our happily ever after.

"I love you, Christy," he says, brushing his mouth across my cheek. "To be able to say that to you freely, let alone feel it, is a gift I will treasure for however long I have left in this world."

"Years and years," I whisper, my fingers curling into his jumper as my heart wishes for it to be true. The words I know he wants to hear are on the tip of my tongue, yet I can't say them. I won't say them, not yet, not until this is all over and I know we'll be free to love each other without fear of repercussions. First I have to figure out a way to get back to them all without Grim and Beast finishing what they'll be starting tonight.

"Hey, stop hogging Christy, she isn't just yours, you know," Konrad says, grinning as Jakub releases me from his arms and I step into his and breathe in his distinctive scent of leather and metal, spice and musk.

"You smell good," I mutter.

"I smell even better," Leon remarks, stepping up behind me and sandwiching me between them both, enveloping me in a warm hug.

Smiling into Konrad's chest I say: "I could get used to this."

"That's the plan, Christy. That's the plan," Leon mutters.

"I'M COMPLETELY STUFFED!" Nala exclaims, sitting back in her chair and rubbing her belly. "How the other half live!"

"Other half?" Konrad chuckles. "Don't pretend you weren't stuffing your face with Cook's food just like the rest of us. Renard always made sure you were fed exactly what we ate. We know this because we made sure of it."

Nala's face falls. "I miss him."

"As do we all," Jakub says softly, his hand resting on my thigh beneath the table. I fold my fingers over his.

"He would be so happy to see you all together like this," Thirteen remarks, reaching over to squeeze Nala's hand.

She smiles up at her, brushing away a stray tear that tracks down her cheek before looking over at me. "The second I met you, I *knew* you'd be the one to change it all. Even when you'd refused my sandwich that first morning you arrived here and glared at me like I was your enemy, I knew."

"Wait, what are you talking about?" Leon asks, glancing between us both. His eyes narrow, but there's no malice, just amusement.

Nala pulls a face. "You were being arseholes leaving her down in the dungeon for so long."

"You devious little bugger..." Leon barks out a laugh, Konrad following suit.

"It makes total sense now," Konrad says, his chuckle fading away as he pierces a carrot baton with his fork, pointing it at me. "And there's me thinking you were a survivalist when all the time this little meddler had been feeding you."

"Christy *is* a survivor," Jakub says, his tone serious, guilt-ridden. "She's had to be."

"You're not angry?" Nala asks.

Jakub shifts in his seat and I feel the tension rolling off him. "I can't deny that the old me would've been, but the person I am today is glad you meddled."

"Someone had to." She shrugs. "Besides, it wasn't just me, Renard helped too. He was my lookout."

That makes all three men smile.

"Well, thank you, Nala, for doing what was right when all we could do was wrong," Jakub says.

"Don't," I say, shaking my head. "Not tonight. No guilt. No regret. Let's keep this light, cheerful. Please?"

"I agree," Konrad says. "We can go over what absolute pricks we've been another time. Today's not the best day for it, agreed?"

Jakub nods. "Agreed."

"Well, I know what will put a smile on Jakub's face," Leon interjects, his hand finding its way to my other thigh and lightly grazing my skin. "Dessert?"

"Ewww, gross," Nala exclaims, dropping her napkin onto the table and standing abruptly. "I think that's our cue to leave, don't you, Thirteen?"

"I think now is the perfect time," she says, glancing over at Jakub, a silent conversation passing between them. Everyone in the room excluding Nala knows what that look means. It's just as well she's so preoccupied with the ball that she misses it.

"I'm so looking forward to dressing up," Nala babbles on.

"This will be the first time attending the ball without being a member of staff. I can't wait."

Jakub coughs into his fist, a look of guilt passing over his features. "Go on, go and get ready," he says, hiding his feelings expertly behind an indulgent smile.

Nala claps her hands together, squealing in excitement before grabbing Thirteen's hand and dragging her toward the door. "We're getting ready together. You should see my dress, it's gorgeous! I must say, the black, gold and white colour scheme is genius," she exclaims. "I'm wearing white... Because, you know, virginal."

"Oh fuck, she's going to be trouble," Konrad exclaims, glancing at Jakub who's scowling.

"Just as well she isn't—"

"I'm sure it's stunning," Leon cuts in before Jakub can say anything further.

"I did try to persuade Thirteen to wear gold instead of black, but she refused," Nala continues, cupping her hand around her mouth and whispering not so quietly even though Thirteen is standing right next to her. "Thirteen insisted on a high neck, floor scraping black dress that leaves *everything* to the imagination."

"I happen to like my dress," she laughs.

"You're dressing for a funeral, not a ball, Thirteen," Nala says, rolling her eyes. We all take a collective breath and Nala frowns. "What did I say?"

"Nothing at all. Come on, let's go," Thirteen says, placing her hand on the small of Nala's back. "We've only got a few hours and I know you'll hog the bathroom for at least three quarters of that time."

Nala grins. "You've got *the* best bathroom. Beats mine any day."

"Speaking of which," Jakub says, "Next week I want you to move into the spare room in our suite. It's much bigger than your current room and has a walk-in wardrobe and a bathroom that is as spacious as Thirteen's..."

"Really?" Nala exclaims.

"Really. You're my sister and this castle is as much yours as it is mine. You don't belong in the servants quarters. You never did."

Nala's eyes well with tears and she runs to Jakub throwing her arms around his neck. "Thank you, thank you, thank you."

"It's no bother," he says gruffly, patting her on the back. "I should've offered earlier. I just had things on my mind..."

She squeals, releasing him. "I get it. Thank you!"

"Go on, go," he says, a smile playing on his lips.

"Wait!" I say, grasping her arm before she can leave.

"What is it? Did you want to get ready with us girls? I just thought perhaps you'd want to spend time with them before your big performance."

"I do, it's not that. I just wanted to..." My voice trails off as I stand, pulling her in for a hug. "Forgive me," I whisper.

"Forgive you? What on earth for?" she replies with a laugh. "I'm *happy* you're together. Haven't I been trying to get you together since you arrived here? I don't begrudge you alone time. I'm not a child. I get what you all need."

I plaster on a smile as I pull back, squeezing her shoulders. "Well, I appreciate it. *We* appreciate it."

"Jakub may have saved me as a baby, but no one needs to treat me like a child. I've grown up in this castle, I'm fully aware of what goes on here. You need to have sex. I get it."

Konrad roars with laughter and my cheeks flush with heat at her honesty and openness.

"Shall we go?" Thirteen asks, her lips quivering with amusement as she looks between us.

"Yes, let's get beautiful," Nala replies, striding across the room and pulling open the door, stepping outside.

The second she's gone, Thirteen cast her eyes at me. "Come to my room when you're ready, I have something for you," she says, and we both know what that something is: a knife laced with poison.

"I will," I reply softly before she closes the door, leaving the four of us to say our goodbyes.

CHAPTER THIRTY-EIGHT

Konrad

"THE BATH'S READY," I say, standing in the doorway to Leon's bathroom, my shoulder pressed against the door frame as I look upon my brothers and the woman I love.

Jakub downs his last mouthful of bourbon, placing the glass on the table while Christy lifts out of Leon's lap, taking his hand in hers before offering her other hand to Jakub.

He blows out a long breath, then grasps her fingers in his as she leads them towards me.

Stepping aside, I begin to quietly undress, watching my brothers do the same.

When Christy starts to remove her dress Leon stops her.

"No, allow us," he urges.

She nods, her hand falling away as Leon steps behind her and sweeps her long hair over one shoulder, unzipping her dress. With my hand pumping my dick in gentle strokes, I watch as his fingers slide over her shoulders and push the material from her skin. It falls to the floor in a puddle of silk and her birthmark flushes a deep burgundy from our combined arousal.

Beneath the dress she wears nothing but a pair of cream cotton knickers and my cock instantly thickens as I marvel at how turned on I am in her presence. I walk around in a perpetual state of arousal, sporting a semi that instantly hardens the moment she bares herself to us.

Just like now.

With her hands by her sides, her fingers lightly grazing her hips, she waits, understanding that in this moment we need to take control.

Leon presses a kiss against her shoulder, his lips stroking across her skin, the darkness of his hair contrasting with her pale skin and halo of flaming tresses. She tips her head to the side, her mouth parting on a moan as he kisses up her neck and catches her earlobe between his teeth, one hand cupping her breast and the other her mound.

"I'm going to make you come whilst my brothers watch. Spread your legs," he commands.

She obeys, her legs parting and allowing Leon to slip two fingers between her folds, rubbing her gently.

Out of the corner of my eye, I watch Jakub step into the sunken bath. He wades to the far end, taking a seat on the sunken ledge, his hand disappearing beneath the water as he watches Leon stroke Christy's pussy. Taking his lead, I step into the bath too, groaning at the warmth and the way Christy's hips grind against Leon's hand.

Jakub nods, his gaze flicking to me briefly before returning to Leon and Christy. Without even having to ask I know what he feels. This is our goodbye, because as much as we believe in Christy, in Thirteen and her ability, there are never any guarantees. Settling down on the ledge beside him, my dick twitches as I watch our brother gently pull apart her pussy lips with his fingers and showing us the deep blush of her pussy before swirling his thumb over her clit. His arms are tight around her, his cheek resting against hers as she stares at Jakub and I, her ghost eyes drinking us in, as though she too needs to commit our faces to memory just like we do hers.

"Fuck," I exclaim, unable to articulate my feelings other than in curse words. She's so goddamn beautiful, so wet and glistening with arousal, so utterly and irrevocably ours.

Turning her head to the side, she looks up at Leon. "Kiss me," she whispers.

"Forever and always," he smiles, before cupping her cheek and kissing her deeply all the while fingering her expertly. She groans into his mouth, her hand coming up to grasp his head, pulling him closer.

They remain like that, her hips grinding against his hand, as they kiss and kiss and kiss until her body begins to shake and her legs wobble from the oncoming orgasm he's drawing out.

"Leon, I want you to fuck Christy," Jakub grinds out, the desperate need in his voice evident. "Show her and us how much you love her. Fuck her until she can't see straight. Take her. Now."

Believe me, I'm right there with Jakub, my own cock weeping precum as I watch Leon break the kiss and walk her over to the wall. He presses her against the stone, her cheek turned to the side as he runs his lips, teeth and tongue over her scarred back, loving the place he was partly responsible for damaging.

When he lowers to his knees behind her, licking between her crack and biting the globe of her arse, she parts her legs for him and arches her lower back. Taking that as the invite it is, he grabs her arse in his tattooed hands and ducks his head licking her from slit to crack and back again. She moans and his dick bobs in answer, the tip engorged and angry, needing release.

"I said fuck her, Leon," Jakub repeats, and Leon flashes him a crooked smile before he rises back upwards, grasps her hips and pulls her back slightly before slamming into her with one hard thrust.

Christy screams from the sudden intrusion, and Leon's spine arches from the tight grip and warmth of her pussy. It's a feeling we've all experienced. Fucking Christy, *loving* Christy is like coming home. No, it is home. *She's* home.

"I can't hold back, Christy," Leon warns.

"Don't. Don't hold back," she murmurs, biting into her lower lip as he wraps one hand around her long hair as he fucks her, *hard*. Christy cries out, alternating between deep, throaty moans and high-pitched mewls. Once again she sings for us and the sound is a melody I'll never tire of.

Despite the tension Leon holds in his muscles, and the look of sheer agony and ecstasy on his face as he slams into her, this isn't about being violent. This is about staking his claim, owning her body as much as she owns his heart. This is about a man terrified of losing the woman he loves and imprinting her on his body as much as his soul.

I get that.

I understand it because it's exactly what I need, too. Fuck, I need her. My fingers grip my dick as I temper my own building orgasm, refusing to come until I'm buried deep inside of her.

Beside me Jakub's breaths fall as heavily as my own as we both watch our brother lose a little of himself as the darkness within him starts to come unshackled.

"I need to look into your eyes," Leon grinds out, dropping Christy's hair.

He pulls out of her and spins her around, hoisting her back up onto his hips so he can slide back into her. Even those few moments withdrawn from her body causes a wild cry to part his lips until he sinks back inside of her wet heat. And right then, as he backs Christy into the wall and drops his forehead to her shoulder, I see the way he fights for control in the clenching of his teeth and the tremble of his body. Christy feels it too, and her hands cup his face, forcing him to look at her.

"I'm on the edge, Christy,' he mutters out, gravel in his voice as the frenzied fucking is replaced with a slow, deep, fuck as though he wants to crawl into her and never ever leave the safety of her body. His arse tightens, his back muscles strain as he cups the back of her head, anguished almost.

Fuck, I feel that, his pain. It punches through my chest and grabs a hold of my heart.

"I know. I feel it too," she replies.

"Aren't you afraid?"

"Of losing you all, more than anything. But I will not allow anything to get between us, not now that I know."

"Know what?" he asks, still fucking her, still quaking.

"I'll tell you when I return." She gives him a smile, then brushes her lips against his before saying: "I want you to fuck me like the devil, but love me like an angel, Leon."

And so he does.

His thrusts become animalistic, tempered only by his love for her. But he's not the only one to lose his control. Christy does too. She fucks him back, her arse slapping against his hips as she rides him. No, as she *claims* him.

She's a warrior. A slayer of monsters. A guardian of hearts. A keeper of souls.

With one last cry Leon slams into her, coming hard.

Seconds later Christy follows suit, her whole body trembling as she comes undone.

"Fuck," Jakub exclaims, shifting in the water beside me. I peel my eyes away from my brother and Christy and turn my attention to Jakub, giving them a moment to come down from their high. He looks haggard, as though the weight of the world is on his shoulders.

"Brother, what is it?"

"I want to fight for her," he mutters as Leon leads Christy into the shower, turns on the spray and begins to wash her. They talk quietly, smiling and laughing softly as we talk. "How can I let her go? Everything in me wants to fucking rip Grim and Beast apart the moment they arrive, but to do so would mean losing her, and I can't do that either."

"I know. I do too, but like you said earlier we have to let this play out the way it's supposed to. She's seen our future."

"She's seen what happens *tonight*, and unless she's keeping something from us, we don't know what's going to happen after that." He sighs heavily. "It goes against everything I am, Kon. I want to fucking keep her. I don't want her out of my sight."

"I get it. Fuck, you know I do. But—"

"She might never come back," he interrupts.

"She'll come back. I fucking know it."

"And if she doesn't..."

"Then we go get her," I say, snapping my mouth shut as Christy and Leon step out of the shower.

"Hey," she says softly, swiping a tendril of wet, tangled hair behind her ear. Water droplets slide over her naked skin and for a moment we're both mesmerised by her.

"Come here," I say, needing to fucking hold her.

I have this real need to take care of her, it's so fucking powerful. I feel it rumbling inside of me. My monster no longer wishes to hurt her but instead it needs to protect her. Like Jakub I want to fight to keep her, but we all know that killing her sister will turn her against us and we can't afford that.

"I need you," I admit, the confession leaving my mouth before I can stop it.

The last time I was inside her I was fighting the monster within me. This time I want to fuck her slow. I want to show her that I'm capable of being gentle. With my eyes glued to her, Christy slowly steps down into the bath. Leon settles into the water at the other end whilst she wades towards us both.

The water is deep enough to float around her tits and a pang of jealousy rushes through my blood at the way it gets to caress her so thoroughly. I mean, fucking insane right? To be jealous of water, but I am. I'm jealous of the way it gets to envelop every inch of her skin, and seep inside of the place I want to drown my cock in.

Impatient, I reach forward and grab her wrist, tugging her to me. She laughs, and the sound is so carefree, so fucking joyous, that hope blooms inside of my chest, making way for a rush of love that snatches my goddamn breath.

Jesus, this woman.

"What?" she questions, gently stroking her fingers over my cheek.

"I was just thinking that I want to spend the rest of my life getting you to smile like that."

"You do?"

"It's going to take a lifetime to make up for what we've done, so yes, Christy, I want to spend that time making you happy."

"I'd like that," she replies, glancing at Jakub who's watching us both with a quiet resolve. I can see she's unsure of what to do, who to go to, and despite the fact that she's in my arms and I want so badly to make love to her, I let her reach for Jakub.

"Jakub?" she asks softly, her hand resting on his shoulder.

"I'm with Konrad."

She frowns. "Talk to me. You don't have to hide your emotions."

"I'm not hiding. You've opened the floodgates. I'm *healing* because of you."

She leans over and presses a kiss against Jakub's lips. "I will come back to you all. Whatever it takes. I promise."

He nods, standing. "Make love to Konrad and when you're done, come find me in my room."

"You're not staying?" she asks, worry knitting her brows together.

"There's something I need to do. Stay with my brothers. They'll take care of you."

"Jakub, do you need me?" I ask.

"No, Kon. Right now Christy does."

"But what about you?" she asks, refusing to let him go.

He places his hand over hers. "We'll pick this back up when you return to us," he says adamantly.

She smiles softly. "Is that a promise?"

"It's a guarantee," he responds, cupping her head in his hands and pledging himself to her with a passionate kiss that leaves her breathless and makes my dick throb.

Christy watches him leave then slowly drops her gaze back to me. Silently, she straddles my lap, her tits brushing against my chest as she lowers herself down over my aching cock. Her gaze remains fixed on mine and I swear I can see our future mapped out in her ghost eyes as she rocks her hips.

It's fucking paradise.

And yet...

And yet, I get a sudden sense of doom.

It's so powerful that I feel it ram into my chest like a motherfucking sledgehammer right at the moment Christy begins to rock against me.

It hurts to feel that way whilst her pussy clenches my dick and she looks at me like I'm someone important, someone worthy of her, but I can't help it.

Fear scatters across my skin at the thought of this ending.

I've always known that paradise was never in the cards for me or my brothers. This incredible, courageous woman might have brought our hearts back to life but she can't scrub away the sins that are tattooed into our very bones.

Bad people don't get happily ever afters.

We don't.

"Christy," I choke out, rocked to my fucking core as I grasp at her, pressing my cheek to her chest and wrapping my arms tightly around her back, wishing that I didn't fucking feel this way, hoping to fuck I'm wrong.

"Shh," she whispers, cupping my head and kissing me, consuming my fears, burying them deep inside of her as she fucks me slow, our bodies making memories that I'll take with me to the grave.

CHAPTER THIRTY-NINE

Christy

"JAKUB, CAN I COME IN?" I ask, pushing open the door to his bedroom.

I'm wearing my gold ballgown, the one I'd seen in my vision. I've no idea where The Masks got it from or how they even knew my size, but it's a perfect fit. The sheer material of the top half of the dress moulds to me like a second skin, my modesty hidden beneath flesh coloured underwear and tiny crystals that glint in the soft candlelight. The skirt is layered with silk and tulle that floats about my legs as I move.

"Please," he replies, standing by the arched window. A cigarette hangs out of his mouth, the blue-grey smoke lifting in the air above his black, tostled hair.

"I didn't know you smoked," I say, moving towards him, my ballet slippers quiet against the wooden floor.

"I don't. This is a special herbal mixture courtesy of Thirteen."

"Like marijuana?"

"It has a similar effect," he replies, dragging in a deep lungful before stubbing the joint out in an ashtray on the window ledge. "Big events like this can be stressful."

"I see," I say, stopping short as I lift my hand and straighten his thin black tie resting against his gold shirt. "We coordinate."

Reaching up, he fingers the gold ribbon woven into my hair. "We do. Except you're far more beautiful. Look at you. You're a vision, Christy."

"Thank you."

"I wasn't sure if the dress would fit you properly..."

"It's perfect."

He stares at me for a long time, his fingers tracing the shell of my ear and over my cheek, before his thumb presses against my bottom lip. "I've been standing here watching our guests arrive and there's a huge part of me that wants to send them away, close the gates and pull up the moat, locking us all in forever. The thought of being separated from you is killing me. How can I part with the woman who brought me back to life? Tell me how I can do that, Christy," he implores.

Grasping the lapels of his jacket, I push my body against his, my stomach tightening with anxiety, my core aching for his touch, my heart pounding with emotion. "Because it's the only chance we have. I know my sister. She will kill you. We have to do this."

"And once you leave, what then?" His vulnerability floors me as he dips his head and brushes his nose along the tip of mine.

"In my mother's letter to Thirteen she said we needed *time*. She didn't just mean time for this connection between us to grow, she meant time to persuade my sister not to come back here and kill you the moment she knows you're alive. I have to leave. I have to persuade her to let *you* live. I have to," I say, pressing my lips against his and kissing him with every single part of me, willing him to do this, to trust me.

When I reluctantly pull back, he presses his eyes shut and nods. "This isn't easy for me. The Brovs are very possessive, *protective* of what belongs to them."

"I know," I reply, because what more can I say.

"I have something for you," he says, dropping his hand and picking up a small leather case that's resting on the table next to the window. Beside it is a shiny black mask, its surface is so reflective that it's almost like the surface of a lake at night time, or a pond... A shudder ripples down my spine as goosebumps scatter over my skin, another portent that I choose to ignore.

"What is it?"

"It's a gift," he replies, flipping open the lid. Inside is the gold mask I'd seen myself wearing in my vision. Up close it's even more beautiful than I remember, with fine gold inlay and beading all around the outer edge. "I want you to wear it. I want you to show the world that you're ours, that you belong to The Masks just like this mask once belonged to my mother."

"Your mother?"

He nods. "When I said I don't remember her, I wasn't lying, but I do remember a story my father told me about her after I found this mask forgotten about in the room now filled with my collection of curiosities."

"What was the story?"

Jakub runs his finger over the mask. It's as reflective as his black mask, the candlelight flickering across its surface. "She was a fan of Phantom of the Opera. My father said she would ask him to take her to see the stage show every time they visited London."

"And he'd do that?"

"Apparently so." Jakub frowns, his eyes glazing over a little as he's taken back in time. "I only have two memories of my father that are not completely horrific. This one, when he told me the story about my mother, and the time he gave me Star. I'd seen the tiniest glimmer of humanity within him on those two occasions." Jakub sighs, and the weight of his past sits heavily on his shoulders.

"I'm sorry."

"Me too," he replies. "You know, she had a favourite quote from the book. It went like this: *If I am the phantom, it is because man's hatred has made me so. If I am to be saved it is because your love redeems me...*" His voice trails off as he lifts the mask out of its case and flips it over. "Engraved into the back of the mask is that exact same quote."

"That's beautiful," I say, taking it from him, my fingertips grazing over the cool metal.

"It is. My father always referred to my mother as a whore. He made me believe that she was nothing special, that she was beneath him, and in his eyes she was. Then I found this and for whatever reason he gave me a small glimpse into the woman she was. This quote, it's significant don't you think?" he asks me.

"Yes, I believe it is."

"Do you think she thought she could save him?"

"Almost certainly," I reply, my heart swelling with compassion for him and sadness for the loss of a woman who he so desperately needed in his life.

"It's funny, when Leon first suggested we become the Masks the day my father shot Star, I had no idea that my mother loved the book and the musical so much. In fact, I knew nothing about her. I found this mask a few years later. It began my obsession with collecting unusual objects."

Jakub places the case back on the table, watching me as I hold the mask up to my face. It covers my unmarred side, revealing my port wine birthmark. He helps me to fix it in place, then when he's done he presses a kiss against my cheek and stands aside so that I can see my reflection in the window.

"It fits you perfectly, just like I thought it would."

"Jakub, how is this even possible?" I ask, marvelling at how this mask seems to be made for me, its edges somehow meeting the shape of my birthmark perfectly.

"How has any of this been possible?" he counters with a wry smile. "You know, when you first revealed your true face to me, I was reminded of this mask. The fact it fits you so perfectly has to mean something. That's what I'm holding on to despite my own fears."

Fate's touch tracks down my spine, making me shiver. "It has to," I agree.

"When I first laid eyes on your true face, I knew you were mine even if I kept denying it. I think you're the most beautiful woman I've seen. You will never hide who you are again. I want everyone to see what I see, Christy."

"No one has ever looked at me the way you all do," I whisper.

"Then they are fools, because the kind of beauty you have doesn't just reside in the surface of your skin or the colour of your hair. It doesn't just dance over your flesh like the freckles that paint your body or shine in the brightness of your eyes. It lives and breathes in the compassion of your heart, the honesty of your words, the courage you're scarred with and the kindness of your touch. You are a remarkable woman, Christy. You humble me."

A well of acceptance fills my chest and I feel the need to tell him how I feel. That I love this man. That I love them all, every broken, damaged part of them. "Jakub, I lo—" I begin, but he takes my hand, shaking his head.

"Don't. Tell me when you return, when you come back for us."

Blinking back the tears pricking my eyes, I nod. "When I return," I agree.

Squeezing my hand once more, he withdraws his fingers and takes a deep, steadying breath before picking up the jet black mask and sliding it over his face. "It's time to go. See you soon, *moja miłość...*"

I tip my head to the side, frowning.

"My love," he repeats, and the man *I* love walks away from me, his words ringing in my ears.

"HOW LONG WILL she be out for?" I ask Thirteen as we both stare at Nala.

She's fast asleep, her white gown spread out over the blue cotton sheets of Thirteen's bed like a swathe of clouds across a summer sky. Ever since I arrived here she's been a breath of fresh air, a friend when I needed one the most. She's a good kid and I hate doing this to her.

"For the whole night. She'll wake up once it's over," Thirteen reassures me.

We fall silent for the moment, the sound of Nala's soft breaths filling the room and somehow helping to soothe the rapid beat of my own heart. "She's going to be so angry she missed the ball," I say, marvelling at how peaceful she looks, how effortlessly beautiful she is.

"She'll be more angry that she wasn't told about the plan," Thirteen says. "She's as fiercely protective of The Masks as they are of her."

I wince at the thought. "There's too many people involved already. We couldn't risk her, too."

"I agree." Thirteen nods, giving my hand a quick, reassuring squeeze before striding over to the counter where all her equipment sits, the train of her black dress floating behind her in a trail of silk as she moves.

Nala was spot-on in her description of Thirteen's dress, it does cover her from head to toe, but what she failed to mention was how form fitting it is, how structured. The boned corset fits her body snuggly showing off her envious hourglass figure. The skirt flows around her in a wisp of smoke as she walks. Her hair is down, curled into soft waves, and the only makeup she wears is a bright red lipstick. She looks stunning, the epitome of a powerful woman, and I can't help but wonder if she's dressed this way not for a funeral—as Nala had suggested—but for the men she denies are her soulmates.

"Five filled me in about One," Thirteen says, as she picks up the knife resting on the countertop and runs the blade through the flickering flame of the candle she just lit. "I won't lie and say I'm not worried about One's state of mind, but I am reassured that Five is going to keep an eye on her for us."

"One doesn't intervene," I say firmly, at least not at the point when I carve my name into The Masks chests with the blade Thirteen is lacing with poison as we speak.

"Good," Thirteen replies, dipping the heated blade into the white liquid. I watch in fascination as the poison bubbles on the surface of the blade, then seems to evaporate into thin air after a few seconds. She repeats the process several times then places the blade on a stone mat to cool before turning to me and grabbing my hands. "I want you to know that I think you're exceptional. What you're doing for The Masks, it's *brave*. To go against the people you love takes courage. I understand the risk you're taking only too well."

"You sound like you're talking from experience. Are you?"

She gives me a sad smile. "That's not a question I can answer right now."

"Thirteen, you're keeping something from us," I say, squeezing her fingers. "What is it?"

"I *can't* tell you. You understand that, right?"

"It's to do with my mother's letter and the Deana-dhe, isn't it?"

"Please, Christy, don't push this. You'll do what you must, and so will I."

"Should I be worried?"

"If you're asking me whether I'm going to betray you, I'm not."

"That wasn't what I meant. I'm concerned about you, Thirteen. You're my friend."

"Please don't be. I knew what I was getting into when I came here a year ago, just like I understood the terms of the Deana-dhe's debt. I'm a big girl, Christy." Releasing my hands, she pulls me in for a hug and my skin prickles with knowing. "I'm going to *miss* you."

"I'll be back before you know it," I say, plastering on a smile that doesn't reach my eyes because this feels like so much more than a goodbye for now. It feels like a goodbye forever.

"No matter what, we'll always remain friends, just like our mothers before us."

"Of course we will," I agree.

"We've got this," she says, sliding the now cooled blade into a tan leather holster, passing it to me.

I hold it in my hands, and despite the lightness of it, what it represents weighs heavily on my conscience. "What if it all goes wrong, Thirteen? What if my sister fires a bullet into their chests just to be certain they're dead? What if I lose them anyway and this was all for nothing?"

"No, don't think like that. It's going to work. It *has* to," she reiterates.

"Yes, it must," I agree, lifting my chin and giving her a firm nod.

"Strap it around your thigh," she instructs. "Keep it on you at all times."

Drawing up my layered skirt, I secure it in place, the layers of silk and tulle hiding the dagger as I drop the material back over my legs. "Done.'"

"Ready?" she asks me.

"As I'll ever be," I respond, and for once in my life I put my trust in Fate and hope that this time she doesn't fuck us all over.

CHAPTER FORTY

Jakub

"JAKUB, the guests are beginning to arrive," Leon calls after me as I stride across the courtyard and towards the Numbers wing of the castle, my dress shoes clicking across the cobbled stone.

"I'm well aware, Leon," I say, spinning on my feet as I look over at him. "I'm just tying up some loose ends. It won't take long."

"Loose ends? I thought we agreed to leave One alone." He reaches up and adjusts his mask, the shiny black surface like inky midnight as he regards me.

"This isn't to do with One. Besides, she's already with the other Numbers getting ready for the show."

"Then what *are* you up to, brother?"

"Trying to fix a mistake. Trying to be better. Do better." I laugh, tipping my head back to the sky at the lightness I feel admitting that. "I've spent my whole life being the villain, the man who inflicts pain, who hurts people. Tonight I want to change that, Leon."

"Seven and Three?" he asks.

"Yes. I owe them an apology. More actually, but it's a start."

"Fair enough," Leon responds, his gaze flipping from me to The Weeping Tree and back again. His hand absentmindedly rubbing over his chest. "She really did bring us back to life, didn't she?"

"Yes, brother. She really did," I reply solemnly, a light breeze tickling the nape of my neck, almost as though the ghost of Marie just traced her fingers over my skin. Perhaps she did.

"Konrad is greeting the guests, and I can cover you for a short while. Don't be too long."

"I won't be." Leon twists on his feet but I call after him. "Wait!"

"Yes?" he asks, cocking his head.

"Any sign of them?"

"No. Not yet, anyway. Perhaps they're not—"

"They're coming," I interrupt. "So keep your eyes sharp."

"Got it, and brother...?"

"Yes?"

Leon fists his fingers and bashes his hand over his heart, once, twice, three times.

I raise my fist and mirror him. "Me too, brother. Me too," I say, before he turns on his heels and strides out of the courtyard, disappearing from sight.

Tapping lightly on the door Three shares with Seven, I wait. Beyond I can hear low voices followed by light footsteps moving towards the door. A moment later it swings open and I come face to face with Seven. Anger flashes in his gaze before he hides it behind a veil of controlled respect. It seems like I'm not the only one who's capable of wearing a mask to hide his emotions.

"I need just a moment of your time," I say, tempering my voice so it sounds less like a command and more of a request.

"Seven, who is it?" Three calls out.

Seven flicks his gaze over his shoulder then back at me. "She isn't healed." This time I see the words he doesn't say written across the tightness of his shoulders, the grit of his jaw and knuckle-white grip on the door.

He wants me to back the fuck off. I don't blame him.

"That's not why I'm here. I just want to talk. Nothing more."

"Seven, who is it?" Three persists, walking towards him. As soon as she sees me her face drops, fear cascading across her features. "Master, to what do we owe the pleasure?"

Seven's grip tightens even more on the doorframe at her welcome. It grates on him.

"I just wanted a moment of your time. I don't have long, I need to get back to my guests."

"Yes, of course. Please, do come in," she says, prying Seven's fingers away from the doorframe. I pretend not to notice how difficult that appeared to have been.

"Can I get you a drink?" Three asks.

"No, thank you," I say, standing in the middle of their living area, feeling more awkward than I ever have in my life. This castle might belong to my brothers and I, but these rooms are their home, the place where they can be themselves behind closed doors...

Or perhaps they're nothing more than a well-decorated prison.

"A seat then?" Three rushes towards the small two-seater, plumping up the cushions.

"I don't need to sit. This won't take long."

"Why are you here then... *Master?*" Seven adds with as much disgust as he can muster.

"Seven," Three whispers, reaching for his hand but he snatches it away, unable to see the hurt look on her face because he's too busy glaring at me. My stomach roils at the wedge I've placed between them, guilt spreads like acid in my gut.

"I wanted to give you this," I say. Reaching into my pocket, I pull out an envelope, handing it to Three. She takes it from me, frowning.

"What's this?"

"A cheque for one million pounds."

She snaps her head up, her eyes widening. "W—what?" she stammers, her hands trembling as she opens up the envelope. On the cheque is her real name. Cassidy King.

"It's a cheque for one million pounds, Cassidy," I repeat, using her real name. Giving her the respect she deserves.

"Why?" Her eyes brim with tears as she shakes her head.

"Because I owe you at least a better future than the past I've given you."

"This is bullshit!" Seven snaps.

"Seven don't," Three whispers, reaching for him, her slim fingers wrapping around his forearm.

"You think you can pay her off for all the damage you've done, is that it?" Seven accuses, his anger spilling over as he takes a step towards me.

"Seven *stop!*" she shouts, the cheque crumpled up in her hand as she grabs his arm.

He shakes her off, his anger a feral thing as he strides towards me. Gripping the lapel of my jacket, he bares his teeth at me. "You forced me to hurt the woman I love, you piece of shit!"

"Seven! Please, STOP!" Cassidy screams, her fear punching a hole in my heart. She thinks I'm going to punish him for his reaction. I won't. I deserve his anger and he deserves an outlet for it.

"I did," I agree, nodding my head. "And I'm sorry for it."

"Sorry? You're sorry?!" he spits, raising his fist, his whole body trembling with rage as he pulls back his arms. "Do you have any fucking idea what you've done? I can't look at Cassy without wanting to rip my own heart out for what I did to her. I can't sleep from the guilt. Can't fucking eat. I should've fought for her!"

"You *saved* me," she cries, her tears streaming down her cheeks. "You saved us!"

Fuck, her pain is more powerful than any punch, any kick. I fucking feel it shred at my insides. I never ever want to be that man again. Fucking never.

"I should've killed you. I want to kill you!" Seven seethes.

"I know," I reply, understanding only too well how it feels to be forced to hurt someone at the whim of a twisted bastard. The guilt, the rage, the pain and anguish. I get it.

"He's trying to make amends, Seven. Let him go," Cassidy begs, pulling at his top.

"Amends?" He laughs, letting me go with a shove and rounding on her. "It's just a piece of paper, Cassy. It means *nothing*. This is our prison, remember? Prisoners don't have the freedom to deposit a cheque in a bank let alone fucking spend any money."

"This is our home," she argues, fear and worry, and so much fucking love for the man she thinks I'm going to hurt, spilling down her cheeks.

"No," he shakes his head. "It's *never* been my home."

"Seven," she cries, her voice lost beneath a broken sob. "Stop this. *Please.*"

"He's right." I say heavily.

Seven turns back around to face me, his eyes narrowing. "What is this, some kind of test? Will we end up in the dungeons beaten to within an inch of our lives for not fulfilling whatever sick fucking game this is? Will you force me to rape the woman I love again to save us both from death?"

"No. I'm giving you both the opportunity to be free," I say, pointing to the cheque. "Take it, leave here. No one will stop you. I give you my word."

"What?" Three frowns, swiping at her tears. "I don't understand."

Seven stares at me in disbelief. "This is *bullshit*. A trick."

"No. It isn't, Jonathon," I say, using his real name as I reach up and remove my mask, revealing my face to them both. Three sucks in a breath and looks away, but Seven holds eye contact. "Tonight will be the Menagerie's last performance. I'll be offering the rest of the Numbers the same opportunity as you both."

Seven grits his jaw. "And yet you show us your face? Now we'll never be able to leave, right?" he accuses.

"On the contrary. I just didn't want my mask to break when you punched me."

"What?" he snaps, his fingers flexing then curling into fists.

"It's the least I deserve. If I didn't have a woman I love waiting for me downstairs, I would let you beat the shit out of me and wouldn't fight back."

"You expect me to believe you've changed?"

"I don't expect anything. Now do what you wanted to do that night and fucking hit me."

And just like I knew he would, Jonathon loses it. He rushes for me, pulling back his fist and slamming it into my face. Knuckles meet bone and I feel the pain like a fucking sledge-hammer to my head as I take the punch, stumbling back from the force. He doesn't stop there, he grips my shirt, shoving me against the wall and punches me twice more. Cassidy rushes forward, her words lost beneath the sound of his anger as he roars in my face.

"You think that me breaking your face will be enough? That giving us our freedom will be enough when you had no fucking right to take it in the first place? That one million pounds will get anywhere close to repaying what you all fucking took from us?"

"No, I don't, but it's a start. I'm *sorry*," I say, swiping at my bloody lip, meaning it, *feeling* it.

"Fuck you!" he responds, letting me go with a shove, as Cassidy grabs his arm and forcefully pulls him away from me.

She pulls him around to face her, clutching his face. "That's enough. It's over," she whispers, standing on her tiptoes and kissing him softly on his lips. "You can go home."

He grasps her back. "Cassy, my home has always been wherever you are," he replies before smashing his lips against hers and kissing her the way only a man hopelessly in love could.

Picking up my mask, I tie it back on, trying not to wince at the fresh cut in my eyebrow from his punches, then reach into my jacket pocket and pull out another envelope. Inside is a cheque made out to Jonathon Driscal for one million pounds, and just like that, Seven has been released from his chains, alongside Three.

"Goodbye, Cassidy, Jonathon," I say, placing the envelope on the table and striding from the room, finally ready to face the music that's been a long time coming.

CHAPTER FORTY-ONE

Christy

STANDING in the shadows of the Grand Hall, I cast my gaze around the space searching for a glimpse of my sister, but despite the elaborate masks everyone is wearing, I know none of them are her. She has a very distinctive rose tattoo that winds up her neck. It's unmistakable.

"Where are you?" I whisper, anxiety washing through my veins as I sweep the hall with my gaze for the hundredth time this past hour.

My eyes briefly pass over the stage where Six is singing the aria in place of Twelve, her voice captivating the audience who stare at her, enraptured. There's a poignancy to her singing, an innate sadness that emanates from her. It filters across the space, a melancholy that only adds to my building anxiety and the already suffocating atmosphere, at least for me.

She too is wearing gold, but her dress has a layer of black

chiffon covering the golden silk skirt and a black bodice with gold flowers sewn across its surface. All of the Numbers are wearing a variation of the same dress in black, gold and white or a combination of all three colours. I'm the only one wearing all gold. Maybe that was intentional on The Masks' part, maybe it wasn't. Either way, in a short while this beautiful gold dress will be stained with their blood.

In another lifetime, not marred by a complicated history with three even more complicated men, I would've stood and stared in wonder at the intricately woven performances each of the Numbers have executed so effortlessly tonight. I would've enjoyed every single second of it. As it is, my thoughts are troubled. Nothing will ever be the same again after tonight. It will either be the start of new beginnings or the end of everything.

My fingers graze over the knife strapped to my leg beneath the material of my skirt, the leather feels strangely warm against my skin and I feel both relief and a deep sense of restlessness at its presence. Our future, mine and The Masks, boils down to one act of kindness masked by an act of cruelty. If it doesn't work we are all lost, The Masks will die and my heart will cease to function. I know this as surely as I know that dawn will break on a new sunrise tomorrow, just like it will every day after without them.

These men who—for such a long time I feared, then hated, then wanted dead—now own my heart as much as I own theirs. In them I have found true acceptance, and in me they've found a home.

Pressing my hand over my heart, my gaze falls on Leon, Jakub and Konrad who are sitting at the table nearest to the stage. They're distinguishable from the rest of the guests not just because of the shiny, ebon masks they wear but because of the connection I share with them. In a room full of a thousand people I'd be able to pick them out. The bond we share is more tangible, more real, and far more visceral than anything I've ever felt before.

I *feel* it.

Like a beacon, I'm drawn to them. Their darkness is no longer pitch black, but scattered with tiny spots of light just like the swathes of silk that decorate this hall and I wonder, briefly, if anyone else sees the change in them like I do, or if all they see are the monsters they once were.

Forcing my gaze away from The Masks, I search the room focusing on each table as I look for men with the same build as Beast and Ford, wondering perhaps if they've separated to be less conspicuous. But my search, yet again, comes up empty.

Yet, I *know* they're in this room, somewhere. Beast had said he saw me dance so if they're not in the audience, that must mean they're...

Oh, God. Of course.

Just as I start to look more closely at the staff milling about the room, Five rests her hand on my arm. "That's your cue," she whispers as One begins to play the opening chords of *Dancing After Death.* "Are you ready?"

"Honestly, no," I respond, forcing my voice to be steadier than I feel.

"You can do this. I have faith in you. We all do."

"Keep them safe, Five," I say, pulling her in for a hug.

"I'll watch over them until you return. I promise you."

With one last dip of my head, I step out of the shadows and into the candlelight, Five's promise ringing in my ears just as Six begins to sing.

As the haunting song floats around the room, I lift up onto my pointes and pirouette across the floor, the skirt of my dress floating around me as I move. I'm supposed to dance my way to the stage before the first verse ends, finishing my performance there, but instead I use this opportunity to move about the grand hall in search of my sister, Beast and Ford.

Candlelight rushes past me in a blur of yellow against the inky backdrop as I twist and turn, just like a comet passing through the night sky. I dance fluidly, adjusting my steps as I make a new path around the Grand Hall, weaving between the tables of guests who all follow my movements, their true identities hidden beneath masks made of silk and lace, bone and metal, wood and paper. Some masks are utterly beautiful but in a way that is more sinister than attractive, with plumes of feathers and jewels embedded across the surface. Others are demonic, monsters come to life. I see twisted faces with horns, bulbous noses and crooked features. Fangs, claws and sharpened teeth. I don't know if it's the way the hall is lit, or the fact I'm dancing and they remain seated, but their masks begin to distort as I move. Twisting and morphing into strange and fantastical creatures you might find in a Grimm fairytale, the ones my sister used to love reading to me as a kid.

Everywhere I look the beautiful sit beside the ugly, the twisted beside the perfect.

And every single one of those masked creatures is focused on me.

Demon. Devil. Monster. Witch. Fairy. Siren.

An audience of humans transformed into mythical beings harbouring secret longings and sinful needs that can only be fulfilled within the walls of a remote castle far away from everyday life. This is their version of heaven, one debauched night filled with alcohol, drugs and sex. For one night they're free to look upon such exquisite beauty, free to enjoy such incredible talent and each other, with like-minded people. They can gorge on it, and those with enough money can buy it. *Have* bought it.

As I dance, I realise that this is just a brief glimpse of another world that lives alongside our own. Where money buys you anonymity, fantasies, *sex*. Here in this castle these men and women can become who they truly are inside, and somehow, rather than making me feel afraid it gives me the strength to continue, to see this night through. Just like them I can put on a mask and become a monster.

Tonight I will be the poisoner of blood, the slayer of hearts. I will take the dagger strapped to my thigh and carve my name into The Masks' chests, scarring them forevermore, saving them from death. I will commit a sin as heinous as any of these men and women here might.

And I will do it out of love.

Giving up on trying to find my family and accepting that I cannot change what will be, I allow myself to be drawn back to the centre of my universe, to The Masks, one last time. Moving fluidly, my limbs feel like melted gold as I dance towards them. My body is my own and yet strangely... it's not.

A warmth spreads out across my skin as my hair flies out behind me, my arms a pair of butterfly's wings as I float around the room. Goosebumps lift the hairs on my arms as One plays the notes so perfectly and Six sings like an angel.

Occasionally a guest will reach out, their fingertips grazing my skin, my skirt, my hair. These people taint me with their touch, their wrongdoings sinking into my skin, imprinting me with visions that I do not seek and have little strength to endure. I had thought my ability to *see* had abandoned me, but alas I was wrong. Yet I don't flinch away. I'm unable to do anything other than dance, my feet moving of their own accord, my brain disconnecting as multiple visions try to drag me under. I fight them off, using movement as a weapon. I can't go under. Not now.

Lifting up onto my pointes I kick my leg into a fouetté turn, refusing to succumb. I dance as though it's my last performance, forcing myself to move, to refuse to submit, but it's a losing battle as the hall fills with the same kind of electricity that infuses the air before a storm. It dances across my skin as my senses become sharper, more defined. Six's voice is clearer, One's notes crisper. I breathe in different scents: a meadow filled with wildflowers, sea-spray on warm sun-kissed skin, a wood burning fire, the sodden earth of a forest damp after rain has fallen. Those scents scoring memories that aren't my own into my mind's eye. Stumbling a little, those smells are replaced with sudden, glaring brightness. The candles on the table become flashes of light, the glinting fairy lights are no longer soft but sharp, almost blinding. Each step I take becomes burdensome, every movement heavy. I no longer float, but drown under the weight of a dozen visions that fight to claim me. But throughout it all I fight to stay awake, with only one thought on my mind. I need to get to the men I love...

CHAPTER FORTY-TWO

Grim

WATCHING Christy collapse to the floor, passing out cold, forces me into action after being held captive by her beautiful dancing. The vision of a woman so far removed from the little sister I'd kept hidden from the world had held me prisoner, unable to do anything other than watch her just like the rest of the bewitched people in this fucking place.

Now I forget our plan. I ignore the fact that it's not the right time to make our move. My protective instinct kicks in as I watch a man we've identified as one of The Masks rush to her side and scoop her up off the floor. He clutches her to his chest as the two remaining Masks rush to their side. One of them, the taller of the three, shouts instructions to the knife thrower who has suddenly appeared on the stage, her gaze fixed not on him but me as the other Mask shoves people out of the way, forging a path through the crowd.

We exchange looks, the knife thrower and I, and in her eyes I recognise a kindred spirit. Shame then that she stands on the other side of the line drawn in the sand between us.

My steps slow as she reaches for a knife strapped to her waist, but I shake my head warning her as my own fingers smooth over the gun hidden beneath the jacket I'm wearing. It's more than anyone else has ever got from me. Wisely she makes the right decision, her hand dropping to her side.

Switching my gaze back to The Masks, I watch them exit the room as the guests start to mutter under their breaths. I thought my clients were dangerous, but these people? They reek of far worse things than drug dealing and racketeering. They smell of forbidden fruit, plucked from orchards that are not their own, their touch rotten to the fucking core. But I'm not here to destroy them. I'm here to end the lives of the men who stole my sister, and right now she's being carried out of the room and taken to fuck knows where.

The piano player, the one with the long dark hair and expressionless eyes, begins to play as the blonde hanging from the trapeze above us starts to swing back and forth, drawing the attention of the audience away from my sister and The Masks.

Like many of the people who move in the circles I do, I've heard of the artists kept prisoner here. Their talent is exceptional and I'm not surprised that the Collector had wanted my friend Pen to add to his collection so badly. Her talent would've shined as bright as the others, so it's just as well we killed the fucker before he could attempt to steal her. Which begs the question as to why I wasn't more careful with Christy. I thought I'd hidden her well enough, but I'd underestimated The Masks.

Speaking of which, I pick up my pace as I move across the hall, afraid that I'll lose sight of her. I don't need to look behind me to know that Beast, Ford and Camden—who offered his help too—are following.

Asia wasn't exactly thrilled that Ford agreed to come, let alone Camden, but despite the complicated history between the two men, of which I'm all too aware, their bond is unbreakable. It's kind of endearing, actually, but the guilt I feel asking for their help is a heavy burden to carry given the danger being here presents. They have a family too, and knowing what could go wrong isn't easy for me to accept.

Which is why it won't go wrong and those fuckers *will* die tonight. We will walk out of here unscathed. All of us. Though I can't say the same for the Deana-dhe, because who the fuck knows where they are right now.

As soon as we entered the castle grounds an hour ago disguised as delivery drivers, we parted ways. Dressed head to toe in black with masks similar to the ones The Masks are wearing now, they entered the flow of guests, blending in with the crowd seamlessly. I've no idea where they are, because they sure as fuck aren't in the hall I've just left. Not that I give a fuck. They're here for their own reasons of which I have no desire to understand. What they do is their business, and I'm smart enough not to pry. Whilst I have a lot of respect for the Deana-dhe, my loyalty lies with my family and they're the *only* people I'll be concerning myself with tonight.

Before stepping out into the hallway, I pick up a serving tray, left discarded on the side table by the door. I'm keen to keep up the pretence of working here for a little while longer, because I really don't need to be stopped by a member of staff and have to kill them if they question who I am. Better for everyone if I appear to be a working cog in this fucking psycho wheel, then when the time is right I can show those motherfuckers exactly why they were fools to fuck with the wrong family.

Keeping an eye on The Masks who have hooked a left further along the corridor, I follow, discarding the tray I was holding on a console table the moment I think it's safe to do so. A quick look over my shoulder confirms Beast, Ford and Camden are still behind me.

Beast gives me a tight nod, his fingers grazing over the knife he has strapped to his chest, hidden beneath the tailored jacket he wears. For a *servant,* he sure looks fucking hot. That man could wear a potato sack and still impress the ladies. Just as well he's mine then because I'd make mashed potatoes out of him if ever dared look in the direction of another woman.

Not that he would.

We fought too hard to get where we are, to build what we have. Besides, I've loved that brute ever since I was seventeen, and even though he denies it, he's loved me for just as long, too. Though he never once overstepped the mark, not until I was an adult anyway. But that's a whole other story that Pen is likely reading to Iris from my diary as we speak. What a bedtime story that's gonna be.

Still knowing our precious baby girl is being taken care of by people I trust allows me to focus on the here and now, which is exactly what I do as I continue to follow The Masks through a maze of corridors. Eventually, they step out onto a cobbled courtyard, a gust of freezing wind whipping into the hallway where I remain hidden, reminding me that we're in the depths of the Scottish Highlands a long, *long* way from home.

"Jakub?" the taller of the three questions as the Mask holding Christy stills.

"She's stirring," he says, dropping his gaze to Christy in his arms.

I hold my hand up, a sign for Beast, Ford and Camden to wait as I decide the best course of action. Right now The Masks have the advantage, given Christy is in their arms and I've no idea whether they're packing any weapons. We might be hidden from view just off the courtyard, which has a huge fucking tree growing in the centre of it, but I'm not going to risk ambushing them whilst Christy's out cold.

"What's happening?" Beast asks, his voice low, his breath whispering over the back of my neck as he steps up close behind me.

"Christy's waking up. He's stopping to check on her," I reply, ignoring the way he always makes me feel whenever he's close by.

"Do you think they've been drugging her? She looked pretty out of it," he asks.

"They better fucking not have," Ford grinds out from somewhere behind Beast.

He's never met Christy, but the moment I told him about her, he'd claimed her as his sister even though strictly speaking they're not blood related. Whilst Christy and I share the same father, Ford and I share the same mother. They're connected by me, both are my half-siblings, but they're unrelated to each other by blood. That didn't matter to him though. As far as he's concerned, we're family and I agree.

"No. I don't think it's that. This is something else," I whisper, watching how the three men gather around her. Their body language speaks of possession, yes, but also something else. They're protective of her. I can see it in the way all three of them look at her. The taller one of the three brushes a strand of hair off her forehead, his fingers smoothing across her skin like she's made of something precious.

She is.

And that just pisses me off more because they've taken what's precious to me and I want her back.

"Is she under?" Beast asks.

"Under what?" Camden pipes up, confused.

I haven't told either of them about my sister's ability to see things so their confusion is understandable, but Beast knows about her gift. Though he's as uncomfortable with it as I am. In our kind of work we deal in what's tangible. We deal with *real life in your face shit*, not visions of things that haven't happened yet.

"Shh!" I grind out under my breath, stress making me snappy. "Just keep a lookout until I tell you to make a move."

Christy moans, her hand flying upwards as she struggles to understand where she is and what's happened to her. The Mask holding her, Jakub, sets her down onto her feet, his arm wrapped around her waist as he supports her weight.

"Can you stand?" he asks her, his slightly accented voice filled with concern.

I narrow my eyes on him. These men have a reputation, and showing compassion for another human being isn't a part of it. On the contrary, these men are conniving fucking monsters and they've had my sister in their lair all this time no doubt doing some psychological damage. My blood boils at the thought.

"I t—think so," she stutters, leaning into his hold.

"Okay, good. Take it easy, you went down hard."

Anger blossoms and it takes every last bit of restraint not to shoot the cunt in the back of the head. As much as a clean kill would be best all around, I've no intention of leaving this place until we've at least got a few hits in before putting a bullet in their brains.

"What happened?" she asks, shaking her head a little, the gold mask she's wearing highlighting her birthmark rather than hiding it. I've always thought Christy beautiful, and to see her baring the part of herself she spent years hiding behind a layer of makeup fills me with a mixture of both pride and concern because I don't know if she's been forced to bare herself this way or has finally accepted her unique kind of beauty.

"We were hoping you'd be able to tell us that," Jakub says, cupping her birthmarked cheek as she stares up at him, blinking. The way he looks at her as he caresses her face, pulls me up sharp. What the fuck does he think he's doing? And more to the point, why is she letting him touch her? Then I remember who these men are and just what she might've had to endure to survive here. The smart thing to do is become whatever they need you to be, and buy some time. She would've known I'd come for her and acted accordingly.

Atta girl.

"You were dancing and then you just collapsed," one of the other Masks says. He reaches for her, pulling her into his arms. I bristle at the overfamiliarity, at the fact she doesn't try to push him away.

"Something doesn't feel right..." she says, her voice trailing off as she looks up at him, concern filling her gaze and something that looks suspiciously like love.

"What's going on?" Beast asks as I continue to watch their interaction.

"Just wait!" I hiss, trying to make sense of what I'm seeing, because either she's a really good actress or she's fallen for the motherfuckers.

"What do you mean, Christy?" One of The Masks asks her, only his question remains unanswered as a woman dressed head-to-toe in black runs into the courtyard, her hair in disarray, red lipstick smudged across her face as tears roll down her cheeks. Even her dress has a tear in it, one sleeve almost ripped right off. Whatever happened to her, it wasn't good.

"Thirteen? What happened?!" Christy cries, pushing out of Jakub's arms and rushing toward her. The girl throws herself into Christy's arms as three familiar men step out into the courtyard directly behind her.

The Deana-dhe.

All three of their gazes are fixed on the woman Christy holds onto and not one of them is wearing the masks they entered the castle with. Arden has a bloody lip, which he swipes at with the back of his hand, a grin pulling up his lips as he focuses his attention on The Masks.

Christy glares at them, making a quick assessment of what's going on. "What did you do to her?" she spits, anger bristling as she hugs the woman she calls Thirteen to her chest.

Arden grins, his eyes dancing with a mixture of delight and venom as he flicks his gaze at Jakub. It dawns on me in that moment that coming here appears to have everything to do with the woman named Thirteen fiercely rubbing at the tears pouring down her cheeks.

The secretive, conniving bastards.

"We did nothing that she didn't ask for," Arden responds coolly.

That statement gets my back up. *Fuck that.* I've always respected the Deana-dhe, but what Arden just said, that's fucking horseshit.

"Grim, what the *fuck* is going on?" Beast insists under his breath, getting more agitated by the second. I reach behind me, grasping his arm in warning.

"The Deana-dhe have just stepped into the courtyard. There's a girl with Christy. I think they've come here for her. Be ready to make a move on my signal," I whisper quickly.

"They've come for a *piece of ass?*"

"Not just any piece of ass given the way the three of them are eye fucking her. Just be ready to go on my signal."

"Got it," he whispers back, and I can feel him shift away from me slightly, talking under his breath to Ford and Camden, passing on my instructions as I continue to watch their interaction.

"Arden Dálaigh we meet at last," Jakub says, removing his mask. His brothers following suit.

"If it isn't the famous Collector's son, Jakub Brov," Arden replies, a sneer pulling up his lip.

"*You're* Arden?" Christy says, her head snapping around as she stares at him like she's seen a ghost. *How the fuck does she know who he is?*

"The one and only. Hello, Christy. It's good to meet you at last," he says, his assessing gaze flicking between Christy and the girl she calls Thirteen.

"I can't say that the feeling is mutual," she responds, her eyes hardening as her gaze flits from Arden to Carrick and Lorcan who flank him. He scowls at that, and I can't help but feel proud of her.

Carrick laughs. "Feisty," he says, removing his mask and rolling his head on his shoulders. "You've got some fire in you, Red. Far more than Thirteen does."

"Shut the fuck up!" Leon snarls, earning him a death glare. "Don't look at her!"

"We'll do whatever the fuck we want," Lorcan replies, smirking. "*Thirteen* belongs to us."

"The *hell* she does," Jakub snaps back.

"Oh didn't she tell you?" Carrick questions, delight dancing in his black eyes as he looks at Thirteen. "We've come to cash in her debt, haven't we, *cailleach?*"

Jakub flinches, but it's the only discernible reaction to what is a surprising turn of events. At least for me. Who is this woman exactly? What fucking debt does she owe the Deana-dhe? What kind of name is Thirteen? And why is Carrick calling her a witch? I wrack my brain trying to work it all out.

"Grim, what the fuck is happening?" Beast hisses, and I can feel his impatience in the way he grips my hips in his large hands. I know him, any minute now he's going to manhandle me out of the way and do some crazy alpha-male, chest-beating bullshit. Not today. Today we do things my way.

I turn around and glare at him before resting my gaze on Camden, ignoring Beast's question as I bark out a command. "I want you to go back to the van, wait for us. Shit's going down and we need a quick getaway. The minute we put those bastards down, I want to be gone. There are too many sick fucks here tonight and I have no plans on dealing with them as well."

Camden's bright blue eyes flash with concern. "I came to fight, Grim. Let me fight."

"Bro, Asia was pissed as fuck that I came, let alone you tagging along. She will have my arse if anything happens to you. Go to the van, we won't be long," Ford says, hiding his concern behind a grin.

Camden shakes his head. "The fuck I will."

Beast rounds on him. "Do as you're fucking told and go get the fucking van ready like Grim asked," he hisses.

"Fine, you old fuck!" Camden grinds out before grasping Ford's shoulder. "Do not fucking die because you know Asia will *kill me* if I come back with you in a bodybag."

"Just go. We got this," Ford reassures him.

"Fine, but if you ain't out within half an hour, I'm coming back for you no matter what," he says firmly, raising a brow at

Beast before twisting on his feet and jogging back the way we came.

"It's like managing a bunch of fucking *delinquents*," I mutter, turning my attention back to the standoff in the courtyard and ignoring Ford's chuckle at my expense.

"Seriously, what the fuck are we waiting for?" Beast grumbles.

"I've learnt to trust my gut over the years, it's never steered me wrong, and right now my gut is telling me to wait. So we wait."

"Got it... *Boss*," Beast adds, knowing full well I fucking hate him calling me that.

Biting back a caustic response, I return my attention to what's unfolding between the opposing sides. There's a time to fight, and there's a time to gather information. Right now, Christy is where I can see her. She's relatively safe and no one is going anywhere. Plus I've got a gun; if any fucker moves towards her threateningly, they're dead.

"Come here, Thirteen," Arden says, crooking his finger at the woman everyone seems to be so interested in.

"Stay where you are!" Jakub snaps, glancing over at her.

She shakes her head at Jakub, pleading with her eyes. Though she doesn't say a word.

Leon, the Mask who has a similar, batshit crazy presence as Carrick, holds his hand up. "Stay put!"

Thirteen untangles herself from Christy's arms. I watch as she slides her hand into Christy's, squeezing her fingers briefly before dropping them and stepping away from her.

"Thirteen?" Christy questions, wrapping her arms around herself. A look passes between them, a whole fucking conversation that I can't interpret, before Christy nods. "Be careful."

Thirteen gathers up her long skirt then makes her way over

to Lorcan. The moment she reaches his side, he grabs her elbow and she looks over at The Masks, swallowing hard.

"What about her debt?" Carrick asks, side-eying Thirteen. "We have a reputation to uphold. Everyone knows what happens if you don't pay up."

"Her debt has been altered," Arden says.

"Since fucking when?" Carrick asks.

"Since right the fuck now." Arden flicks his gaze to Lorcan. "Get her out of here. Carrick and I will finish this."

Lorcan nods, picks up Thirteen and chucks her over his shoulder.

Then all hell breaks loose.

CHAPTER FORTY-THREE

Christy

EVERYTHING HAPPENS SO FAST.

One minute I'm standing between the two warring sides and the next I'm being lifted off my feet and dropped beside one of the stone pillars on the other side of the courtyard.

"You stay out of the way, Christy! Do not intervene!" Leon instructs, before spinning on his feet and diving back into the fray.

"Wait!" I call after him, knowing that I have to let this happen, and hating myself for it.

How can I watch the people I care about rip each other to shreds? How can I pretend their pain doesn't affect me? How can I just stand here and do nothing?

"Stop!" I shout. "Just stop!"

But no one hears me.

The sound of their cries are deafening.

Their rage is palpable.

It's thick and cloying. It's a chokehold around my throat.

My cries go unheard, my pleas are ignored and I'm forced to watch the carnage unfold, praying and hoping that this is over quickly.

"You little prick!" Beast roars as Konrad punches him in the jaw.

Flashes of movement merge with sounds of violence, all of it mixing up into a cacophony of carnage. My sister punches Jakub, his head snapping back from the force. Leon ducks beneath Ford's fist and lands an uppercut to his jaw. Konrad receives a kick to his stomach, Carrick's foot like a sledgehammer.

I catch glimpses of Beast, Kate and Ford as they fight. They're my family.

I see Leon, Jakub and Konrad unleash their monsters. They're my heart.

I watch Arden and Carrick seek their revenge. They're strangers.

It's five against three, unfair odds at the best of times, let alone battling against some of the best bare knuckle fighters in the world. Yet, despite the odds, The Masks hold their own, landing punches and giving as good as they get. It tears me apart watching this all unfold. I feel every punch, every split lip and broken rib, every black eye and swollen cheek. When Jakub is thrown to the floor, I *feel* the pain of the deep gash that splits open his skin from his eyebrow to his hairline. I can't stop the sob that escapes my mouth as his eyes roll back in his head from the impact, knocked out cold. I want so badly to go to him, but I have to keep up the pretence. I have to be the woman who hates them. I have to.

Now it's five against two.

Fists fly, bones crack, skin splits, bruises bloom and blood spills.

The sharp glint of a knife flashes in the air, and Konrad's scream rips through my chest, the cut to his face mirroring the one I feel across my fleshy, tormented heart. My hand slams over my mouth as my knees buckle, dropping me to the floor.

There's so much blood.

It pours from their faces, drips over their clothes and splatters the cobblestones.

So much blood. So much violence. So much hate.

I want to fucking scream. I want to rip my hair out.

I want them to stop. Just please fucking stop!

But still they fight.

On and on it goes, a battle with no end, a war with no victors, only countless victims. And just like The Weeping Tree I bear witness to it all. I stand here and watch helplessly, knowing I can't step in, that I can't do anything to stop it. Worse than that, I *have* to let it happen.

Leon and Konrad do what they can to protect Jakub, but their energy is waning. No man can take the hits they have and keep standing. Their fight is admirable. Their protective instincts are strong, but it doesn't matter.

They lose anyway. I know this.

Konrad falls next. The sound of his knees hitting the stone is as loud as a thundercrack. His shoulders drop, his hands falling forward as blood drips from the slash across his face. He crawls towards Jakub earning a kick in the stomach from Carrick that drops him to the ground. Konrad coughs, spitting up blood adding to the already growing pool beneath him. Carrick kicks him again and if it wasn't for Leon's roar of anguish my own would've filled the courtyard. It's so filled with pain that I feel his heart breaking as surely as mine is now.

With one last powerful punch, Leon slams his fist into Beast's jaw then twists on his feet and runs for Carrick, dodging Kate and Ford and shoving his shoulder into Carrick's stomach. They fall to the floor in a tangle of limbs, but somehow Leon gets the upper hand. His fierceness explodes, and he rains down punches like fireballs from hell.

It doesn't last long.

"That's enough, dickwad!" Beast snarls, grasping him by the scruff of the neck and yanking him backwards, pressing a knife to his throat.

With a sharp intake of breath I watch the love of my sister's life holding the love of mine in his death grip. "Enough!" I command, pushing up onto my feet. Leon instantly stills, his eyes meeting mine as I shake my head minutely. "It's over."

"It's not over until they're dead!" Arden snarls, swiping at a streak of blood dripping from his split lip, across his chin.

"He's got a point," Beast remarks with a smile. "Shall I do the honours?"

"No," I shake my head, forcing hate into my eyes and focusing it on Leon. I have to make this convincing. I have to get them to believe. "*I* want to do it. I want to kill them."

"What?" Carrick asks, pushing up onto his feet, his dark eyes narrowing.

"They took me away from my family. They've kept me prisoner in this place," I spit, glancing at Kate who is staring at me in a way that makes me feel more than a little uncomfortable, as though she's assessing the truth of my words. She thinks she knows me, and perhaps that was once true, but I'm different now. I've changed. I'm able to put on a mask when I need to.

"You don't have it in you," Carrick says.

"I'm pretty sure she does," Ford says, dragging Konrad to his feet, a gun pressed to his temple. He groans and it takes every last ounce of self-restraint not to go to him. Behind him Jakub is still out cold, oblivious to what's happening around him.

Swallowing hard, I focus my attention on Carrick who looks at me as though I'm beneath him. It pisses me off. "Don't presume to know what I'm capable of. I've survived this place, haven't I?"

"Indeed," Arden agrees with a nod of respect.

"This is *my* right."

"And your need for vengeance, that would be the *Dálaigh* blood running through your veins," Arden remarks knowingly.

"The fuck?!" Beast exclaims, looking between us both. "What're you talking about, Arden?"

Kate frowns. "Explain."

"Christy is my cousin. Her mother, Nessa *Dálaigh*, is my late father's sister. Isn't that so?" He cocks his head to the side, watching me carefully.

"Yes," I agree.

"Well, you couldn't fucking make this shit up," Beast exclaims, shaking his head, the movement causing the knife he's still holding against Leon's throat to cut a little deeper. I grit my teeth, forcing myself not to react. "Fucking brothers and sisters and cousins and shit." Beast looks over at Arden. "Next you'll be telling me I'm your long lost father."

Kate whips her head around and glares at Beast. "Not fucking funny."

Arden grins, baring bloody teeth at us all. "I knew there was a reason I liked you, Beast. Now slice his motherfucking throat."

"No! They're *mine*. Tie them to the tree," I growl, jerking my head towards The Weeping Tree.

Arden raises a brow, "We might be family but you do not have the last say here."

"What will it take?" I ask.

"Christy..." Kate warns, a flash of worry in her eyes.

"You deal in debts, right?" I ask, ignoring her. "What will it take for me to have the pleasure of ending these fuckers lives," I say, refusing to look at Leon or Konrad who are staring at me so intensely I can feel the heat of their gazes burn my skin.

Carrick tips his head back and laughs. "This is turning out to be a pretty fucking entertaining night."

"You want it that badly?"

"Yes."

"No!" Kate argues, striding over to me. She stands before me and shakes her head. "What the hell do you think you're doing?"

"What does it look like? I'm seeking vengeance. It's mine. Not yours. Not Beast's. Not Arden's but *mine*. You have no idea what I've been through with these men. Don't interfere." My heart pounds in my chest, willing them to believe me.

"Well, shit. Our little Christy has grown some major balls. Good for you, girl," Beast says, earning him another glare from Kate who twists on her feet and points at Arden.

"She's your blood, Arden, and as far as I'm aware there's very few of you left. Let her have this. Besides, you got what you came here for tonight, haven't you?"

Arden squints his eyes at me, considering for a moment. "Who is she to you?"

"Have you taken something? They're fucking sisters," Beast pipes up, pulling a face.

"I'm not talking about Grim," Arden replies, his gaze still focused on me.

"Thirteen's my *friend*. I care about her."

He nods. "Then these are my terms. I will let you have the pleasure of killing these fuckers but when it comes to the day she asks you for help, I want you to deny her."

"What the hell is this?" Kate asks. "Who *is* Thirteen exactly? And why would she need Christy's help? What do you intend to do with her?"

"That's our business. Not yours," Carrick responds this time. "I suggest you keep your nose out of it."

Kate bares her teeth, but she doesn't argue.

"Those are my terms, cousin," Arden offers.

My throat constricts, my stomach tightening in knots. How can I do that? How can I possibly turn my back on Thirteen if she asked me for help? My mother had said in her letter to me that Fate would catch up with her and that I should be a friend when that happens. So what kind of person would I be to deny her help when she needed it the most. I can't do that. I won't.

"No."

"Fine," Arden says, flicking his gaze from me to Beast. "Do it."

"Wait!" I hold my hand up, my heart hammering against my rib cage. "There's an object in this castle I believe you'd be interested in obtaining. I will tell you where it is so long as you allow me to kill these men."

"What object?"

"There's a knife. Its handle is made of human skin."

"And why the fuck would I want that?" Arden asks.

I point to the butterfly tattooed onto his neck. "Your father had a tattoo just like that one, didn't he?"

"Fuuuuckkk!" Beast exclaims.

Arden's skin pales and Carrick grips his arm, steadying him.

"We've both lost people we love. The man who killed your father is dead. My sister saw to that. You've had your revenge, albeit through her, but I still need mine. Let me have this and I will tell you where to find the knife."

"I could *make* you tell me," he counters.

I shake my head. "You could try, but you won't. Besides, Grim and Ford have a gun. You don't. So let's stop fucking around and make a deal. I'll tell you where to find the knife, and you give me the retribution I deserve." Arden grits his jaw, then nods, a note of respect flickering across his face. "Oh, and for the record, not only will I come running when Thirteen asks me to, you won't stand in my way unless you want me to inform her family just exactly how you've treated her over the years."

"She talked about us?" he asks, a flicker of emotion tracking across his face before he shuts it down.

I shake my head. "Thirteen isn't the only *cailleach* here, but you know that already, don't you?"

"You're more of a Dálaigh than I'd first thought."

I shrug, feigning more confidence that I feel. "Well?"

"Where can I find it?" he asks.

"Ground floor, east wing. Find the room that gives a view of the terrace gardens. There's a door that exits that room and leads to a hallway beyond. Take a right and you'll find Jakub's room of curiosities at the end of that hallway. The knife is in the same glass cabinet that's filled with human bones and jewellery."

Arden nods then flicks his gaze to Kate. "Make sure they're dead."

"Done," she agrees.

"I suggest you hurry, mate," Beast interjects, "Because once these fuckers are dead, we're out of here, and I don't know about you but we're not hanging around to find out if those sick fucks in that ballroom have balls big enough to murder as they do to fuck a pretty woman. There are two hundred of them and only three of you and I don't care how good at fighting you are, there's no way you'd be able to take them all on."

"He's got a point. We got what we came for," Carrick says. "Let's grab the knife and get the fuck out of here."

"It was good to meet you," Arden says to me, before turning his attention to Konrad and Leon who've remained quiet this whole time. A slow smile pulls up his lip. "I'll be seeing you in Hell."

With that, Arden and Carrick turn on their heels and exit the courtyard, leaving me to walk the path Fate has paved so thoroughly with blood.

CHAPTER FORTY-FOUR

Leon

"YOU MOTHERFUCKERS DESERVE to be hanged for what you've done to Christy. Stealing her from her family and peddling her to your fucking sicko clients like a piece of meat. She should be dancing for the Royal fucking Ballet, not for you bastards at this motherfucking ball," Beast says, as Grim and the man they call Ford make sure the cable ties wrapped around our wrists are securely fixed to the bolts embedded in The Weeping Tree.

Beside me, Jakub is out cold, his head lolling between his shoulders, a deep gash running from his hairline to his right eyebrow. Konrad isn't faring much better, the old scar on his cheek torn open and weeping blood. He coughs, and more blood releases from his mouth. I don't feel too great myself, and I'm pretty sure I've got a broken rib or three. But none of that matters. We are where we're supposed to be.

"Do it. It's no less than we deserve," Konrad mutters.

Grim, who's standing closest to Konrad grabs his face, her finger pressing into the newly open wound as she sneers at him. "Get ready to say hello to your forefathers, prick, because they'll be seeing you very, very soon."

Konrad mutters something indistinguishable under his breath, but my attention is drawn to Christy standing on the other side of the courtyard. Fuck, she's been so brave tonight standing up to Arden like she did. Our eyes meet and hers flicker with pain. It hurts her to see us like this as she stands there with her arms wrapped around her chest, shivering uncontrollably.

Beast steps forward, getting in my line of sight. He smiles, punching me in the stomach. I double over and gag, my wrists pulling against the restraints just as Grim raises her fist and punches Konrad in the face. Not to be left out, Ford punches an unconscious Jakub in the kidney before spitting at his feet.

"Please," Christy whispers, holding her hand up for them to stop.

"Christy?" her sister questions.

They exchange looks and Christy's expression morphs from one of anguish to one of hate. It's so convincing that it even makes me flinch. She strides across the courtyard, her golden dress floating about her, a knife clutched in her hand.

Grim steps out of her way, glancing at Ford. "Give her room, Ford," she says.

"Just let us shoot the fuckers and be done with it, Christy. It's time to go home," Beast says, rolling his head on his shoulders.

Konrad lifts his head, looking at Christy. His face is swollen, the jagged gash on his face still sleeping blood. "We deserve to die," Konrad says, his voice gravelly, hoarse with pain. "I won't try to stop you."

"Dipshit, you're handcuffed to a tree," Beast retorts. "You couldn't stop us even if you wanted to."

Maybe it's all the punches to my head, but I laugh, I can't help it. "He's got a point, Kon."

Konrad ignores me, glancing at Jakub before speaking. "If we wanted to stop you, we would've by now. We were expecting you."

"Are you trying to tell me that you don't deserve to die just because you 'allowed' us to beat the shit out of you?" Beast says, making quote marks with his fingers, "Is that it? Cuz as far as I'm concerned, you three pricks couldn't fight your way out of a paper bag."

"No, that's not what I'm saying," Konrad replies firmly, flicking his gaze back to Christy.

"Then what? Because I dunno about everyone else here, but I'm over this shitstain of a night already. I wanna go home to my daughter with my family intact, knowing that you scum-buckets have been wiped off the face of the earth."

Konrad heaves out a shaky breath. "It was inevitable that men like us wouldn't survive in this world for long. I don't blame any of you for coming here tonight for Christy. I get it," he stresses, glancing at me then at Jakub, who begins to stir. Slowly he tracks his gaze back to Christy. "But the only person here that has the right to kill us is you, Christy, the person we hurt the most. The woman we love."

"Love?" Grim spits the word out, her eyes narrowing. "You don't know the meaning of the word, you fucking psychopath."

"That's where you're wrong," I say, smiling despite the blood dripping into my mouth. "Christy taught us."

Beast, Grim and Ford all look over at Christy, and I realise my mistake too late. She's supposed to fucking hate us. *Fuck!*

"Stop talking," she whispers, her voice steady even though her hands are shaking.

Jakub stirs, his head lifting, puffy eyelids opening as he tries to focus. "End this," he mutters, more aware of what's happening around him than I'd given him credit for.

Christy wobbles on her feet, dragging in a ragged breath. Her expression falters and we all see her compassion replacing the anger. Grim notices it too, her brows pulling together in a frown, but lucky for us she thinks we're trying to manipulate Christy, not encourage her to see this through to the bitter end.

"This is emotional warfare, Christy. They're trying to fuck with you. You don't need to do a damn thing."

"No! I'm the one who should do it. *Me*," she replies fiercely. "Jakub's right, I need to end this once and for all."

"Atta girl," Beast says, a grin pulling up his lips. "You're more like your sister than I've given you credit for."

Focusing on the three of us, Christy steps forward, holding the blade laced with poison in front of her. She goes to Konrad first and with trembling fingers silently unbuttons his shirt. From my vantage point I can see her silently mouth the word *sorry* as she presses the blade against his skin, carving her name into his chest. Konrad groans, his head falling back against the bark. I've no idea how long it will be before the poison begins to take effect, but I hope for all our sakes it's quick.

Jakub is next, but the wound to his head keeps dragging him into unconsciousness and he barely makes a sound, let alone registers Christy cutting into his chest. Her whispered apology is lost to the wind lifting up her hair and whistling through the courtyard.

When she reaches me her expression falters, as she slides her hands beneath the torn material of my shirt and traces her fingers over her name already carved into my chest. Tears brim in her eyes and she blinks them back furiously.

"Do it," I urge her, pressing my chest against the tip of the knife.

"Leon," she whispers, leaning in close, close enough for me to whisper in her ear.

"We do not fear the darkness, Christy, not now that we've found our source of light. I love you."

She swallows hard, blinking back her tears as she cuts my skin, the poison flowing into my bloodstream with every slice. When she's finished, she steps back, her arms falling to her side as a calmness settles over her features. "You told me that your hearts belong to me, that I brought them back to life. Well, I claim those hearts now. They're *mine*."

And she's right, they are.

"Yours," we all respond as a blast of wind passes through the courtyard raising goosebumps on my arms. My body wracks with shivers as the poison begins to take hold but I fight it off, my attention caught by the blade of a knife glinting in the moonlight, an intruder hiding within the shadows on the other side of the courtyard.

No! I try to shout but no words will come, my voice stolen by poison, my muscles turned to stone.

"Look, Christy, as much as I love your flair for the dramatic and all that, these fuckers need to die. If you want their hearts, I'd gladly cut them out for you. It's a messy fucking job, but it's not like I ain't done it before," Beast says, drawing her attention away from me and the words of warning that refuse to form on my tongue.

"But they *will* die," she replies softly, dropping the blade to the ground. It clatters to the cobblestones, masking the intruder's footfalls, distracting everyone. "This blade is laced with poison."

I hear One's demented cry of anguish just as darkness claims me.

CHAPTER FORTY-FIVE

Christy

"NOOOOOOOO!"

I spin on my feet, my skirt whipping out around my legs as One rushes towards me, blade in hand. Her makeup is smudged, her hair wild about her head, a crazed look in her eyes.

She's a woman scorned. A woman in pain. A woman who has lost everything.

And in those few short seconds before the knife impales itself in my chest, I'm given a glimpse into a future that doesn't include me, a parting gift from Fate, so utterly cruel in its beauty.

I see my aunt and uncle dancing in their kitchen, their lined cheeks pressed against each other as their favourite song plays on the radio.

I see Iris as a teenager, her pretty face lit up with laughter as she watches something funny on the television.

I see Kate and Beast sitting at a table talking animatedly with a group of friends, a baby with bright green eyes and a shock of dark curly hair being doted on by four handsome men and a woman with a pretty smile.

I see Two in a black cocktail dress sipping a Martini and talking softly to a man who's looking at her like she's the centre of his universe.

I see Three and Seven on stage in a club, she's dancing, he's singing. They're both smiling.

I see Four and Eight standing on a balcony overlooking the Eiffel Tower, their arms wrapped around each other.

I see Five teaching a little girl with long dark hair like hers how to throw a knife.

I see Six singing in the Royal Albert Hall filled to the brim with an enraptured audience.

I see Nine, Ten and Eleven stepping out of a cottage on a warm summer's day, laughing at how their puppies tumble and play in the long grass.

I see Thirteen in an overgrown garden, a determined look on her face as she pulls up weeds and churns the dirt with her bare hands.

I see Nala with a paint brush in her hand, standing in front of a mural in the Grand Hall, a gentle smile on her face.

I see Jakub walking through the forest surrounding the castle, lost to his thoughts.

I see Leon swimming in the lake beneath our feet, the cool water sliding over his naked skin.

I see Konrad playing an acoustic guitar, his eyes shut as he strums the strings.

I see the three of them dressed in smart black suits, standing by a graveside, the branches of a willow tree hanging just above their heads.

I see The Masks alive and well and all I can think of is one thing...

I never did get to tell them that I love them.

CHAPTER FORTY-SIX

Jakub

ONE MONTH LATER.

"IS THIS IT?" Konrad asks as we take a right turn into Mortlake Cemetery in London.

"Yes, this is the place we'll find her," I reply, checking the address on my phone for the hundredth time since we picked up the rental car from the airport.

It's been a long journey to get here, and I don't just mean from Ardelby Castle. Until a few days ago, I wasn't certain if I wanted to see her grave. Then I realised that this trip wasn't just about me and my needs, but those of my family too, and I wasn't about to turn my back on that. Not after we've come so far together.

"Her grave is situated in the far corner of the cemetery

beneath a willow tree," Leon confirms, checking the map we were sent detailing the exact location. "Ready?"

"You?" I ask him.

"I'm good," he replies. "Kon?"

"Yeah, me too," he nods, opening the door to the car and stepping out onto the gravel.

We're still working on communicating our feelings better and it's been a long, bumpy road but day by day we're getting there all, thanks to the woman who sacrificed everything for us.

There won't be a day that goes by when I don't thank the universe for bringing Christy to us and no matter how painful the journey, I will never regret it.

With a steadying breath I pick up the bunch of white lilies and follow my brothers through the graveyard. It's well-tended, the grass clipped short. There isn't a piece of litter in sight. Just knowing she's resting somewhere so well looked after eases the ache in my chest a little.

"There's the willow tree," Leon points out, as I rub the heel of my palm over the centre of my chest.

Cutting a right, we head along the shingle path towards it. It's an impressive tree, with a thick, circular trunk, the ends of the branches grazing the grass below. In summer when the branches are covered in leaves, I've no doubt it would make the perfect place to hide beneath and talk to the dead in peace and quiet. A lot of people find cemeteries creepy, I don't. The dead have no power to hurt you, it's the living who you need to watch out for. Pushing aside the curtain of branches, I rest my gaze on the marble gravestone, a fresh bunch of roses already resting against it.

"Looks like someone beat us to it," Leon says, his voice thick with emotion.

"Christy," I whisper, dropping to my knees and running my

fingers over the epitaph engraved into the stone. I stare at the words, my fingers running over the grooves before reading it out loud. *"If I am the phantom, it is because man's hatred has made me so. If I am to be saved it is because your love redeems me..."* My voice trails off as a deep sense of peace settles inside of my chest. "Thank you for finding her for me."

"You're so welcome, Jakub."

I lift my gaze from my mother's name carved into the marble gravestone to the woman I love as she steps out from behind the huge trunk, her red hair lifting in the breeze as she looks at each of us in turn. It was a miracle she even found this grave, and honestly I never expected my mother to even have one, let alone be buried in London. Perhaps somewhere deep down inside my father had the tiniest glimmer of humanity which allowed him to do this. I suspect she was buried so far away because he never wanted to be reminded of that humanity. Either way, I'm glad to have found her even if the only real memory I have of my mother is her smell.

"Christy," I repeat, my heart lurching as I stand

"I've missed you all so, so much," she whispers before running into my open arms.

"Fuck, you've no idea how crazy we've been without you," I respond, burying my nose in her hair and swearing to myself that we'll never, *ever* be parted again.

"ARE you positive they're not going to fire a bullet in our brains the second we enter the club?" Konrad asks, scrubbing a hand over his face as he looks up at the club's name, *Tales*, lit in bright red neon lights above the door. "Because I'm pretty sure coming back from the dead only works once you know.

I'm not about to tempt fate again, it was a close call the last time."

"Beast said that he locked all the guns away and stuffed the key down his arse crack, and Kate said she'd rather cut her own tongue out than go searching for it. So I think you're safe," Christy replies, grinning.

Her smile is like the midday sun in summer and I bask in the glow of it. How lucky are we to be here with her like this? I won't ever take this gift of a new start for granted for as long as I live.

"You're so damn beautiful when you smile, do you know that?" I say, taking her hand in mine before Leon can pull her back into his arms.

"Arsehole," he mutters with a smirk, before grasping Christy's face in his hands and kissing her until she's breathless and panting. "Two can play at that game."

"Three, *three* can play that game," Konrad adds with a wink as he holds open the door, and lightly slaps Christy on the arse as she passes him by. "Just wait until we get you home."

"All in good time," Christy responds. "First my sister."

"Lead the way," I say, ready and more than willing to build a few bridges, starting with the family of the woman we love. "It's been a long time coming."

Truthfully, it's been torture the last four weeks without her. Waking up after the poison had left our system wasn't a painful experience because of the very thorough way we were beaten, it was having to recover without Christy. It was knowing she'd been hurt and not being able to go to her the second we had the strength to do so. Just thinking about the moment I woke up after the poison had finally worn off gives me fucking anxiety...

. . .

"IS IT OVER?" *I ask, blinking back the lingering heavy fog as I stare up at Five.*

"Yes, it's over," she replies, patting my hand.

"Where are Leon and Konrad?"

"They're resting now. Six is with Leon and Nala is with Konrad. We've fixed them up as best we can. They'll be okay. As will you."

"And Christy?" I ask, knowing she's left with her family just like we'd planned, but asking anyway. Five's gaze flickers with apprehension, and despite the fact my whole body hurts, I force myself upright, breathing heavily from the effort. "Five, tell me!"

"One slipped away from The Wolf—"

"What?!" I snap.

"By the time I'd realised, she'd already stolen a knife from the kitchen and had set out to find you. When she found you in the courtyard tied to The Weeping Tree, she came to her own conclusions and attacked Christy."

"No! No!" I shout, my whole body trembling as I grip at Five, my fingers squeezing her shoulders. "Please don't fucking tell me she's gone. Please, please, please!"

"She's okay. I promise!" Five says quickly. "She's okay, Jakub."

A sob breaks free from my lips as I collapse back onto the bed, the agony of my battered body is nothing compared to the thought Christy has been hurt. "What happened?"

"One stabbed Christy just beneath the collarbone. It could've been fatal but it wasn't, all major arteries were missed. Thirteen patched her up enough for them to leave."

"Thirteen? But I thought..."

"She'd left with the Deana-dhe?" Five shakes her head. "Arden wanted to be certain that you were dead before they left, so they came back to the courtyard to check. He killed One before

I could intervene, slit her throat for attacking Christy. He used the knife with the human skin handle to do it."

"Then it's me who owes him a debt," I mutter, grateful to my arch nemesis for doing what I should've done myself. "Do we know how Christy is now?"

"Charles called here an hour ago," Five replies. "He picked up a message between Grim and a man named Hudson Freed. She was flown from Edinburgh Castle to a private hospital in London. She's okay, Jakub."

"I never thought I'd be thanking God for anything, but thank God."

"Quite," she replies, smiling a little.

"And what about Thirteen and the Deana-dhe?" I ask.

"She left with them voluntarily..." Her voice trails off as she sighs heavily.

"What is it?"

"On the night when Christy died, Thirteen gave me a letter to look after. She asked me to give it to you once she'd left the castle but instructed me to tell you that you shouldn't open it until you were reunited with Christy and have resolved your issues with her family. She said that part was really important," Five says, reaching into the leather pouch attached to the holster strapped across her chest and pulling out an envelope, handing it to me.

I glance down at the handwriting, Thirteen's this time. "Then I shall honour that wish."

Five smiles. "Good. She also said you need to give Christy time to make things right with her sister."

"That's not going to be easy, for any of us."

"She said you might say that," Five replies with another smile. "And she told me to tell you that patience is a virtue, and given you've all shown the ability to regain some other key *virtues over the past few months, you should be able to handle this one easily."*

"Then she really doesn't know us all that well," I reply with a grumble, groaning as I shift to get more comfortable.

"I think you're wrong. I think she knows you all very well indeed," Five replies, pulling the blanket up over my chest. "Can I get you anything?"

"A way to contact Christy would be good," I say, my eyelids beginning to droop as exhaustion takes hold. "If I can't be with her right now, then there's no way I'm going more than a day without speaking to her..."

SHAKING my head free of the memory, I follow Christy and my brothers into the club feeling cautiously hopeful. Christy has spent the last month working on Grim and Beast. I know in the early days after she told them we were in fact alive, Grim had wanted to finish what they'd started, but somehow Christy had managed to persuade her not to act, and more importantly not to tell the Deana-dhe we were still living and breathing. Over time Christy had worn her down enough to get her to listen, and after several conversations and lots of heated disagreements, we ended up here, at the infamous *Tales,* to make peace officially.

"You okay?" Christy asks me, as we step into the main area of the club.

"Apart from needing to be alone with you, I'm good."

"Soon," she whispers, squeezing my hand.

Inside, the club is deceptively spacious, with a large central dancefloor and a raised stage situated at the back of the club. The walls are painted a deep scarlet with matching velvet booths dotted around the space, and to the far right of the club is a huge bar with a mirrored wall behind it and shelves lined with bottles of liquor.

Music is being played through the speaker system, the volume turned low as we make our way over to the booth furthest from the door. I can hear people talking and a rumble of laughter, but it is neither of those things that makes my steps falter.

"What's that?" I ask, pointing to a prosthetic arm resting on a stool beside the booth.

"That? Oh, that's Dax's arm. He's just popped in to see Beast after picking it up from the shop. He's a good guy, you'll like him."

"Who's Dax?" Leon asks, the possessive note in his voice unmistakable.

"That'd be me," a man covered neck to toe in tattoos replies as he slides out from the booth we're heading towards and holds out his hand to shake, Beast getting up behind him. They're both huge men, intimidating I'm sure to many. Not to me. Though after our encounter with Beast, I do have a heavy dose of respect for him.

"Don't mind Dax, he's 'armless," Beast says, with a smirk.

"Seriously, *old man*, it's been over two years of the same damn joke. You need to get a better repertoire," Dax retorts, holding his hand out to me.

"It's a pleasure to meet you," I reply, taking his hand and giving it a firm shake.

Dax nods his head, offering his hand to my brothers who shake it in turn. "I must admit, you're not what I expected."

"And what did you expect?" Konrad asks.

"Someone more like The Collector. He was a sick fuck, had a bad aura. Know what I mean?"

"If they were more like The Collector, they'd be dead...

Permanently," Grim says as she strides across the dance floor with two more men in tow. One of them has a shock of white blonde hair and piercing blue eyes, the other is dark-skinned, with curly hair and sharp green eyes that assess us all. "This is York and Xeno, our friends."

"We come in peace," Leon says tensely.

The blonde, York, holds up his hand and makes a v-shape with his fingers. "Live long and prosper," he says with a grin.

"You fucking idiot," the man they call Xeno grumbles under his breath.

I frown, looking at Christy who's trying to hide her smile but failing. "What's going on?"

"Star Trek," she replies, like I should know what that even means.

York drops his hand. "Okay then, straight over your heads. Don't you have a television in that castle of yours?"

"We don't, but we do have two libraries," Konrad replies.

York pulls a face. "Well then, shall we sit? I'm dying for a drink."

Beast leans over and whacks York around the back of the head. "This is Grim's club, arsehole, we wait for her to start proceedings."

"Proceedings?" Leon questions, as bemused as I am. I expected more of a battle, honestly, not this strange banter that I don't really understand. A month ago we were beating the crap out of each other, and now we are in the same room having a conversation like decent, civilised people.

"Ignore Beast, he's trying to broaden his vocabulary because he's scared Iris's first full sentence is going to include the words cunt, prick, arsehole and dicknugget," York explains, dodging a punch this time, laughing raucously as he slides into the booth.

Grim rolls her eyes. "Am I the only adult here this afternoon? Take a seat," she instructs, straight down to business. There's no denying the distrust in her eyes. I don't blame her in the slightest. In fact, I'd be concerned if there wasn't at least a little bit of hostility. I don't know what Christy said to persuade Grim to at least be open to the idea of peace between our families, but whatever it was, it worked.

I take a seat, Christy sliding in beside me, Leon and Konrad after her. Opposite, Beast, Grim, York and Xeno sit. Dax picks up his prosthetic arm and perches on the stool, laying it across his lap as a girl who looks to be about eighteen brings over a tray of glasses and a bottle of bourbon. She smiles at us all as she passes them out, pouring a generous shot into each glass.

"Thank you, Lena," Grim says, with a smile.

"Hey Christy," Lena says as she looks between her and us. "Are these your men?"

Christy nods. "They are."

"Well, if you hadn't already guessed, I'm Lena, Pen Scott's younger sister. She was the one your dad tried to kidnap a few years back..." She raises her brow and cocks her hip. "And these loveable rogues are my sister's boyfriends. Well, three of them at least. Zayn is with Pen over at their club, Twisted Bullet, looking after Iris because we do *not* trust you three around a baby."

"Speaking of which," Grim interrupts. "Pen and Zayn just called. They've got a huge delivery they need to deal with, and according to Pen, Gray isn't much of a babysitter. You wouldn't mind heading over there?"

"Sure thing."

"I'll be over to pick our little princess up just as soon as we've got shit sorted here," Beast adds.

Lena nods, giving Christy's arm a quick squeeze before she turns on her heel and strides away. Stopping when she gets to the middle of the dance floor Lena frustratingly interjects, "Oh, and you know you can totally take Gray back. I don't need him hanging around anymore, I'm quite capable of looking after myself these days."

"Tell that to those punks sniffing around you like you're crack and they're addicts," Xeno remarks, lifting a brow.

Lena rolls her eyes. "They're not punks, they're *musicians*, and my friends. And I stopped needing a babysitter two bloody years ago, thank you very much," she says with a huff as she exits the club.

Beast smirks. "Tell that to the lovesick fool."

"Ah fuck, he doesn't does he?" Dax asks, looking at Beast and pulling a face. "Pen isn't going to be happy about that."

"You've got to be blind, deaf and dumb if you ain't noticed that Gray has got the hots for your girl's baby sister."

"Would you stop discussing Lena's love life? We've got more pressing issues to discuss right now!" Grim snaps, "Starting with why I shouldn't just pop each of you with a bullet right now and be done with it." She glances between us, waiting for our response.

"Kate!" Christy exclaims.

"Chill, sweetheart. Grim's just joking, aren't you, love?" Beast says, and Grim mutters something under her breath that sounds a lot like, *I don't joke.*

"Kate, we've talked about this..." Christy's voice trails off as she grasps my hand, and squeezes Leon's thigh beneath the table, reassuring us both as best she can.

"I'm getting soft," Grim mumbles with a heavy sigh before laying her hands flat on the table and meeting my gaze. "By all rights, you should be dead. The only reason you aren't is because Christy took the time to explain why you shouldn't be." Grim looks at her sister and nods. "She explained that you've disbanded The Menagerie. That you've given each of the Numbers security, freedom and a chance to start over."

"That's right. We have."

"Last week Christy introduced Pen and I to Cassidy and her boyfriend Jonathon. I believe you know them better as Three and Seven."

"I do," I say, glancing at Christy who gives me a warm smile. "You never said."

"They came to London a couple of weeks ago visiting Jonathon's family," Christy explains. "I met up with them last week and they explained that whilst they can live relatively comfortably with the money you gave them, they miss performing. Pen has offered them a job at their club. They start next week."

"I'm happy for them," I say, truly meaning it.

"Cassidy is an incredible dancer," Dax says. "We're happy to have her."

"Yeah, and her fella can't half belt out a note. Pen started bawling when she heard him sing for the first time," York adds.

"Jonathon has that effect. He's an exceptional artist," Leon adds.

"In our line of work, it isn't easy to give up something you've taken so long to build," Grim says. "I respect your decision to give the Numbers a chance to start over. It shows your willingness to be better men than your father was just like Christy has been telling me all this time. That being said..." Her voice trails off as she reaches for a gun holstered on her hip and places it on the table between us. "I won't tolerate any kind of lapse into old behaviours, do you understand me?"

"Perfectly," Leon says, answering for all three of us.

"Kate, there's no need for this," Christy says, a note of anger in her voice that doesn't go unnoticed.

"There absolutely is," she argues. "You're my baby sister and no matter what, I will always look out for you. If that means reminding these men every now and then what I'm capable of, then so be it. This peace is only as good as your word. Break my trust and I will kill you."

"We appreciate that," Konrad says respectfully. "And I know I can speak for my brothers when I say, we wouldn't expect anything less. You have our word. We are not those men anymore, at least not to those we love."

Grim scowls, but I quickly interrupt. "What Konrad is trying to say is that we will love and care for Christy the right way from this moment onwards. You don't ever have to fear for her, but we are not so far removed from the men we were if anyone tried to hurt her again. You and I both know that just because we've laid down our masks doesn't mean that others have forgotten who we are. Speaking of which..."

I slip my hand into my jacket pocket and pull out the letter Five gave to me from Thirteen and slide it across the table to Christy.

"What's this?" she asks, flipping it over.

"Thirteen gave this letter to Five with instructions not to read it until we'd all made peace," I explain.

"Sounds ominous," York says, knocking back his shot of bourbon.

I'd have to admit that I'd agree with him there. This letter has been burning a hole in my pocket ever since Five gave it to me. It most definitely tested my patience, that's for sure.

"You gonna open it or what?" Beast asks, tapping his finger against the side of his glass.

"Patience is a virtue, you know," Christy says, unknowingly repeating the exact same message Five passed onto me from Thirteen. I can't help but smile.

Sliding her finger under the flap, Christy pulls out the letter and begins to read.

TO MY DEAR FRIENDS,

If you're reading this, you've either ignored me completely and failed at being patient or you broke the cycle just like Nessa knew you would, just like I did. If I know you all as well as I think I do, I'm guessing the latter.

Despite the letters from Nessa, I had known you were meant for each other from the very first moment you introduced Christy to us all in the Grand Hall. I believed in your love from the very beginning. I'm so, so happy you get to have your happily ever after.

I also know that you will be furious at me for leaving with the Deana-dhe and that you've most likely tried to search for me and failed.

Please stop.

Don't look for me. For us.

Don't meddle in our story.

As far as the Deana-dhe are concerned you're dead, and that's the way we need it to stay for as long as possible. It won't last, they know too many people, have fingers in too many pies but, like you, I need time with these men to convince them that you should be left alone to live your lives without having to look over your shoulders every day for the rest of them.

It won't be easy, nothing ever is with Arden, Lorcan and Carrick, but I'm up for the challenge, and I'm determined to keep them distracted for as long as possible.

I guess you're probably wondering how we met? All you really need to know is that The Deana-dhe and I have a compli-cated history, one filled with as many ups and downs as yours. A long time ago, when we were stupid kids high on diamonds—a drug I invented, by the way—we made a blood pact that bound us together in a way that can't be undone. We even sought out a 'cailleach' to bless it. Turns out she wasn't a fraud like I'd thought and that blessings weren't really her thing. But what's a curse between enemies, right?

That's if you believe in those kinds of things of course... For a long time I hadn't. Then I got a letter from a woman I'd never met, knowing things no one else did, and I realised that anything is possible. Anyway, I hope one day to be able to tell you our story face to face, but in the meantime I want you to let us be.

Please. It's important.

We all have our paths to follow whether we believe in Fate or magic or curses or nothing at all. This is my journey, mine and the Deana-dhe's, and I have to see it through.

Which leads me onto another important point. Grim and Beast, I need to ask you a favour...

CHRISTY LOOKS up from the letter and across to her sister, a question in her gaze.

Grim shakes her head. "I've no idea. None," she says. "Keep reading."

YOU EACH OWE the Deana-dhe a debt and when they come asking for payment I want you to deny them. They're not as powerful as everyone believes, and the only reason people follow through with their debts is because of fear. Like all people gifted in the art of manipulation, they use your own fears against you. Don't let them do that.

In the meantime, I will do everything I can to keep them distracted. I will play along with their games and pretend to fear them whilst fulfilling this debt they believe I owe. Diamonds are my specialty but it takes time to make them, which works for all of us, don't you think? I will also try my damndest to cure us of this curse that the witch saw fit to burden us with all those years ago, relieving us of this connection none of us wish to have.

In short, I will do everything to protect your love for as long as I possibly can.

Take care of each other.

Thirteen x

"WHAT ARE DIAMONDS?" Christy asks, the moment she finishes reading.

"A very potent hallucinogenic drug," Xeno explains, glancing at York.

York smirks. "Some even say mind-altering, and if you fuck whilst using them. Well..." He mimics a brain exploding and we all get the idea. I'm not surprised, I've experienced Thirteen's drugs before, they have that kind of effect.

"Diamonds can be crushed and smoked in a joint or taken whole like a pill," Xeno continues, knocking back the last of his bourbon. "They're called diamonds because they look like them in their barest form.

Leon shifts in his seat. "Sounds like you're talking from experience."

"Our paths have crossed with the Deana-dhe before," Xeno replies. "Diamonds are potent. Your friend is extraordinarily talented, and very, *very* valuable because of that."

"Indeed," Grim remarks, cutting her gaze to me. "What's Thirteen's real name, Jakub?"

"Cynthia O'Farrell," I reply, confirming what she already knows to be true. In all honesty, I'm surprised she doesn't know already, though I'm guessing by the way Christy shifts in her seat that she kept that information a secret on purpose.

"Wait, what the fuck? That's *Connall's* niece."

"Who's Connall?" I ask.

"He's my fucking mate, and his family, the O'Briens, own all of the Irish pubs in London."

"Shiiiiittt," York exclaims. "I thought the Deana-dhe were tight with the O'Briens."

"So did they," Beast replies. "Fuck! They've been trying to get Cynthia back from Niall for years since Aoife was murdered. They're gonna go ape-shit when I tell them that the Deana-dhe have her."

"No!" Grim snaps.

"What?"

"I said no. This is between us."

"Ah Jesus, fuck," he exclaims running his thick tattooed fingers through his hair. "They're our friends."

"And Christy is my *sister*," she counters. "We'll keep a close eye on the situation. If at any point we get wind of things going south. We'll step in. Let this play out the way Thirteen, *Cynthia*, asked. I get the feeling that she's a lot stronger than people have given her credit for."

"She is," I agree. "Thirteen... *Cynthia* can hold her own. She's always been able to. She grew up with the infamous Masks as friends after all."

"You know she actually killed Carrick once," Christy adds a smile in her voice. "Brought him back too, obviously."

"She did what?" I ask, my lips quivering with a smile.

"It's how she figured out how to make the poison. She just

altered the ingredients a little. Apparently Carrick was being a dick to her at the time, so she poisoned him."

"Well, well, well, I'm loving this woman more and more," Beast says with a chuckle. "Looks like the Deana-dhe need to pull on their big boy pants with this one."

"Looks like it," I agree, bursting out with laughter alongside everyone else around the table.

Eventually our laughter dies down and Grim picks up her gun reholstering it. "Well, I guess you want to get home?" she says, and if I'm not mistaken, her eyes glaze over a little with tears which she blinks back furiously the second she sees me notice.

"Our flight leaves in a few hours, so we should be heading back to the airport."

She nods, turning her attention to Christy. "I give you my blessing, but if they step out of line I will—"

"Kill them, we know."

"I'm just a phone call away, okay?"

"I know that too," Christy replies, giving her a wobbly smile. "I love you, Kate."

"Love you, too."

"Well, that went far more smoothly than I'd thought it would," Beast says, lifting his glass in the air and grinning. "Cheers to new beginnings."

We all lift our glasses.

"To new beginnings..."

LATER THAT NIGHT as we make love to Christy in our room above the library, I thank Fate for bringing her to us. Our route to each other may have been a difficult one, but it has taught us so many things. How to be human, how to accept and give kindness, how to find compassion, how to conquer our pasts and fight the darkness within, and most importantly, how to *love*.

Right now we're a quartet of groans and moans. A cacophony of sounds. A beautiful melody of lust, affection, and desire. We're tongues, lips, and mouths. We're a perfect symphony of a thousand heartfelt kisses. We're touches made of fire and heat, passion and possession, forgiveness and compassion. We're inexplicably bound to one another, completely devoted, and utterly in love.

"I love you," Christy murmurs, her face flush from her orgasm as we sit in a circle around her on the bed. She traces her finger gently over her name imprinted onto each of our chests then looks up at Leon.

"I love you, Leon, for the man that you are now and the angel who saved me... *twice*," she adds with a smile, brushing her lips tenderly over his.

"I love you, Konrad, for fighting the monster and becoming the man you were always supposed to be," she says, kissing him gently before shifting on her knees to face me.

"And I love you, Jakub, for being the first Brov brave enough to break the cycle, just like that little boy always knew you could."

And at that moment as she looks at us all with hope in her eyes, I feel a sense of peace in my heart knowing that we're more than a number, more than a mask. We're people with hearts and souls and *feelings*.

We're free.

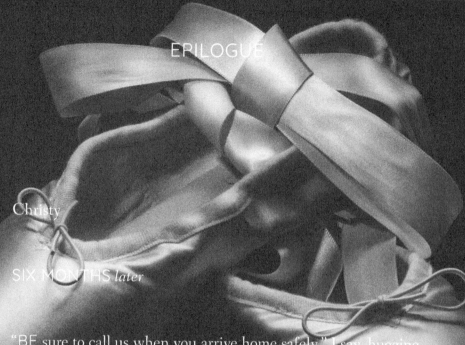

Christy

SIX MONTHS *later*

"BE sure to call us when you arrive home safely," I say, hugging my aunt and uncle, wishing they didn't have to go so soon.

"We will, darling," Sandy replies, sliding her hand into Frank's. She glances back up at Ardelby Castle, still marvelling at how impressive it is, before focusing back on Jakub, Leon and Konrad who hang back slightly, allowing us to say goodbye.

"Thank you for having us. Your home is beautiful."

"Our offer still remains," Jakub says, stepping forward to shake Frank's hand and accept a kiss from Sandy. "We have plenty of room."

Frank slaps Jakub on the back, grinning, "As much as your offer is tempting, we like having our own place. Besides, I'm not sure you'd appreciate us dancing in your kitchen at midnight in our undercrackers."

"Oh I don't know, it sounds entertaining," Jakub jokes, grinning.

Frank chuckles. "Seriously though, we're happy where we are. We have friends we don't want to leave behind, and when you get to our age they're few and far between."

"Well, if you ever change your mind..." Konrad offers.

"We know where to find you," Sandy finishes for him, her cheeks flushing a little as Konrad kisses her on the cheek. It's sweet how giggly she gets around them. My Aunt Sandy has always been one to appreciate a good looking man, and now she has three more to flirt with. "Well, we should go!"

"See you soon, okay?" I say, pulling her in for one last hug before reluctantly letting her go.

"Before you know it!" she waves.

They climb into the car, and I don't take my eyes off the vehicle until it turns left at the end of the long drive, disappearing from view.

"You okay?" Leon asks me, wrapping his arm around my waist and pulling me into his side as we head back to the castle. "I know how much you miss them when they're gone."

I lean into his hold. "I'm fine. Besides, it'll only be a few weeks until Grim and Beast arrive with Iris."

"They're definitely coming then?" Konrad asks, holding open the door that leads into the entrance hallway. He looks surprised. Honestly, I am too. I never thought I'd see the day.

"Yep. She finally trusts you all enough to visit."

"I'm not sure she'll ever completely trust us," Jakub says, heading towards the parlour to the right of the hallway.

"She's a tough nut to crack, for sure, but believe me this is a huge step. Another ten years of good behaviour and you'll have the perfect relationship," I joke as we follow him into the room. I drop down onto the leather sofa beneath the window, Leon settling on my left and Konrad to my right. They both place a warm hand on each thigh whilst Jakub picks up a bottle of scotch.

"Anyone like a drink?"

"It's only two o'clock, Jakub. Was it that bad having my aunt and uncle stay here?" I quip.

"No, not at all. I meant what I said. We have so much space here."

"I know, I'm kidding," I reply, my spine tingling as Leon's hand slides higher up my thigh. Out of the corner of my eye I can see him smirking, we only had sex this morning but he's insatiable. They all are. Not that I mind. Sex for us isn't just about climaxing, it's about forging a bond based on mutual pleasure and connection. It's about loving each other in so many different ways. Though my favourite will always and forever be the tuning fork. Who knew?

"You might want to reconsider that drink," Five says, stepping into the room.

"Hey, Five, what's up?" I ask, greeting her with a smile. I've loved having her here, she's been a wonderful friend to both Nala and me, and even though we wanted to call her by her real name, she made it perfectly clear that Five is her preference, and so Five she remains. "I thought you were spending the afternoon with Nala teaching her some knife throwing skills."

"I was," she replies, entering the room and shutting the door behind her, a serious expression on her face. "But something important came up." She smoothes her hand over her jeans, an anxious tell that we've all come to recognise. Five rarely gets anxious, so whatever this is, it's big.

"What is it?" Leon asks, tracking her as she walks across the room and takes a seat on the armchair opposite us.

"Charles just called. He's picked up some chatter."

"And what chatter is that?"

"Looks like the honeymoon period is over. The Deana-dhe know you're alive."

"Fuck!" Konrad exclaims, swiping a hand over his face.

"We always knew this day would come. We're prepared," Jakub says, trying to reassure us all even though I see the flicker of concern in his eyes, too.

"That's not the only thing that's a cause for concern," Five says, casting a look at me.

My skin immediately covers in goosebumps. "What's the other thing?" I ask.

"Thirteen is missing."

"What?!" I exclaim.

"What do you mean she's missing?" Jakub says.

"I mean exactly that. Someone took her from the Deana-dhe."

"Who?" Leon demands, shifting forward in his seat, all thought about sex gone from his mind, from mine too.

"Charles hasn't been able to find that out, but he wanted you to know he's looking into it as we speak. He's going to call as soon as he finds out."

Before we can even process this new information the telephone on the bureau trills with an incoming call, making me jump.

"It's as though he's tapped the room," Jakub jokes darkly, striding over to the phone and snatching up the handset. For a moment he just listens, then he presses the loudspeaker button, a familiar voice echoing around the room.

"The Skull Brotherhood have Cyn," Arden says, his voice tight. "And we need your help getting her back."

The End

TO FIND out what happens between Cyn and the mysterious Deana-dhe, and how she ends up in the hands of the Skull Brotherhood, check out their story starting with **Debts and Diamonds** releasing in Autumn 2022.

AND FOR THOSE of you who've always loved Grim and Beast and want their story. Well, you're in luck! The long awaited **Tales You Win** is available now. Read on for an excerpt.

TALES YOU WIN

EXCERPT FROM BOOK ONE OF GRIM &
BEAST'S DUET

PROLOGUE

Grim

Dear Iris,

I'm not great with words. I act. That's what I'm doing now.

You see, my sweet baby girl, I have a sister. Her name's Christy and she's in trouble.

Real bad trouble.

Some men have taken her, stolen her away and locked her up in their castle.

They're bad, bad men and they'll hurt her.

I have to rescue her. I have to bring her home.

That's what I do. I protect my own. Family means everything to me. Everything.

Which means I have to do the one thing I hoped never to do and that's leave you behind. I can't put you in danger.

I won't.

Instead, I'm trusting my friend Pen and her men, Xeno, Dax, Zayn and York to take care of you whilst I'm gone. They're good people, the best. They will love you and care for you whilst your dad and I go slay the monsters.

You're too young to understand how dangerous this is. We might never come back. It hurts my heart to admit that I may be making a choice where you are left an orphan with no parents.

It hurts me beyond repair, and I will live with the wound forever, whether I live or die.

But I have to go. We have to go, your dad and me.

I have entrusted you to my friends who will love you until we return, and if we don't... will love you always.

If this is the end of your dad's and my story, then so be it.

Either way, I've left you a gift.

It's my story.

Actually, it's our love story.

Your dad's and mine.

His words, and mine. His memories and my memories, all scrawled down on the pages of these notebooks.

You see, Iris, a long time ago a coin was thrown.

A coin that would decide my fate.

Tales you win.

Heads you lose.

I won, and my dad, your grandfather, lost.

Though admittedly it didn't feel that way at the time.

What I do know is that everything happens for a reason. Your dad and I were always supposed to be together, it just took a while to get there.

This might not be the perfect fairy tale, but it is our fairy tale, and now it's yours.

Ma x

CHAPTER ONE

It started with a... ~~kiss~~ fight.

Kate

"Fists up, protect your face, keep light on your toes," the growly bastard yells at me.

"I'm trying!" I snap, stomping my foot against the canvas in frustration as I drop my guard and glare at Beast, my dad's enforcer and my fucking bodyguard. Sweat trickles down my spine and between my tits, causing my t-shirt to stick to my chest and back.

"Has *Princess* Kate had enough for one day?" he asks, snorting with laughter as he pulls off the boxing pad and tussles my hair with his huge hands. We've been training regularly for the last six months and I'm getting stronger and fitter with every session, but Beast still runs me ragged.

"It's *Grim*," I protest, slapping his hands away.

Beast cocks his head. "Nope, still *Princess* to me."

"I'm not a princess, you arsehole!"

He chuckles. "Yeah, yeah. Now are we done?"

"Not nearly, *Roger*," I retort, shoving him off me and using his given name because I know it pisses him off. Ever since my dad aka *The Boss*, aka Carter Davidson, aka the ruler of Tales— an underground fight club—started calling me Grim after my love of reading Grimms' Fairy Tales, Beast and the other men who work for my father started calling me Princess.

It's fucking annoying.

His smile drops. "You ain't too old to be put over my knee and given a spanking. Don't push your luck, kid."

Kid? Okay, that's worse than being called Princess, the fucking twat. In a month I'll be eighteen. Besides, I haven't been a kid for a very long time. Comes with the territory of being a gangster's daughter.

"Ha! As if you would. I think my dad would have a few things to say about an *old* wanker like you getting his rocks off over spanking a *kid*!" I sass back, knowing I'm pushing all his buttons and loving every minute of it. Firstly, he's not all that older than me, maybe around twenty-three. Secondly, he'd never raise a hand to me, unless it's in the ring and he's teaching me how to defend myself. Thirdly, he might be a fucking maniac and kill people for a living, but he isn't a predator. The guy's a straight up saint when it comes to women. In fact, I've heard he's a gentleman, except in bed when, apparently, he's an animal or rather a *beast*, but only to women who are well over the age of consent. Not that I've asked around or anything. My cheeks flush at the thought, and I preoccupy myself with trying to pull off my gloves, which is no easy feat when you don't have the use of your fingers.

"You know that mouth of yours is gonna get you in a shit-load of trouble one of these days," Beast remarks, chucking the boxing pads he was holding at Dom—my dad's third in command—who catches them easily.

The reflexes on that man are insane. I witnessed him catching a knife by the blade once. Straight up thought it was going to bury itself in his forehead. It didn't, though. Dom's got a four inch scar on his palm for the trouble. In fact, he's covered in them. He's been involved in more fights than the local tomcat and that tomcat takes on *dogs*. Both of them are certifiably insane, like all my dad's men, or 'soldiers' as he calls them. Funnily enough he looks like more of a beast than Beast does with a shorn head, squashed nose from it being broken so many times, and missing half an ear from when it was ripped off by an opposing fighter in the cage.

Yeah, the fights get bloody at Tales.

"What do you mean *going* to get her in a shitload of trouble?" Dom asks, winking at me whilst I glare back at him. "She's already causing a fucking problem with the local hoodrats. That fucker Hudson came over today sniffing around for Princess."

"Hud is my friend, not a *hoodrat,* and I am NOT a princess!"

"Touchy subject, Princess?" Dom teases.

"Fuck you, *Dom-I've-got-a-limp-dick,*" I retort with a wan smile.

"Oh Princess, my dick most definitely limps. Have you seen the way it drags across the floor when I walk?"

Beast roars with laughter as my eyes stupidly drop to Dom's crotch and the very sizeable bulge he has there. What is it with these men and their dick appreciation? If I had a sack of skin swinging between my legs like some elephant trunk, I wouldn't be bragging about it. Fucking ugly if you ask me. I much prefer tits. Not that I have any... Maybe I'm a lesbian? I mull that thought over as I glance back at Beast who is watching me with a sudden intensity that makes my skin cover in goosebumps, my stomach lurch and my traitorous pussy tingle. Okay, so definitely into men then.

"Fuck sake," I mutter under my breath.

"What's the matter, Princess, cat got your tongue?" Beast asks, his voice low and lethal sounding.

I gulp. "Nope. Perfectly fucking fine, thank you very much," I reply, arching a brow.

"I'll leave you to lock up and get Princess home, yeah?" Dom asks, completely ignoring me and smirking at Beast.

"Yep. I got this," Beast replies, turning his attention back to me as the door to the gym slams shut and Dom leaves us alone together. He stares at me, his leaf-green eyes bright in the fluorescent lights as I continue to struggle to remove my boxing gloves. "So you were saying something about me getting off on spanking kids?"

"It was a *joke*," I say, rolling my eyes and turning my back on him as I stride over to the other side of the ring. Only I don't make it that far as Beast lifts me up and chucks me over his shoulder. "WHAT ARE YOU DOING!" I scream from my upside-down position, my face practically pressed against his ridiculously firm arse.

"I thought that was obvious," he retorts with a low, rumbly chuckle that has my insides fucking squirming.

Jesus, I need to get a grip. I do not like *Roger Smith*, a bland name for a man who's far from it. "My dad will kill you if you even think about raising a hand to me." I punch him on his arse and the back of his tree-trunk thighs. The fucker doesn't even flinch.

"Your father has given me free rein to do whatever the fuck I want..." he warns, his voice dropping an octave or two and sounding far more sexy than it has any right to. *"...Inside the ring."*

"Fuck that, you moron! Put me down!"

He chuckles, clearing his throat, then drops me unceremoniously onto the stool situated in the corner of the ring. I let out a whoosh of air from the impact and immediately stand, not liking, or perhaps liking too much, the fact that he's towering over me all sweaty and big and fucking sexy as sin. He's tall. Six foot five to my five foot seven. A fucking giant, no... *Beast.*

"Urgh, you're an arsehole!" I say, punching him as hard as I can on the nearest bodily part which happens to be his very wide, abnormally firm, stomach. I mean there's six packs and then there's *six packs*, and his happens to be accompanied with a V muscle that turns all women's insides liquid. Except mine, because once you've seen one, you've seen them all, and every fighter at Tales has one.

So I'm immune.

Except his muscles are covered in tattoos, and my immunity stops there. Tattoos are my weak spot and I happen to find them insanely attractive. My eyes rove over his bare chest, all slick with sweat as I drink in the familiar geometric patterns that criss-cross his chest and stomach, and the single eye staring at me from his right pec. Not to mention the beautifully detailed side profile of a lion, its gaze focusing on his navel. God, his tattoos are fucking epic...

"Are you gaping at my dick?" Beast asks, chuckling.

"What? No!" I reply, quickly lifting my gaze and rubbing at my sweaty, *flushed* cheeks.

"Then don't be staring like that, Princess. You might give a man the wrong impression," he says, placing his large, bear-sized hands on my shoulders. "Sit!"

I sit.

Dropping to his knees before me, he reaches for my gloved hands and starts untying them. His thick fingers are nimble and mesmerising despite their size, and don't even get me started on his hands with his wide palms, the thick wrists, the veins and the tattoos. You know what they say about a man and his hands... Wait, perhaps it's the feet? Fuck, whatever. Either way, big hands, big dick.

"I don't fancy you, Roger, if that's what you're getting at," I say, lying through my teeth. "Your physique might turn the average bimbo with fewer brain cells than a gnat on, but not me. I prefer my men with more upstairs. Know what I mean?"

Beast scoffs and I can't help but smile at the way he yanks at the string of my gloves. "Are we back to that Hudson prick again? Jumped-up shit who thinks he's gonna run the world, that one. More balls than a rugby team playing at Twickenham stadium, but a lot less sense."

"Hud is *smart*," I counter. "Don't underestimate him."

"Princess, I make a habit of never underestimating anyone because I *am* smart."

"Says the man who has ride or die tattooed on his lower stomach. Yeah, smart. More like fucking *obvious*," I scoff. "Is that the male equivalent of a tramp stamp?"

Beast's fingers still. "No, just the fucking truth. I'm a ride or die kinda man, both in life and in the bedroom. Any woman I invite into my bed can vouch for that," he says, and I have to grit my teeth and lock down the urge to squirm. I do not want to give him the satisfaction.

"Well, whatever. I prefer the smarts. Besides, Hudson's about a thousand times more attractive than you..." And whilst that's not strictly true as they're both equally attractive, just in different ways, he doesn't need to know that.

Beast snorts, back to concentrating on what he's doing. "If

you're trying to offend me, don't bother, Princess. I'm not interested in the slightest. You're my boss's daughter, *underage* and entirely off fucking limits. So let's just get back to being cool, okay?"

"What, as opposed to hot? Are you saying I'm *hot*, Roger? Do you want a nice tight piece of underage arse?" I don't know why I push him like this, but I can't seem to help myself. Not to mention the fact I'll be eighteen in a couple of months and officially classified as an adult, so there's that. This time he does look up, and I swallow hard at the look of anger in his eyes.

"Even if you were of fucking age, I still wouldn't touch you."

"You do realise that the age of consent in the UK is sixteen, right?" I say, taunting him.

"I don't give a fuck what the law says. My age of consent is firmly fixed at twenty, got it?"

"Why twenty? You're also considered an adult at eighteen in this country."

"Just because..." he replies, refusing to explain. "Besides, you're not my type."

Removing my gloves, his fingers curling around my wrists, all warm and firm and, surprisingly, soft. For a couple of seconds he just stares at the spot where our skin touches and I wonder if he feels it too, that electric current humming between us.

"No?" I question softly, my heart racing in my chest as he leans in close. I'm pretty sure he can feel my pulse racing under his fingers.

"No," he repeats, whispering in my ear. "I like my women with a bit of meat on their bones. Come back to me when you've turned into one, yeah?" I suck in an offended breath and he laughs, letting me go. "I'll call you a cab," he says, standing abruptly.

"I thought *you* were taking me home?"

"Nope." He strides over to the other side of the ring and ducks between the ropes, dropping to the floor.

"Where are you going?" I shout after him, hating the way my voice catches and my skin burns from his touch.

"I've got work to do."

"What work?" I ask, frowning.

"Carter has got wind of some news he ain't happy with. Nothing to concern yourself with."

"News?"

Beast ignores me "Babysitting duties are up. Catch you later, *Princess*."

And with that he's gone.

"It's Grim!" I yell after him.

Staring at the door that Beast just left through, I grind my teeth. He's the only one of my dad's men who knows how to really push my buttons, the arrogant, cocky bastard. Then again he's the only one of my dad's men that really knows me at all. As I try to calm my thrashing heart, I reassure myself with the fact that there will come a time when I'll be queen of this fight club and Beast will be answering to me. Though whether that's as my lover or as my soldier isn't clear just yet.

Tales You Win is available now to read.

AUTHOR NOTE

Well there we have it! The Masks and Christy's love story has come to an end. Getting into the heads of such dark and troubled characters is draining. I both loved and hated The Masks for all that they were.

This story was about their redemption. It was about being better men and learning to be human when you've spent your whole life being taught the opposite of compassion, love and kindness.

Christy is, and will remain, one of my strongest female characters to date. She absolutely held up that mirror one thousand percent and made them *see*.

I hope you enjoyed their story despite all the ups and downs, the trauma and the hardship. I believe in their love. I hope you do too!

And who is looking forward to Grim and Beast's and the Deana-dhe's stories?

If you follow me you'll know that the Deana-dhe was always going to get their story. The second they appeared in the

Academy of Stardom series I just knew I needed more of them. When I tell you they leapt off the page, they absolutely did, and their relationship with Thirteen aka Cynthia is off the charts smouldering and angsty and all the good stuff!

Likewise, Grim and Beast have been around since the Academy of Misfits trilogy and I always knew that one day they'd share their story. I'm having so much fun with these characters. Their banter and sexual chemistry is off the charts! Be prepared for a funny, angsty, steamy read!

Special thanks to Crystal Carroll for coming up with the name - The Brònach Masquerade Ball.

Thanks to my Beta team, Lisa, Jen, Gina and Janet all of whom kept me going when I found parts of this story too hard to write. Thanks to my PA, Alpha reader, and all round badass friend Courtney Dunham for never failing to support me. Girl, you're my ride or die.

And finally, thank you to my readers. The fact that you're still here warms my heart. Thank you for reading, for believing in me, for all the reader graphics, reviews and words of encouragement. I will forever be grateful to you all.

If this is the first book you've read by me, then you're in luck! All of my contemporary books so far are set in the same world and characters often cross over from one series to the next. Here is my recommended reading order:

The Brothers Freed trilogy - start with Avalanche of Desire

Academy of Misfits trilogy - start with Delinquent

Beyond The Horizon (M/F standalone)

Finding Their Muse series - start with Steps

Academy of Stardom series - start with Freestyle

The Dancer and The Masks Duet

Grim & Beast's Duet

The Deana-dhe Duet

(bully/academy reverse harem)

#1 Delinquent

#2 Reject

#3 Family

Finding Their Muse

(dark contemporary reverse harem)

#1 Steps

#2 Strokes

#3 Strings

#4 Symphony

#5 Finding Their Muse boxset

The Brothers Freed Series

(contemporary reverse harem)

#1 Avalanche of Desire

#2 Storm of Seduction

#3 Dawn of Love

#4 Brothers Freed Boxset

Contemporary Standalone's

Beyond the Horizon

For all up to date book releases please visit

www.beapaige.co.uk

ABOUT THE AUTHOR

Bea Paige lives a very secretive life in London... She likes red wine and Haribo sweets (preferably together) and occasionally swings around poles when the mood takes her.

Bea loves to write about love and all the different facets of such a powerful emotion. When she's not writing about love and passion, you'll find her reading about it and ugly crying.

Bea is always writing, and new ideas seem to appear at the most unlikely time, like in the shower or when driving her car.

She has lots more books planned, so be sure to subscribe to her newsletter:
    beapaige.co.uk/newsletter-sign-up

Made in the USA
Middletown, DE
14 August 2023

36690812R00305